The Mark of The Dragonfly

Jaleigh Johnson

A YEARLING BOOK

Text copyright © 2014 by Jaleigh Johnson
Cover art copyright © 2014 by Nigel Quarless
Map illustration copyright © 2014 by Brandon Dorman

Visit us on the Web! randomhousekids.com

Educators and librarians, for a variety of teaching tools, visit us at RHTeachersLibrarians.com

The Library of Congress has cataloged the hardcover edition of this work as follows:
Johnson, Jaleigh.
The mark of the dragonfly / Jaleigh Johnson. — First edition.
pages cm
Summary: Since her father's death in a factory in the Dragonfly territories, thirteen-year-old Piper has eked out a living as a scrapper in Merrow Kingdom, but the arrival of a mysterious girl sends her on a dangerous journey to distant lands.
ISBN 978-0-385-37615-0 (hc) — ISBN 978-0-385-37645-7 (glb) —
ISBN 978-0-385-37646-4 (ebook) [I. Fantasy.] I. Title.
PZ7.J63214Mar 2014
[Fic]—dc23
2013019716

ISBN 978-0-385-37647-1 (pbk.)

Printed in the United States of America

10 9 8 7 6 5 4 3 2 1

First Yearling Edition 2015

To Tim, for being the hero of my favorite story. You know the one.

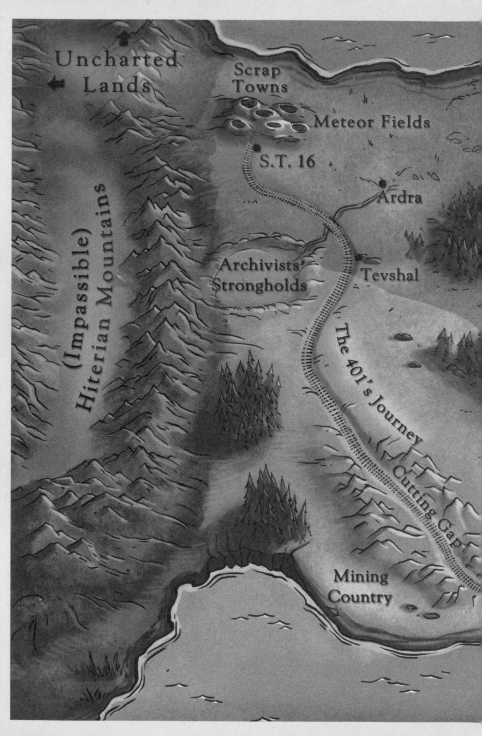

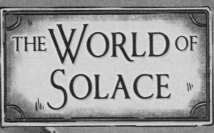

THE WORLD OF SOLACE

MERROW
KINGDOM

DRAGONFLY
TERRITORIES

● Noveen

Uncharted
Lands ➔

⇒ ONE ⇐

Scrap Town Number Sixteen
Merrow Kingdom

Micah brought the music box to her on the night of the meteor storm. Piper never slept on these nights, when debris from other worlds fell from the sky. Restlessness kept her awake in bed, staring at the slanted ceiling of her tiny house. She counted the widening cracks in the gray scrub-pine planks and then counted the seconds as they ticked by on the tarnished silver watch she wore around her neck. Beneath her cotton nightdress, the metal lay warm and comfortable against her skin. Micah's knock made her lose count, but the watch ticked on steadily.

She pulled on a pair of her father's old boots, slung his brown coat over her nightdress, and opened the door. Wind blew a harsh breath of snow and ice crystals into her face. Piper wiped her eyes and fixed a look of annoyance on the boy huddled in the doorway.

"I must be seeing things," Piper said. "This can't be Micah Howell standing at my door, dragging me out of bed in the drop dead of night. Look at me—I'm stunned stiff. I'm speechless."

Micah snorted. "That'll be the day, then. Let me in, Piper, will ya?" He stomped snow off his boots. "Stinks out here, and it's so cold my teeth are cracking together."

"That's your own fault for being out on a storm night. Most scrappers have the sense to stay inside." He was right, though. The air already reeked of brimstone. The storm was coming. Piper moved to let him in, then shut the door behind him. He immediately ran to the cast-iron stove to warm his hands. Piper nudged him aside and adjusted the dampers. "Hand me a log before you make yourself at home," she said. It was her habit to pretend to be bothered by her friend, even though she was happy to see him.

Micah handed her a piece of wood from the basket near the stove and reached into the bulky sack he had slung over his shoulder. "I brought it, just like I said I would."

"That's great, kid, but I thought you were going to bring it a few hours ago—you know, before I made a comfortable nest in the middle of my bed." Piper tended the stove, and then she went to the window and looked out at the sky, which had begun to lighten, though it was still several hours until dawn. The moon waxed a sickly greenish color, as it always did before the meteors fell, making the clouds around it look like swelling bruises on the sky.

Piper's skin itched. She had the urge to go outside and watch the fields, to see the first of the meteors streak from the sky, but it was too cold, too dangerous. And besides, she'd promised to fix Micah's toy.

A musical box—Piper rolled her eyes. Machines couldn't make proper music. You needed a person for that.

She lit an extra kerosene lamp and placed it on the small kitchen table. Piston rings, bolts, and cylinders littered its surface. Piper shifted these aside, wishing she had a bigger work space, one she didn't also have to eat at. "Let's see it, then."

Micah set the music box between them. "Isn't she beautiful?" he said, his fingers lingering on the lid. It was decorated with a painted figure of a woman in a white silk robe. She reclined on a strip of grass, her long black hair falling around her waist. At her back grew a tree full to bursting with pink blossoms that hung over her like a veil.

Whoever had made the music box was a skilled artist. Piper could practically smell the flowers, each one hand-painted in white, coral, and cerise. In a few places, the paint had cracked and faded, but those were hardly noticeable. Overall, it was an incredible piece. Micah had been lucky to find it.

"But she won't sing?" Piper lifted the lid to get a look

at the musical components. She'd seen contraptions like these before. A series of pins arranged on a metal cylinder struck the teeth of a steel comb while the cylinder turned, making the tinkling notes of a song. She'd heard this type of music and had always thought the sound was a little annoying. "Did you clean the inside after you dug it out of the crater?"

"Course I did." The boy was indignant. "You think I'm stupid?"

Piper glanced up from the box and raised an eyebrow.

"Ha-ha. You watch—the coin I get from that thing will feed my family and me for a month. She'll look smart in one of those fancy mansions in Ardra. Don't you think she will, Piper?" His excitement faltered, and he looked at her anxiously.

"Yeah, it'll look smart. Just make sure you find a buyer with a stiff hip at the market," Piper said. "They're the ones who'll be looking for these kinds of pretties." She felt the cylinder and its tiny pins. Micah had done a decent job cleaning it, but flecks of dirt still caked the comb, and something was keeping the cylinder from turning. She heard the soft, strangled notes of a song trying to play.

"Why a stiff hip?" Micah asked. He had a thin face and a stubby nose that always scrunched up when he was confused.

"It means he's got a lot of coin on his belt." Piper swayed back and forth in her chair like a drunk man to illustrate what she meant. "Poor thing, he can't walk right with all that money weighing him down. You have to know what to look for or you'll never make any decent coin."

"I've sold stuff before," Micah said. "I did all right."

"A handful of trinkets at most—you're still a puppy at this game."

"Am not!" At eleven, Micah hated it when he was made to feel young.

Piper went on as if she hadn't heard him. "Every trader's got a different story. Greasy fingers means you're dealing with a machinist." She waggled her stained fingers at him significantly. "She'll be looking for spare parts. The ones who come in from Ardra will want iron, always iron. If you have books or pictures to sell, you want an archivist. Stiff hips have money to waste. You can sell them just about anything if you can convince them it's a one of a kind."

"Oh, I forgot! I have a book to sell too," Micah said. He rummaged in the sack and pulled out a red leather-bound book with spidery cracks on the spine. The smell of aged paper tickled Piper's nose. Embossed on the front cover was a picture of a girl and a small dog. Next to her stood a grinning scarecrow, a lion, and a man who looked like he was made entirely of metal. "I can't read any of the words. What do you think?"

Piper examined the book. "If it's a language they've never seen before, the archivists will go nuts. Can't be a very good story, though—that picture doesn't make much sense."

Micah shrugged. "I don't care, as long as it's worth something."

"Don't worry. Archivists always pay good," Piper said. She didn't know much about them, only that their life's work was collecting meteor-storm artifacts in order to learn as much as they could about the other worlds. Piper had heard stories about their museums, vast vaults built in mountain strongholds to the southwest. They didn't much care for outsiders either. As far as Piper was concerned, they could be as mysterious as they wanted, as long as their prices were fair. And they would love the condition of Micah's book.

"Where did you find these?" Piper asked, comparing Micah's two items. "The book's got most of its pages, and I've never seen a music box this pretty. There's hardly a scratch on it."

"Got it at the last harvest," Micah said proudly. "I beat everybody else to it—found it in a crater, just under the ice dragon's tail." He gestured vaguely to the north, where the Hiterian Mountains rose up sharply to snow-covered peaks and marked the northern border of the Merrow Kingdom. On clear days when clouds didn't obscure the view, if you closed one eye and put your thumb over the top of the jagged peaks and valleys, the spaces between flesh and rock formed the rough shape of a dragon with one wing dipping, as if the mythical beast had frozen in midflight.

Below the dragon lay the harvesting fields, a crescent-shaped stretch of land that covered roughly fifty miles of cratered plains and foothills. For as long as anyone could remember, the meteor storms had happened there on each full moon.

Over the years, the scrap towns had grown up on the outskirts. People had become scavengers, scrappers digging out whatever the storms brought from other worlds, hoping to find some machine, artifact, or trinket, like Micah's, that was worth selling at the trade markets. Becoming a scrapper was a way for people to make a living, though not a very good one. Most things that fell from the sky were hopelessly broken. The storms were so violent it was a mystery how any objects remained intact after they hit the earth.

"How did you get out there so fast?" Piper asked suspiciously. Micah was nimble, but neither he nor his brother ever ate really well, so they didn't have as much energy as some of the other scrappers in town. At thirteen, Piper was stronger and faster, and she made extra coin from fixing machines people brought her from the fields.

"Well, I might've gone up the mountain before the storm was over," Micah said guiltily.

Piper almost dropped the music box. "You're telling

me you went out to the fields before the meteors were done falling?"

Micah waved his hands as if trying to hold off a different kind of storm. "Just once, and I promise I was careful! Mom and Dad were away fishing at the lake, so it was just me and Jory at home. We went to the shelter together, but I told Jory I was going to be with you so I could sneak off. I was scared of the storm at first, but once I squeezed under some rock ledges, I didn't have to worry about the meteors."

Micah and Jory's parents would have had a fit if they knew what Micah was up to, Piper thought. But they were fishermen who went south to the Meljoy lakes every other week for the trout and pike while Jory, the eldest, looked after Micah. Fishing was what really kept Micah's family fed, not scavenging in the scrap fields, but Micah always thought he'd find some priceless trinket, something valuable enough to sell and bring his parents home for good.

"Oh, well, that's fine," Piper said, though it wasn't. "For a minute there, I was worried, but now that I know you had some pebbles to protect you from the *deadly meteors raining from the heavens,* I won't think any more about it. So how about let's go back to the part where you snuck off and used *me* to lie to your brother?" Piper caught Micah by his shirt collar and shook him. "You know going out in a storm is illegal, not to mention a hundred and fifty kinds of dangerous. Do you want to get your skull smashed? It'd probably smarten you up, a couple good knocks to the head."

"Let go, Piper!" Micah wriggled in her grasp and bared his teeth as if he might bite her. Piper let him go, but she scowled fiercely at him until he turned red from his hollow cheeks to the tips of his ears. "I told you I kept under the rocks. I was safe," he insisted.

"It's not just the meteors you have to worry about," Piper said, exasperated. "Meteors bring the dust too, or did you not see the green clouds hanging in the air like pretty little death curtains?"

"I wore gloves," he protested, and wilted under her black glare.

"I don't care if you picked that box up with your brain like the sarnuns do!" Piper poked his temple until he slapped her hand away. "There's a reason the Consortium crams everybody down into the shelter during a storm, Micah. You have to wait for the wind to blow the meteor dust away, or you're just breathing poison. The thickest gloves in the world won't protect your lungs from that stuff."

"No *human* ever died from that," Micah said stubbornly.

"It'll kill you slower than a meteor to the head, sure, but it's just as nasty as the black smoke that belches out of the factories in Noveen," she said. Her voice wavered. "You knew people from this town who died of *that*."

"I'm sorry, Piper," the boy said, subdued. "But I'm

not as fast as the others. If I don't get out there first, there's nothing good left."

"Sure there is. There's plenty of good stuff if you know where to look."

Micah didn't answer, just stared at the music box with a defiant, hungry look. Piper sighed. Boys were so stubborn. Her father used to say he thanked the goddess every day that he'd had a girl. Boys were too much trouble. "Look, I'll prove it to you," she said. "When the storm's over, we'll go out together—you and me. I'll get you a trinket that'll make this music box look like a cheap windup toy."

Micah's face brightened. "You'd do that?"

Piper smiled. "Absolutely, if only so I don't have to step over your smashed skull in the field. Now hush up a minute. I think I found your problem." Piper rested her fingers on the music box's cylinder. The tinny vibration of the strangled music beat a little rhythm against her fingertips. She felt the steel teeth, which were supposed to pluck the pins on the cylinder and create the melody. One of the teeth had a clot of dirt stuck on the end, which had crusted on the cylinder and kept it from turning. Piper reached into the box with her smallest finger, but she couldn't scrape the dirt off without risking damage to the fragile tooth. "Go get my tool belt, will you?" she said to Micah. "It's under the bed."

The boy crawled over, pushed aside a stack of dog-eared, greasy-fingerprinted repair manuals, and reached underneath the bed to grab the small tool belt. It was little more than a thick leather strap with pockets sewn all over it. Her father had made it for her a long time ago when she'd first started fiddling with machines. Back then, all their nuts, bolts, and gear wheels had seemed like fun mysteries that needed solving. She'd had no idea her talent would one day become what fed her.

Piper took out a small horsehair brush. As gently as she could, she rubbed the bristles over the comb, dislodging the dirt from them and the cylinder. "What I'm doing here will probably bend or break off part of the tooth—these pieces look pretty old—so it might miss a note or two, but just tell the buyer it's all part of the song. Here, I'm done," she said, handing the box back to Micah.

Micah lifted the box lid and looked at the cylinder. "Which tooth?" Piper pointed to the place, but the boy shook his head. "It looks the same as the others, doesn't even look bent. How'd you do that without leaving a mark?"

"Look, you said to fix it, so I fixed it," Piper said crossly. "Stop bothering me and try it out."

He took hold of the windup key and turned it until it wouldn't move anymore. When he let go, a tinkling melody drifted out of the box, soft and—Piper had to admit it—sweet, with no missing notes at all. The boy's eyes widened. "How do you do it, Piper?"

"I told you how."

"Yeah, but . . ." He hesitated, and Piper's stomach clenched. She knew what was coming. "People in town say you're weird with the machines. You're like a healer with them. Only, when the healer treats a bad cut, it always leaves a scar. When you fix the machines, it doesn't leave a mark."

"Machines are easier to fix than people," Piper said, trying to shrug it off. "A lot louder and dirtier too—well, sometimes, at least."

"But you even fixed that watch," Micah persisted. He lifted the trinket from around Piper's neck and held it in the palm of his hand. "When I gave that to you, I was sure you'd never get it going again. Now it looks almost new."

Piper didn't have an argument for that one. Micah was right. The watch had been in pieces when he brought it to her. Micah's brother had taken it from a small crater at the edge of the harvesting fields. He'd gathered up as many of the broken pieces as he could, but it looked like some scrapper had trampled the watch in his rush to get on to bigger treasures. Piper spent weeks working on it, painstakingly reinserting its brass gears, escapement, and mainspring into the case. Her patience paid off the day she heard the distinctive ticking sound coming from the thing. Micah ended up giving the watch to her as a gift.

What she never told Micah or anyone else was that in the months after her father died, when she desperately needed coin that he was no longer able to provide, she'd tried to sell the watch to a stiff hip from Ardra. The trader brought the watch back a week later, claiming Piper had cheated him, that the thing didn't work. Piper gave him his money back, though it had almost killed her to do it. A few days later, the watch inexplicably started ticking again. Twice more Piper tried to sell it, but both times the traders brought it back, angrily waving the broken thing in her face. Apparently, the watch had decided not to work for anyone but Piper. She'd never figured out why.

Piper knew she should be proud of her talent, and she was, but it made her nervous the way people whispered about her when they thought she couldn't hear. They claimed that there were many machines only Piper could fix, and that made some people angry, as if she were taking something away from them by being so good at her work. How could the best machinist in the scrap town be so young, with no training beyond her father's guidance and her own tinkering? That was what they whispered. Even Micah looked at her strangely sometimes, as he was doing now, and Piper hated it.

"It's getting late—or early, I guess," she said. "You'd better head home." The storm was coming, and she had to be ready. She didn't have time to worry about stupid rumors. Piper held open the sack for Micah to put the music box in it. "Look, promise me you won't take less than twelve for that thing, and make sure you tell anyone who looks at it that it plays a pretty song. They'll want to hear all about it."

The melody had dwindled to a few meek notes. Micah pressed his ear against the box. "But I don't know anything about the song. It's from another world."

Piper threw up her hands, but she was smiling. A little bit of the tension went out of her. "Of course you don't know it, but that doesn't mean you can't make something up, you dumb puppy. Tell them it's probably an old song from a world of poets, a lover's lament."

"Lover's lemon?" Micah said dubiously.

"*Lament*," Piper said. "Didn't you learn anything in the Consortium school? It means regret or something. Trust me, they'll eat it up." She shooed him toward the door. "Go on."

Micah ran when Piper pretended to kick him out with her oversized boot. "Thanks, Piper," he said, grinning. "Mom and Dad are coming back tomorrow night. I'll bring you some fish from their catch!"

As soon as he disappeared around the corner, Piper shut the door, shed her nightdress, and put on trousers and a thick cotton shirt, adding another layer of socks to the ones she already wore so her father's boots would fit tighter. Luckily—or unluckily, depending on how you looked at it—she'd always had big feet. She'd outgrown her own boots months ago. Her father's coat, however, didn't fit her at all. The tail dragged on the ground, and the sleeves bunched at her elbows. It hung loose on her and she was always catching it on things, tearing holes and leaving threads hanging out. The garment looked more like a dog's shaggy coat than a jacket. She adored it.

After she dressed, Piper checked the stove again and hauled water in from the well. She filled the teakettle and set it on the stove to boil. From a cupboard, she took a box of tea and measured out a small amount to add when the water was done. For the rest of her breakfast, she got out the loaf of bread she'd made the day before and tore off two large chunks.

Every now and then, she threw an uneasy glance out the window. The green light in the sky grew brighter with each passing hour, and the smell of brimstone thickened in the air, mingling with the scent of woodsmoke from the stove. By her guess, the meteor storm would break just before dawn, which gave her a couple more hours to get ready and get to the shelter.

She packed a satchel with cloths, heavy leather gloves, a pair of goggles to keep any lingering dust out of her eyes, and a couple of rice balls she'd bought from the market. She went over every item twice to make sure she hadn't forgotten anything that she'd have to come back for later. As soon as the storm was over, she needed to be among the first out to the fields for the harvesting— Micah would slow her down—she had to be ready to run as soon as the green light faded from the sky.

She felt a twinge of guilt for lying to him, but the truth was too depressing. The fastest scrappers did always snatch up most of the valuable stuff. It only took thirty minutes after a storm ended to be left with junk. That's how good the scrap towns had gotten at scavenging the objects that fell from the sky. If you didn't get a move on, there was no point digging through the craters. There was nothing valuable left.

Outside, Piper heard doors opening and closing up and down the street and footsteps passing by her house. A few people called out her name as they passed by her door to make sure she was awake and moving. She didn't know who they were exactly—she never opened the door when they called to her—but they'd been doing it since the day her dad left the kingdom to go south to work in the machine factory in Noveen, and they'd kept doing it after he died. Piper wondered if her dad had asked them to look out for her while he was away. They never offered to share food with her—generosity only went so far in a scrap town—but she appreciated the little show of friendship, especially in a town where most people never bothered to learn their neighbors' names.

Many of the scrappers were nomads by nature, and superstitious. If they didn't have any luck scavenging in their first few months in a scrap town, they moved on to the next one. They were always sure that all they needed was a change of scenery for a change in luck. As a result, there were always empty houses around town as scrappers cleared out and squatters moved in. Piper figured they all eventually ended up back where they started, with no better luck than when they'd begun.

Her satchel packed, Piper poured the hot tea through a strainer into her favorite fat yellow mug. Curls of cinnamon-laced steam rose in the air. After an impatient minute waiting for the tea to cool, she drank it down, burning her tongue as usual. The scent was amazing, but the flavor was weak. She needed fresh leaves, but it was too much of a luxury to buy them when she still had a little bit left in the box. When she'd finished the bread and drained her second cup, she left her mug on the table next to the machine parts and went out to join the other scrappers on their way to the shelter.

Frigid night wind burned against her face. Piper pulled her dad's thick coat around her and hugged herself to hold in the warmth. Nearly Thirdmonth, she thought disgustedly, and winter still held the northern towns in a death grip. The shelter would be a little warmer with the heat of all the bodies, but Piper didn't like the idea of so many people crammed together in a hole.

In the distance, on the southern edge of town, green moonlight illuminated the sweeping, snow-covered roof of the Trade Consortium pavilion, the immense structure overshadowing the scrub-pine houses of the townspeople. Made of sturdier oak and pika wood shipped by rail from Ardra's lumberyards, the pavilion housed the weekly trade markets sponsored by the Consortium.

Behind it were the trade offices and multistory dwellings for Consortium representatives. The columned pavilion separated the two parts of the town like bars. Piper looked toward the center of town and saw Arno Weir standing next to an open metal door set into the ground.

He saw her approach and pulled his lips back in a gap-toothed smile. "There's my little machinist! Have you finished working on my steam engine yet?" As he spoke, he crossed her name off a list he clutched in his left hand.

The population of the town was constantly changing, so it was hard to keep track of people and make sure they got to the shelter, but Weir knew everyone. He ran a general store out of his house and could tell you—for a price—which were the fairest traders at the market. If the town had been big enough to have a mayor, Weir would have been it. He was also one of Piper's best customers.

"It's going to take me another week," Piper told him, "and it's going to cost you double." That engine was a clunky little beast, more trouble than it was probably worth, but Piper loved a challenge. Not that she'd ever admit that to Weir. If he thought she was having too much fun tinkering with the machines, he'd try to make her work for free. Piper *never* worked for free.

Weir clicked his tongue and put on a morose expression. "You trying to cheat me again, Piper? What would your father say?"

"He'd tell you you're a bad actor," Piper said. "You forgot to say it was a smaller model—the ones used on short-range, semi-rigid supply gliders. Those things are twitchy—don't work right half the time—and you know it. You also conveniently forgot to mention that there were sarnun stretch coils all over it."

"No, no, no, I didn't see anything like that—"

Piper crossed her arms and smothered a grin. She couldn't help it. She loved a good bargaining match, and she also enjoyed making Weir squirm. "Come on, Weir, you know this isn't my first dance. You stripped the coils off, but the chemicals leave traces everywhere. You can't miss them. They smell like dog vomit."

"Do they really?" Weir said, dropping his innocent expression. "I mean— Aw, darn it, Piper!"

"Look, you know I like a good chemical accelerant as much as the next girl, but if you add too many seasonings, it spoils the soup," Piper said. And really, it was shameful to muck up a perfectly good machine with chemicals and embellishments to make it go faster and run longer than it ought to. Why couldn't people learn to be more respectful? "More time, more money, or I can bring the engine back tomorrow and we'll call the deal off," she said.

"Not so hasty!" Weir cried, putting extra mournfulness in his tone. Piper rolled her eyes. "How can I argue with you? You're magic with the machines. I'll give you twenty extra and another week. Fair?"

Piper nodded curtly. Normally she would have held out for more, but she wanted to shut him up. The last thing she needed was Weir praising her—loudly—in public about her talents. Just like Micah and that stupid watch. There wasn't anything special about being a good machinist. Keeping her customers happy kept food in her belly, so she had to be good at her work. That was all there was to it.

"Move on," said a deep voice behind Piper. "You're holding up the line."

"Sorry," Piper said, glancing over her shoulder. A guard wearing the blue livery of the Trade Consortium frowned at her. The frown emphasized his long mustache and saggy cheeks. A hound-dog look. He wore a revolver at his belt—you didn't see many of those in the north, where iron was scarce—and a crossbow on his back.

The Trade Consortium was an independent organization sanctioned by the Merrow Kingdom to keep order in the scrap towns by settling disputes. They also hired men to make sure the scrappers didn't fight each other over what they took from the harvesting fields. The more scrappers who harvested, the more goods there were to trade at the markets, and the Consortium took a cut of every sale. In return, they made sure each town had a couple of healers—if you had the coin to afford them—a school for the youngest children, and decent roads, and when fights did break out, the Consortium came down hard and stopped them. Those attentions stabilized the towns and helped them thrive as much as they could, but still poverty reigned and a perpetual feeling of despair hovered over the harvesting fields like the poisonous dust. Order was good, but it didn't make daily living any easier.

Piper passed Arno Weir and entered the shelter. The townspeople trooped single file down a set of earthen stairs into the dark. Being in the shelter had always felt to Piper like being buried alive. She'd never been able to stop the crawly feeling that came over her skin when she was in the shelter with the earth above her head. Forcing down the flutter of nerves in her stomach, she followed the crowd.

Gathering like this was the closest the town ever got to an official function outside market days. She assumed all the scrap towns had shelters similar to this one, though she'd never been to any of the others. The problem was people built their houses closer and closer to the harvesting fields every year, so close that sometimes the meteors flew wide and demolished them like piles of matchsticks. The Consortium warned people against doing this, not only because of the meteors but also because of the dust, but they didn't care enough to try to stop them. If only people would hold themselves back, just a little, not be so eager to get killed, there'd be no need to gather everybody underground.

Piper heard Arno Weir's heavy boot tread on the stairs. "Looks like that's all of us," he said, and the metal door clanged shut, making Piper jump. Candle lanterns filled the cramped space, illuminating the haggard, wind-burned faces of the townspeople. Smoke and the odor of unwashed bodies quickly soured the air.

This last part of the night—the waiting—was the worst. Everyone was quiet for a while, but as soon as the crashes and booms of the first meteors sounded outside, it started. Mothers juggled their children, and the youngest ones started to cry because they were tired and hungry and didn't like being underground in the stink and smoke any more than Piper did. Men fidgeted, stomped their feet for warmth, while some chewed their smelly sarnun tobacco and remarked to nobody in particular that it sounded like there were more meteors than usual.

"Be a good harvest this time, wait and see," Weir said. He removed a dirty handkerchief from his pocket and blew his nose loudly.

Piper gritted her teeth to keep from screaming. Scrappers with mouths bigger than their brains—their talk was always the same. Everyone had a story of a friend of a friend of a friend who'd made a fortune in the fields after a huge storm. Piper knew it for trash. It was never a better harvest. Nobody ever found a trinket that made them rich, got them out of the scrap town and into a fancy mansion. Every person gathered in that hole had been born in a scrap town, and they'd probably die in one too.

But not Piper.

She had vowed it on the day she learned her dad was never coming back from the factory. Once she had enough money for a train ticket, she was leaving for Ardra. It was the capital of the Merrow Kingdom, the seat of the royal family, and the best place for someone with Piper's skills. She'd find a machinist's shop, a small one, and hire on for repair work for as long as they needed her. If Ardra didn't suit her, she'd just keep traveling until she found the right place.

No matter what happened, Piper had sworn—to herself and to her dad—she'd never work in a factory down south, and she wouldn't live out her life in a scrap town. She wanted to see more of the world than this one tiny, frigid corner.

Absorbed in her thoughts, she almost didn't hear the alarmed cry that rang out from the back of the shelter. Jory, Micah's older brother, ran up to her, his lantern swinging wildly in the darkness. "Where's Micah?"

⇒ TWO ⇐

A cold knot of dread settled in Piper's stomach. "Isn't he with you?" The boy wouldn't be that stupid—not after she'd promised to help him . . . would he?

"He said he was coming to the shelter with you." Jory swung his lantern around, as if he could root out Micah from one of the dark corners. The shifting light reflected off the faces of the townspeople, many of whom had turned to watch the disturbance.

"Weir, didn't you check his name off the list?" one of them said.

The merchant strode forward, glancing at his papers by the light of Jory's lantern. "Yes, here it is—name's checked off. He must have slipped away after I counted him." He fixed Jory with a look of deep concern. "I'm so sorry, boy. So careless of me."

Piper knew better than that—and so did everyone

else in the shelter. Weir's sharp eyes never missed any-thing that went on in town, and he'd never "accidentally" let someone slip past him, especially if it meant that per-son might find something valuable in the fields before he had his chance to scavenge—unless that person had promised him a cut in exchange for his looking the other way. She couldn't prove it, though, so she kept quiet and instead turned to Jory.

"He probably went back home for something and got caught by the storm," she lied. The truth would only make Jory panic. "You run and see, and I'll go to my house to make sure he didn't stop there."

"You can't leave," Weir protested. "You know the rules."

"We're not going to scavenge," Jory said angrily. "I just want to find my brother."

"It doesn't matter where you go," Weir said. "If you're outside the shelter during a storm, the Consortium will treat it as a crime. You'll be imprisoned."

"But what if Micah gets hurt?" Jory shouted.

They were wasting time, Piper thought, worry twist-ing her gut. Minute by minute, the storm grew stronger, and Micah was out in it. Micah, the boy she'd known since he was a toddler. He used to be afraid of the shelter when he was small. He would cry in his mother's arms until Piper made faces at him and got him giggling. And some days, especially lately, Micah was the only one who could make Piper laugh. They took care of each other.

Micah's parents and Jory had looked after Piper when her dad went south to the factory so Piper didn't have to live in one of the worker dormitories. Rumors circulated that they were horrible, with workers sleeping ten to a room in hammocks strung together like sausages. They'd spared Piper that, and had continued to watch over her after her dad died.

Piper made a silent decision—and tried to ignore the voice in her head screaming that she was every kind of crazy for defying the Consortium.

"You know, I've never seen the inside of a Consortium prison," she remarked. "Think the food's any good?" Before anyone could react, she turned and pounded up the shelter stairs. Jory started to follow, but Weir and two other men grabbed him and held him back. Ignoring the townspeople's shouts, Piper threw aside the metal bar that secured the door and shoved it open. Hands reached for her, but she scrambled away and burst out into the cold night air, slamming the door behind her.

Light bathed her, so bright it was like midday. Piper shielded her eyes until they adjusted. When she lowered her arm, her mouth dropped open.

Green streaks of light rained from the sky. Against the backdrop of the dark mountains, it looked like the end of the world. She saw the outline of the ice dragon clearly by the light of the falling meteors. The air burned with the stench of brimstone and dust, making her eyes water. Out of breath, Piper sucked in the fumes, coughed, and instinctively spat to expel the poison from her body. Luckily, Micah was right about the dust. Breathing in small amounts wouldn't kill a person, but long-term exposure to multiple storms was dangerous. No way was she going to test how far her body would tolerate the stuff.

Piper looked back to the shelter to see if anyone had chased her, but the door stayed closed. No one would follow her into this storm. They'd be crazy to take the risk. The Consortium would find her later and punish her.

"Micah!" she screamed, even though she knew the boy would already be in the fields and too far away to hear her. Blindly, she ran through the town, cutting a path through yards, trampling wire fences and dormant gardens, making her way to the foothills. Micah said the last time he'd been in the fields he'd taken cover under the rock ledges. If he had a drop of sense, which Piper wasn't at all counting on, he'd use the same path this time.

At the edge of town, Piper found a set of fresh tracks. The land was completely devastated. The assaults by the meteors meant no trees or grasses would ever take root here, and wild animals avoided it even when the air wasn't choked with poisonous dust. Craters littered the ground, some of them glowing with a faint emerald light. Piper didn't stop to look at what treasures they might contain, though for an instant, she was tempted. She'd been poor for so long it was hard to step over what might be a trinket worth a month's supply of food.

The pockmarked ground made the footing chancy, but Piper couldn't slow down. She jumped from the lip of one crater to the next, her foot sinking in mud and snow. Her ankle twisted. She fell on her hands and knees. Stifling a cry of pain, she got up and went on, half running, half limping.

"Micah, if you can hear me, I'm going to beat you until you can't hold a thought in your head! They'll slide right out your ears!" Piper's voice squeaked with rising panic. She was well into the fields now, and the craters were getting much bigger.

A teeth-rattling explosion shook the ground to her left, spraying her with mud and snow. Piper wiped the debris from her eyes as another fit of coughing overtook her. The green mist hung thickly in the air, threads of it drifting toward the snowy foothills.

"Piper, over here!"

Whirling, Piper saw Micah waving to her frantically from beneath a narrow rock outcropping. She ran for the protection of the ledge, though with the meteors falling around her, it seemed a hundred miles away. "Stay there!" she shouted when Micah started to come out to meet her. Fiery pain shot up her ankle. She bit her lip and kept running, trying not to look up at the sky and the green death hanging over her head. Forget about beating him; Piper was going to make Micah wish he'd never been born.

Her ankle gave out just as she reached him, and she went down on her knees again. Micah hauled her under the ledge by her armpits. The ledge was barely enough to cover both their bodies. Piper could imagine a meteor shattering the flimsy rock and pulverizing the two of them at any minute.

"Are you"—she could barely speak, teeth chattering with cold and fear—"out of your mind? I told you we'd scavenge together when it was safe!"

"I know, but I just couldn't stand to wait. I think this is the biggest one ever, Piper," Micah said, his body trembling with excitement. He pointed to the violent sky. "Look at the size of those meteors."

"I *am* looking at them!" Piper shouted. "I'm looking at the humongous, deadly meteors raining from the sky, wondering why we're not safe and warm in the shelter right now instead of cowering under this rock!"

Micah ignored her ranting. "We're not the only ones who came out early. See that?" He pointed to the field, where dark shapes moved slowly in the direction of the town. "It's a trade caravan—two wagons. Got here a few minutes ago. They think they're going to get the jump on the whole town, but they didn't notice me."

"A caravan?" Piper asked as she turned to look. "It can't be." No one in his right mind would bring a caravan into the middle of a meteor storm. Piper had never heard of such a thing.

But Micah was right. In the distance, a pair of high-walled wagons pulled by four sintees rolled across the shattered ground. The shaggy, half-blind beasts stumbled often among the craters, their trunks outstretched to feel the terrain while their bellies dragged the ground. The traders were probably too busy watching the skies to guide them. Sintees were a bad choice for caravan animals, but they were the only beasts Piper knew of that might tolerate a meteor storm without balking. They were too deaf, blind, and stupid to know any better.

"Whoever they are, if they don't manage to get themselves killed, the Consortium will ban them from the trade markets for good," Piper said. "Why would they risk coming out here? They've always let the scrappers do the dirty work of harvesting."

"Hoo, boy! See that gap in the clouds? It looks like a huge hole in the sky!" Micah wasn't listening to her or paying attention to the caravan any longer. The falling meteors had transfixed him. "Do you think that's where Hiteria went through?"

"What—the goddess?" Distracted, Piper shook her head. "That's a bedtime story, Micah. It's not real."

"I know, but they say when she left Solace, she tore open the sky." Micah shook Piper's shoulder to make her pay attention to where he was pointing. A swelling vortex of green clouds hung over their heads. At its center was a vast darkness devoid of stars. "Isn't that a big enough opening for a goddess to fly through?" he demanded.

Piper stared up at the shattered sky and tried to push past the fear that had her clenching her teeth and digging her nails into her palms. Micah had a point. She'd never seen anything like this before. People in the scrap towns made up all kinds of stories to explain how the strange objects came into their world. Some believed it was the goddess's doing, while others thought the objects had been forgotten in their own worlds and somehow slipped through the cracks into this one. Piper didn't know about the latter story, but as a tiny speck cowering before the unimaginable sight above her, she could believe a goddess had ripped a celestial tear so big that it allowed things from distant worlds to fall through.

Then she glimpsed a spark of green in the center of the darkness. With a dawning horror, Piper was pulled from her daydream of goddesses to—reality. A huge meteor, the largest she'd yet seen, roared from the darkness at the center of the swirling vortex, heading straight for the slowly moving wagons.

There was no way the traders would be able to get clear in time. The meteor was falling too fast. Micah dug his fingers into her arm, and Piper watched in horror as they jumped from the wagons. Too slow. The meteor looked as big as a horse, and the screaming sound it made as it neared echoed the cries of the doomed caravan.

Piper threw her body over Micah's and covered her ears as they fell to the ground.

The world erupted in a ball of heat and light. The meteor's impact shuddered through the ground, sending debris from their stone shelter falling all around them. Piper squeezed her eyes shut, praying the ledge would protect them. Micah wrapped his arms around her in a painful grip and yelled something incoherent.

They stayed like that, terrified, until gradually the storm passed. The whole thing was over in less than twenty minutes, but it felt like Piper spent an eternity pressed against Micah under the small rock ledge. As the minutes ticked by, the impacts grew fewer, and finally an eerie quiet fell over the field, broken only by the ringing in Piper's ears. She knew it was truly over by the smell of the air. Each breath passed more easily into her lungs, until the cold mountain wind finally chased the last of the green dust and brimstone stench away to the south. It would probably take another hour or so for the mist to blow out of town. The scrappers would stay in the shelter until then.

Piper opened her eyes, eased away from Micah, and looked across the field. As she expected, the enormous meteorite had torn the caravan apart. The battered shell of the second wagon was intact, but a sintee head and two wheels were all that was left of the first. "I don't think you'll have to worry about the traders taking any of your treasures, Micah," she whispered, her voice shaking, a lump rising in her throat.

Micah didn't answer.

Piper turned back to the boy. He still lay on the ground, his body scrunched underneath the rock shelter, eyes closed. He wasn't moving. "Micah?" she asked, silently adding, *Open your eyes.* A sick feeling clawed at Piper's stomach. Why wasn't he answering her?

Gently, Piper eased his body out into the light. The sky was no longer green but gray with a line of pink on the horizon. Micah was breathing but unconscious. Blood streaked the right side of his face and soaked the hair near his temple. Some of the caravan debris must have hit him in the head. All those jokes Piper had made about getting his skull smashed . . .

Tears blurred her vision, and her throat got tight. With trembling hands, she felt Micah's chest. A strong heartbeat; but with a head wound, that might not last. She ran her hands up and down his body, looking for more injuries. "Tell me what's wrong, Micah," Piper sobbed. "Tell me where you're hurt, and I'll fix it, I'll—"

How would she fix it? She was a machinist. Machines were so much easier to fix than people were—hadn't she told Micah that herself? Piper put her head in her hands. She didn't even have her tools with her. She had nothing.

Except the caravan. Piper's head snapped up. Traders from the big cities were wealthier than any person in the scrap town could ever hope to be. Their caravans carried extra food, supplies, and medicine. It would have taken a miracle for any of it to have survived the storm, but Piper needed to check.

Ignoring the pain in her ankle, Piper pushed herself to her feet and ran unsteadily across the field to the ruined caravan. The bodies of the two traders lay nearby, but she didn't look at them. Instead, she went to the remains of the second wagon. She hadn't noticed it at first, but now she realized a good portion of the wagon had escaped the meteorite.

"Let's see what you've got here," Piper said out loud. She rubbed the tears from her eyes and got down on her hands and knees to tear into the wagon. With every breath she drew, anger bubbled up inside her. "See what we can scavenge off of you. You make us animals, clawing at each other, killing ourselves for food down here in the scrap heaps, so let's see what we can take from you." Piper hated that she couldn't stop crying, but Micah's blood-covered face was all she could see in her mind.

Someone had tied the goods down in the back of the wagon, under a thick black tarp, and the storm had tangled the tarp in the wreckage. Piper lifted her shirt and took a knife from a small sheath strung on her belt next to the coins she'd been saving. She punched a hole in the tarp and dragged the blade down toward her. The cloth parted easily, and the contents of the wagon spilled out onto the ground.

Medicine kits, food packs with meat kept on ice, and clothes fell into her lap. Not just any clothes, either, but the thin, bright-colored stuff the southerners liked to wear. To Piper, all those sky blues, fiery yellows, and ivories looked foreign and strange set against meteor green, but Micah wouldn't have been able to contain himself at seeing all the pretties.

Piper carefully laid the medicine kits aside and cut away the rest of the tarp. She would use it as a litter to take Micah back to town. The tarp seemed to be the only thing holding the wagon together. Once she freed it, the wagon collapsed.

An arm fell across Piper's lap.

With great effort, she held in a scream. Scrambling back, she let the arm drop to the ground. Piper tore the tarp away and uncovered the body of a girl lying in the wreckage.

Judging by the face, she appeared to be only a year or two younger than Piper, but she was smaller, delicate-boned and frail. She wore petticoats and a pale yellow dress with flowers embroidered on the collar. Mud and snow had ruined these, and her wet skirt clung to her legs. Her dark hair hung in braids coiled at the back of her neck. Several strands had come free and lay limply across her cheek.

For the second time that day, Piper found herself checking for wounds, her hands tracing the girl's limbs and face, looking for the cause of her death. It took her a minute to realize the girl's skin was still warm. When Piper reached her chest, she drew back in shock at the steady rise and fall, the breath that blew softly on her fingers.

The girl was alive.

≋ THREE ≋

The tarp was just big enough to carry Micah and the girl. Briefly, Piper considered leaving the two of them to go get help—it was risky to move Micah, especially if he had a head wound—but the howling, frigid wind made her decide against that. The sooner she got them both back to town and got them warm, the better.

Piper took as much medicine and food from the caravan as she could carry, which wasn't much, but once she got back to town, she would tell Micah's brother where to find the rest. She'd taken bandages from one of the medicine packs and used them to wrap Micah's head, but she could see no visible wound on the girl. She did a quick search but found no other bodies in the caravan wreckage. If there were any other passengers, they'd either escaped the meteorite impact and run off—or there was nothing left of them.

She dragged her burden out of the fields, trying to be gentle as possible as she passed over the crater-marked earth. When she finally reached the town limits, she was half fainting with exhaustion, and a fiery ball of pain had settled around her ankle.

The townspeople were still in the shelter, which meant all the healers were there too. Piper didn't think she had the strength to get both Micah and the girl all the way to the center of town. Her own house was closer. That would have to do.

She dragged the tarp across her yard, kicked open her front door, and pulled it into the house. Her legs wobbled as she lifted the girl by the armpits and propped her up by the stove, the warmest spot in the house. Piper put Micah beside her, then stripped the two blankets off her bed, one for each of them. As far as Piper could guess, the girl would be fine—she'd probably just passed out from the force of the meteor blast or from the thick fumes in the air. She'd been the lucky one. But Micah needed help, now.

Voices filled the air, breaking the heavy silence that had settled over the fields in the wake of the storm. Stumbling, Piper went back outside. While she'd been tending to the injured, the rest of the town had emerged from the shelter and were now running for the fields. Piper was torn. She could try to chase down one of the healers or go find Jory and bring him here, but that meant leaving Micah. A wave of panic washed over her at the thought of leaving her friend alone, even for a few minutes. What if he woke up and she wasn't there? What if he got worse and he was all alone?

Just like her father—alone when he died. She hadn't been able to be with him.

Piper clamped her jaw tight to stifle a whimper. She'd brought Micah this far—she had to get him home to his brother.

Her arms leaden, Piper put Micah back on the tarp and dragged it outside. She headed toward the center of town, shouting frantically for Jory as she went. Halfway there, she met him running.

"What happened?" Jory's face went ashen when he saw his brother lying on the tarp.

"He got hit in the head. It was a meteor . . . or . . . maybe debris—just help me!" Piper stammered. She'd been calm before because she had to be, for Micah, but she could feel herself starting to come apart. "We have to get him inside and warm."

Jory had been staring at Micah—lifeless and pale, blood soaking through his bandages as he lay on the tarp—but Piper's words galvanized him. He took one end of the tarp and helped her drag it to his house, which thankfully wasn't far. She didn't think she could have made it back to her own house.

"There's a caravan wrecked in the fields," Piper said haltingly. Even with Jory pulling most of Micah's weight, her arms shook with weariness, and her breath came in sharp gasps that burned in her chest. "Meteorites destroyed most of it, but I found some medicine packs, food, and clothes. I couldn't carry it all. You should go back and get them." Piper waited for him to say something, but he didn't even look at her. His face was frozen in a mask of shock. "Are you listening, Jory? Get the healer for Micah, then go out to the fields and get the medicine packs. You can use them to pay for the healer. Do you hear me?"

"I hear you," Jory said hoarsely, coming out of his trance. "We need to get him inside first. I'll take his head and shoulders; you lift his legs. Once we get him there, we'll put him in bed and I'll go."

As gently as she could, Piper did as he told her. She couldn't stand seeing Jory like this—she'd never seen him look so scared. "I'm telling you, there's a week's supply of food out there in the fields," she said, trying to distract him from his brother. "So much I couldn't carry it all. If you hurry, you can get the rest before anyone sees the caravan wreck." She babbled on, her voice shaking, but she couldn't make herself shut up. She just kept telling Jory to go get the medicine packs, to use them to pay for a healer, as if that would somehow make up for the fact that his brother was unconscious with a bleeding head wound and maybe wouldn't wake up. But Piper kept repeating the words until her throat was so tight she couldn't talk anymore. Then she noticed that, aside from them, the house was empty.

"I forgot—your parents aren't home yet," she croaked. They didn't know their little boy was hurt, that they might never see him alive again.

"They won't be back until tomorrow," Jory said. Gently, they laid Micah down on his bed. Jory covered him with a blanket.

As soon as Micah was tucked in, Jory headed for the door. His face was still deathly pale, but he spoke calmly. "You'll stay with him, won't you, Piper? I'll be back as soon as I find a healer."

Mute, Piper nodded. She wouldn't leave him alone. When Jory left, she stood beside the bed, looking down at Micah. "I'm sorry," she whispered. "I should have looked after you better." She was older, stronger; she was supposed to protect him, but she'd failed. What would Micah's parents think of her? They always said Micah looked up to Piper like a big sister.

She stared at Micah for a long time, willing him to open his eyes, to point and laugh at her for crying and carrying on like this. But he never moved. There was only silence in the room until the door opened and Jory was back with one of the healers in tow.

The older man was much more finely dressed than Piper and Jory, his tailored suit as nice as any worn by the Trade Consortium representatives. He elbowed Piper aside and pulled up a chair beside the bed. Jory stood on Micah's other side, watching anxiously as the healer examined his brother.

Piper wanted to stay to hear what the healer would say about Micah's injury, but she suddenly remembered the girl. If she woke up while Piper was gone, she wouldn't know where she was or what had happened to her.

"I have to go," she told Jory. "There was a girl unconscious in the caravan wreck. I brought her back with Micah and left her at my house. I need to check on her."

Jory nodded. He looked like he was still in shock. "Does she need a healer?" he asked.

"I don't think so," Piper said. "But . . . will you tell me if Micah—if anything changes?" She didn't want to think the worst and tried to block the thought that Micah could die from her mind.

"I will." Jory had already turned away, his attention fixed on his brother.

Piper wiped her face. There was nothing more she could do. Reluctantly, she slipped out the door.

Piper's steps got heavier as she trudged back to her house. Her ankle still ached, but she didn't think it was a bad sprain. When she was finally home, she locked and barred the door behind her, pressed her back against it, and slid to the floor in a quivering heap. Through her tears, she saw that the girl was still asleep by the stove, her chest rising and falling in a regular rhythm.

Exhausted, Piper curled up on her side, burying herself deep in her dad's coat. The worn fabric used to smell like him, his warmth, but now all she smelled was her own sweat and sour echoes of the green dust. She closed her eyes and tried to shut it all out, to bring back her father. Eventually, she fell asleep.

She woke to a mewling cry. Piper sat up stiffly, her back against the door, hand reaching instinctively for her knife. Her mind was still fuzzy, but through the haze, she saw the girl thrashing and twisting under the blanket. Her eyes were closed. She must have been having a nightmare.

"No! No, keep it away!" she cried. Her voice was terribly hoarse—Piper barely understood the words. The girl pawed the air frantically, reaching toward the hot stove.

Piper scrambled across the floor and got hold of the girl's hands. That only made things worse. The girl fought back with wild punches. Piper took a hit to the eye and saw stars. All the while, the girl's cries grew louder. The house had thin walls; Piper was glad all the townspeople were out in the fields. If they'd been at home, someone was bound to think she was beating the girl.

"Stop it!" Piper hissed as the girl continued to thrash in her sleep. "You're safe, do you hear me? Listen, the scrapper you're punching is the one who saved you!" She dodged another blow. "One more like that and I swear—" Flailing knuckles glanced off her jaw. "I should have left you in that field!" Piper was too tired and worried to deal with this mess.

For all her wild terror, the girl was still weak and Piper finally got a secure hold on her. With soothing motions, she rubbed the girl's trembling hands, trying to show her that she wasn't dangerous. Gradually, her cries grew fainter, and Piper began to relax her hold. She pushed up the sleeve of the girl's dress, intending to check her pulse, and gasped.

Inked on the girl's forearm was a tattoo roughly the size of a matchbook. The design was a dragonfly, but instead of a normal insect, this one was made of mechanical parts. Transparent wings veined with iridescent wires and minuscule springs curled around the girl's arm. Gears and cogs composed its multifaceted eyes, and the dragonfly's metallic green body was a piston that tapered toward the bend of her elbow. A skilled artist had painted the dark-haired woman on Micah's music box, but whoever had done the dragonfly design was a true master. The inks alone had to have cost a fortune.

It was the mark of the Dragonfly.

Piper had never seen one, but she'd heard of the famous tattoos. The mechanical dragonfly was the symbol of Aron, the king of the Dragonfly territories, which lay directly to the south of the Merrow Kingdom.

The two powers had been rivals for as long as anyone could remember, competing over resources and land, with the Merrow Kingdom usually being the more aggressive. In fact, rumor had it the Merrow Kingdom had been making and stockpiling weapons and had been plotting to try to take over part or all of the Dragonfly territories—until Aron caused the iron shortage.

A well-known inventor and explorer, King Aron had set up factories all over the Dragonfly territories in the last five years, with the sole purpose of building a fleet of airships and ocean steamers to explore the uncharted lands of Solace. The world's future lay in exploration and expansion, he claimed. But for the longest time, that expansion had been halted by a range of impassable mountains to the north and west, and by oceans to the south and east. Expeditions that tried to cross the mountains were stopped by avalanches and peaks so high and cold that they froze the blood in a person's veins. And the wooden sailing ships that set out to find new lands across the sea were battered by storms and vicious currents. They returned in failure—if they returned at all.

King Aron intended to change all that, with steamships that would weather any ocean storm, and airships that would pass over the highest mountains in safety and comfort. But to accomplish his goal, he needed iron— lots of iron. Lucky for him, most of the iron mines in Solace were located in his kingdom, but to ensure he had a large enough supply, and at the same time to prevent the Merrow Kingdom from building mass quantities of weapons to attack his country, Aron had stopped trading iron to the Merrow Kingdom. Instead, he funneled it all into his factories. Ending this trade had left the Merrow Kingdom with a shortage that put thousands out of work and soured relations between the two kingdoms to the point that many feared a war would erupt anyway. But King Aron continued with his shipbuilding, claiming that finding new lands and resources was the key to lasting peace. He built the largest factory of all in Noveen, his capital city—the place where Piper's father had gone to work, and died.

The dragonfly tattoos were only given to two groups of people: Aron's advisory council, of which there were four members, and those who were under the king's protection. This usually included the rich and powerful, although no one knew exactly how many bore the mark. The symbol itself had originated with Aron's family. One of his oldest family crests was a pair of sabers crossed to look like the wings of a dragonfly, which had started the tradition of the people referring to the reigning monarch as the Dragonfly. Over the years, the symbol had changed as technology evolved, but Aron was still called the Dragonfly. Done in a mixture of rare inks, the tattoos were almost impossible for outsiders to duplicate. Piper could tell by the swirling metallic colors—emeralds and coppers so vivid they sparkled like jewels—that the mark was genuine. Whoever this girl was, she must be under Aron's protection, so she was obviously very important. Her king was one of the most powerful men in Solace.

And Piper's father's murderer.

Not directly, of course. But King Aron had built the factory in Noveen, the monster that had swallowed Piper's father up and made him breathe poisonous black smoke until his lungs couldn't take it anymore. After her father died, Piper had spent many sleepless nights imagining her journey to the capital, how she would burn Aron's precious factory to the ground.

And now look at her, still living in the scrap town, tending and comforting a spoiled capital girl. Yet the girl couldn't be more than eleven or twelve years old, and in the grip of the nightmare, she'd seemed much younger, terrified half out of her mind.

Carefully, Piper adjusted the girl's sleeve to cover the tattoo. What was a girl under Aron's protection—one so young!—doing on a caravan in the harvesting fields during a meteor storm? Who else might have been on the caravan with her? Was she with her family? Had any of them escaped? Piper sucked in a breath—surely not Aron himself? No, she couldn't believe that. The scrap towns didn't get much news except what the traders brought with them, but they talked plenty about Aron. Rumor had it that he didn't condone scavenging from the scrap fields. He even encouraged people to come from the Merrow Kingdom as her father had done, to work in his factories, shaping iron for his fleet.

He wants us poor, Piper thought—poor and working for him.

"That still doesn't explain where you came from." Piper spoke softly to the girl, nudging her a bit. "Can you hear me? Can you wake up?"

No answer. The girl had drifted into a deep sleep, but whatever nightmare she'd been having hadn't let go of her yet. Her eyelids twitched, and every so often, her body stiffened as if she expected an attack. Piper started to move away, wanting to give the girl space, but in her sleep, she clutched at Piper's wrists and made an unhappy little mewling sound. Piper sighed and settled down next to her. The floor was cold. She freed one of her hands long enough to reach for more wood for the stove.

Outside, she heard the first stirrings of the townspeople coming back from the fields. Voices raised in agitation drifted past her door. She caught snatches of their conversations—mostly about Micah and the caravan, how neither of them had any business being out there in the storm and how the Consortium was going to punish the survivors. Anger swelled in Piper's chest. They had no right to gossip about Micah. He was just a kid. And none of them had run out of that shelter to help him. They'd stayed huddled in the dark like rats.

That was the problem with this town. Nobody really cared about helping anybody else. They were all drifters, scavengers hoping to make a fortune or at least some quick coin. Nobody ever thought about trying to build a real life here. Even the houses were temporary structures built as quickly and as cheaply as possible. In some ways, Piper knew she was just as bad as the rest. After her father died, she'd stopped going outside unless it was necessary. She kept to herself and rarely talked to anyone except Micah and his family. Now even that connection might be gone for good.

And what would happen when the girl woke up? Piper didn't need another mouth to feed, and a girl from the Dragonfly territories wasn't likely to want to stay in the scrap towns any longer than she had to. She could go to the Consortium and tell them what happened, but they were already going to be looking for Piper to answer for the stunt she'd pulled escaping from the shelter. Why hurry that process along? Still, as someone marked by Aron, the girl was obviously important. Someone was bound to be interested in where she was and what had happened to the caravan.

Piper lifted the girl's sleeve and looked at the tattoo again. Outside, the shrill call of a distant steam whistle caught her attention. It was the 401. The train came through the scrap town once a month, ferrying goods and passengers on a north-south route through the Merrow Kingdom and the Dragonfly territories, where it originated. It was scheduled to come in at midday. Piper hadn't realized it was so late. A gnawing hunger clawed at her insides. She hadn't eaten anything since her quick breakfast of bread and tea.

"I bet you're going to be hungry too if you ever decide to wake up," Piper grumbled at the girl. "Well, we can't sit here cuddling all day, and I'm going to need my hands if you want food."

She eased out of the girl's tight grip and breathed a sigh of relief when the girl didn't make a fuss. Piper took the rice balls out of her satchel and ate both while she fetched another bucket of water from the well. Then she got out an old dented pot with a bent handle and set it on the kitchen table. Micah's parents had returned from their last fishing trip with a bundle of sturgeon for her. She kept it in an ice chest in the corner farthest away from the stove. She took two fillets from it and a bunch of leeks and potatoes that she'd bought at the trade market. Altogether, she thought she had enough to make a decent fish soup for her and the girl.

Piper hadn't cooked for two in a long time.

A little while later, she had fishy-smelling fingers and a blister on her thumb from peeling potatoes, but her ingredients were chopped and simmering in the pot on the stove. The aroma of cooking vegetables and fish broth brought a raw ache to Piper's stomach. She tried to ignore the sensation and washed her hands and face in the water bucket. Her brown hair fell in wet spirals against her temples, and she caught a strong whiff of brimstone and sweat. Wrinkling her nose, Piper stripped off her coat and shirt. She kept a bar of soap and a few other toiletries in a small cabinet at the foot of her bed. She used the soap to wash her hair and her upper body, scraping the dirt and dust remnants off her tan skin. After she'd finished, she changed into a spare shirt and stripped off her pants to wash her legs. When she was satisfied that she no longer smelled like the meteor storm, she hung her coat on a hook on the door and went to check on the soup.

Piper didn't realize the girl's eyes were open until she was standing right next to the stove. The girl had woken without a sound, and she lay silently where Piper had left her, clutching Piper's knife in her hands.

≈ FOUR ≈

Piper went straight for the knife on her belt, but of course, it wasn't there. It must have fallen out of its sheath while she was washing, she realized. And now the girl held it in both her hands as she watched Piper's every move with huge brown eyes.

When she was little, Piper used to bring home stray cats and beg her father to let her keep them. He always said no, not only because they couldn't afford to feed them, but also because of their temperaments. The townspeople called them devil cats because they were half crazy with hunger and fear of the humans. They'd leave scratches and bites up and down Piper's arms every time she tried to pick them up. The look in their eyes was the same look the girl was giving Piper.

I should have learned my lesson back then, Piper thought. *No more bringing home strays.*

Piper held up her empty hands. "I'm not going to hurt you," she said softly. "You were in an accident. Your caravan—" She hesitated. Now probably wasn't the best time to tell the girl that the rest of her companions were gone. For all Piper knew, her parents might have been among the dead. Her stomach twisted at that thought. "I brought you here to get better," Piper said at last. "Are you hungry?" She pointed to the bubbling broth on the stove. Tempt it with food—the best way to tame any wild creature.

Against her will, the girl turned her attention to the food. Piper saw the naked desire in her eyes, and the hands holding the knife trembled. "I'll get you a bowl and spoon," Piper said, turning slowly to a shelf on the wall. She made sure she could still see the girl out of the corner of her eye. "But you'll have to put the knife down to eat."

The girl watched as Piper took a wooden bowl and spoon off the shelf. Her eyes followed Piper to the stove, where she carefully ladled out soup from the pot. Herbs floated on top of the broth and steam rose from the bowl in fragrant clouds. Piper ignored the growls of her own stomach and held the food out to the girl.

After a moment's hesitation, the girl dropped the knife and snatched the bowl from Piper's hands. She plunged the spoon into the broth and shoveled it into her mouth.

"Careful!" Piper said. "Blow on it first, it's—"

The girl's eyes widened an instant before she spat out the scalding mouthful. A shower of broth and leeks hit Piper in the face.

"—hot," the girl said in a small, croaky voice.

Silence fell. A log shifted in the stove, and the pot of broth continued to simmer. With a detached calm, Piper reached up, picked a leek out of her hair and dropped it back in the pot. Waste not. She took the bowl from the girl and blew on the broth several times to cool it, then she handed it back and smoothly retrieved her knife from the floor. The girl was too busy eating to notice.

Piper watched her for a long time when she should have been eating her own meal. She was absorbed in trying to figure out how, in the space of a few short hours, her life had gone so completely lopsided that she found herself standing in her house, fish broth dripping down her face, watching her dinner be gobbled up by a girl who was protected by King Aron, the person she hated most in the world.

Try as she might, she couldn't come up with a satisfactory answer, so Piper ladled up some soup and ate it at the kitchen table while the girl stuck close to the stove. When Piper finished, she stood and went to get her coat. She used the sleeve to wipe the rest of the broth off her face. She knew without looking that the girl was watching her. "I'm going out," she said, "but I'll be back soon, and then we'll talk about . . . what happened. Eat as much as you want, but don't go outside, you understand? I don't want you getting lost while I'm gone."

The girl didn't answer, and Piper wondered how much she understood. Piper herself spoke in the Trader's Speech, and the girl had used the same tongue just now. Was she a simpleton, or just afraid because she'd woken in a strange place to an unfamiliar face? Either way, it didn't make any difference to Piper. She needed to get the girl out of here, find a way to send her back south to the Dragonfly territories. The first step would be to get a letter out on the 401, let the king know what had happened to the girl. She could look into doing that much now. Then she needed to check on Micah. She couldn't stand not knowing how he was.

Piper bundled the big coat around her and headed for the train station, a worn, two-story brick building on the outskirts of town. The 401 had pulled alongside, sunlight gleaming off its tracks and driving wheels.

Despite all the other things on her mind, excitement fluttered through Piper at the sight of the immense black steam engine with its mile-long tail of boxcars and passenger carriers. Though aged, the 401 was still an impressive specimen. Every time it came to town, Piper itched to get her hands on the old girl to see what secrets she held in her metal heart.

And there were secrets. Piper could tell just by look-ing. Dozens of strange pipes, vents, and valves covered the train's exterior, far more than should have been needed to operate the various systems of an ordinary train, and an extra layer of thick armor plates had been bolted to each of the cars. Stories floated around town that the best machinists in the Dragonfly territories had fitted the train with a formidable set of defenses, and that it hauled cargo through some of the most dangerous lands in Solace, fending off sky raiders and saboteurs along the way.

Whether the stories were true or not, Piper thought the 401 was a heavy, stern-looking, capable old girl—one who'd seen practically every corner of Solace—and Piper envied the big train and everyone who had ever traveled on her. Her crew had seen more of the world than Piper was ever likely to.

But maybe that didn't have to be true, Piper thought as an idea came to her. Her heart beat excitedly as she considered it. Getting an express letter all the way to Noveen was going to cost a small fortune, yet wouldn't the capital be very interested to learn that she'd rescued one of Aron's marked people from the harvesting fields? Interested and maybe grateful enough to reward Piper with the money she needed to get out of the scrap town for good.

Running through the possibilities in her head, she was almost to the station when she heard a male voice call her name. Turning, she saw Jory running toward her, his blond hair flapping in his face. Piper swallowed. What if he was coming to tell her bad news about Micah? For just a second, a tiny part of her wanted to run away, even though she was desperate to know how Micah was doing. She pushed her fear aside and greeted Jory when he stopped, out of breath, in front of her.

"I was on my way to your house when I saw you headed out of town," he said. "Micah's still unconscious, but the healer thinks he's going to be all right."

"Thank the goddess!" Piper breathed. Light-headed with relief, she didn't immediately notice the worried expression on Jory's face. "What's wrong?" she demanded. "You said he was going to be all right."

"It's not that," Jory said. "I came to find you because there's a man wandering around in town—says he was with the caravan. He's looking for the rest of his people, asking if anyone found anything in the wreckage."

"Another survivor?" Piper felt a quick surge of relief. That meant the girl wasn't alone. It also meant Piper wouldn't have to spend the money to send a message after all, and she could get rid of the girl—and maybe get her reward—much sooner than she'd expected. Finally, things seemed to be looking up. "Where is he?" Piper asked.

"I don't know," Jory said. He shot an uneasy glance back toward the town. "I didn't tell him about you finding the girl."

"Why not, for goddess's sake?" Piper felt a flash of irritation. "It's not as if she can stay here."

"I know that, but I didn't like him, Piper. He wasn't friendly." Worry furrowed Jory's brow. "I didn't like the look in his eyes either."

"He's from the cities," Piper said scornfully. "His type doesn't like to mix with us scrappers. Of course he's uncomfortable."

Jory didn't look convinced. "Why's he here, then? Why did that caravan go out in the storm? I never heard of anyone from the cities doing something that stupid." He bit his lip. "And Micah, he never should have—" Jory's voice cracked.

Piper laid a hand awkwardly on his shoulder. "Once this story gets out, nobody will ever try it again," she said. "Thanks for telling me about the man."

Jory nodded. "Watch yourself," he said seriously. "If you need help—"

"I'll get by." But his offer made warmth spread through Piper's chest. Even though his brother was hurt, Jory still thought to look after her. "You just take care of Micah." Piper stepped away from him. Again, tears stung her eyes. She'd come so close to losing Micah. But she didn't have time to cry anymore. "Take care of yourself too," she added as she turned and headed in the direction of her house.

Since she no longer needed to arrange to send a message, Piper decided to check back in on the girl and then go looking for the other survivor. Maybe hearing that one of her companions was close by would make the girl a little less afraid of her.

When Piper opened her front door, her mouth fell open. Had she fallen and hit her head? Come to the wrong house? She couldn't believe what she was seeing.

The place was a shambles. Pillows stripped off the bed, all the plates, bowls, and cups taken down off the shelf and scattered on the floor. The little blue chest of drawers by her bed was only a shell. Someone had pulled all the drawers out and strewn her clothes across the room. Her tool belt was empty, her precious tools piled in a heap by the stove. Piper didn't have many possessions, but those she did have were all over the floor, leaving barely enough space to walk. In the middle of the chaos sat the girl, sorting through a stack of pictures Piper's father had drawn while he was away working at the factory. He'd tucked one in with every letter he'd sent to her.

At first, Piper was too shocked to feel anything. She stripped off her coat and let it fall to the floor. Then she saw the girl with her fingers all over her father's pictures, how she traced the lines curiously, wonderingly. Her sleeves were pushed up, and Piper saw the dragonfly tattoo peeking out of one. A burning sensation started deep in her gut and slowly spread until her blood pounded a harsh rhythm in her ears.

She crossed the room in two strides and slapped the pictures out of the girl's hands. The girl looked up in surprise that quickly turned to confusion when she saw Piper's furious face.

"What do you think you're doing?" Piper said, fighting to keep her voice level. "You have no right to touch my things!"

The girl blinked. "But I fixed them," she said.

"Fixed them!"

The girl nodded vigorously. "You see, everything was hidden. Hidden away in the boxes"—she pointed to the empty chest of drawers—"or hidden away on the shelves." She crawled over to the cups and bowls and began lining them up in rows in front of the stove. "Now you can see where everything is, remember the name for everything, although the furniture is still a problem . . ." With a clatter, she dropped the cups and wandered over to the bed. She spread her arms as if measuring. "I don't understand the logic at all."

"Understand?" Piper said through gritted teeth. "Understand this—if you ever put your grubby little hands on my things again, I'll—"

"The problem is size!" the girl said, interrupting her. "Everything is too big." She stabbed a finger at the bed, then at Piper. "The bed is too big for one person. Your boots are too big, and your coat is absolutely hopeless." She spoke very fast. "It's all out of proportion. Nothing fits. Nothing makes sense." She looked at Piper with a pleading expression. "It *has* to make sense."

I was wrong, Piper realized. *This girl is the one with the head injury.* "Who *are* you?" Piper demanded. "And what did you do with the girl who was here before—the quiet one with the knife? I think I liked her better."

But the girl wasn't listening. She gathered up the pictures Piper had slapped out of her hands. "Now, *these* make sense. Graceful lines, proportions perfect—and I've seen these buildings before, though I don't know their names." She held up a drawing of the factory where Piper's father had worked. "What is this place?"

"The factory at the capital," Piper said. She sat on the floor next to the girl. "Noveen—it's in the Dragonfly territories—that's where you came from. Don't you remember?"

The girl stared at the drawings as if she might burn holes through them with her eyes. "I remember pictures, objects, voices—a clock on the wall, ring the bell for tea, the white dress, no, the yellow one, look at the sunset colors, the waterfall, the scale models, send the guards away, shall we have music, hold her there, put the needle in just so—" She sucked in a breath and threw the picture down. "No, no, that's painful." She looked at Piper helplessly. "They're all jumbled. I can't sort them out."

"Slow down," Piper said. "A little while ago I thought

you didn't speak at all, and now your mouth has a life of its own. Let's start with something easy. Do you remember your name?"

"My name?" She looked at the other pictures as if they might give her a clue. "Of course. In theory. Hypothetically. Everything has to have a name. Look at the picture of the salamander—now say the word. Picture of the dog—now say 'dog.' I said them every time, over and over, but they couldn't hear me. Why couldn't they hear?"

She ran out of breath, trembling, squeezing the drawings in her hands. Piper didn't understand half of what came out of her mouth, but the girl was obviously suffering. She looked at Piper, half afraid, half in a dream, and Piper sighed. "It's all right," Piper said. She picked up a cracked mirror off the floor. She usually kept it hanging on the wall, but for whatever reason the girl had moved that too. Piper held it up in front of the girl's face. "Can you tell me who's in this picture?"

The girl stared at the mirror. Slowly, she nodded, and in a dreamy voice said, "Anna."

≈ FIVE ≈

"Hello, Anna. My name is Piper."

Piper held out her hand to the girl, who took hold of it, but instead of shaking, she held on tight. "Piper," the girl repeated. "Piper. This is where you live?"

"Yes. We're in Scrap Town Number Sixteen, in the Merrow Kingdom," Piper said. She waited, but none of this information seemed to register. The girl looked at her with a blank expression. "Scrap Town Sixteen. See, they don't give them proper names, just numbers on the map because there're so many." And more seemed to crop up every day. Still there was nothing, no sign of recognition from the girl. "You know what the Merrow Kingdom is, right?" Piper said, a little desperately.

This stirred something. The girl—Anna—pointed to the drawing of the factory. "Merrow Kingdom—that's *not* where that is," she said.

"There are factories in the Merrow Kingdom," Piper said, though factories in places like Ardra primarily made weapons, not ships, and most of them had been shut down as a result of the iron shortage. "But the place in the drawing is in one of the Dragonfly territories. Do you know the difference?"

The girl thought about it and nodded. "I remember— the Merrow Kingdom is the north. Dragonfly is the south. To the west live the archivists. The crown over it all is the scrap fields. We are all . . . Solace."

"Good to know you're not as far gone as I thought," Piper said. "Listen, you've had a shock. The explosion knocked you out and probably shook up your memory. I'm sure it'll all come back to you as soon as I bring your friend here."

"Friend?" Anna repeated the word as if it were something ominous, and the expression on her face turned cautious. "What friend?"

"You were with a caravan," Piper explained. It was time for the truth, no matter how much it might hurt. "Goddess knows what you were doing out in the fields. Most of the people on it were killed by a meteorite. I'm sorry."

Piper patted the girl's shoulder. She expected Anna to be upset, but if she felt anything at hearing about the deaths, she didn't show it. Instead, Anna began softly humming a tune. Piper didn't recognize it until she added words. "*Hurry hurry, make the journey, come across. Unwanted things, forgotten things, they all end up in Solace. Unwanted things, forgotten things, they all come home to Solace.*"

She was repeating the old children's rhyme. Piper remembered hearing kids in the scrap town skip rope to it when she was a little girl. She'd done it a few times herself. "That's right. In the scrap fields, the earth and the sky—something about them is different from the rest of Solace. The boundary between worlds is thin there, and on certain nights, it dissolves completely. That's where the meteors come from. No one knows how it got that way—some people say it happened when the goddess left the world after she created Solace—but the first machines came from the scrap fields, from other worlds."

"All theoretical," Anna said, shaking her head. "Maybe mythical. But it's accepted, so we can't do anything to change it, can we? That's what they say."

Piper raised an eyebrow. "'They' say that, huh? I don't suppose you remember who 'they' are? People on the caravan? At least one other person who was on it survived. He's probably looking for you right now."

"I don't remember," Anna said. She put the pictures down and went to sit by the stove. Tucking her knees beneath her chin, she said, "I remember the wagon, the bumps and the cold, but I don't remember any faces." She looked around the room. "I still don't understand why it's so big. Makes it difficult to think when everything's out of proportion."

"Out of—" Piper looked around the room, at her father's coat, his boots—now hers—and suddenly realized what the girl meant. "Most of this stuff belonged to my father. Sure, it doesn't fit me, but I don't have anything else," she said, irritated and a little self-conscious.

"Your father?" Anna brightened. "Where is he? With him in the room, the proportions would be perfect."

"No argument there," Piper said softly. She picked up the drawings and her father's letters that Anna had scattered over the floor, gathering them carefully into a bundle. "He used to be a foundry worker in Ardra until Aron decided to stop trading iron to the Merrow Kingdom because he needed all of it in his own factories. Pretty greedy, right? I mean, how much iron does one king need?" She felt that ugly burning sensation in her gut again and fought to quell it. "Anyway, people like my father lost work and turned to scrapping in the harvesting fields to get by. We weren't making enough money, though, and since the Merrow Kingdom didn't care enough to help the people who were out of work—they're too busy trying to make weapons without iron—Dad went south to the Dragonfly territories to work at one of the big factories in Noveen, hoped that eventually he'd save enough to buy us a house there. He sent letters and money every week until about a year ago, when he died."

"He died?" Anna's forehead wrinkled, as if this didn't make sense to her. "How?"

"Breathing the factory smoke made him sick—I didn't know for sure he was dead at first. The letters and money stopped coming. Then I got a letter from the factory boss. He said the illness came on so quick there was nothing they could do. They buried him in one of the cemeteries down south." Piper shrugged, trying to be nonchalant, but the memory of seeing Micah's fragile body in the fields, the absence of her own father's body, made her sick inside. At least if the worst happened, Micah's family would have something to bury. The people who died in the factories were only sent home if their families could pay to have the body shipped. Since she couldn't, Piper had laid a wreath of flowers behind the house and pretended it was a grave.

"I'm sorry," Anna said. Her cheeks turned pink. "Sorry for touching the pictures. I was wrapped up in the analytical, not the social. I should have asked before I tried to make sense of them."

"Forget it," Piper said. She shook out a wadded-up shirt that had been lying on the floor. "If you're feeling better, maybe you could help me straighten things up in here?"

A sudden, loud knocking made them both jump. Piper's first thought, before she remembered, was that it was Micah—he was the one who came to see her most often, rapping urgently at the door just like that, as if he couldn't wait to get inside—but she quickly reminded herself that that was impossible. Micah was still unconscious and recovering at home.

Goddess, she hoped it wasn't the Consortium already. She knew that sooner or later she was going to have to answer for running out of the shelter into the storm, but she didn't think they'd get around to punishing her this soon. Piper glanced at Anna and saw her eyeing the door uneasily.

"It's all right," Piper said, wanting to reassure the girl. "Stay by the stove where it's warm, and I'll see who it is."

Piper went to the door, unlocked it, and lifted the bar. She opened the door partway to see a man standing on the threshold. He was dressed in the remains of a suit and trousers that had once been very fine but were now torn and bloodstained. His right arm rested in a sling made out of part of the suit. His face was gaunt, as if he hadn't slept or eaten in days. A black beard contrasted sharply with his pale white skin.

Automatically, Piper slid sideways a step, putting the protection of the door between her and the man. She didn't recognize him, and she knew most of the faces of the current crop of scrappers in town. Strangers didn't necessarily mean trouble, but sometimes the hungry or hurt ones were desperate, and they weren't above breaking into houses for food and warmth. This man looked like he was in sore need of both. But his injured arm might also mean that this was the other survivor of the caravan that Jory had mentioned. Piper hoped so, anyway.

Before she could open her mouth to ask him what he wanted, the man spoke.

"Are you Piper Linny?" he asked, a mixture of hope and impatience in his voice. "I was told this is her house."

"That's me," Piper said cautiously. "What is it you want?"

"Is she here?" the man asked. His voice quivered, suddenly excited. "I was on a caravan in the fields when the meteors hit. I thought everyone else died, but I was told you found a girl, that she survived. Please, may I see her?" He took a step forward and lifted his good hand as if to push the door open.

"Whoa." Piper set her foot against the door and rested her hand on the knife in her belt, making sure he saw the gesture. She could tell he was upset and worried, and though she felt for him, she didn't like the idea of him pushing his way into the house. Injured or not, he was still a stranger. "It's all right," she said, "just calm down. Yes, she's here, and she's alive."

"Thank the goddess!" The man sighed and rubbed his good hand over his face. Piper noticed a tremble in his fingers. "Please," he said, "I have to see her. I was so frightened."

Piper bit her lip and looked the man up and down again. "Okay, but give me a minute to check on her first before I let you in."

Piper waited for him to take a step back before she closed the door. She should have been relieved—the man had come to her, saving her the trouble of searching for him. All she had to do now was give him the girl and—hopefully—collect her reward. But Jory was right. Something about the man didn't sit right with her. He seemed so anxious, like he was about to jump out of his skin. She told herself she was imagining things and that he was just eager to make sure that Anna was all right.

"Anna, the man I told you about—the one who was on the caravan with you—is here. If you're feeling up to it, he really wants to see—" She stopped. Anna wasn't sitting by the stove anymore. She'd pressed herself into the farthest corner of the room and was staring at the door with an expression of sheer terror on her face.

"Don't let him in," she said. Her voice was barely a whisper. "Don't let in the wolf."

Confusion gripped Piper. "Anna, what's wrong?" Piper crossed the room and crouched in front of the girl, taking her by the shoulders. The girl's breath came in quick, panicked gulps. She shook her head violently from side to side.

"No, no, no, no," she moaned. "The wolf found me. He caught my scent. Now I'm the prey. I'm acting just like the prey, but I can't stop!"

"What are you talking about?" Piper demanded. The wild expression on the girl's face frightened and confused her. "Who is he? Anna, *who is he?*"

"We have to escape. Fight or flight. Always flight—it's the only way when you compare the odds." Whimpering, Anna struggled out of Piper's grip and stood up. She grabbed Piper's coat and shoved it into her hands. "Get out while we still can."

"I'm not going anywhere until you tell me what's going on." But Piper put on the coat. It was, after all, best to be prepared for anything.

A loud, urgent knocking sounded again at the door, and the man's voice came through the thin wood. "Listen to me. You must let me see her, my Anna." Piper heard the impatience in his tone, but she thought now it bordered on anger.

Anna danced in place, looking as if she might bolt for the window. "We have to run!" she insisted.

"We're not going anywhere," Piper said firmly. "Look, I'll talk to him, get him to go away until you've calmed down."

She returned to the door, shooting a quick glance over her shoulder to make sure Anna wasn't going to try to run off. That was all she needed, to end up chasing the girl all over the scrap town. Why was she so panicked? Piper had thought she'd be relieved to see the man, that maybe it would jog her memory seeing someone she knew. She'd never expected the raw fear that shone in Anna's eyes.

Cautiously, Piper opened the door a few inches, wide enough to see the man fidgeting on the threshold. When he saw her, his lips pursed anxiously. "May I see her now?"

"I think you're going to have to come back later," Piper said. "She says she doesn't want to see you right now and—"

Her voice trailed off as an expression of shock spread across the man's face. "She's awake?" he cried. "You spoke to her?"

Before Piper could reply, the man was moving; he threw his hip against the door and shoved it open, pushing Piper off balance. Piper tried to push back, but he was bigger than she was, and he'd caught her by surprise. She didn't even have time to go for her knife.

Once he was inside the door, the man's gaze fell on Anna. His face went paler, if that was possible, and his shocked expression melted into wonderment. "Anna. My beautiful child, you're alive. You're *looking* at me! Those lovely eyes, they see me."

Piper saw tears well up in his eyes. Was Anna his daughter? she wondered. They didn't exactly look alike. The man's transformation from shocked to affectionate was so sudden and complete, but the way he looked at Anna—the possessiveness in his expression—sent a chill up Piper's back. He gazed at Anna rapturously, as if she were some sort of precious object. It felt wrong, very wrong.

Glassy-eyed, the man took a tentative step toward Anna. Anna reacted immediately, pressing herself against the opposite wall. Her head whipped wildly from side to side, and her body tensed, prepared to flee.

"Don't be afraid, my Anna," the man said soothingly. "You're safe. I'm here to take you home."

At the mention of "home," Anna began to tremble violently. She slid to the floor, locked her arms around her knees, and curled into a protective ball.

Piper couldn't stand to see her so terrified. Even when her own father had yelled at her for doing something stupid—which was fairly often—she'd never been anywhere near as afraid of him as Anna was of this man. No way was he her father.

Before he could move any closer to Anna, Piper darted between the two of them. Being so close to the man reemphasized how much bigger than her he was. *Smart, Piper, really smart*, she told herself. *This is the kind of crazy you save for special occasions.*

"She doesn't want to go with you," Piper said, fighting to keep her voice steady. "I think you should leave. The Trade Consortium's already going to be after you for dragging a caravan out to the fields during a meteor storm. When they find out you've broken into my house, it'll just make things worse."

"The Consortium?" the man said. "You think the Consortium will protect you?"

Piper thought her threat might make a dent, make him come to his senses, but instead, he smiled at her like a parent listening to a boastful child. That smile shook

Piper more than seeing Anna's terrified reaction to the man. The smile emphasized his eyes—and even through the tears, the depths of the man's eyes were cold, just like a predator's.

Anna was right. The wolf was in the house, and they were the prey.

Taking a deep breath, Piper stepped forward. It was a monumental effort to move *toward* the threat. Her feet felt weighted down, but she had to try to get back in control of the situation somehow. "This is my house," she said. "I won't let you barge in here and threaten me." The quaver in her voice betrayed her fear. She weighed the situation. She had a knife, and he had a broken arm, but he was still much bigger than both of the girls were. Escape was their best option, except Piper had no idea how they were going to get past him. There was only the one door, which he stood in front of, and they wouldn't be able to get out a window before he caught them.

The man's smile disappeared. He regarded Piper with narrowed eyes. "That child is mine," he said calmly, "and I'm taking her with me. Step aside or I will make you."

Time ground to a halt. Piper didn't know whether it was fear that kept her rooted in place in front of Anna or the hope that the man wouldn't really hurt her, that he must be bluffing.

It only took an instant to find out that he wasn't.

The man lunged at Piper. Piper raised her knife, but he slapped it out of her hand. He grabbed her roughly by the shoulder and shoved her aside. Pain exploded in Piper's head and down her back as she hit the wall. She fell to the floor and lay there, head spinning, trying to protect herself from more blows. Distantly, she heard a scream.

"Stop! Don't hurt her!" It was Anna. Piper watched as the girl sprang up from the floor and grabbed the man's bad arm. He faltered when she touched him. He turned to her, reaching for her with that same wondering, rapturous expression on his face.

"My Anna . . ."

Hearing him say her name, so softly, like a caress, gave Piper new life. She pushed herself up from the floor, ignoring the screaming pain in her head. She didn't have her knife, so she grabbed the closest thing at hand—the pot of fish soup. Anna must have taken it off the stove while she was gone. She'd eaten almost all of it too. *Glutton.* That was Piper's last thought as she brought the pot up and hit the man in the back of the head.

He might have been able to withstand the blow if he'd been stronger, but he was injured, and the shock of seeing Anna had obviously affected him. The blow sent him to his knees and splashed the remaining fish soup all over the wall, and then the man collapsed on his stomach in the middle of the room.

It seemed like a long time that Anna and Piper stood frozen, staring down at the man's unconscious body. A log in the stove popped, and Piper jumped. The sound got her moving. She dropped the pot and grabbed her knife off the floor. Next, she found her satchel. Inside she still had the medicine and food packs she'd taken from the caravan. Luckily, Anna hadn't unpacked those in her mad scavenger hunt through the house. She stuffed in her father's letters and drawings, a few extra shirts, and her only other pair of pants that still fit. By the time she was done, the satchel was heavy and bulky. Last, she grabbed her tool belt, replaced the tools Anna had scattered all over the floor, and fastened the belt around her waist. With her satchel slung over her shoulder, she grabbed Anna by the hand.

"You said it—fight or flight. We're getting out of here."

≈ SIX ≈

Darkness was falling as Piper and Anna reached the edge of town. Piper went through their options in her head, discarding most as soon as she thought of them. Jory had offered his help, but he was no match for that man, and he still had Micah to care for. She didn't trust anyone else in the town to go to for help. The Trade Consortium was supposed to protect the scrappers, but even their officials could be bought with enough coin. The man's clothes may have been torn and bloody, but he was a stiff hip if Piper had ever seen one.

The next scrap town on the map, Number Seventeen, was only a few miles away, but even if they could get help there, Piper knew Anna would never make it that far. The girl was already shivering in her flimsy dress, and her shoes weren't made for hard walking, let alone running in the dark over uncertain ground.

The 401's whistle rang out in the night. Piper felt it reverberate through her body, and with it came a surge of hope.

"It's still here." Gasping, Piper skidded to a stop and changed direction, heading for the station. "Come on, we're getting on that train."

How she would accomplish that, Piper had absolutely no idea. She didn't have nearly enough coin for one ticket, let alone two, but the train was their best hope of getting far away before the man woke up and came after them.

Beside her, Anna stumbled and fell to her knees. Piper heard her bite back a cry of pain. "I'm all right," she said when Piper helped her up. "You should keep going. I'm holding you back—slowest member of the herd."

"We're not separating," Piper said.

"But it doesn't make sense—"

"Not much of anything makes sense around here," Piper said impatiently, "especially today." She gripped Anna's hand securely and they were off again. They didn't slow down until they got near enough to the station to slip into the shadows. Piper crouched low to the ground in hopes they wouldn't be seen, and headed toward the back of the train, where she thought the mail-carrier cars were. Piper figured it was the best place to try sneaking on. There wouldn't be as much traffic back there as in the passenger section, and those cars wouldn't be as heavily guarded as the boxcars carrying the trade cargo.

They came up alongside the last row of cars. Piper stayed crouched for a moment, listening for signs of people. Thankfully, all was quiet. Of course, even if they managed to get aboard unseen, there was still the small matter of the train's legendary defenses. What was the penalty for a scrapper stowing away on board a train? Three lifetimes in prison or just two? Piper smiled grimly.

"What are you . . . smiling about?" Anna asked, still out of breath from their run. "It doesn't make sense . . . for you to be . . . smiling while . . . we're in danger."

"Don't worry about it—and stop saying that none of this makes sense!" Piper drew her knife and pointed with it to a gap between two cars. "That's where we'll try to get in. Lie down there by the tracks until I tell you when it's safe to climb up."

Anna obeyed, crawling on her belly onto the sloping rock hill near the train tracks. As soon as Piper saw she was safely out of sight, she climbed up the metal ladder attached to the car and grabbed hold of the heavy canvas bellows that protected the vestibule between cars. She brought her knife up and, before she lost her nerve, sliced an opening in the canvas.

A warning bell erupted from somewhere deep within the train. Piper flinched, almost dropping her knife. She figured there'd be protection on the doors, but she'd never dreamed that a little scratch would set off an alarm. "We're in trouble," she called down to Anna, trying to keep her voice low. "Stay there and don't move."

"Come down," Anna whispered fearfully.

Piper shook her head. "It's too late to turn back." She hooked an arm around a ladder rung, gripped the knife handle in both hands, and pulled, widening the slit in the canvas until it was half the length of her body. Her heart pounded in time with the warning bell.

"Piper, look out!"

Piper raised her knife, prepared to fend off an attack, but there was no one there. Then she heard it, a high-pitched whine like a machine warming up. The sound was coming from a line of four pipes running alongside the car. They ended in an open vent right beside where Piper clung to the ladder. Scorch marks covered the wall of the car near the vent.

Fire, Piper thought as panic spread through her chest. She cursed her own stupidity. She should have expected a trap like this. They were flame vents, part of the train's defenses triggered by the alarm. It looked like the pipes were designed to shoot gouts of fire out the vents at raiders trying to board the train.

"Stay down!" Piper yelled at Anna, forgetting to be quiet. She started to jump off the ladder to get clear of the vent, but her coat sleeve caught on one of the iron bolts that held the ladder in place. The force jolted her, and the knife slid from her hands. Her sleeve tore, the threads twisting around the protruding bolt. Piper swore and tried to pull the cloth loose, but jerking her arm only made the threads twist tighter. The whining sound grew deafening. Piper didn't want a taste of the fire that was about to shoot out of that vent. She gave up pulling the sleeve and tried to slip out of the bulky coat. At the same time, an intense heat built at her back.

She wasn't going to make it. A strangled cry rose in her throat. She thrust out her hand to cover the vent, even though she knew it was futile. Nothing could hold back the fire. Piper closed her eyes and braced for the worst.

Please, stop. Please, please don't fire.

Behind the mechanical whine came a roaring sound that filled Piper's ears. Suddenly, both sounds gave way to a shuddering groan, and abruptly the pipes fell silent. Piper opened her eyes. The vents were dark. The heat was gone. She felt only the cold night air on her sweat-soaked face. Even the warning bell had stopped. The machinery must have malfunctioned.

"Are you all right?" Anna asked.

Piper was so relieved she felt like crying. She released a shuddering breath and reached down for Anna's hand. "Hurry," she said, hauling the other girl up onto the car. "I don't trust that thing to stay broken, and somebody had to have heard the warning bell. We need to find a place to hide."

Anna had retrieved Piper's knife. With it, Piper freed her coat from the bolt, though she had to cut half the sleeve away to do it. She held open the canvas while Anna crawled through and then followed her inside. They went left through a door and found themselves in an empty boxcar.

"Can we stay here?" Anna asked.

"No, it's too wide open," Piper said. "Let's go right, toward the back of the train." She turned and went back through the vestibule to the other door. Shoving it open, she started to plow forward and realized—too late—that the car they'd entered wasn't empty.

Piper suddenly found herself staring into a pair of startled green eyes. She skidded to a stop and stumbled when Anna bumped into her from behind. The eyes belonged to a boy standing alone in the middle of the car. He looked to be about Piper's age, dressed in torn overalls and a brown shirt. A bean-shaped blot of soot darkened his left cheek, and his bare feet were filthy. When he saw Piper, in an instant, the expression in his eyes shifted from surprise to anger. He broke into a run toward them.

"You there! Stop!" he yelled.

Piper slammed the door on him. "Go!" she screamed, and the two girls turned and ran back the other way. They passed through the empty boxcar and on into the mail car. Piper heard the boy's footsteps pounding behind them. He was fast, fast enough to catch up before they found a place to hide. "Keep going!"

The next car was full of cargo and food supplies for the train. Piper didn't have time to stop and look as they tore through the car. A guard standing at the far door turned when he heard their footsteps. Piper kept running, using her momentum to throw herself at the guard. She hit the guard in the side and knocked him sprawling beside the door. Anna ran past and opened the door for them. Piper lost her balance, but the smaller girl grabbed her by the shoulder to steady her and they ran on.

"This is no good," Piper said. Her chest burned, and she knew Anna must be worse off. "We're running toward the front of the train. There'll be more people and more guards; we can't hide up here."

Proving her words, they ran into the next car to find three guards. They were inspecting some cargo and didn't immediately see the girls. Piper grabbed Anna and turned her around.

"Where are we going now?" Anna asked. Sweat ran down her face. She looked as if she were about to drop. "We're not making any progress forward or backward. Those chasing us, on the other hand—"

"I know, I know! Back to the mail car," Piper said. Maybe they could tackle the boy, overwhelm him as they'd done to the guard. "We have to—"

Just then, the boy burst into the car. The guards at

the other door looked up. "Get them—they're stow-aways!" the boy shouted. Before Piper could run, the boy grabbed her wrist and twisted it behind her back. Anna tried to push him away, but the guards ran forward and lifted her by the waist. She kicked the air futilely. "Throw them off the train," the boy said.

"You don't understand. It's not safe out there." Piper struggled, but the boy only squeezed her wrist until she yelped in pain. "If you throw us off the train, we're dead."

"You're lucky we don't give you to the Consortium," the boy said, "or drag you off to the capital, charge you with destroying government property."

"If they want it protected, maybe the capital should put *men* in charge of the 401, not boys," Piper sneered. She stamped her heel on the top of his foot. The boy grunted, but he didn't let her go. How could he be so strong? He was thin as a scarecrow and no taller than she was. Piper twisted around to look at the boy. Up close, she saw two ugly scars slashed his neck just above his collarbone. His pupils dilated, flashing yellow at the edges. The change caught her off guard and she blinked, but when she looked again, they were the normal black color. She must have imagined it.

"Off you go," the boy growled.

The guards took out a set of manacles and bound Piper's wrists in front of her. They went to do the same to Anna, pushing up the sleeves of her dress. Piper stopped struggling. Instead, she prayed they would remove the bindings once they were off the train. At least then they would have a chance to run again.

Watching the guards, the boy suddenly let out a soft cry. "What is that?" he demanded.

The guards looked at each other, confused. Piper turned and saw the dragonfly tattoo exposed on Anna's arm. Then she remembered what the boy had said about charging them with destroying government property.

Of course—she was an idiot not to have realized it sooner. The 401 originated from the Dragonfly territories, which meant King Aron likely owned the train and employed all its workers. They would recognize the tattoo and its significance right away. Piper sucked in a breath as hope stirred in her chest. Maybe, if they put on a good enough show, they could still get out of this.

"Anna!" Piper hissed. "What are you doing? I told you to keep that covered!"

Anna glanced blankly at the tattoo, then at Piper. "I don't remember you telling me—"

"Quiet!" Piper said. "Don't say a word."

"Wait a minute. That can't be genuine," the boy said. "Bring her over here," he told the guards. "I want to see that tattoo up close."

They led Anna over to the boy, who removed her manacles so he could examine the tattoo. Piper noticed that he had large calloused hands. If not for the soot on his face, the dirty bare feet, and the expression of suspicious anger in his eyes, he might have almost been good-looking. Almost.

He stared at Anna's tattoo for a long time with narrowed eyes, running his finger over the shimmering wings and body, as if he could wipe the ink away and prove the tattoo was a fake. Abruptly, he released her and nodded to the guards. "It's genuine. Let them go."

The guards hesitated. "Are you sure?" the larger one ventured.

"Do it," the boy said stiffly. "They're under the king's protection."

Piper's knees went weak with relief. She never thought she'd be glad for Aron's influence, even indirectly. The guards removed her manacles, and she rubbed the feeling back into her wrists.

"What does it mean, Piper?" Anna asked. "A minute ago they were like predators, chasing us down, hemming us in, but now they're acting differently . . . because of this." She looked at the tattoo as if she'd never seen it before. Piper quickly took the girl's hand and rolled down her sleeve to cover the tattoo. This would be tricky. To avoid attracting suspicion, she needed the guards and the boy to believe that they actually worked for Aron and knew what they were doing—instead of being two scared girls running for their lives up and down a train.

And if they believe we're working for Aron, Piper thought, hope rising within her, *they'll have to help us, at least let us*

leave on the 401. They wouldn't dare defy their king by deny-
ing us safe passage on the train.

"Our secret is out," Piper said, affecting a tone of res-
ignation, as if they'd been caught playacting. It was the
best thing she could think of to cover Anna's confusion.
Her amnesia would be a bit too hard to explain at this
point. "No need to pretend anymore, Anna—they know
you're working for Aron."

"But what—" Anna stared at her blankly.

"Never mind," Piper said, shooting Anna a look to
try to keep her quiet. She couldn't let the girl give them
away. "What's important is that these men understand
we're here on *secret business* for the Dragonfly territories."
She tried to sound as mysterious as possible—which
wasn't hard, since she was making her story up as she
went along. "And we need their help."

"Secret business?" the boy echoed, disbelief plain in
his voice. He rolled his eyes and laughed. "Maybe the
Dragonfly territories should send *women* to represent
them, not girls."

Irritating as he was, Piper gave him points for turning her insult around. But she still had the advantage.
"You saw for yourself the tattoo is genuine. I think that
entitles us to a little more respect—and an apology." *All*
right, that last one might have been asking too much.

Piper and the boy stared each other down, tense, neither one willing to blink. Piper tried to look confident,

but her stomach churned with nerves. "Where's *your* tattoo?" the boy challenged.

Piper gritted her teeth. "I don't have one." She ignored the annoying little *aha!* flicker in the boy's eyes and scrambled to think of an explanation, preferably one that sounded at least a tiny bit plausible. "Look, I'm this girl's protector." Piper's mind raced. Goddess, what was she saying? Where did that come from? "Isn't that right, Anna?"

Awkward silence fell over the car. Piper realized she'd just potentially put her fate in the hands of a girl with no memory, whose next sentence might or might not make any sense.

Oh, I am such an idiot.

"It's true," Anna finally said, and Piper let out her breath, relieved. "She's my protector."

The boy's eyes narrowed. His jaw worked, as if he was holding back a flood of words—hopefully not something like *You two are the world's worst liars!*—Piper thought. "I see" was what he ended up saying. "In that case, we apologize for mishandling you." The boy stared at Anna as he spoke and ignored Piper completely. "How can we be of service in your *secret business?*" he asked, the disbelief still in his voice.

Piper started to answer him, but then she realized they were all waiting for Anna to speak. As far as they were concerned, Anna was the one in charge here. Piper was just the scrapper. Piper's face burned with anger and humiliation. She didn't have a tattoo, so in their eyes she wasn't even worth talking to.

Anna glanced uncertainly at her, and Piper tried to smile encouragement, but inwardly she prayed that the girl wouldn't start going on about wolves and proportions—theoretical, hypothetical blabbering again.

"Piper and I want to leave this town on the train," Anna said at last. She hesitated before she continued. "We want to go to the capital. Yes, we want to go to Noveen." She looked at Piper again. "It's the logical place, the only one that makes sense."

Piper sighed in relief. She gave the boy a bright smile. "Couldn't have said it better."

"All right," the boy said. "Noveen is at the end of our route. But it would be best if you told us who or what you need protection from so we can be prepared."

"A wolf," Anna murmured, shuddering. Her eyes lost focus as the memory took hold of her.

"What?" the boy asked, looking confused.

"Never mind," Piper said hastily. She didn't want them to know about the man chasing them. Knowing about him would bring up too many questions Piper couldn't answer. "That's our business. You said you're already going to the capital—great. We just want to tag along."

"Just using us for a ride, huh?" A muscle in the boy's jaw twitched, and his angry scowl deepened. "Can you at least tell us your full names, or are they a secret too?"

Piper thought about it. She didn't want to give him her full name, even though she didn't think it was smart to push him much further. The fact that he seemed suddenly angrier surprised her. She knew he didn't fully believe their story, but why should he care about taking on a couple of extra passengers? It didn't cost him anything. "I'm Piper. This is Anna."

"Fine, then." The boy turned to the guards. "You can go. I'll take care of things from here."

"Are you sure?" one of the guards said, eyeing the girls warily.

The boy nodded. "I can handle them." He looked at Piper and Anna. His expression was neutral now, but Piper sensed the anger still simmering beneath the surface. Where did it come from? "I'll show you to your private car," he said.

Piper couldn't believe the ploy had worked. The relief that came over her left her feeling shaky. They were going to get out of this. "Thank you," she said, then realized what she'd just heard. "Wait, hold on, did you say our private car?"

The boy nodded at Anna. "Anyone who has the mark of the Dragonfly is treated as a representative of King Aron himself," he said formally, as if he were in the presence of the king. "He or she is entitled to full access of the train and all its services for as long as necessary. I do wish you hadn't waited so long to make your identities known," he added with a hint of scorn in his voice as he turned to Piper. "We might have avoided all this unpleasantness."

Piper realized he was still suspicious of her, even after seeing the tattoo and knowing Anna was under the king's protection. Piper couldn't help it. Her anger flared. It was she who didn't fit into the picture. "I told you our business is secret, and even if it wasn't, maybe we didn't trust that you'd let someone like me on the train. How many scrappers do you take on as passengers up here in the mountains?"

"None," the boy said flatly. Oh yes, he was suspicious of her all right. "But as long as you're with her, you're welcome here too." His tone left Piper no doubt that if Anna weren't here, he'd take great pleasure in throwing her off the train himself. "My name is Gee," the boy continued. "I'm in charge of security. If you need anything while you're here, talk to me. Now, if you'll follow me."

Without waiting for them to reply, Gee strode off quickly toward the front of the train. He was all business, and judging by how fast he was moving, he was clearly anxious to get rid of them. Piper and Anna hurried to follow, Anna sticking close to Piper's side as if she was afraid Piper was going to suddenly disappear.

"Will we be safe now?" Anna whispered.

Piper didn't know. She didn't want to lie, but she also didn't want to frighten the girl any more than she had to.

"It looks like for the moment. We caught some luck back there," Piper said. She glanced at Gee's back, the rigid set of his shoulders. "I think he likes us."

Anna brightened. "Really?"

"Oh, absolutely," Piper said, trying to sound cheerful. *Not at all.*

As they walked, Piper felt the train begin to move. The whistle blew a final time. After passing through another storage car, they entered the passenger section. Several passengers and train personnel milled about, turning the seats from their upright daytime positions into upper and lower beds with privacy curtains for nighttime sleeping. Piper looked out the windows to see the houses of the scrap town slowly passing by, fewer and fewer until they were clear of them.

That was it. In another minute, they'd left Scrap Town Sixteen behind. Piper realized with a jolt that her dearest dream—to ride out of the scrap town—had come true in a heartbeat and she'd nearly missed it. She stopped and stared out the window, watching the snow-covered hills roll by and the town get smaller in the distance.

And then it dawned on her what she was really leaving. Micah was back there too, and every minute she was getting farther away from him. The realization hit Piper, and she put her hand against the cold window, staring back at the town as loss gripped her chest. Everything had happened so fast, she hadn't realized what leaving the scrap town would actually mean. She was leaving

Micah behind, and she hadn't even gotten to see him wake up. She wouldn't be there to see that he recovered from his injuries. Worse than that, Micah wouldn't know what happened to her. He would wake up and find out she was gone, with no explanation and her house a shambles. He would be so worried about her.

"Piper, what's wrong?" Anna stopped a little ahead of her. Gee stopped too and turned back to wait for them. He sighed impatiently but said nothing.

"I'm all right. I was just looking at the scenery." With an effort, Piper turned away from the window and caught up with them, but her legs felt shaky, her steps uncertain. She was free of the scrap town, but it wasn't the clean break she'd thought it would be when she used to dream about leaving. She was going to miss Micah terribly.

Gee led them through several more passenger cars and common areas until they reached a car near the front of the train. A narrow hallway ran the length of the left-hand side, but the entire right side was enclosed. Piper assumed it was another passenger car set up for nighttime, but this one had real walls instead of privacy curtains. Gee opened the one door to the enclosure and stood aside to let them go in.

Piper's mouth fell slack as she entered. They stood in a large private suite. To her right was a sitting area with a plush sofa bolted to the floor. Opposite was a small polished dining table flanked by two chairs.

Outside the huge windows, the scenery raced by as the train picked up speed. Near the front of the suite were two plump berths, upper and lower, and a private washroom. Piper's tiny house could have fit into the car a couple of times.

"Is this acceptable?" Gee asked stiffly. His tone still carried traces of anger.

Piper could only nod. She was too busy staring at the beds, the furniture, and the bowl of apples, oranges, and grapes sitting on the dining table. Without another word, Gee turned and left the suite, slamming the door much harder than necessary.

Anna glanced at Piper uncertainly. "It really doesn't seem like he likes us," she observed.

"I think you're right." Piper sighed. "Well, it doesn't matter. I'm just happy we made it this far. Might as well make ourselves comfortable." She shook her head. She still couldn't believe the size of the room.

Anna grabbed an apple from the bowl of fruit on the table and bit into it eagerly. Juice dripped down her chin. "This tastes amazing." She offered an orange to Piper, but Piper shook her head. She knew she should eat, but she wasn't at all hungry. After everything that had happened, her stomach just wouldn't settle down.

Dropping her satchel, she walked over to the sofa and knelt on the cushions, leaning against the sofa back so she could press her cheek against the window. She was trying to look back at the scrap town.

She told herself it was only Micah she missed, not the town itself. Number Sixteen wasn't home. The only real connection she had with the place was in the memories she'd shared with her father, and he was gone. Her mother had died when Piper was too young to remember her.

Nothing should be holding her back. She was safe, she had a bed to sleep in—a very nice bed—and she was on her way to the capital. Her plans for her future hadn't changed. In fact, they'd improved. A private suite for the trip to Noveen. Arno Weir would have swallowed his tongue at seeing those fluffy sofa cushions. And she would get to see a nice little slice of the world along the way. Once Anna was safely home, Piper would collect her reward and set off to find work as a machinist, just like she'd planned. The whole thing felt like a dream.

An image of the man from the caravan flashed through Piper's mind, and fear took hold of her.

Piper gripped the sofa back and pressed her forehead against the window. Her breath peppered the glass with little fog clouds. All right, so maybe things weren't perfect. Maybe she'd just had a world of trouble dumped in her lap along with her dreams, but she was too exhausted to sort it all out right now.

Piper turned her back on the window and sank into the couch. Anna had put the half-eaten apple back in the bowl and was sitting at the table, sleeve rolled up, tracing the lines of the dragonfly tattoo. "You'd better keep that hidden," Piper said. "It came in handy today, but we don't want to attract too much attention."

"I didn't know I had this," Anna said. Fear quavered in her voice. "There are too many blank pages. Nothing's comprehensive. Why are there so many blank spots, Piper? I heard the name Aron once when I was asleep, but I don't know his face, so the picture's unfinished. But I *should* know his face because you say he put this picture on me." Tears ran down the girl's cheeks. "It doesn't make sense! I know you told me not to say that, but it's true. None of this feels real."

"Hey, take it easy." Piper went over to the table and took Anna by the shoulders. She steered her across the cabin, over to the lower berth, and sat next to her. "You knew you needed to go to the capital, didn't you? You told those security men exactly what you wanted."

Anna nodded slowly. "It feels like the right place," she agreed, but she still looked miserable. "I just don't know why."

"Well, it's a start," Piper said. "Look, what you need is sleep. We've both been through a lot today. Tomorrow, we'll work on your memory."

Anna reached across the bed and slid her cold hand into Piper's. "I'm glad you're my protector," she said. "You're fierce like a mother goshawk."

Piper laughed self-consciously. She didn't know what to make of that compliment. "Sure, sure, that's what they all say," she joked, but Anna didn't seem to hear her. The girl's eyelids drooped; she was already half asleep. Piper moved aside so Anna could lie down. Seeing her stretched out like that, Piper realized for the first time how dirty they both were. The hem of Anna's dress was torn in several places, the skirt covered in mud. Piper's coat sleeve was torn all the way to the elbow, and the knees of her pants were muddy and ripped.

"Maybe we should wash off some of this muck before we go to sleep," she said, but Anna didn't answer. She was asleep. Piper sighed and covered her with the blanket folded at the end of the bed. The dress was a loss. She would have to find Anna something else to wear. Maybe there were merchants on the train. She figured she could trade the medicine packs for clothing. "Now I'm a nursemaid," she grumbled. "Micah would laugh if he could see me." But saying Micah's name out loud made his absence hurt even more.

Piper got up and wandered back over to the table, took an orange from the bowl, and forced herself to eat a few pieces. As soon as the tart juice hit her tongue, she realized just how hungry she was. She finished the orange, ate an apple and a bunch of grapes, and tried to think of the last time she'd had fresh fruit. *Wild blackberries, that was it*, she remembered. Her father used to find patches when he was out hunting, but even those were rare. As far as Piper was concerned, the fruit was a feast, all the different flavors converging. She savored each bite.

When she'd finished eating, she stripped off her coat and slipped out of her muddied pants. Wearing only a shirt and her underthings, she climbed into the upper berth and closed the curtains. On the other side of the bed was another, smaller window. Piper propped up her pillow and lay on her side to look out into the darkness. They were still in sight of the mountains, heading south. Noveen was on the coast, a long way away. Piper had never seen the ocean. She drifted off to sleep imagining what it might be like, one big mass of blue, a saltwater bath. Did blackberries grow in the south? she wondered.

"You should be worried," Gee said.

Jeyne Steel wiped her hands on her pants, turned from the coal bunker, and regarded her security chief. Gee was tall but scrawny. It was hard to believe he could move half a ton of coal all by himself and hardly break a sweat. "Green-Eye, are you *still* talking about those two? Please tell me that it's two different passengers you're worried about now, because you're coming dangerously close to wasting my time."

Gee's cheeks flushed. "They're not passengers, they're stowaways, and I'm telling you, they've got trouble written all over them."

"Well, they did manage to get past you," Jeyne said,

scowling. "Speaking of which, what happened to the defenses back there?"

"The flamethrowers didn't fire, and something killed the alarm," Gee said angrily. "Ask your fireman what went wrong."

"Is he still talking about this?" Trimble looked up from the firebox and grinned at Gee. Flames burned hot at Trimble's back, but he ignored them. Jeyne often said that between the fireman who was immune to fire and Gee the chamelin, her crew would fit just as comfortably in the capital circus as on the 401.

"What happened to the third-tier defenses?" Gee demanded. "Those girls should never have gotten as far onto the train as they did."

"I checked them over twice," Trimble said. "Nothing's wrong. In fact, everything's working great back there now. Must have just been a misfire."

"Check them again when you're finished up here," Jeyne told him. "No more misfires on this trip. And you," she said, before Gee could open his mouth again, "I don't want to hear any more about this. If trouble from two little girls is all I have to worry about, I'll kiss the goddess's feet—figuratively speaking." She mopped sweat off her brow with a handkerchief and then used the cloth to tie back her thin gray hair. "The only thing you should be thinking about right now is getting this train and its cargo through Cutting Gap," she told Gee. "No distractions."

"I'll be ready," Gee said, but his green eyes were yellow around the pupils. The color change always gave away his anger.

"Good. Now get out of here," Jeyne said. "I'm tired of looking at both of you."

"Hey, what'd I do?" Trimble said. His black hair stood up in sweaty spikes all over his head. He pulled his goggles over his eyes and ducked his head back in the firebox.

Gee went to the window opposite the engineer's seat and climbed out of the engine cab. He crawled up to the roof and stripped off his overalls and shirt, tossing them back through the window before he changed form. The eyes were the first to shift, the pupils turning a lambent greenish yellow and immediately adjusting to the darkness. His feet and hands widened and extended into claws, which made little shrieks as they ground against the cab's metal roof. His body thickened and sprouted a wiry coat of green hair; his skin darkened to match. Bone spurs burst from his spine, and his face hardened, taking on an angular, lizard-like appearance. Finally, he crouched down and braced himself, and in a spasm of pain, wings burst from his back, stretching to a span of over twelve feet.

He caught the wind and let it lift him off the car. Despite his weight, his wings beat the air gracefully, carrying him easily. Below him, the train wound through the darkness like a mechanical snake. He flew up and down the line of cars, looking for anything out of the ordinary. Not that he expected to see anything. The mountains were too distant to hide ambushes or sky raiders. Besides, they hadn't taken on enough cargo yet to make an attack worthwhile. Jeyne was right. Cutting Gap would be the real test, but they were still several days away from that obstacle.

Gee found himself hovering over the private car where the stowaways were probably asleep by now. No matter what Jeyne said, Gee knew trouble when he saw it, and those two had it pouring out their ears. Especially the older one, the scrapper. She had something inside her that burned. Gee had seen it in her eyes. He might have admired her passion if it wasn't obvious that she and the other girl were hiding something. They were both on the run, and odds were that whatever was giving chase would follow them onto the train.

Into his home.

Gee had spent nearly his whole life on the 401, working one job or another until Jeyne gave him the security chief spot. But he had always protected the train, its passengers, and crew. They all knew him and trusted him. Jeyne and Trimble were his family, the only one he'd ever known. And he wasn't about to let anything threaten his home, whether it was marked by the Dragonfly or not.

Since when had Aron ever cared about the 401

anyway? To Gee's knowledge, the king had never even traveled on the train. He was too busy holed up in his estate in Noveen, running his factories and building his steamships to conquer the oceans and the skies. Everything had to be bigger, better, more efficient. If Aron had his way, someday soon the 401 would be obsolete, abandoned.

Gee rose higher into the air, releasing a howl of frustration and anguish that echoed back at him from the mountains. Why couldn't the factories just stop and the train keep moving, traveling forever? He wished for it, but deep down he knew things weren't that simple.

Aron might have planned to blaze a path to the uncharted lands with his ships, but it was the Merrow Kingdom's aggression that had started all the trouble. They'd spent their iron developing weapons and war machines, building up their military to the point that King Aron's people whispered that an invasion was coming, that the Merrow Kingdom was looking to expand by conquering the Dragonfly territories.

To protect his kingdom, Aron halted the iron trade with Merrow and accelerated his own shipbuilding to get his plans for exploration under way, but Gee wondered how much that would really accomplish in the long term. Merrow was furious over it all, and if trade wasn't restored soon, war would come anyway. Thousands of people had already suffered because of the rivalry between the two kingdoms; war would make the suffering a hundred times worse.

But there was nothing Gee could do about any of that. All he could do was protect the 401 and its people.

The wind buffeted him. Gee smelled snow in the air. The cold didn't penetrate his tough hide, but the struggle against the wind was beginning to tire him out. He drifted down and landed on the roof of the stowaways' car. He didn't bother to soften his impact. Let them hear the noise and think there were strange, sinister things out in the dark. Gee chuckled, a sound like stones scraping together, and folded his wings around him.

≈ SEVEN ≈

Piper awoke to sunlight shining directly in her eyes. At first, she didn't understand where it was coming from. The windows of her house were always dirty and muted the light. She rubbed the sleep from her eyes and rolled over. Her cheek met with a wonderful softness, a pillow so full and luxurious she thought she might drown in it. She looked down at the sheets and blankets covering her body, and then she became aware of the gentle rocking movement of the train. The events of the previous night came rushing back.

It hadn't been a dream. She was on the 401 bound for the capital. Her new life. And as she came fully awake, Piper realized she smelled food. Heavenly, mouthwatering scents of meat and warm bread. Dazed, Piper stumbled out of bed and made her way over to the sitting area.

Someone had placed a large tray on the table; it held two heaping plates of scrambled eggs, sausage, corned beef, and fried cassava, along with two cups and a pot of black tea.

Anna was already sitting at the table in an oversized white bathrobe, her hands clasped in her lap as if she could barely contain herself. "Someone knocked on the door earlier with this," she exclaimed. "I didn't want to wake you up because you were sleeping so soundly, but I knew it would be rude to start eating without you, so I waited and watched you closely all the while you slept."

"That was nice," Piper said. Anna was really kind of sweet, Piper thought. Sure, the idea of someone staring at her while she slept was a little creepy, but the girl's intentions were good.

"Of course, I can understand you sleeping so long," Anna chattered on. "I don't think I've ever slept in a bed as comfortable as that one—not that I can remember, anyway. Can you believe the pillow! Oh, and I found this in the washroom." She lifted the robe sleeve. "My dress smelled awful, so I threw it away. The robe is much more comfortable. Do you want something to eat?"

Now that she'd had some rest, Anna sounded more like a frantic hummingbird than ever. Piper fell into the chair next to her and reached for the teapot. "Yes." She smiled. "Let's eat."

Anna beamed.

For the next half hour, Piper was in heaven. The

tea scorched her tongue, hot and fresh and strong with spices, and the sausages burst when she cut into them, dripping with juices. Her father had rarely been able to afford meat. The meteor storms chased most game away from the scrap towns. Traders could bring it in on ice, but that was expensive, and most people couldn't afford to keep livestock in the scrap towns. Their food came from the lakes and whatever crops they coaxed out of the short growing season. Now, in the course of one morning, Piper was eating sausage and eggs, and drinking the freshest tea she'd ever tasted. And as a bonus, eating meant Anna couldn't talk, so there was blessed silence throughout the meal.

When Piper finished eating, she poured more tea for herself and Anna, then she took her cup and went to sit on the sofa in front of the window.

"What are you looking at?" Anna asked, her mouth full of food. She had eaten everything on her plate plus some of Piper's food. Piper didn't know where she was putting it all.

"I don't want to miss it," Piper said, gesturing outside. She watched the brown winter fields roll by, buildings with roofs covered in snow. "I've never been outside the scrap town before. I want to see everything."

Anna left her plate and came to sit next to Piper. "I'm sorry I made you leave your home. I should have said that before. You saved me, and what did I do to thank you? I took you out of your nest. The wolf came and—made you leave."

"That's one way of putting it." Piper caught the look of misery creeping into the girl's eyes and patted her arm hastily. "It's all right," she said. "Everything important about that place I took with me." Which wasn't true, Piper thought, an image of Micah coming into her mind, but she didn't want the girl feeling guilty about things that weren't her fault. "Right now I'm more worried about the wolf—er, the man from the caravan."

That part was definitely true. Despite the soft bed and the incredible pillow, Piper hadn't slept well. She'd told Anna not to worry, but all night her dreams were filled with the man and the look in his eyes when he shoved her against the wall. Piper didn't know how far he'd go if she kept getting in his way. And now he'd be awake and looking for them. It was only a matter of time before he figured out they'd left town on the 401.

Anna stared at her hands. "I tried to remember some more this morning. There were little bursts and pops, things that looked familiar—like this." She pushed up the robe sleeve and looked at the dragonfly tattoo. "I remember it hurt when I got this. I remember the pain but not the reason they put it on me. Reaction, not reason—what does that mean?"

"I don't know," Piper said. "What about the man? He said he's your father. Is that true?"

A sickened expression came over Anna's face. "He can't be."

"But you don't remember?"

"If he's my father, I don't want to remember."

"Anna, you have to try," Piper insisted. "He's not going to stop looking for us."

"But . . . we're safe on the train, aren't we?" Anna's voice rose in panic. "He can't get to us here. A train moves at an average speed of forty-five miles an hour, but a human man, even running, moves at an average speed of—"

Piper shook her head. "Anna, think. This train carries a ton of cargo. It's going to stop. In fact, I think we'll be making a whole lot of stops between here and Noveen. The 401 spent hours just at the scrap town station loading and unloading cargo for the Consortium. And what if we have engine trouble? All of that will slow us down. Meanwhile, that man will be looking to catch the first express train he can find—one on a different track that doesn't carry freight—and then he'll be moving a lot faster than us." Judging by his clothes, Piper thought the man had more than enough coin for several express tickets. "Eventually, he'll catch up and try to head us off at one of the bigger towns."

"Then we need to get off the train!" Anna cried, jumping up from the sofa. "Hide somewhere so he can't find us. Fight-or-flight all over again, and it's always flight!"

"Fine, it's always flight, but then what?" Piper

snapped, losing patience. "Where will we find shelter? It's winter, for goddess's sake, and you're wearing a bathrobe. The money and food I have won't last us a week. This, right here"—she spread her arms, encompassing the private car and the tray of food—"is a miracle, and this train is our best chance to make it to the capital. But if you can remember anything at all about the wolf— who he is and what he wants with you, *anything* that might help us—you need to tell me."

Once she was done, Piper immediately regretted her outburst. She'd spent all this time trying to reassure Anna, to keep her calm, and now she'd ruined it because she couldn't keep her own fear of the wolf in check.

Piper's heart sank as Anna shrank into herself, clutching the sleeves of her robe until the fabric threatened to tear. "I'm sorry. I wish I could remember," Anna said in a choked voice. "I tried. When I woke up, I tried to remember why he scared me so much, but it's like there's a wall around him that I can't get through. I just know his voice. In my dreams, I hear it all the time. He's dangerous, and he's not . . . normal."

Piper laughed without humor. "Yeah, I definitely picked up on both of those things."

"I'm sorry," Anna repeated in a small voice.

"It's all right," Piper said, suddenly ashamed. She had no idea what Anna might have been through before she ended up in the harvest fields. Maybe it was better if she didn't remember everything about the man. "I'm sorry, Anna, I shouldn't have snapped at you," Piper said. "Whenever I get scared, I act like a bully. My dad used to say that. You should just tell me to shut up when that happens."

Anna's eyes got big. "I would never do that!"

Piper laughed again, this time with more feeling. "Oh, you'll learn to. Listen, why don't you stay here and have some more tea? I'm going to go and see if I can get you some other clothes. You'll need something to wear outside this room. I also need to find out where the train's going to be stopping. Probably Tevshal, at least— that's one of the bigger cities. People there don't scavenge from the meteor storms like the scrap towns do. It's too far away."

"But why go there?" Anna asked. "I thought we had to stay on the train."

"We do, but—" Piper hesitated. An idea occurred to her, but she wasn't so sure it was a good one. "Well, there's a sarnun woman in Tevshal called Raenoll. The traders who come to Scrap Town Sixteen used to tell stories about her. Do you know what a sarnun is?"

"I—" Anna stared out the window for a long moment, concentrating. "They live underground, and they speak to each other without words. Their bodies are weak, but their minds are strong, hyperdeveloped— telepathic, telekinetic. Is that right?"

"Well," Piper said sheepishly, "I was just going to point out that their minds are a lot different from a human's, but what you said is better. Anyway, the traders sometimes take things they've bought from the scrap towns, the things that come from other worlds, and show them to Raenoll. They say she can touch an object and tell things about it, like who the owner was, what the world looked like where the object came from, things like that. I guess there are some invisible fingerprints left on the object that only she can see. Some of what she says doesn't make any sense, but having a story to put with an object helps drive up the price when the traders sell it. The better the story, the higher the price." Like having a name for the song Micah's music box played. Piper swallowed a lump in her throat when she thought of that late-night visit. She hoped Micah was doing all right. "Anyway, it's possible Raenoll might be able to tell us something about you," Piper said.

"But I'm not an object," Anna pointed out.

"Well, no, but the idea is the same," Piper said. "You're a mystery, the same way the objects that fall from the sky are mysteries."

"Yes." Anna nodded thoughtfully. "But I'm not an object."

"Right, but we don't know very much about you, the same way we don't know about the things that come from other worlds, so we have to figure it out on our own. I've heard people say Raenoll can sometimes translate bits of language that stump even the archivists, and they spend all their lives studying this stuff. Maybe she can unlock a memory that'll let you remember the rest on your own," Piper said.

"But I'm not an—"

"*An object*—yes, I know that!" Piper put her hands on Anna's shoulders and took several deep breaths to keep from shaking the girl. "Repetitive, annoying, and strange, but definitely not an object. Look, this is the only thing I can think of to try. I don't even know if we'll be able to afford her, but we have to do something. I don't want to just sit around and wait for the wolf to catch up to us. Do you understand?"

Anna was quiet for a minute as she thought it over, but finally she nodded. "You're right," she said. "If it'll help, I'll do it."

"Are you sure?" Piper said. "You won't be scared?"

"I trust you."

Piper's stomach clenched when she heard those words. She hadn't lied, not exactly—she did believe their best chance at helping Anna lay in reaching the capital. Since she was marked with the dragonfly tattoo, Anna was important enough that someone at the royal embassy was bound to know who she was. Someone there would be able to help her piece together her memory, maybe find her family if she had any left—Piper didn't believe the man from the caravan was Anna's father. But she hadn't told Anna her whole motivation—about the reward she still hoped she would get. Anna trusted her, but would she feel differently if she knew Piper was acting as much for herself as for Anna? She felt the stab of guilt but forced those feelings aside. It didn't matter why she was doing this—she was here, wasn't she? Right now, that was the most important thing.

After breakfast, Piper spent a few minutes in the washroom trying to make herself and her clothes look presentable before she left Anna and went out to explore the train. Now that she wasn't worried about running for her life, she was able to get a decent look at the interior of the passenger section. Gaslight fixtures lined the walls, some a bit tarnished with age, and the cushiony, velvet-covered seats on either side of the car were a bit worn, but to Piper that made them look more comfortable and inviting, not stuffy and formal like she'd expected.

Humans and a few sarnuns sat near the windows. The humans mostly ignored her, but one of the sarnuns turned as she went past. Blue-skinned, he had chalk-white eyes, three slits for a nose, and a tiny mouth cavity. The skin around his nose slits fluttered up and down when he breathed, but otherwise his smooth face was still, expressionless.

The first time Piper had ever seen a sarnun, that blank, cold expression had frightened her. She'd heard Arno Weir say never to trust a coldskin in any negotiation because you couldn't make them sweat. But Piper had learned to understand why they looked that way.

Sarnuns communicated mind to mind, and their emotions came through by the movement of their feelers. This one's stirred and angled toward Piper as she edged past, but not so much that he was being impolite. Pointing feelers too directly was the sarnun equivalent of staring.

Piper had never quite gotten used to seeing those thin bluish-white tentacles hanging past their shoulders in place of hair. Few sarnun traders came to the scrap towns. The meteor dust was particularly damaging to their lungs, and even minimal exposure hardened their feelers, prematurely aging them. Most of this one's feelers were soft and glistening with moisture, but a few had calcified and hung stiff against his neck. Counting the stiff cords, Piper guessed the sarnun was about sixteen years old, which would make him an adult, as sarnuns normally only lived into their sixties.

Nodding as she walked by, Piper saw the sarnun's tentacles lift briefly in greeting.

The next car had a green sign above the door that said OBSERVATION LOUNGE. Armchairs faced the big windows on either side of the car, their floral patterns sun-faded but still pretty. In the middle of the car was a horseshoe-shaped bar area with dozens of glass bottles and crystal decanters arranged in cabinets against the wall.

More passengers gathered here, the humans laughing and talking while nursing cups of coffee or kelpra juice. The burnt-leaf smell of japmel cigar smoke lingered in the air. A group of sarnuns sat in silence by the windows, their bodies pressed close together in an intimate circle as they spoke mind to mind. The other passengers could only guess what they were talking about—Piper supposed eavesdropping was never a problem for the sarnuns, at least not outside their own kind.

Piper opened the door at the other end of the car and almost bounced off Gee's chest.

Quickly, they both stepped back, and for a moment, they just stared at each other. Gee didn't look any happier to see her in the light of a new day, although Piper noticed his green eyes were much more vivid than they'd seemed last night in the darkness of the cargo section. She caught herself staring at them for a few seconds longer than was strictly polite.

Not that the pretty color made up for anything. He was still sooty, scarred, and barefoot. The bean-shaped soot mark on his face had migrated south to his chin sometime in the night and now more resembled a smooshed teakettle. Worst of all, he still glowered at Piper as if she were a piece of scrap he wanted to pitch out a window.

"Excuse me," she said icily, pushing past him.

Gee put a hand on her arm, startling her. "Can I talk to you for a minute?"

"I don't think that's a good idea," Piper answered coldly.

"Why not?" he asked, sounding suspicious.

Piper glanced down at his hand on her arm, and he let her go. "Oh, I don't know," she said. "I don't have a shiny, special tattoo to protect me, so maybe I'm afraid I'll end up 'accidentally' falling off the train at some point in the conversation."

He scowled at her. "I told you I can't do that." He leaned around her and closed the door to the observation lounge, sealing them between cars. Piper tensed, but he didn't touch her again. "You're pretty jumpy," Gee said, eyeing her carefully. "Is there something you're afraid of?"

"Wait, now you're concerned about me?" Piper sniffed disdainfully. She didn't believe that for a minute, not when he'd been ready to toss them off the train as if they were so much trash the night before. "Don't strain yourself with worry."

Gee's frown deepened. "I'm not worried for you, but if there's a threat to this train, I need to know about it. So let's pretend for a minute that I actually believe you and your friend are important people on some secret mission for King Aron. You can at least tell me what you're running from."

"I really can't." Technically, it was only half a lie—Piper had no idea who the man with the caravan was or what he wanted with Anna. But even if she had known what he was after, she wasn't about to share her troubles with Gee. It was crystal clear that Anna's tattoo was the only thing keeping him civil. "Can I go?" she said. "I need to find a porter."

But Gee didn't seem inclined to move, and Piper wouldn't give him the satisfaction of trying to squeeze around him in the narrow space, so they just stood, toe to toe, glaring at each other, until Gee said, "What do you need from the porter?"

Piper sighed and crossed her arms. "Are we going to stop at Tevshal?"

He seemed surprised by the question. "Yes. Why?"

"Sightseeing," Piper said, and ignored Gee's eye roll. "When will we get there?"

He shuffled his feet and ran a hand through his already mussed hair. Muttering under his breath, he stared at her as if he was fighting some inner battle. Piper wondered what else she'd done to bother him. "We'll be there in about two days," Gee said finally, "but I can tell you that you won't want to get off the train there."

"Why not?" Piper asked, suspicious. "I thought you'd be jumping for joy to get rid of us for a while."

"Believe me, in any other town I would, but we've heard rumors from some of the passengers that there's going to be a slave market at Tevshal sometime in the next few days," Gee said. "We don't know exactly where— someplace outside town—but that means Tevshal will be crawling with slavers. We're telling all the passengers to stay on the train unless they live in town or it's an emergency."

Piper bit her lip, hesitating. She hadn't expected this obstacle. Slavers were nothing to mess around with. But surely if she and Anna were careful, kept to the main streets where there were lots of people, they'd be safe enough. "This *is* an emergency," she said at last.

"Really? So it's emergency sightseeing?" Gee looked like he wanted to strangle her.

Piper threw up her hands, tired of lying and tired of how easily he saw through those lies. "Exactly. I have this crazy desire to see the perfumeries and the night eye flowers. I hear they're beautiful this time of year."

"Don't be stupid!" Gee's pupils flashed yellow. Startled by the change, Piper took an involuntary step back and bumped her elbow against the door. "Have you ever seen a slave market?" Gee snarled. He plowed on, not waiting for an answer. "More coin changes hands there than in the richest legal trade markets in the capital, and the government hasn't been able to shut any of them down. Do you know why?"

"Probably because they don't care enough to try," Piper said, her anger rising to match his.

He barked a laugh. "And you say you work for the Dragonfly territories. You don't know much about what goes on in the world, do you? It's because the slavers know exactly what they're doing. The locations of the markets change all the time. Slavers have their own secret cant to talk to each other, so they're always a step ahead of the law, and whomever they can't outsmart, they buy off. They make a fortune because they've turned kidnapping and bribery into an art." Gee stared at her, his lips pressed into a thin line. "You were raised in the scrap towns—did you know they collect the green dust from the harvesting fields?"

"That's impossible," Piper said with a laugh. "No one would risk breathing that poison just to try to bottle it up."

"The dust is worth a lot to a slaver," Gee said. "They combine it with other chemicals to make a tranquilizer. They pack it tight in these little sacks and tie each end of a rope to them to make bolas. When they throw them at a moving target, it trips them up and sprays them with the dust at the same time, very neat and tidy." His hands clenched into fists. "The dust doesn't knock you out or anything, it just makes your head go all fuzzy, like you're in a fog. You can't run away; you can't yell for help. You just stand there in a daze while they round you up, march you off to the market, and auction you off to the highest bidder. Slave markets are very quick and quiet, and not a place you ever want to be."

"If you're trying to scare me, it's not going to work," Piper lied. Inwardly, she had to admit it was working pretty well. As much as she hated it, maybe Gee was right. If they encountered slavers, they could end up in a situation far more dangerous even than running into the wolf. On the other hand, this might be her best chance to help Anna recover her memories. She just couldn't pass that up. "We'll take our chances," she said. "We have to get off at Tevshal."

Gee sighed and closed his eyes. When he opened them, Piper saw they were still yellow around the pupils. He managed to keep his voice level as he spoke. "You know, as a passenger on this train, you're under my protection. I may not like it, but if you need help, if someone's after you—"

"What?" Piper almost yelled it. "You're going to protect us?" Anger burned in her chest, the same uncontrollable, consuming emotion she'd tasted when she saw Anna touching her father's drawings. "Do you know what the 'protection' of the government—Merrow or Dragonfly—is worth to us scrappers? You know how often anyone in charge comes up to the mountains to see how we live, how we dig up bits and pieces of broken machines, trinkets covered in toxic dust, just to sell them to the capital folks for a few coins? The Merrow Kingdom doesn't care that thousands of its people are starving. And what do you do down in the Dragonfly territories with all that iron you kept? You build more ugly factories—metal and smoke! Life's hard and dirty, and there's barely enough money to live on. Keep your protection, because we don't need it."

Heart pounding, Piper shoved past him and banged through the door to the other car. She glanced back once, but he wasn't following her. Through the window in the doorway, she saw he was still standing between the cars, not moving. She had no idea what he might be thinking. For her part, Piper was shaking. She sat down in one of the empty passenger seats and let out a long breath. She tried to calm down, but it wasn't easy.

She'd never realized how much anger she still had churning inside her. She thought she'd gotten over it in the months since her father's death, or at least buried it so deep that it couldn't touch her, but here it was, coiled snakelike in her chest. The intensity of it frightened her. Every nerve in her body had reacted to Gee's words, lashing out. She knew she wasn't really angry at him but at the Dragonfly territories, Aron, and the Merrow Kingdom—all the powerful people who didn't seem to care if she starved, died in a factory, or was killed in a meteor storm, people who thought she was nothing but a worthless scrapper. The only thing she wanted to do was pour all that anger and rage onto someone else so it couldn't poison her anymore.

The strange thing was that he'd let her. He'd stood there and let her rant at him without saying a word. When she'd regained some of her composure, Piper laughed weakly at her own stupidity. If Gee hadn't wanted to toss her off the train before, he surely was dying to now.

She waited until Gee left the vestibule before she made her way back to the suite. She didn't want to have to face him again. She couldn't trust herself to be civil, though a part of her regretted taking so much of her anger out on him. He was doing his job, and naturally, he saw her as a threat, an invader.

Piper shook her head. No one knew better than she that she didn't belong here. A scrapper staying in a private train car, eating fresh fruit and being served a breakfast fit for royalty—she wouldn't have believed it if she'd heard the story from Arno Weir or one of the other scrappers.

When she got back to the suite, she was surprised to see the porter standing at the door talking to Anna. He was an elderly man with a shiny bald spot, dressed in a navy blue jacket and black pants. He listened with a polite, bland expression as Anna talked and gestured animatedly about something. Piper had to look down to hide her smile. Seeing Anna's excited expression helped dissolve some of her anger. Piper didn't know how she managed it, but when Anna wasn't being annoying, she had an air about her that made Piper want to grin. Kind of like a puppy.

"Piper!" Anna said when she saw her. "This is Mr. Jalin. I was just telling him what you said, that I couldn't wear this bathrobe around the train, and he agreed with you."

"Wholeheartedly, miss," said Mr. Jalin, his lips twitching.

"So I asked him if there was anything else I could wear besides a bathrobe, and he told me there's a clothing merchant traveling on the train—Ms. Varvol. She sells dresses, coats, petticoats, hats, trousers, shirts—"

Piper held up a hand to stop the flood. "That's great, Anna." She looked at Mr. Jalin. "Can you tell us where to find Ms. Varvol?"

"She spends most of her time in the dining car or the library," he told her. When Piper thanked him, the porter turned to Anna. "Is there anything else I can do for you, miss?"

Anna shook her head. "Thank you very much."

Mr. Jalin inclined his head to them both and moved off to the passenger cars. Piper followed Anna back inside their room and flopped down on the sofa. "Well, at least something's gone right today. We'll go see Ms. Varvol at lunch. I just hope she doesn't charge much."

"Oh!" Anna, who had just sat down next to Piper on the sofa, suddenly sprang up and reached into her robe pocket. "I almost forgot. I have to show you something." She drew out a leather money belt. "I forgot I was wearing this. I saw it when I took off my dress. It weighed me down so much, I didn't want to put it back on, but I thought I'd better keep it in case we needed it."

She held the belt out to Piper. Threaded onto it was a row of rectangular gold coins. Piper's heart stopped when she saw them. Ten, twenty, thirty—Piper lost count.

"Where . . . did you . . . get those?" Piper had never seen so much money in one place before. She reached out and caressed the gold coins, running her finger along their smooth surfaces. There was enough money on that belt to feed everyone in Scrap Town Sixteen for a year.

Anna shrugged. "I don't know where they came from," she said. "Is it because of the dragonfly tattoo that I have them, do you think?"

"I . . . maybe. I don't know." Piper was having trouble concentrating. She couldn't take her eyes off the coins. "You'd better hide them someplace safe. You don't want anyone to steal them." Goddess, it would be like stealing a new life.

"Oh, well then, you have them. You'll keep them safer than I could." Anna held the money belt out to her. Piper swallowed hard and reached to take it. "Are you all right?" Anna asked. She touched Piper's hands. "Your palms are sweating, and your body is shaking. Are you cold? You might have a fever. Are you hot, Piper?"

Piper shook her head. "No, I'm fine," she answered, but all she could think was, who was this girl? How could she be so calm, just hand over a small fortune in gold coins as if it were nothing? Did she not understand what something like this meant to a scrapper who had to worry about starving or freezing to death in her house because she didn't have the coin for food and firewood? Did she not care? Maybe, where she was from, money in these amounts was common, or was it that she just trusted Piper to take care of it for her, as she trusted her for everything else?

"Are you sure you're all right, Piper?" Anna gripped Piper's hand worriedly. "Doesn't this solve our problem about the clothes?"

Piper laughed finally, though still uneasy. "It solves the clothing problem and a few others," she said. *With this kind of money, we would never have needed to sneak onto the train. We could have marched on like queens.* "We'll get clothes from Ms. Varvol, and we'll easily get an appointment with Raenoll once we get to Tevshal."

As long as they avoided the slave market, she added to herself. Even if the slavers gathered far outside the city limits, there was still a significant danger for two girls walking alone on the streets. Large crowds were the places to be, and they needed to stay as close to the train station as possible. Knowing that they carried such a large sum of coin didn't make things any easier, but as long as they didn't flash the gold around, she thought they would be relatively safe.

Piper sat on the sofa for a long time, holding the money belt, staring at the rows of gleaming gold.

At lunch, Piper went to the dining car to look for Ms. Varvol. She wasn't hard to spot—her long, straight black hair was tucked beneath a flamboyant purple hat with hipa bird feathers on the brim, and she wore an expensive-looking jade gown. When Piper walked up to her, she was sorting through a thick book of fabric samples, using a magnifying glass to inspect each fiber of the cloth closely.

She looked up when Piper stopped at her table. "Yes?"

"Ms. Varvol?" Piper asked, feeling suddenly nervous standing next to the elegant woman.

The woman eyed her up and down, from the tangled spirals of her hair to her oversized coat to her muddy boots, which Piper thought she'd cleaned up fairly well, but from the woman's wrinkled nose, she guessed she was wrong. "I have no coin to spare, little one," Ms. Varvol said, and made a shooing motion with her hand. Her fingers were large and thick, the rolls of flesh almost burying a small square emerald on her left index finger.

"I'm not here to beg," Piper said, forcing herself to be polite. "The porter told me you sell clothing. I need to buy a dress, a warm coat, and some shoes." She hesitated. "Also a pair of trousers and a shirt." She couldn't part with her dad's coat. She didn't want to replace *any* of her old clothes, actually—she felt at home in them—but if she was going to be traveling with Anna, she needed to look like she belonged in the girl's company. They'd draw less attention if they looked like they came from the same social class.

Ms. Varvol went back to looking at her fabric samples. "Show me your coin, and then you can have some of my time," she said. "As you can see, I'm extremely busy."

"Oh, I can see that," Piper said sarcastically. She

reached into her innermost jacket pocket, where she'd stowed Anna's money belt. She took two gold coins off the belt—not enough to raise suspicions, but enough to get the woman's attention—and held them under Ms. Varvol's magnifying glass.

The woman glanced up sharply. Her expression of impatience melted into a sugary smile. "My dear! Come and sit down. I'll order us a glass of kelpra juice, and we'll talk measurements. I have just the dress to complement your skin tone. You'll be lovely."

"The dress isn't for me," Piper said. "It's for a friend of mine. Listen, do you mind coming back to our suite? You can measure her there." Piper had the satisfaction of seeing the woman's eyes widen before she nodded vigorously.

"But of course, my dear. Just let me gather my supplies." The woman bundled up her fabrics, grabbed a large case sitting on the seat next to her, and stood to follow Piper back to their car.

As Piper led the way back to the suite, she wondered, was this what it was like to have money—every conversation so easy, everyone so eager to please? The rich people in the cities must be absurdly spoiled. They never had to work at being polite or try to convince others to take them seriously. All they had to do to get what they wanted was flash some coin, and everyone jumped to serve them. One had to treat them that way, didn't they, in order to get one's own bit of coin? False civility and money changing hands—a show, that was all it was—but Piper had never been on the other side before.

Now Piper was the stiff hip. Anna had put all that coin into her hands with nothing but the utmost trust that she would use it to help her. Piper felt the horrible burden of that trust roiling inside her.

You can step off the train at Tevshal and disappear into the crowd, and no one will ever find you. The wolf isn't looking for you; he's looking for Anna. You could take those coins, get on an express train, and be halfway to Ardra before Anna even thinks to notice you're missing. A new life, just waiting for you to take it. You will never go hungry again, and you will never have to go near a factory.

Her heart raced at the thought. To be safe, to have the security of money wrapped around her like an impenetrable shield—then she imagined the look on Anna's face when she realized that Piper had abandoned her, that she was truly alone. Shame washed away Piper's excitement. Even at his lowest point, her father had never resorted to stealing coin to feed them, though he could have, easily. Bandit camps and sky raiders thrived by attacking trains and trade caravans, and they were always looking for men to replenish their numbers. Piper had seen them in town talking to Arno Weir more than once. She knew that the merchant would have pointed them to her father in a heartbeat if he'd thought her father would have been interested in joining up.

Yet, choosing to stay honest had driven her father to

the factory, to his death. What had honesty gotten him in the end? It had left Piper an orphan and forced her to care for herself any way she could.

The thoughts nagged at her all during Anna's fitting. Piper was still reluctant to replace her old clothes, but Anna insisted that she be fitted with new pairs of trousers and shirts. Piper tried to focus on picking out some clothes from Ms. Varvol's case, but all the subtle shades of browns and blacks looked the same to her. In the end, Ms. Varvol selected two pairs of sandy-colored trousers and two white shirts of the softest material Piper had ever felt. She thought she hardly looked like herself in these new outfits. She'd never had creases down the front of her trousers, or a shirt tailored to fit the curves of her body. Anna was so excited to see the transformation she abandoned the idea of a dress and petticoats for herself and asked for outfits like Piper's.

A small skirmish erupted over her dad's old coat and boots, but Piper flat-out refused to part with either of them. They compromised—Ms. Varvol took the coat and patched the torn places, all the while looking as if she was secretly planning to burn the garment. There was nothing to do about the boots. Ms. Varvol refused to look at them, so Piper wrapped them in one of her old shirts and stored them in her satchel along with her tools and the medicine and food packs. She let herself be fitted for brand-new leather boots, which she had to admit were far more comfortable than her father's oversized ones, but still she felt like she was betraying her father somehow, discarding pieces of his memory.

Piper blinked back sudden, unwelcome tears as Ms. Varvol tied the bootlaces and sat back on her heels to admire her work. "There, aren't you pretty?" she said.

Pretty? Piper supposed so. If Gee saw her now for the first time, he would never know she was a scrapper. Well, until she opened her mouth. Anyway, wasn't this what she wanted? To shed all vestiges of the scrap town and her old life? She'd never felt more disconnected from them than she did at this moment.

So why did it feel wrong?

⊰ EIGHT ⊱

Two days later, just after dark, the train arrived at Tevshal. Thoughts of Anna's money and what she could do with it hadn't stopped running through Piper's head, but thankfully, when they stepped off the train, the city itself distracted her.

Her father used to call Tevshal the Silver City or the Night Eye. Human town houses and sarnun vaults weaved together along the narrow streets, lit by the night eye flowers that spilled from baskets hung on wrought-iron posts. Unique to the city, the white blossoms only opened at night and gave off a silver glow brighter than any lantern. With the vaults and townhomes all bundled together in the light, the city reminded Piper of a tightly knotted metal star.

Absorbed by the twinkling glows, the flowers

swaying in the night breeze, Piper didn't realize that Anna was tugging on her coat sleeve. She turned to look at the girl. "Sorry, what?"

"I said did you see their bell shapes?" Anna asked excitedly. "Like a little candle turned upside down. The flowers only grow here. It's the combination of uniquely enriched soil, temperate climate, and the large population of sarnuns in the city."

"What are you talking about?" Piper asked in surprise. "Do you remember being here before?"

Anna shook her head. "I found a book on rare flowers in the train's library. There's a fascinating section on the night eye's bioluminescence and its connection to sarnun physiology."

Biolu—what? Piper thought, glancing at Anna in confusion. How did the girl remember all that? She steered them onto one of the main streets. "All right. Er, I don't know what any of that means," she said. "Maybe you could tell me about it later, after we find Raenoll."

Anna didn't seem to hear her and simply continued chattering away. "Apparently, their vision is poor when compared to a human's, but a sarnun's *feelers* have *twenty times* the number of olfactory receptors we do," she said. "Because of that, they value unique fragrances. The market for perfume in Tevshal is the largest in the Merrow Kingdom. The sarnuns make it and sell it not just among their own kind but also to the humans, even though we can't appreciate all the subtleties they put into it."

She knows an awful lot about sarnuns too, Piper thought, surprised. She guided Anna by the shoulder, half afraid the girl was going to step out in front of a carriage, so absorbed was she in her recitation. How many books had Anna managed to read in the last two days, Piper wondered, and how was she remembering everything in them?

"Most of the merchants near the train station are sarnun," Piper remarked, trying to get Anna's attention onto something else. "Looks like business is good."

"Chemicals from the sarnun perfumeries seeped into the soil over time," Anna droned on, "and modified several species of existing flora to produce the biolumi-nescence, but the reaction was most evident in the night-blooming flora, obviously. Isn't that fascinating, Piper?"

"Sure, almost as impressive as your ability to soak up all that information and yet completely ignore me when I tell you to save it for later," Piper said. "Anna, you need to focus. Why don't you fix that amazing brain on helping me find Raenoll's place?"

Piper figured the most likely place to start looking would be in the merchant district, near the sarnun per-fumeries. Tevshal was very different from Scrap Town Sixteen, Piper realized as they walked. It was much big-ger and cleaner, with sturdy, beautiful buildings, and the people—an equal mix of humans and sarnuns—seemed happier, more prosperous. Probably because Tevshal's major business was perfume, so they'd been much less affected by the iron shortage than other places in the Merrow Kingdom.

As they pressed further into the knot of buildings, the sarnun influence in the city became more apparent. The sarnun shops were stone tunnel vaults with copper pipes running along the outside. More silver flowers grew in arches over the doorways. According to signs on the doors, the merchants and their families lived beneath the shops in underground tunnels snaking throughout the city. Sarnuns preferred the cool, damp dark of the underground and shied away from the sun because it was hard on their skin. Aboveground, it was impossible to tell where one shop ended and another began. They all spilled together in the long, narrow vaults. Evidently, the sarnuns didn't believe in walls the way humans did. Of course, since the sarnuns communicated mind to mind, they probably didn't see the need for physical barriers either.

Piper glanced uneasily behind them. It was after dark and they were deep in the city, out of sight of the train station. This was the best time for the slavers to be out looking for targets. The only bit of good luck was that the streets were still bustling with foot traffic and sintee-drawn carriages, and it seemed the shops were in no danger of closing anytime soon. It was a safe bet slavers wouldn't try to snatch them while there were so many potential witnesses around.

An avenue of glowing silver flowers led them to an

open, cobblestoned square lined with shops and res-
taurants. Cheerful organ music flowed from a garden
in the center of the square. Following the music, they
entered an area of sculpted hedges surrounding a large
carousel where a myriad of animals cavorted in frozen
poses. Charging horses, sintees, grapa hounds, and grizzly bears turned in a circle, their metallic skins reflecting
the night eye flowers and lighting up the square with dazzling copper and silver glows. Piper's mouth fell open.
She'd never seen a carousel in real life, only in pictures
or miniatures. This one was ten times as impressive as
any of those.

"Look at that!" Anna cried, poised to bolt to the carousel.

"Wait." Piper grabbed the girl's arm. "I don't want us
to lose each other in the crowd. I told you, this place is
dangerous."

"I know, but it's a system of simultaneous moving
parts—rotating platform, supporting sweeps, and sus-
pended, posed figures, all of it powered by the steam
engine in the center. Look, you can see the smoke." She
pointed to the carousel's domed top, where the steam
and smoke escaped like a whistling teapot. "And look!
The animals can blink and turn their heads. I wonder
how they're accomplishing that. Really, it's a beautiful
set of integrated systems that—"

Piper held up a hand. "You're doing it again."

Anna blinked. "Doing what?"

"Talking like a book, like you—" Piper stopped herself, realizing what must be going on. "Did you read a book on rare carousels too?"

"No, I just . . . I know it, somehow." Anna stared at the carousel, transfixed and confused. She tugged on Piper's arm. "Can I ride it? Please, Piper, can I?"

Piper sighed. "At least that sounded normal. It's your money; you can ride on it if you want, just don't wander off afterward. Come right back here."

She gave Anna a couple of coins and went to wait beside the hedges while the girl bought a ticket. The ticket taker opened the gate, and Anna climbed on the back of one of the big grapa hounds. Piper would have chosen a horse herself. They looked much nobler and more beautiful, with their curlicued copper manes flying in an imaginary wind—not that she was interested in riding on carousels. The grapas were just too fat, and their lumpy tusks always made them look a little silly. But Anna clung happily to the metal beast's back and grinned at Piper as the platform started to turn.

All dressed up and sparkly, yet Anna was right: at its heart, the carousel was an impressive machine. Piper strolled around the fence to get a better view. She paused when she noticed the engineer standing near the ticket booth.

"How are you making the heads and eyes move?" she asked him by way of introduction. "Individual mainsprings?"

The engineer looked surprised, but then he nodded. "I wind 'em all up before every other ride, same time I check the pressure on the engine—got an eighty-seven-key Alcastra organ up there too to take care of."

Piper let out a whistle—that was a lot to keep an eye on at once. "Impressive." She watched a thick-bodied bear with a jeweled saddle pass by and narrowed her eyes at it. "You might want to check Mr. Grizzly there when the ride's done. Something's off with his hanger—it's wobbling. Might be a problem with the crank."

"How do you—" Blinking, the engineer looked where she pointed. Slowly, he nodded. "Good eye you've got. I'll check it out."

"Lot of systems to manage for one carousel ride," Piper said, but she thought it would make for an enjoyable challenge.

He grunted. "Don't I know it. Something's always busting on this thing."

Piper's gaze roamed over the carousel again. "Other than the bear, it looks like it's running pretty good to me."

"First time ever," the engineer said, scratching at the beard stubble on his chin. "Can't figure out what I did right this time."

Piper understood his confusion. *I've had my own experience with touchy machines,* she thought, feeling the weight of the pocket watch she wore around her neck. "Well, good job anyway," she said. "I'd better be going."

She waved goodbye to the engineer, who tipped his hat to her. She wandered among the hedges, past a small fountain with a stone mermaid reclining on a rock, and she sat down on a bench to rest, making sure she still had a clear view of Anna on the carousel.

Across the square, a man and a woman came out of a candy shop carrying four caramel apples on sticks. Two little boys younger than Micah waited eagerly on a bench outside the shop. They jumped up and ran to their parents, hands reaching for the caramel treats.

Piper watched them sitting next to their parents. They looked so happy, she thought, all clustered in an intimate little group. The youngest boy had to have his mother help him hold the stick while he bit into the apple. He came away laughing with a caramel-covered chin. The woman smiled and wiped his chin with her fingers. She glanced up and caught Piper's eye. Piper dropped her gaze.

Her shiny new leather boots filled her vision, and suddenly Piper felt tears threatening again. She clutched her father's coat close around her for comfort. It was a warm night, much warmer than in the northern towns. She might have gone without the heavy coat, but the thought of that made her feel even worse.

For the longest time, all Piper had wanted was to escape from the scrap town and start a new life, but now that she had, she felt more alone than ever. Her father was still dead, and she was saddled with a strange, talkative capital girl with a belt full of coins who was being chased by a crazy man. They were in a town that, for all its pretty sights, was crawling with slavers, and the only hope they had for getting information was from a sarnun that Piper wasn't even sure she could find. Her father would have known how to handle all of this, but it was too much for her.

Anna waved to her again from the carousel, and as the machine slowed and came to a halt, Piper waved back. She wiped the corners of her eyes and stood up.

Probably the craziest part of all was that she was actually starting to like this strange girl, Piper thought as Anna hopped off the grapa hound and ran toward her. Piper thought she was going to bowl right over her, but at the last minute, Anna stopped and threw her arms around Piper's shoulders, giving her a fierce hug. Piper was so surprised, for a minute she just stood there with her arms awkwardly trapped by her sides. Tightness spread in her chest that had nothing to do with the girl's grip.

"Careful, you'll break me," Piper said with a light laugh as she untangled herself from Anna's arms. She smiled wryly. "I take it you liked the ride?"

"Oh!" Anna spun in a circle. "That was—"

"Amazing?" Piper guessed. "Fascinating?"

Anna grinned. "Fun."

"Good. Now we need to go find Raenoll," Piper said. "No more stalling."

"Oh, I forgot," Anna said, her face brightening. "I saw a sign for the place while I was on the carousel. It's down a little alley just off the square." She pointed to one of the paths leading out of the garden. "That way."

"Nice work, Anna," Piper said, grinning in relief. That was one less problem, anyway. "Lead the way."

Anna took Piper's hand and led her to the opposite side of the square from the candy shop and down a stretch of tunnel vault. Sure enough, three doors in was a sign that had a picture of a white eye. Beneath it was written RAENOLL THE SEER in both the Trader's Speech and the sarnun language.

They approached the door. Piper reached under her shirt and pulled out her pocket watch. "It's later than I thought," she said worriedly. "I hope she's still seeing customers. I guess we'll find out."

Anna looked at the watch curiously. "I didn't know you wore that. It's beautiful."

"Thanks. It's been with me a while," Piper said. "I fixed it. That's what I do—I'm a machinist. I guess I never told you that."

"That must be hard work," Anna said. "Did you have to study for a long time to learn to fix machines?"

"Not really. My dad taught me a little, but I've always had a knack for knowing what's wrong with a machine. I can tell sometimes before I touch it. Then, the more I touch it, the more I know how to fix it, and the machines always seem to respond to me. Just like the watch—for some reason, it won't work for anyone but me." Piper laughed uneasily. She'd never talked this much about her talent to anyone but her dad. "I bet you're going to say that doesn't make any sense."

Anna looked thoughtful. "No, I think it makes perfect sense. You've cared for it. The watch is a part of you. It feels safe with you."

"Great. The pocket watch cares for me," Piper said, sighing. It wasn't quite the same as having a human care for her. "I suppose it's as good an explanation as any for what I can do. Anyway, we're wasting time. We should see if Raenoll's home so we can get this done and get back to the 401," she said. She stepped forward and rapped on the door.

"Come in, please."

Piper could swear she heard the voice, accompanied by a watery echo, with her ears, though in actuality the sarnun had projected the invitation into her mind. Piper reached for the door handle, but the door swung open on its own, startling her. Night eye blossoms growing along the walls illuminated a set of stairs leading down deep into the earth.

"Piper, are you sure about this?" Anna said. "Her voice hurts my head."

Piper reached out and found Anna's trembling hand waiting for her. "We'll be fine. I'm right here with you. I'm not leaving."

As she said the words, Piper heard the truth in them,

and in that moment, she made a decision that silenced all the thoughts that had been running through her head lately. She wouldn't abandon Anna for a belt stuffed with coins. *That's not who I am,* she thought. She would help Anna get to the capital and do what she could to protect her from the wolf. Maybe in the end there would still be a reward in it for her, and she could get started on her new life.

Piper squeezed Anna's hand reassuringly, and they descended the stairs.

"You want to run that by me again, Green-Eye? I'm a little bit confused." Trimble picked up a hot coal and tossed it idly from hand to hand. Beside him, Gee stared out the window at the silver lights of Tevshal's merchant district.

"I just asked if you'd seen them come back to the train, Fireman. It's a simple question," Gee said irritably.

"Oh, I understood the question, just not your reason for asking it," drawled Trimble. "I thought you wanted to get rid of those girls."

"I do," Gee said. "The older one's got a temper that's just waiting to blow like one of your experiments, and the younger one . . . well, she just never stops talking. If they're working for Aron, I'll eat my wings. They're hiding something, I'm telling you."

"So why do you keep looking for them out there?"

Trimble threw the hot coal back into the firebox and turned to check the boiler pressure. Sweat poured down his face. He pulled down his goggles to keep the moisture out of his eyes.

"Just because I want them off the train doesn't mean I want them to end up on the slave market," Gee said, absently rubbing the scars on his neck. "I'm not a monster. I mean . . . you know what I mean."

"Never said you were, my friend." Trimble wiped the sweat from his forehead. "Jeyne's checking the boxcars to make sure everything's in place for Cutting Gap. She won't need you for a while. Why don't you fly over the city, get some air? You might see them."

Gee snorted. "Why bother? She said she didn't want me to protect them." He remembered the look on Piper's face when she'd shouted at him, her voice filling that tiny vestibule. Brown eyes burning, she'd looked at him as if she hated him. Her expression conjured a memory of a time, years ago, when he'd looked and shouted at Jeyne Steel the same way.

"What do you expect me to do? I don't have anywhere else to go!"

Gee shook the memory away.

"Well, if you're not going out, do you want to help me shovel some of this lovely ash?" Trimble asked hopefully. "Wonderful stuff, really—heavy gray dust everywhere, smelly, makes you cough. It'll be fun."

"Actually, maybe I will make a few circles around

the town," Gee said hastily, unbuttoning his shirt. Anything was better than shoveling ash. "Just to make sure no one else is trying to sneak onto the train. Can't be too careful."

"Of course not," Trimble said dryly. "I'll be here covered in coal dust and sweat if you need me." He sighed theatrically and reached for a shovel.

Gee slid out the window and dropped into the shadows beside the engine. He was more comfortable transforming under cover of darkness. Chamelins weren't a common sight, even in the midlands and the north, and they tended to remain in human form for the majority of their life spans. In many ways, it made life easier. In his beast form, Gee couldn't speak in any language humans understood, and he was more susceptible to illness and infection. More than anything, the transformation itself was what kept chamelins in their human forms. Witnessing a human change into a beast was an unsettling experience for the other races. They tended to react with fear at best, violence in the worst cases.

Gee had heard stories of chamelins killed by mobs in the south where the people mistook them for monsters. Though he felt relatively safe in these lands, Gee avoided transforming when he could, and at all other times he tried his best to hide until the change was complete.

Heady floral scents filled his nostrils, and the noise coming from Tevshal grew louder as Gee's senses shifted. He spread his wings and took off, soaring over the 401's

nose and into the town, trusting the darkness to conceal him.

Circling the area once or twice couldn't hurt.
Whether or not the girls wanted his protection, Gee was
responsible for the passengers on board the 401, and he
took his job seriously. Over the years, he'd learned to
trust his instincts, and tonight he felt a sense of foreboding in his gut. Something bad was about to happen.

⇒ NINE ⇐

At the bottom of the stairs, a hallway branched off to the left and right. Night eyes lit the way in both directions, but Piper felt an invisible pull, like a string around her waist, drawing her to the left. Beside her, Anna fidgeted as if she too felt the phantom string.

They walked slowly down the hall, Piper casting nervous glances behind her every few steps, though she didn't know exactly why she was anxious. Maybe it was because she had heard the sarnun's voice in her head, yet so far, Raenoll's house appeared to be empty.

The hallway ended, opening up into a sitting room with a large rug laid out on the earthen floor. A padded bench and two comfortable-looking chairs took up most of the space, and white sheets covered the curved walls and ceiling. It made the room look stark and uninviting. Only a handful of the night eyes lit the room, so the space was dim, but Piper could see, and feel by the damp chill, that there was no fireplace, and she shivered.

It was a few moments before she noticed, seated in one of the chairs, a shrunken old sarnun woman. Her dry, leathery blue skin barely held her bones, and her feelers were nearly all calcified. Only two remained mobile, and they lifted toward Piper and Anna in a feeble greeting.

Piper nodded in return. "Raenoll?" she asked.

The woman nodded. "You are welcome here," she said. The echo of her mind voice seemed louder now that they were in the same room. Piper wondered if sarnuns were able to communicate with each other over long distances, speaking from city to city, country to country. She tried to imagine all those voices traveling hundreds of miles, overlapping and jumbled.

"We're sorry for coming here so late," Piper said, "but we aren't going to be in Tevshal very long, and we need your help."

"I understand. You have an object for me to identify?" Raenoll asked.

Out of the corner of her eye, Piper saw Anna squirm. "Not an object," she said firmly, "a person. See, my friend here has lost her memory. She doesn't know who she is or where she comes from. We were hoping you might be able to . . . look at her, or something, and see if you can tell us about her."

Raenoll gestured to the bench and waited for Piper

and Anna to sit down. "I can promise you nothing," she said. "My power lies in reading purpose—destiny, if you will. The purpose of an object is fixed. Its destiny rarely changes, and so it is a simple matter to divine where it has been and where it is going. A person is mutable, an entity that changes and evolves. Their destinies are similarly uncertain, but occasionally I am able to catch glimpses, flashes of their purpose and future."

"That's all we ask," Piper said hopefully.

"A challenge of this nature undertaken so late at night—it will of course affect the price."

Piper had been waiting for this part. Sarnuns were master bargainers, and though they couldn't read human minds, they read their facial expressions so well that it was almost impossible to bluff them. Piper knew they had enough money to meet any price Raenoll named, but she had no intention of letting a sarnun grandmother wring them out. It was a matter of scrapper pride. "Sure, sure, the extra coin's a given," she said, "but you just said you can't guarantee results. I don't buy a fish if it smells rotten, and I won't hand over a fistful of coins for a machine I don't even know will work."

"You would like a test, then?" The sarnun's feelers swayed back and forth in what looked to Piper like a considering motion. Finally, she answered. "Accepted. Give me an object that is dear to you."

Piper reached inside her shirt and pulled out the

pocket watch. She took off the chain and handed it to the sarnun. "This came from Scrap Town Sixteen in the north," she said.

"You are a long way from home," Raenoll said as she took the watch. It looked big and heavy in her shriveled hands. Piper had heard sarnuns were so physically weak that they couldn't lift anything heavier than a soup pot. There were other stories, though, of what they could move with their minds.

"What can you tell me about it?" Piper asked.

Raenoll's feelers brushed the watch face tentatively. She closed her eyes.

The blank room suddenly came to life, startling Piper.

A man's face appeared on the white-sheeted wall closest to Piper. Piper turned, her hand automatically reaching for her knife before she realized the man wasn't real. It was only a blurry picture fading in and out but with more details slowly appearing in the background. Gradually, the picture widened, covering all the sheets in the room like wet paint poured across a canvas. Objects took shape. Behind the man loomed an immense square tower and the largest clock Piper had ever seen. A river flowed nearby, and other figures walked in and out of the picture, but they were mostly indistinct shapes, little blots of gray and black.

"The man who owned this watch cast it off in the

river," Raenoll said, opening her eyes. "Broken beyond repair, he said. It drifted away, forgotten, and when it came to you in this world, it was in pieces."

The scene was a wonder, Piper thought. She folded her arms, forcing herself to look at Raenoll instead of the sheets. She didn't want the sarnun to see how captivated she was by the moving pictures, but it was almost impossible not to stare at the man and the strange, ominous-looking tower rising behind him. Beside her, Anna watched the images with her hands half covering her eyes, her mouth open in awe.

So much for subtlety.

"You put on a good show," Piper admitted, and thought she saw Raenoll's feelers vibrate in the sarnun equivalent of a smile. "But how do we know you didn't just dream all this up to impress us? Maybe you show these same pictures to every stiff-hip trader who comes knocking." Piper didn't really think that was the case, but she had to try the bluff. She didn't want Raenoll to know how impressed she truly was by the stunning sights the sarnun had put on display.

Abruptly, the pictures on the sheets disappeared, and the sarnun's voice rang shrill in Piper's mind. "You call me a charlatan!" she screeched, and Piper winced. "Would a charlatan know that you tried three times yourself to cast off this watch, and three times you failed? It owes you its existence. Without you it *is* broken beyond repair." The sarnun's feelers moved agitatedly around her face. "Would a charlatan tell you that, scrapper child?"

Piper was too shocked to come up with a clever reply. Raenoll knew her whole history with the watch—it was as if the sarnun had opened a window into Piper's mind. She felt Anna tugging on her sleeve. "What's wrong, Piper?"

"Nothing," Piper said, recovering her composure. "I just realized this is going to cost a lot more than I expected, but she's the real thing."

The sarnun's feelers vibrated again. She handed the watch back to Piper. "Shall we say twenty?"

"Agreed," Piper said, wincing. She'd never paid so much for anything in her life. She pulled out the money belt and counted the rectangular coins, then gave them to Raenoll. "Tell me about Anna," she said.

"Now come over here, child," Raenoll said, gesturing to Anna. "Sit before me."

Piper felt Anna shrink from the sarnun. She'd been expecting this too. She gave Anna a reassuring smile. "Anna, remember what I said. I'll be right here with you. You're safe."

"I'm not afraid of her," Anna whispered.

"Then what's wrong?"

Anna looked at her nervously. "What if she shows me something bad? What if I'm a bad person—another wolf?"

"That's impossible," Piper said, and she meant it.

Anna was a mystery, it was true, but Piper had never sensed any deception or malice in her. She grinned. "It's true you talk funny, you eat like a grapa hound, and you're incredibly annoying, but I'm actually starting to get used to all that."

"But—"

"What I'm saying is, you're not a bad person, Anna." Piper squeezed her hand. "Trust me. I've got excellent instincts for these things."

Anna nodded, but still she moved slowly to sit on the rug in front of Raenoll. The girl looked like a fly cuddling up to a spider, Piper thought. The sarnun leaned over so her feelers could brush the top of Anna's head, and Anna tensed, but she didn't draw away.

"Close your eyes," Raenoll instructed. "Try to clear your mind and think of nothing at all."

Obediently, Anna closed her eyes. Piper watched the blank sheets hanging on the walls around them, her own body tense in expectation.

A flash of color saturated the white canvases. Piper tried to make out what was in the picture, but it disappeared too fast for her to see any details. Then the room fell into darkness, with only the tiny lights of the silver flowers shining on the walls. The sheets had gone completely black.

"What's happening?" Piper whispered, worried that Raenoll's power wasn't going to work. "What is that?"

"Piper?" Anna sounded frightened. "What's going on?"

"Both of you be silent," Raenoll said sharply. "Concentrate, and keep your eyes closed, child."

Anna whimpered softly. Piper perched on the edge of the bench, resisting the urge to go over and slap the sarnun's tentacles away from the girl.

A rush of motion passed over the dark canvases, and the blackness shrank to become a massive building made up of gray stone blocks. Piper squinted, trying to make sense of the new picture, which took up almost all the blank space on the sheets and filled the room with a gloomy haze.

Iron staircases ran up and down the sides of the building, and a film of dirt covered the few windows offset in the stone. There were trees surrounding the structure— their branches a mix of dead and living leaves, as if the shadow of the building was gradually suffocating them. Piper finally realized what the building was when she saw the thick black smoke rising from chimneys along its roof, and her stomach dropped.

Piper coughed as if trying to expel phantom smoke from her lungs. Her father had been too kind in his drawing of the factory. The image on the walls was a place of despair.

"That's Noveen," Piper said, trying to keep the sadness out of her voice. "We were right, Anna. You're from the capital." She didn't mention the factory or the deadly smoke.

Another flurry of motion crossed the walls, and the factory shrank to reveal a bird's-eye view of the city. Piper watched as the land rose, leaving behind the haze of factory smoke, up a cliff side and over to a view of the ocean. The beauty of it, such a sharp contrast to the factory, stole her breath. It was so stunning she hoped for the image to widen so she could get a better view of the blue-green expanse, but the view stopped on a beautiful mansion situated at the top of the cliff. White stonework and columns formed the backdrop for a vibrant garden and a large stone fountain in front of the house. Unlike the factory, the mansion was all lightness and windows, and there wasn't a hint of smoke to mar the pristine landscape.

Was that Anna's home? Piper didn't want to disturb Raenoll by asking the question. She figured that it had to be her house, though. Anna's fancy yellow dress, and the money she'd been carrying—this was exactly the kind of place where Piper expected someone like her to live.

The mansion faded, and this time the sheets stayed blank. Raenoll lifted her feelers from Anna's head and sighed. "You may open your eyes, child. You did very well."

Anna opened her eyes and blinked sleepily up at the sarnun. She seemed calmer now too. Piper checked her watch. They'd been here for almost an hour, though it had felt like only a few minutes. The 401 wouldn't leave for a while yet, but they needed to be heading back before it got any later. "Is that all you see?" she asked Raenoll.

The sarnun nodded. "As I told you, with people, there are many uncertainties."

At least she'd confirmed that Piper was doing the right thing by taking Anna to Noveen. Piper was reassured by that, but on the other hand, they'd learned nothing about who the man from the caravan was or why he was after Anna. Piper had hoped they might get some clue there.

"We need to go," Piper said, glancing nervously at her watch again. "We should get back to the train."

Anna stood up, looking at Piper worriedly. "What did she see?" she asked.

"Someplace good," Piper assured her. "I'll tell you about it later—when we get back on the train. Thanks for all your help," she told the sarnun.

"Before you go," Raenoll said, "may I speak to you alone?" She glanced at Anna. "Wait at the bottom of the stairs, child. I won't keep your friend long."

Anna looked at Piper uncertainly, as if she was nervous about leaving her. Piper wondered why Raenoll wanted to send the girl out of the room when she could just speak directly into Piper's mind. She hesitated, then nodded toward the door. "Go ahead, Anna. I'll be right behind you."

"All right," Anna said reluctantly. She left the room, disappearing down the hall.

Piper waited nervously for Raenoll to speak. Could she have seen something else, something that she hadn't put on the walls? she wondered. The sarnun's expression was impossible to read, but her feelers had again adopted that swaying, considering motion, as if she was choosing her words very carefully.

Piper's nervousness made her impatient. "So?" she asked. "Why do you have to talk to me alone? Couldn't you just say what you wanted to say into only my mind?"

"Yes," Raenoll said carefully. "But humans often have poor control over their emotional responses. I was afraid your face would give you away, and I did not want to alarm the child."

Piper's stomach twisted. "Alarm her with what?" she asked.

"That child is very fragile," Raenoll said. "You should know that if you abandon her, she will certainly die."

Piper sank back down on the bench, clutching the edge for support. Raenoll was right. Her expression *would* have given her away. She leaned toward the sarnun. "But how can you know that? You said there were too many uncertainties."

The sarnun's feelers didn't move, but Piper somehow sensed the woman's confusion. "There are. I have tried to read human destinies before, but she is by far the most difficult subject I have encountered. None of it is clear, except that the two of you are connected. She needs you." Raenoll paused, and for a long moment, her mind voice was silent. "There is something strange about her, but I sense she is valuable. That is why you are helping her, I assume?"

Piper felt her face flush. "Maybe you don't know as much as you think."

The sarnun's feelers became utterly still. "I sense the reward you will receive for helping the child get to Noveen will be greater than anything you can imagine." Her mind voice was flat, cold. Piper felt a tremor go through her body, a feeling similar to what she'd experienced when she saw Anna's money belt. But the sarnun wasn't finished speaking. "It will also be horrifying to you. Neither of you will be able to stand it."

Knots of fear and anger welled up in Piper. "Well, isn't that nice? So what you're saying is, if I leave Anna, she's going to die, but if I help her, something terrible is going to happen to us anyway? What kind of a stupid destiny is that?"

The sarnun shook her head. "It may not happen that way."

Piper stood up, her hands clenched into fists. "Can you try to be more specific, then, or do you just enjoy playing around in people's heads?" She kept her voice down so it wouldn't carry out to the hallway, but her body shook with anger.

"You know nothing about me, scrapper child," Raenoll said, but there was no anger in her words. "If I could see a clear path, I would point you to it. I know you are afraid—"

"Of course I'm afraid!" Piper said in a strangled voice. "Anna's depending on me. There's a man who's ready to kill me to get to her, and my only plan was to get her to Noveen first so she'd be safe. Fine, so maybe I *do* want a reward, but why not? After that, she'll be safe and taken care of, and I'll be alone again!" She covered her mouth, realizing what she'd said, but it was too late to stop the words.

Piper turned and ran from the room.

The sarnun's mind voice followed her into the hall. "Do not be rash, child. You are strong enough to save your friend. Do so on your own terms."

"I don't know how," Piper said miserably. She waited, hoping the sarnun would reply, offer her help, reassurance . . . something.

But Raenoll's voice faded, and Piper was alone in her head.

Anna was sitting on the steps waiting for her. Piper didn't pause, just pulled her to her feet by the bend of her elbow as she went past. "Let's get out of here," she said, and Anna seemed eager to follow.

Of course she wants to go with me, Piper thought. *Didn't*

I tell her to trust me? Except it didn't matter whether Piper was worthy of that trust or not—either way, according to the sarnun, something bad was going to happen.

At the top of the stairs, Piper shoved the alley door open angrily. To her surprise, the door shoved back, hitting her shoulder with enough force to knock her off balance. Before Piper could recover, an arm snaked around the door and grabbed her, pulling her roughly into the dark alley. Another arm covered her mouth so she couldn't scream. And from somewhere next to her, she heard Anna utter a frightened squeak that quickly cut off.

≈ TEN ≈

Piper clawed at the arm holding her, scratching at it like a wild animal. Her attacker cursed, but he didn't let go. Piper tried to elbow him in the stomach, but he quickly pinned her arms to her sides with his free hand. He hauled her deeper into the alley, where another man waited in the shadows. Piper caught a brief glimpse of a dirty, unshaven face before the hand at her mouth fell away and a dark hood came down over her head. She felt hot breath at her ear, and a voice whispered, "If you scream or try to run, your friend's going to get hurt. Remember that." Piper stiffened, but she made no sound. Other arms grabbed her ankles and lifted her off her feet.

She heard the rattle of carriage wheels from farther down the alley. As the sound drew closer, Piper smelled the heavy scent of horse sweat and heard the whuffing

sound of the beasts' breathing. A door opened somewhere to her right, and the men lifted her up and set
her down on her back on something soft. A few seconds
later, she heard a thump and Anna's soft whimper. The
men had put her in the carriage too, probably on the seat
across from Piper.

"Tie their hands and feet," a voice called from somewhere above her—likely the carriage driver.

"Been a lot easier just to use the dust," said the man
who'd been holding her. Three voices chuckled. There
were at least four of them, and there was no doubt about
it, they were slavers. They must have followed them to
Raenoll's place and waited for them there. Piper's heart
beat frantically in her chest as she fought to stay calm.

"Man said no dust—least he paid us extra to do it the
hard way," said the driver.

Piper froze. *The man.* It had to be the man from the
caravan. But how had he found them? Piper felt a burst
of fresh panic. She wasn't sure which was worse: being
sold on the slave market or being delivered right into the
wolf's hands.

One of the slavers grabbed her ankles, lashing them
together so tightly she winced in pain. He did the same
with her hands, and as he drew away, his fingers brushed
her weighted coat pocket.

"Well, well. What's this here?" The slaver reached
inside Piper's coat and yanked out Anna's money belt.

She could hear the coins jangle as he pawed through it and whistled softly. "It's all gold, every bit of it. Who *are* these two?"

"Doesn't matter who they are," said the driver. "Take the gold—we'll divide it up later. Let's get going."

It was only a moment until the door slammed shut and the carriage began to move. Piper listened, but she didn't hear any of the other men. She and Anna were alone in the carriage. "Anna, can you hear me?" she whispered.

"Yes." The muffled voice came from the other side of the carriage.

They'd tied her hands behind her back, but the hood was a little loose, so Piper turned on her side and used the edge of the seat to work the cloth off her head. She breathed in fresh air, shook her hair away from her face, and looked around.

She was lying on a padded bench in an enclosed carriage. Heavy black curtains covered the windows. The only light came from a small sprig of night eyes in a pot fastened to the carriage door. Anna lay on the bench across from her, hooded, her hands and feet similarly tied.

"Don't worry," Piper whispered. "I'm going to get us out of here."

"Chances aren't good," Anna said breathlessly. "The knots are too tight. Cow hitch, square knots, perfect loops—we're the cows, and they're taking us to the slaughter."

"That's good," Piper said. "Keep talking strange—that way I'll know that you're not panicking."

"I'm scared." The girl's voice was smaller and it made Piper's chest feel tight.

"I am too," Piper admitted. She levered herself upright on the bench. Anna was right. The knots were tight; her fingertips were already starting to go numb. She looked down at her feet and saw a glimmer of metal at her waist. Her breath caught. "I don't believe it," she whispered.

"What is it?" Anna angled her hooded face toward Piper.

"They didn't take my knife," Piper said. "Idiots must not have seen it on my belt, or they were too distracted taking your gold. Anna, try to sit up if you can, and lean toward me. We have to hurry."

"I'll try." Anna pushed herself up clumsily to a sitting position and leaned forward. "Like this?"

"Perfect." Piper pivoted until she got her fingertips on the hood covering Anna's head. She pulled it off and then slid to the edge of the bench. "Turn around and see if you can get your fingers on my knife."

Anna knelt on the floor of the carriage and turned, straining to reach Piper's belt. The carriage hit a bump; Piper was sent sprawling back against the seat and Anna banged her head against the window. The road was getting rougher, which told Piper that they must be headed out of the city. And that they were running out of time.

Anna leaned back and grasped the knife handle. "I've got it," she whispered excitedly.

"Great, now try to hold the blade with the point toward me. Let's see if we can saw these ropes off."

Anna hesitated for a moment, then her words came fast. "But, Piper, taking into consideration the speed of the carriage we're traveling in combined with the roughness of the terrain, having an exposed knife within inches of your skin—"

"Yes, yes," Piper hissed, "sharp knife, bumpy carriage, high risk of stabbing—all bad. We're already in it up to our ears, might as well pile on some more trouble."

"Right. Sorry." Anna gripped the knife handle and turned the blade parallel to the floor. "Ready," she said.

Bracing herself as best she could between the bench and the floor, Piper reached back and rubbed her bound wrists against the exposed knife blade. She could feel the fibers snapping and the tension loosening. Thankfully, she always kept her knife sharp, and the ropes fell away quickly, though she also managed to slice up the sleeves of her dad's coat again, undoing all of Ms. Varvol's repair work.

She massaged some feeling back into her wrists and turned and took the knife from Anna. "Try to hold still," she said. She cut the ropes from Anna's wrists in two neat slices and then went to work on their feet. A minute later, they were both free.

"Should we try to jump out?" Anna asked, nodding at the door.

Piper pushed back one of the curtains and looked outside. Moonlight shone on open fields and scattered tree copses. In the distance was Tevshal, the lights still shining brightly against the darkness.

"We're not far from the city," she said, "but the carriage is moving pretty fast." Piper ran through their options. If they jumped, they could walk back to Tevshal—it was dark enough that they might not be noticed. But if they hit the ground wrong, one or both of them could end up with a broken leg, which would leave them at the mercy of whoever found them. The other option was a long shot. "If we can get to the driver, knock him off his seat somehow, we could take the carriage back to town."

Anna opened her mouth to reply, but whatever she was going to say was lost in a loud crash. The carriage tipped sideways, throwing Piper and Anna against the windows. The driver shouted in alarm at the same time something heavy banged against the carriage roof right above Piper's head, and the carriage came to a dead stop.

"Are you all right?" Piper whispered, helping Anna sit up.

"I think so." Anna was dazed and bleeding from a shallow cut on her forehead. Piper wiped away the blood and checked her over quickly, then scrambled for the door and kicked it open.

"We're going to make a run for it," Piper said. "Stay close!" She jumped to the ground and turned back, offering the smaller girl her hand.

Anna took it and hopped out. "What hit the carriage?" she asked.

Piper pulled her along the side of the carriage to avoid being seen, but the driver was gone, and so were the horses. The driver's seat had three long, deep gouges in the wood that looked like claw marks, and the carriage roof had a huge dent in its center. Piper stared at the marks and a shiver of fear ran down her back.

"Could have been a dravisht raptor," she said. "I hear some of them have claws as long as your arm."

Anna's mouth fell open. "If it carried off a full-grown man with an average weight of a hundred and seventy-five pounds, taking into account the length of the claws, I calculate the size of the raptor has to be—"

"Forget I said that," Piper cut in. She didn't want to think about how big the creature might be. "Whatever it is, we don't want to be here when it comes back."

Piper grabbed Anna by the arm and pulled her away from the carriage. They took off across the field toward the city. The wind blew cold on Piper's face as she ran, though it wasn't nearly as biting as she was used to in her scrap town by the mountains.

The night air burned in Piper's lungs, and after a few minutes, both girls were panting. If they were going to make it to the city, they would have to rest, but the moonlight was too bright and the field too exposed to stop out in the open, so she angled west, heading for a copse of trees.

Ducking among the dense oaks and pikas, Piper slowed and let Anna catch her breath. "We'll stay here a minute," she said as she lifted one of the pika's low branches aside. They grew right down to the ground, and their bluish leaves effectively blotted out the moonlight overhead. Anna followed and sat down beside her. Above them, Piper could hear bird rustlings, and a nighthawk cried out, then took flight. "Somebody doesn't want to share his tree." Piper laughed, but she was too tired to put much heart into it.

"You're trying to make me feel better, aren't you?" Anna said. "Is that why you laugh and make jokes when we're in trouble? You don't want me to be scared?"

"I'm trying not to be scared either," Piper admitted. She glanced toward Tevshal, but the city still seemed a hundred miles away.

Anna followed her gaze. "We've been gone a long time," she said. "What if the train leaves without us?"

"They won't," Piper said firmly. "I heard the porter say the 401 won't leave until near midnight. We've still got a few hours." It felt like she was trying to convince herself as much as Anna. In truth, Piper was scared to think about what would happen if the 401 left them in Tevshal.

"You think we'll make it in time?"

Piper heard the fear in Anna's voice and she forced a crooked smile. "I got us out of that carriage, didn't I?" Of course, Piper *had* had help from whatever had landed on the roof and was probably still out there prowling around for fresh meat right now, but why dwell on the details?

Another rustling sound, louder, made Piper spin. This time it was coming from the field. Piper froze, facing the direction of the sound, and Anna grabbed her hand, squeezing it in alarm.

"Maybe it's another bird?" Anna offered meekly.

Piper shook her head and put her hand over the girl's mouth before she could speak again. She lifted aside a clump of pika leaves and squinted into the darkness.

Shapes moved in the field—two shadows on her left, one to the right. Human shadows. And the figures were coming closer. It was more slavers. They must have been waiting to meet the carriage. Piper considered for a moment, but she knew there was really only one option. The copse was too small to hide in. They would have to make a run for it.

"Anna." Piper lifted her hand from Anna's mouth and spoke very softly. "I'm going to distract them. While I do, I want you to run toward the city as fast as you can. Don't stop until you get to the train. Do you understand?"

"No!" Anna nearly yelped. "They'll catch you. I'm not going to run while they take you away!"

"We don't have time to argue!" Piper pried the girl's fingers from her arm and hauled her none too gently to her feet. "Do what I say, Anna, please," she said desperately.

Shouts echoed from the field. The slavers had heard them. They were running toward the copse now, and Piper was sure they'd be surrounded at any moment. Piper pushed Anna out in front of her, and together they burst from the trees and broke into a run. Piper made sure Anna was headed toward Tevshal; then she turned and ran in the opposite direction, screaming at the top of her lungs.

Two of the slavers immediately turned at the sound and gave chase. The third kept after Anna, but she had a good head start on him. Piper kept on screaming and running, glancing back every few seconds to see if Anna was still ahead of her pursuer. Piper was frightened, but at the same time elated that she'd kept two of the slavers away from the younger girl.

Then, to her left, she heard a loud whirring sound. Piper looked back and saw that one of the slavers chasing her had stopped. He was whipping a length of rope with weighted sacks at both ends in a circle above his head. Piper had a good idea what was in those sacks.

It looked like the slavers had decided to use the dust after all.

Piper skidded to a stop and changed directions. Her only chance was to make herself an impossible target. She ran and stopped, ran and stopped, each time changing direction slightly until she had doubled back and was running toward the city. She saw Anna in the distance, still running strong. Behind Piper, the slaver grunted as he threw the bolas and the whirring sound closed in on her.

Piper threw herself to the side and hit the ground, rolling. She heard the weighted sacks pass over her head and hit the ground several feet away. One of the sacks burst, spewing an ugly, greenish-yellow cloud into the air. Piper covered her nose and rolled away. Luck was on her side. The wind blew in the opposite direction, carrying the cloud toward the second slaver, forming a poisonous wall between them. The slaver cursed at his partner and covered his mouth and nose.

But Piper didn't have time to rest. The slaver who'd thrown the bolas was reaching for a holster on his belt. Piper got to her feet but almost tripped on the other sack, which had landed near her but hadn't burst. Piper grabbed the sack and stuffed it in her pocket at the same time as she heard the crack of a revolver.

"Stop right there!"

Piper froze in terror. She was caught. The slaver had fired the shot into the air and now trained the revolver on her. His partner came up on her left. He carried no re-volver but had a length of rope in his hands. Piper knew she couldn't escape a second time, but maybe Anna still had a chance.

"Forget the rope." Out of breath, the slaver motioned with his revolver. "Use the dust."

The rope man reached in his pocket. Gee's words pounded like alarm bells in Piper's head. *"You can't run away, you can't yell for help, you just stand there in a daze while they round you up, march you off to the market, and auction you to the highest bidder."*

"No." Piper didn't realize she'd breathed the word aloud until the slaver cocked the revolver and took a step forward.

"You've got nowhere to go," he growled. "Don't do anything stupid."

Piper stared at the gun, her gaze moving slowly along the length of the black barrel. Images of her standing helpless in a crowd of slavers passed through her mind. They waved coins and clustered around her. A loud whine filled Piper's ears. She thought the sound came from her own throat, a scream suppressed only by the teeth she clamped on her bottom lip.

Then the slaver's gun exploded.

The cylinder and hinge burst from the gun's frame, showering ammunition everywhere, and the hammer slipped from under the slaver's thumb. He cursed and dropped the pieces of the weapon on the ground.

Relief made Piper dizzy, and she stumbled. As she fought to clear her head, she saw what remained of the gun's frame lying on the ground. The slaver hadn't fired. She'd heard no report. The weapon had just exploded— exactly when she'd needed it to.

Run. Piper snapped back to herself. *You have to run.* She turned and took off before the slavers recovered from their shock.

Fatigue slowed her, but she forced herself to keep going, cold wind burning in her ears, feet pounding the ground. The lights of Tevshal were getting closer. And ahead of her, Piper could see that Anna was almost to the city limits.

Piper was beginning to think they might make it after all when she realized the distance between her and Anna was shrinking. Anna was tiring, slowing down. As Piper watched, the third slaver closed in on the girl. He had his bolas out, whipping them above his head, ready to throw. She would never be able to dodge them.

At that moment, a dark shape appeared in the sky above Anna.

Piper stopped dead.

In the moonlight, the creature looked equal parts lizard, bird, and man, with eyes that glowed green and leathery wings that stretched to a huge span on either side of its body. On the ground, it would walk on two legs, but in the air . . . As Piper watched, terrified, the creature dipped in a smooth arc and snatched Anna up in its claws.

"No!" Piper screamed.

A heavy weight slammed into her from behind. Piper hit the ground hard with the slaver on top of her, wrestling her hands behind her back. She didn't bother to struggle; she was too busy watching the sky, tears blurring her vision, as the creature carried Anna up into the clouds and far out of reach. Soon they were only a moving speck against the moonlight, and then they disappeared completely.

Piper dropped her face against the ground. The smell of dirt and cold grass filled her nostrils as shuddering sobs racked her body.

The slaver hauled her to her feet. Fiery pain shot up her arms. She didn't resist when he pushed her to the base of a nearby oak tree, where the other two men stood catching their breath. Her legs were so tired they shook. She was sure they would give out completely if the slaver hadn't been holding her up.

"Fight's finally gone out of this one, hasn't it?" he said, smirking. "We won't need the dust to make her obey now."

"Won't need it anyway," said the slaver who'd been chasing Anna. "Our man will be here for her any minute."

Piper barely heard them. Chest heaving, she stared

up at the sky, but nothing moved except ragged clouds passing over the moon.

They stood like that for a few minutes before she heard the sound of approaching footsteps. She squinted into the darkness and saw a man hurrying across the field toward them. Piper thought at first it was just another slaver—until the man spoke, sending a chill up her back.

"Where's the other one, Tuloc?" he asked. "I told you there were two."

"Master Doloman, sir," the slaver holding Piper replied, "we've had some trouble."

"Doloman," Piper said to herself. So that was the wolf's name. Strength flooded back into her limbs as he came into view. "How did you find us?" she asked.

"Hello again, scrapper." In the moonlight, Doloman's beard looked thicker than it had at her house, yet still unkempt. He'd changed clothes, though, and was now dressed in a fine-looking gray suit, but his arm was still in a sling, and dark circles ringed his eyes, making him look half-demon in the shadows. "You led me on a chase, but I caught an express train in Evansdown and managed to arrive in Tevshal a few hours before the 401." He addressed the slavers. "Where is the other one?" he demanded. "I want her brought to me at once."

The slavers exchanged uneasy glances. Tears ran down her face, but Piper had the sudden urge to laugh hysterically. Doloman hadn't seen what happened in the field.

"Your men lost her," Piper said, her voice raw. "She's gone for good this time."

Doloman went pale, his lips quivering with rage. "Find her," he hissed. "Spread out and search the field. She has to be here somewhere."

The slavers started to argue, but Piper interrupted, her fury boiling over. "What do you want with her?" she cried. "I don't believe for a minute she's your daughter— she's terrified of you. What did you do to her?"

For a moment, Doloman's rage melted into genuine surprise. "Terrified of me? But I tried to help her. When she came into my care, she was half dead. I only wanted to heal her. When the storm destroyed the caravan, I thought I had lost her forever, and then I saw her with you—alive and well. It was a miracle."

"You're lying," Piper spat. Anna might have lost her memory, but other than that, she'd been fine until Doloman showed up. "There's more you're not telling. Why were you out in that storm with the caravan? What were you doing in the scrap town?" she pressed.

Doloman's eyes narrowed. He glanced at the slavers. "I told you to find the girl!" he barked. "Stop wasting time!"

"That *thing* took her," the man holding Piper said, glancing anxiously at the sky. "It got Ori too."

"What?" Doloman shrieked.

"A monster," Piper said, choking back a sob. "And it's all your fault!"

Doloman took two steps forward and grabbed Piper by the throat, pulling her up on her toes as he dragged her closer. He stared into her eyes with so much loathing, it was as if he were staring down an insect he longed to crush.

Piper's lungs seized, and she choked for air. Without breath, everything inside her was grinding to a halt. Darkness crept in at the edges of her vision, and her thoughts fragmented. *He's going to kill me this time*, she realized. She clawed at Doloman's arm, but he didn't loosen his grip.

As darkness closed in, Piper thought she heard a distant whooshing sound, like the beating of massive wings. . . .

"Look out!" screamed one of the slavers, and Doloman's hand at Piper's throat was suddenly gone.

Piper dropped to the ground, coughing and sucking in air. At the same time a dark, winged shape landed in their midst, sending Doloman and the slavers scattering. Piper looked up; the creature's massive body blotted out the moonlight. It towered over her, green eyes shining with a strange, hypnotic light. A clawed hand reached out for her. And that was when Piper squeezed her eyes shut and waited for the beast to tear into her.

She waited, but in the silence she heard the whirring

sound of bolas and Doloman's harsh voice barking orders to the slavers. Piper opened her eyes in time to see the creature turning toward the men. It let out a loud, deep roar that had Piper covering her ears and curling into a ball.

That was all the slavers could take. They dropped their weapons and ran, sprinting across the field toward the city. But Doloman didn't run. With his good arm, he grabbed one of the slavers' discarded bolas. He whipped it around once and released it right into the creature's face.

The bag exploded against the beast's chest and released a thick cloud of dust. Flapping its wings wildly, the creature took flight. Piper rolled away, both from the dust and the enormous beating wings.

But instead of lifting up into the sky, the creature let out a choked roar and crashed back to the earth, its wings caught underneath its body. Piper watched the thing try to get up, but it couldn't breathe. Instead of being stupefied by the dust, the beast was choking on it.

With the creature no longer a threat, Doloman turned on Piper. She tried to scramble to her feet, but she knew she couldn't outrun him. She barely had her breath back, and she was so weak that her vision was starting to blur again.

Piper reached into her pocket for the one weapon she had left. She pulled out the sack she'd taken from the bolas and hurled it at Doloman.

The dust bag exploded, and Piper watched as Doloman inhaled the greenish-yellow cloud. His eyes immediately glazed over, and he sank down on the ground, twitching feebly as he fought the effects of the poison. In less than a minute, he lay still, staring blankly up at the sky.

Piper crawled to her feet and staggered over to his still form. She stood, watching him for a moment to make sure he wasn't going to get up, but it looked as if the dust had him completely. His lips moved, but the sound that came out was barely above a whisper. Piper leaned down so she could hear what he was trying to say.

"Anna . . . you must . . . come home . . . to me. . . . You must . . ." He sounded desperate.

"She's not coming home," Piper said bitterly. "She's dead. *You killed her.*" But Doloman's glassy expression remained fixed on the sky.

Piper didn't know how long the dust would keep him helpless. She had to get as far away as she could before it wore off. She turned from Doloman and saw the creature on the ground, still choking on the dust, its wings beating weakly. It was clearly suffering.

Good, Piper thought, rage burning inside her. Let it suffer the way Anna had suffered. Piper's hand went to her knife. She drew the blade from its sheath and stalked over to the creature. As if it sensed her presence, the beast rolled onto its back and stared up at her with those strange glowing eyes.

"She was smaller than all of us," Piper said. She didn't know whether the creature understood her or not, and she didn't care. "Why did you have to take her? I was trying to keep her safe!" Her voice broke, and tears blinded her. "To take her home."

Piper raised the knife in both hands, fighting to hold it steady. Let the beast suffer for a few seconds more, and then she would put it out of its misery. She met its eyes again. Their glow had diminished, and she was startled by what she saw—was that compassion in its expression?

Suddenly the creature's skin rippled. Its body went rigid, wingtips pointing toward the sky. Then the appendages began to shrink. First the wings, and then its arms and legs began to draw in toward its body. The dark green skin faded to an olive tone, and the bones of the creature's face shrank and reshaped right before Piper's eyes. Dark hair sprouted from the creature's head, falling across a face that was now unmistakably human.

Gee's face.

Piper's hands dropped to her sides. She bit her lip to keep from sobbing aloud in relief. Gee was a chamelin. Piper had heard stories from her father about such shape-shifters, but she'd never seen one before. She'd just assumed the creature that had attacked the carriage was a wild beast, a monster, but chamelins didn't hunt humans. Her father had told her that too. In fact, they often lived among them in their human forms—like Gee must have been doing.

Now that Piper knew the creature's identity, everything else began to fall into place. Somehow, Gee must have seen the slavers take them and followed from the air. Once they were outside the city, he'd attacked the carriage driver and given them a chance to escape. A monster hadn't taken Anna. Gee had saved her; he'd probably flown her all the way to the 401. Then he'd come back for Piper.

And now he'd returned to his human form—and he was naked.

Piper's face got very warm. Quickly, she averted her eyes and slipped off her dad's coat. She knelt beside Gee and covered him. Gee tried to sit up, but another fit of racking coughs overtook him, and he fell back, spitting a mouthful of green bile onto the dirt.

The dust must affect chamelins differently, Piper guessed. It seemed like Gee had inhaled a ton of the stuff, but it hadn't stupefied him. Piper helped him to a sitting position and wrapped an arm around his chest, supporting him as best she could while he coughed up more of the dust. Finally, he drew in a shuddering breath and wiped his mouth.

"Thanks," he said. His voice was hoarse. "I'd hoped for"—he coughed again—"a cleaner rescue. I didn't see the other slaver coming—put the dust right down my throat. What about you? You all right?"

The sound of voices pulled Piper's attention away from Gee, and she looked up to see a trio of figures running across the field in their direction. They carried lanterns with fire in them, not night eye flowers.

"There they are!" one of them shouted. "Piper!"

It was Anna. Piper still half supported Gee, but when she heard the girl's voice, her strength gave out. She rested her head against Gee's back and started to cry again.

"It's all right," Gee murmured. "She's safe. I promise. You're both safe."

≈ ELEVEN ≈

The next few minutes were a blur. Piper managed to get herself under control before Anna came running at her, throwing her arms around her and squeezing all the breath out of her again.

"I thought they were going to take you away," Anna sobbed. Her tears made tracks down Piper's neck. "I told Gee to hurry."

"He had incredible timing," Piper said, smiling. Gently, she loosened Anna's grip. The two people who'd followed Anna across the field were helping Gee to his feet. Piper had never seen either of them before. One was a man wearing gray overalls eaten up with so many black singe marks she wondered how the fabric held together. His spiky hair stuck out all over his head, and his face, smooth and white as an egg where it wasn't obscured by soot, looked friendly. He wore a wide belt affixed with dozens of leather loops. Each of the loops held a small glass vial with a rubber stopper. Liquids of various colors floated inside the vials.

The woman standing next to him was dressed in similar gray overalls—minus the singe marks—and was much older. What drew Piper's attention was the woman's right arm. From the elbow down, it was made of not flesh but steel and brass. Piper had seen the prosthetics that healers used, but those had been made of wood or simple metal shapes like hooks. This woman's limb had a wrist joint and five hinged metal fingers. Piper watched her use the limb to steady Gee on his feet. Then the woman turned to Piper.

"So, you're the two troublemakers I've been hearing so much about," the woman said. Her voice was gruff, but Piper detected no anger in it. "You can call me Jeyne. I'm the 401's engineer. You already know Gee, and that's my fireman, Trimble."

"We call her Jeyne Steel," Trimble said, grinning warmly. "She loves that."

Jeyne ignored him. "I talked to the authorities in town after Gee dropped off that carriage driver. They're coming to round up the rest of the slavers. They seemed surprised when I told them where you were. According to their information, the slave market was supposed to be on the other side of town. Guess this bunch got lost."

"Bad luck for us," Piper said, as if that were all there was to it. She didn't mention or look at Doloman, hoping that maybe Jeyne wouldn't ask too many questions about their ordeal.

"Luck, huh? I guess we'll see." Jeyne nodded to the fireman. "Trimble, you take the girls on back to the train. Gee and I will be along shortly, and then we're going to have a nice long chat about what happened out here tonight." She gave Piper a piercing look. "Does that suit you?"

Clearly, a cryptic story about being on a secret mission wasn't going to work this time—Jeyne had seen through her, and Piper knew it was time to confess. The engineer didn't strike her as the kind of person she could fool with a lie. Besides, Gee had just pulled their butts out of the fire and hurt himself in the process. They owed him and his friends some trust.

Piper looked Jeyne in the eye and nodded slowly. "That's fair," she said.

"Good." The older woman's severe expression softened a bit. "Go on, then. You must be exhausted after all you've been through."

Trimble led the way back to the train while Piper and Anna trailed behind. Anna refused to let go of Piper's hand the whole way, but Piper didn't complain. She was too tired and too relieved that they were safe. For her part, Anna didn't seem nearly as affected by their ordeal. Even after she'd been kidnapped by slavers, banged around in a carriage, and carried off by a beast, Anna was back to her normal self, chattering away at full speed.

". . . one minute my feet were running on the ground, and the next they were running through the air. That's not logical at all, I thought. I'm not a bird, but then I looked up and realized I'd grown wings! Of course, that's not logical either, I told myself. Spontaneous hybridization from human to bird isn't possible, not by any science we know. Then *that* got me thinking about the chamelins—and at the same time how high we were in the air—and somehow I knew it was Gee carrying me. I don't know how I knew. Maybe it's because his eyes are green when he's a boy and when he's a beast. Anyway, then I wasn't scared at all. Piper, were you scared of Gee in his other form?"

"Not for a second," Piper said. She'd die before she admitted that her heart threatened to pound right out of her chest when she saw that creature land in the middle of the field.

"You're a brave one," Trimble said, shooting Piper a knowing grin. "Gee looks fierce in his beastie form, and he grumbles enough when he's human to make you want to push him off the train at full steam, but he's all right. He's protective of the train, and thank the goddess for it, I say. We might not be running if it weren't for Gee."

His tone was jovial, but Piper heard the feeling underlying the fireman's words. "I thought the chamelins all lived in the west with the archivists," she said. "What's Gee doing here so far from his own kind?"

"He has his reasons. You'd have to ask him about that, though. It's his own story to tell," Trimble said.

Trimble's answer made Piper even more curious about Gee. She opened her mouth to ask another question, but suddenly she stumbled on the uneven ground and almost fell. Her feet felt like they were weighted down with rocks, and her throat ached where Doloman had grabbed her. Jeyne was right. Piper was so exhausted she didn't know how much farther she could walk.

Thankfully, they were almost to the train. Piper never thought she'd be so relieved to see the big steam engine again. Inside, her bed was waiting for her, soft and warm and, most importantly, safe. A few minutes ago, Piper had thought the only bed she'd be sleeping in was the dirty wood floor of a slaver's wagon. Instead, she almost felt like she was coming home, back when her father was there. Those days she'd always felt safe when she slept. Tears stung her eyes at the thought, and Piper wiped them away impatiently. She was crying entirely too often these days. She was sure it was Anna's fault, somehow.

As much as Piper wanted to sleep, she knew she had a lot of explaining to do first. Trimble led them toward the front of the train to a car that contained a small office with a cluttered desk, an upper and lower berth near the windows, and a tiny washroom.

"Jeyne and I sleep here," Trimble said, "so we can be near the engine in case there's trouble." He pointed to the lower berth. "That's my place. Take a seat, and Jeyne'll be here in a minute." He left the car and closed the door behind him.

Piper sank down on the bed, and Anna settled in next to her. In the glow of the gaslights, Piper noticed dark circles under Anna's eyes. She was more tired than Piper had realized.

"Go ahead and lie down," Piper told her. "I don't think Trimble will mind." She fluffed up the fireman's pillow and helped Anna slip off her shoes. The girl curled up on her side, and Piper sat on the edge of the bed next to her. She thought Anna would drift off immediately, but a few minutes later, she felt the girl's fingers on her arm.

"You never told me what Raenoll said." Anna looked up at Piper through half-closed eyes. "What did she see in her vision?"

Piper had been expecting—and dreading—the question, though she hadn't expected Anna to ask it so soon, so it caught her off guard. "Raenoll? After everything that's happened tonight, the seer is who you're thinking about?" Piper forced a laugh, but she was just stalling.

How much could she tell Anna? She couldn't reveal what Raenoll had told her about what would happen to Anna if Piper abandoned her, that much was certain. Piper didn't know what to think of the seer's cryptic words herself. According to Raenoll's prediction, if she took Anna to Noveen, her reward would be that something terrible would happen, something neither of them could live with. But what other choice did they have? If that mansion was where Anna came from, the answers they needed were there.

"I think she saw your home in her vision," Piper said at last, hoping that it turned out to be the truth. She described to Anna the sculpted gardens, the fountain, and the beautiful columned house overlooking the ocean. Piper hoped that it was as beautiful in real life as in the vision. Surely a place like that was too huge and fine for someone like Doloman to live there. It was the perfect house for Anna, big enough for parents and a small army of brothers and sisters. Piper wanted desperately to believe that Anna had a home and a family like that, a place safe from Doloman and his slavers.

While Piper talked, Anna's eyelids drooped, but she smiled when Piper finished. "That's nice," she said. "I don't remember that house, but maybe it *is* home. I hope so. I'm glad we went to the seer, Piper."

Piper didn't answer, letting Anna drift off to sleep. In the silence, she found herself thinking not about Raenoll, but about Doloman. She tried not to, wanted nothing more than to block out all that had happened, but she kept feeling his hand at her throat. Piper's fingers brushed lightly over her neck. Tomorrow there would be bruises on the tender skin. Doloman would have choked the life out of her if Gee hadn't come when he did.

Gee, a chamelin. Imagine that. Though up until now

she'd never seen one, Piper's father had told her stories about a chamelin who used to live near the scrap town. He'd said the creature was solitary, which was odd because chamelins were family oriented and protective by nature. They lived in large groups, establishing their colonies near archivist strongholds. When Piper asked her father why, he'd told her no one knew for sure, but the most likely reason was that the archivists valued protection too. They worked in groups to preserve the knowledge and culture that came from other worlds. Books, musical compositions, art—the archivists guarded all those objects as precious artifacts. The chamelins in turn protected the archivists.

Her father told her he felt sorry for the chamelin, that he'd probably lost his family group and was looking for another, but since the people in the scrap towns rarely interacted outside their own families, he wasn't going to find what he was looking for there. Eventually, he left, and her father never saw him again. Piper wondered if Gee had had a similar experience.

The flickering gaslights in the suite made her sleepy. Piper was just contemplating lying down next to Anna when the door opened, and Gee and Jeyne walked in, grim expressions on their faces.

Piper tensed, unsure what to say as Jeyne came to stand in front of her. "You've both had a rough night, so I won't keep you here long, but I need some sort of explanation," she said. Her tone was businesslike, but there was an edge to it. "Gee followed you from the train. He said those slavers didn't just grab you at random. They were looking for you specifically, and they went to a lot of trouble to get you. I need to know why so I can protect both you and this train."

She waited for Piper to speak. Gee leaned against the wall, but he wasn't looking at Piper. He was pale, and looked sick from breathing in the dust. Piper felt the weight of the debt she owed him. She cleared her throat. "They were after Anna," she said, then she started talking.

She told them what had happened the night of the meteor storm, about Micah's injury, how she'd found Anna in the caravan wreckage and brought her back to her house, how the other caravan survivor had eventually tracked them there. "We jumped on the train right after he attacked us," Piper explained. "The only thing Anna remembers clearly is the factory in the capital, so that's where we're headed."

"That's why you went to Raenoll," Gee said, speaking for the first time. "You thought she could help Anna remember who she is."

"That's right," Piper said, "but it wasn't worth getting caught by the slavers. I should have listened to you," she said, glancing at Gee.

Jeyne looked at her thoughtfully. "You've come a long way on your own," she said. "You have family back north?"

Piper shook her head. "It's just me."

"And Anna has no idea who this man is who's after her?" Gee asked.

"I found out tonight his name is Doloman," Piper said. "That's all we know." She sighed. At least maybe that nightmare was over. With any luck, he was sitting in a Tevshal jail right now with the other slavers and couldn't hurt either of them.

"Doloman?" Jeyne said. She looked at Gee and their alarmed expressions churned up dread in Piper's gut.

"What is it?" Piper said. She rubbed slick palms together and tried to push back her growing fear. What else was about to go wrong?

"Well," Jeyne said, "that makes for a thornier problem, doesn't it?" Before Piper could speak, she held up a hand. "Your friend has the tattoo of the Dragonfly territories, is that right?"

"That's right," Piper said. "Whatever else she is, she's protected by King Aron." She glanced at Gee. "I wasn't lying about that part."

"That doesn't solve anything," Gee said tersely, but he was addressing Jeyne, not Piper. "We're still obligated—"

"I'll decide what I'm obligated to do on this train, thank you," Jeyne said curtly. Her expression softened when she looked at Piper. "Gee here is upset because he knows the 401 is bound to cooperate with anyone who has the dragonfly tattoo on account of it being King

Aron who pays our wages and keeps this train running. The problem is that Doloman also has the mark of the Dragonfly."

Piper's heart stuttered in her chest. Suddenly, she couldn't catch her breath. It was as if Doloman were there choking her again. "You mean . . ."

"Yeah, I mean. *Master* Doloman—that's his title—is a member of King Aron's advisory council. In addition to that, he's the king's chief machinist. That pretty much makes him the second most powerful person in the Dragonfly territories."

Piper was at a loss for words. All she could manage to utter was a faint "I didn't know."

"There's no reason you would," Gee said. "You're not from the Dragonfly territories, and Master Doloman's very secretive about himself and his work for Aron. He hardly ever goes out in public." He glanced at Jeyne. "We've never met him, but he was one of the men who built the 401."

"He's an engineering genius," Jeyne said grudgingly.

"He's your boss." Piper gripped the edge of the bed for support. "That's what Gee meant when he said you were obligated. When they find out who he is in Tevshal, they'll let him go. Then he'll come here, and you'll have to turn us in."

What would happen to her then? What would happen to Anna? Doloman would likely take her to Noveen, and Piper would be the one thrown in a jail cell for the rest of her life for assaulting Aron's chief machinist. She'd been an idiot to think their troubles with Doloman were over, but this was worse than anything she could have imagined.

Jeyne turned to Gee. "Why don't you head up front and let Trimble know that we need to get under way as soon as possible. I'll join him in a minute."

Gee hesitated, his lips pinched as if he wanted to argue, but something in Jeyne's expression stopped him, because he nodded and headed for the door. He shot one last, long glance at Piper that made her look down at her feet uncomfortably. When she looked up, he'd left the car.

"What are you going to do?" she asked Jeyne.

The older woman didn't immediately answer, which made Piper's stomach clench. Jeyne pulled a chair out from the desk and sat down across from the bed. She regarded Piper thoughtfully. "I haven't decided yet," she said finally. "On the one hand, Gee's right. Now that I know that it's Master Doloman after you, I'm required to turn you over to him. If I don't and King Aron finds out, there's a good chance this train will get shut down, and we're all out of a job. Goddess knows we're running on borrowed time already, what with the factories spewing out parts for airships and ocean steamers faster than you can say 'exploration through innovation.'" She sniffed. "That's King Aron's favorite saying. On the other hand, Master Doloman's guilty of kidnapping and consorting with slavers, which is something I won't tolerate no matter who he is."

"But if he's such an important person, why didn't he just have the authorities in Tevshal pull us off the train as soon as we got to the city?" Piper asked, confused. "Why did he hire the slavers?"

"I'm asking myself the same question," Jeyne said, rubbing her temples. "He must not want the authorities knowing about you two. Slavers take their coin and don't ask questions, and if Master Doloman wants to recover Anna quietly and get rid of you at the same time, selling you to the slavers is the perfect way to do it." She clasped her hands together, cupping metal over skin. "But if it's true he doesn't want to attract attention, it's a safe bet he won't risk coming on the train and demanding that we hand you over, especially after what happened tonight. And that gives us a reprieve."

Piper considered this. Jeyne was probably right—if he hadn't already, Doloman probably wouldn't risk coming after them openly, but whatever sanctuary the train provided wasn't going to last forever. "He'll just wait and come after us when we get to Noveen," Piper murmured. "He knows that's the train's last stop. He knows that it's Anna's home too, that that's where she'll want to go." And how perfect for Doloman. Big city like Noveen—Aron's chief machinist probably knew all kinds of unsavory types like the slavers who would be willing to help him kidnap two girls. The safe feeling

Piper had had earlier when they'd gotten back on the 401 fled her utterly. "We have to get off the train. It's too dangerous to stay here—and we can't go to the capital."

"Hold on a minute." Jeyne held up her hand. "You're not caught yet," she said.

"But—"

"No, *listen*. What if I decided to pretend you didn't tell me that it's Master Doloman who's after you?" Jeyne said. "The train can stay on schedule to the capital, and once we get there, we'll come up with a plan to hide you from him. What do you think about that?"

Piper hesitated. Jeyne's plan sounded reasonable, but why would the woman go out of her way to help them, and defy one of King Aron's advisors in the process? It seemed too good to be true. "You'd be risking a lot." Piper's voice quavered, betraying fear and hope. Would Jeyne and the others really stick their necks out for them like that? And if she did, how was Piper ever going to square all these debts?

"You took a risk too," Jeyne said. "You could have handed Anna over to Master Doloman that night he showed up at your house, saved yourself a world of trouble. Why didn't you?"

"I'm not that kind of scrapper," Piper said. "She was alone and scared. Who else was going to help her?"

Beside her, Anna shifted and sighed in her sleep. Piper started to pull one of Trimble's blankets over her, but Jeyne came and knelt beside the bed, stopping her.

Piper realized she was looking at Anna's tattoo, which was exposed when Anna rolled over.

"That's the Dragonfly's mark, no mistake there," Jeyne murmured softly. "Can't figure why Master Doloman's hunting one of his own, though. Doesn't make sense."

"That's what Anna always says." Piper smoothed the hair out of the girl's eyes where it had come loose from her braids. "Nothing makes sense anymore." A thought occurred to her. "Doloman said Anna is his daughter. Do you know if that's true?"

Jeyne raised an eyebrow. "Master Doloman's got no daughter that I've ever heard of. He's married to his machines."

"He looked at her like she was his daughter," Piper said. She thought back to when he'd appeared at her house. He'd been overjoyed—beside himself—to see Anna that night. But the crazed look had been there too. "Doloman scares her. I've never seen anyone that scared of another person."

"Then it's a good thing she found you," Jeyne said. She stood, drew a handkerchief out of her pocket, and mopped her face with it. "You should go and get some rest. Leave Anna. When she rouses, I'll have Trimble take her back to your room."

Piper hesitated. "I don't know if that's a good idea. If she wakes up and I'm not here . . ." Piper stopped herself. Since when had she become such a mother hen?

What was it Anna had called her, a mother goshawk? Not much better—she really was going soft.

"I'll check in on her every now and then," Jeyne assured her. "She'll be safe. As long as the two of you stay on the train, you'll both be safe. I can promise you that."

Looking into Jeyne's determined face, Piper believed her. "Thank you. I—" She swallowed. She couldn't promise repayment because she had no money now that Anna's gold had been taken. Simple gratitude didn't seem like nearly enough, but for now, it would have to do. "Thank you."

"You're welcome." Jeyne stuffed the handkerchief back in her pocket and nodded at the door. "Go on, now."

Piper stood and wobbled a little on her feet. Jeyne reached out with her metal arm and steadied her. Piper expected the steel prosthetic to be cold, but the metal was warm against her skin. She nodded her thanks, cast one more glance at Anna, then left the car.

She told herself she was going to take a long shower to wash off the dirt and wipe away the memory of the slaver's rope on her, but Piper only managed to strip off her clothes before the room started to spin. She climbed to the upper berth and drew the covers over her head. Strangely, her last thought before she fell asleep was that Gee still had her father's coat.

≈ TWELVE ≈

Gee stood on the open-air observation deck at the back of the train, leaning against the iron rail as a grove of cypress trees rushed past. They had entered the southern territories—the Dragonfly territories—King Aron's country. Before long, the air would grow unbearably hot and thick with the tang of salt water. He'd never liked the coast. Gee preferred the north countries—the cold, solid mountains and the pewter color of the sky before it snowed. He loved to fly in that weather.

He shifted, Piper's coat draped over his right arm. It was far too big for her, Gee noticed, but that hardly mattered. She wouldn't need to wear it in the south.

Behind him, the door slid open. Gee didn't have to look to know that it was Trimble. Even in Gee's weaker form, the smell of the fireman's sweat was like a beacon.

"Off to scout?" Trimble asked.

"In a minute," Gee replied. "I was resting."

"You sure you got all the dust out of your lungs?" The fireman stood next to him, fingering one of the glass vials at his belt. Thick yellow liquid filled the vial, and when Trimble popped the stopper with his thumb, Gee smelled burnt peanuts. "This antidote's good enough for humans. It might be a little weaker inside you, but it'll help the burning."

"I'm all right," Gee said. He coughed once. "If that stuff tastes as bad as it smells, I'd rather have the burning cough."

"Suit yourself." Trimble put the vial back on his belt. "Jeyne says not to go too far tonight, and I agree. You need to rest."

"We'll be in Cutting Gap in three days," Gee answered. "None of us has time to rest."

"The cargo will be safe," Trimble said. He ran a hand through his sooty hair. "The defenses are working perfectly—fact is, everything on this train is humming along better than I've ever seen it—and there'll be guards in just about every car."

Gee shook his head. "You'd think they were guarding solid gold, not machine parts. I don't know why we don't just give the raiders some. They'll sell the stuff for scrap and be able to feed themselves decently for once. It'd save King Aron a lot of coin in the end. He wouldn't have to hire so many guards."

Trimble raised an eyebrow. "You think they'd sell

the parts to buy food? More likely they'd use them to build a dozen more gliders and hit us even harder next run. There's no room for compromise in this game, friend."

"No, not when they're willing to die for the cargo—or kill for it." Gee shot him a sidelong glance. "Each and every run, we have to boost our defenses. The train's becoming a weapon in itself. Things didn't used to be like this, did they?"

"I can't remember anymore." Trimble blew out a sigh. "All I know is if we don't do our jobs, by the end of this run we won't have jobs. They'll replace us with crueler people, the ones who shoot back even when they don't need to." He looked at Gee. "Is that why you went out after those girls—your conscience nagging you?"

"I should have listened to her," Gee said. He combed his fingers through the loose threads on Piper's coat sleeve. "Those girls needed protection, just like I did once."

"You couldn't have known," Trimble said. "They didn't exactly confide in us."

"Yes, they did—the night they came aboard the train. Piper told me that if I threw them off, they were dead. Tonight, they almost were." Gee let the threads hang free. "I should have tried harder to keep them away from Tevshal, from the slavers."

"You like her." A smile creased Trimble's face.

"Piper, I mean," he added. "I can see why. You two are a lot the same."

Gee blushed. "Actually, I was thinking she's more like you."

The fireman frowned. "What do you mean by that?"

"When I was flying to get Anna, I saw that one of the slavers had a gun on Piper and then—" Gee stopped. He decided he didn't want to share his theory with Trimble. Not until he'd had more time to think about it. "Never mind. We'll talk about it later. And I *don't* like her," he added. "Not in the way you think."

"Whatever you say, but you can't protect them from Master Doloman forever," Trimble said. "Once we get to the capital, they'll have to get off, and then they'll have to go into hiding. There's no other way to avoid him."

"I know," Gee said sharply. It had been bothering him ever since he found out who it was the girls were running from. "You think I haven't already thought about that? I'd get them off sooner if there were any decent towns I could fly them to, but there aren't. Aron ruined them when he strip-mined everything in the area to get his iron. There're hardly any safe places left anywhere."

"Well, they're safe enough here for now," Trimble said. "Master Doloman will be a while recovering from the dust Piper threw in his face, and the authorities will have to confirm his identity before they let him go back to Noveen. We have some time." He stared into the distance. "Too bad Jeyne couldn't buy the 401, run it as an independent operation. We could take on the cargo and passengers we wanted, maybe bypass Cutting Gap completely. It'd make for longer runs, but it'd be worth it."

"You're dreaming," Gee said. "Jeyne doesn't have any more coin than the rest of us. We get by with what we have, same as always."

"You're right." Trimble sighed, pushed off the rail and headed for the door. "You want me to give that coat back to Piper on my way up front?"

"No," Gee said. "Let them sleep. I'll give it to her in the morning."

" 'Let them sleep,' he says. That's the problem," Trimble muttered. "One of them is sleeping in my bed. Got her own suite, but she ends up snug in my cot."

Trimble shook his head as he went back inside. As soon as Gee was alone, he started to cough again. He'd been holding the coughs in so as not to worry Trimble, and they felt like hot coals pressed against the inside of his chest. He bent over the rail and hacked until his lungs threatened to burst. The train tracks peeled away beneath his feet in a sickening blur. He closed his eyes and held on to the rail tight with both hands.

When the fit finally passed, Gee straightened and rubbed a hand over his burning chest. Maybe he should have tried Trimble's antidote. His alchemical experiments generally worked—except for the times when they exploded. At any rate, the fireman was right. He needed to rest and get back his strength before they hit Cutting Gap. After that, he would worry about what to do for Piper and Anna.

He hoped three days would be enough time to recover. He'd need all the strength he could get.

Piper woke to a gray sky and rain streaking the windows. The train had stopped, and when Piper crawled to the window to look outside, she saw they were in Molwey. That meant they were out of the Merrow Kingdom and already deep into the Dragonfly territories.

She rubbed her eyes and leaned over the edge of the bed to see if Anna was awake yet. When she saw the empty, made-up berth, everything from the previous night came back to her.

Anna was sleeping in Jeyne and Trimble's room. She and Piper were running from King Aron's chief machinist on board one of Aron's own trains.

Piper flopped back on the bed. Not the smartest scheme she'd ever come up with, she thought, but at least they were safe again for the moment. Jeyne Steel had promised to look after Anna, and Piper believed she would. But their presence here put everyone else who worked on the train at risk. If Doloman or Aron found out that the 401's crew was protecting them, they'd be in as much trouble as Piper. The sooner they got to Noveen and sorted out who Anna really was, the better it would be for everyone.

Though she was still tired from the previous night, Piper pulled herself out of bed, showered, dressed, and was headed out to check on Anna when a voice called to her from the hall. She turned to see the porter, Mr. Jalin.

"I'm sorry to disturb you, miss," Jalin said. He fidgeted and kept shooting glances over his shoulder. "It's just . . . your companion . . ."

"Anna?" Piper was suddenly on edge. "Is she all right?" She took an involuntary step toward him, her hand raised.

"She's fine," Jalin said quickly. "Miss Anna is in the library, but I'm afraid there's a problem. She's been . . . rearranging things."

The way he said "rearranging" got Piper's attention. Considering what the girl had done to her own house, she didn't want to know what was going on in the library. Piper smiled. "So she's started moving things around. Is she going on about proportions and fixing things?"

"Yes, that's it." Jalin's expression looked as if his neck button were fastened too tight. "I hoped you might look in on her and make sure—"

"I'll take care of it." Piper patted the beleaguered man on the arm and moved past him. She'd best get to Anna before she dismantled the whole library. Still, Piper slowed when she reached the dining car, savoring the breakfast smells as her stomach rumbled.

Piper noticed then that the car was almost empty. It should have been packed at this hour, but there were only a handful of humans sitting quietly in their seats, most of them staring intently out the windows instead of eating. And no sarnuns to speak of. When Piper slid the door to the next car open, several of the passengers jumped. A strange tension filled the air, a feeling of expectation that resembled a scrap town just before a meteor storm. Uneasiness immediately swept over her, and Piper's guard came up.

Head down, she walked quickly through the car. At the other end, Piper saw the door marked LIBRARY. She slid it open, then closed it behind her.

Glass-fronted book cabinets lined both walls, and a pair of windows between them let in the natural light. Cushioned leather armchairs were situated around the room, and permeating everything was the smell of old books and ink.

When Piper stepped into the library, she saw immediately what had put Jalin into such a panic. Every one of the cabinet doors stood ajar, and the bookshelves were empty.

Anna sat on the floor in the middle of the room, a large leather-bound book open in her lap. Arranged around her were the rest of the books, dozens of them, stacked in towers that were almost as tall as Piper. Anna had turned the spines to face her.

She looked up when Piper walked into the car, and

smiled enormously. "You're awake. You must see this, Piper." She gestured excitedly for her to sit down, so Piper took a seat in one of the armchairs. "The room was all wrong. You couldn't see any of the books behind the glass because of the reflective surface. I think that's why so few people come in here, but I've fixed all that. Accounting for average height and the angle of the sun coming in the windows, I've created the ideal spot here in the middle of the room for reading. You can see all the book titles, and everything is in easy reach. What do you think?"

Piper heard the 401 blow its whistle, a long, loud burst of warning. She crossed her arms and fought to keep from laughing. "Well, Anna, as you like to say, it's a good idea in theory, but I can see one or two little problems."

"Really?" Anna's forehead scrunched in consternation. "What's wrong with it? I accounted for both human and sarnun reading styles, if that's what you're worried about."

The train started to move, slowly at first, but quickly picked up speed. Piper leaned back in her chair as the car started its rhythmic swaying from side to side. The book towers swayed with it. A second before the first one toppled, Anna's eyes widened. "Oh," she squeaked, and scrambled to her feet.

Books began to crash to the floor all over the room,

despite Anna's valiant attempts to steady the towers. She managed to save one, wrapping her thin arms around the books, but that made her lose her balance and Piper had to jump up and grab her before she fell.

"Let it go," Piper advised, pulling Anna toward another chair. Reluctantly, the girl complied, and the last tower fell over with a loud crash. They were knee-deep in books.

"I thought I accounted for everything," Anna said gloomily.

"You did—everything but a library that moves," Piper said. "Don't worry about it. I'll help you get the books straightened up."

They spent the next hour going through the piles, sorting the books alphabetically and by subject, putting them back in the cabinets. When Piper got to the book she'd seen Anna reading, she examined it.

"*Encyclopedia of Predator and Prey Animals*," she read off the cover. "What were you looking up in here?"

"Nothing specific, but when I started reading the book, it triggered a memory." Anna took it from Piper and flipped to an entry near the beginning. On the left-hand page was a sketch of a wolf. "The picture and these words—I remember someone reading them to me before I went to sleep at night." She pointed to a paragraph, and Piper read it aloud.

"'Stress responses in prey animals—the frozen

muscle response and the instinct to fight a predator or seek escape. Fight or flight.'" Piper remembered Anna repeating those words the night they escaped the scrap town.

Running from Doloman—*the wolf.*

The hairs on the back of Piper's neck stood up. "Someone read this to you?" she asked. "Do you remember who? Or where you were?"

Anna shook her head. "When you read it just now, I didn't hear the wolf's voice in my head. But I don't hear your voice either, or mine. It's different."

"Different how?" Piper pressed, her excitement building. Anna was finally starting to remember something about her past. "Is it a male voice or a female voice?"

Anna thought for a minute. "Male," she said.

"Old or young?"

"Old—very old."

Maybe her father or grandfather, Piper thought. "Well, this is good news. Maybe it's a sign your memory's going to come back soon," Piper said. "Do you think you'd know the voice if you heard it again?"

Anna smiled. "Oh yes. I'd know it right away. It's a nice voice. Not that yours isn't nice," she added quickly, flushing. "I didn't mean—"

"Don't worry. Reading isn't my best skill." Piper closed the book with a thump. "And this isn't what I'd choose for bedtime reading either. I like adventure stories. What about the other books? Do you recognize any of them?"

They went through the shelves in more detail, and Anna pointed out two titles in the reference section. "These," she said. *"Frey's Encyclopedia of General Knowledge and Brosstoi's Scientific Procedures."*

Piper blinked at the titles. "Well, that maybe explains some things." What if Anna's strange outbursts of knowledge came as a result of someone reading to her from encyclopedias and scientific texts like these? Instead of memorizing beloved bedtime stories, Anna had soaked up a variety of scientific and technical knowledge. "Do you want to take one of them back to our suite?" Piper asked. "You can read it after breakfast."

Anna didn't answer. She fingered the cuff of her shirt. "I remembered something else while I was reading the books," she said quietly.

"What is it? Something bad?" Piper put a hand on Anna's arm, at the same time trying to push away her own sudden anxiety. "When you fidget like that, it usually means you're upset about something."

"Maybe." Anna stood up and turned her back to Piper. She lifted her braids to reveal a large crescent-shaped scar on the back of her neck. "I never noticed it before, and I don't know why, but while I was reading the book, I suddenly remembered it was there."

Piper reached out and gently traced the rough flesh.

It looked like the scar from a deep, jagged cut, one that no healer had ever treated. "Do you remember how you got it?"

Anna shook her head and let the braids fall back into place. "I didn't want to remember it."

"What do you mean?" Piper said.

"The wolf—Doloman—used to talk about it," Anna said. "I heard his voice in my head. He talked about the scar a lot."

"Do you think he gave it to you?" Piper asked, and anger tightened her gut. "Did he hurt you?"

"I don't think he gave it to me . . . but I think he hurt me *because* of it," she said carefully. "I remember cold metal and sharp pains like fire all over my skin." She shuddered. "I don't want to remember it, Piper."

"It's all right," Piper soothed, "then don't." Inwardly, a wave of sadness seized her. What had Doloman done to Anna? Was it something so terrible that her mind had put up a wall around the memories? "Look, we know enough about Doloman to know he's dangerous," she said. "Concentrate on that other voice, the nice one. Maybe the person who read to you is part of your family. He probably read to you in that big house on the cliff."

"Do you think so?" Anna said hopefully.

Piper shrugged. "One thing's for sure—if he is up there, I'm going to tell him he has lousy taste in bedtime stories," she answered, grinning.

Anna smiled too. "You're doing it again, making me feel better with your jokes. I haven't thought about last night at all since you came in the room. When I'm with you, I'm not scared."

"That's good," Piper said. Her smile widened. She wanted Anna to feel safe. "You let me do the worrying for both of us."

"It's just . . ." Anna's smile faded. "You keep getting in trouble because of me, and last night Gee got hurt because of me. I don't understand why you're all doing this. You left your home, Piper, put yourself in danger just to help me. So much has happened, but this makes the least sense of all. You don't know me, but you act like a mother bird. Well, maybe not a mother—you're too young, aren't you? It's not logical."

"Not to mention I can't fly," Piper said dryly.

"You're more like a sister," Anna said. She looked thoughtful. "I don't think I have a sister. I don't remember a sister's voice, and nobody ever looked after me the way you do."

"I never had a sister either," Piper said. "But you annoy me like I imagine a sister would, and you're an awful lot of work." Anna put her face in her hands as if she was about to cry, and Piper reached out and squeezed her shoulder. "Hey now. I was joking again." She scooted closer and put an arm around the younger girl. "Last night was rough, but we got through it. From now on, we play things smart and stay on the train. Jeyne

Steel's going to look after us until we get to the capital. Once we're there, we'll find someone to help us."

Piper spoke with confidence, but she didn't know if she really believed they'd find help in Noveen. If King Aron's chief machinist was after them, who would give them sanctuary? They had to hope that Anna really did have family at the house on top of the cliff, someone powerful who could protect them once Doloman caught up to them again. Because that was sure to happen.

And she had to hope Raenoll's grim prediction didn't come true.

No, Piper decided. She wouldn't let it. She cared about Anna, and last night, Piper thought she'd lost her friend. She vowed she wouldn't let that happen again. She'd make sure she got Anna all the way to the capital, and that she was safe.

Even if it meant Anna would leave Piper and rejoin her family.

Anna laid her head on Piper's shoulder, and they sat for a while in silence. Piper found herself thinking about King Aron. Where did he fit into all this? He lived in the capital. If they went to him, would he be a friend or an enemy? Anna and Doloman both bore his mark. He owed loyalty to both of them.

At least in theory—as Anna would say.

No, it was too risky to go to the king. Anna was just a kid, and according to Jeyne Steel, Doloman was practically Aron's second in command. Their only option was to find Anna's family—if she had one. And for her sake, Piper hoped she did.

After breakfast, Anna wanted to go back to her reading spot in the library. Piper didn't really feel like sitting still, so she decided to take a walk to the back of the train. She told herself she just wanted to stretch her legs, but she found herself looking around for Gee as she explored. She hadn't seen the security chief since the night before, and she felt like she owed him an apology. Really, she owed him a lot more than that, but Piper could only swallow so much of her pride in one day.

When Piper got to the door of the cargo section, a guard stopped her at the vestibule. "I'm sorry, miss, but this area is off-limits to passengers," he said. He spoke politely, but his body squarely blocked her path. He wore that same expression of nervous expectation she'd seen on the faces of the passengers earlier.

"I'm looking for Gee," Piper explained. "Have you seen him?"

"He's meeting with the senior guards," the man said. He looked her over. "You're one of the girls marked by the Dragonfly, aren't you?"

Piper hesitated. Saying yes would probably get her past the guard, but at this point, she decided the truth was best, and anyway, she was tired of lying. "I'm not marked, but I'm traveling with someone who is," she said. She turned to go, but before she retreated the man stopped her.

"Wait here," the guard said. He turned, opened the boxcar door, and shouted to someone Piper couldn't see. "Go tell the chief one of the girls is here asking for him."

A few minutes later, Gee's scarecrow figure appeared in the doorway. Today, his soot smudge floated above his left eyebrow in the shape of a carrot. He looked tired and pale, but he smiled at Piper. "Just the person I wanted to see."

His smile was startling. It softened his face, made him less intimidating—or maybe it was because she'd seen him naked. That was an equalizer. Piper wasn't sure whether that would make her apology easier or harder. "I don't want to bother you," she said, feeling her cheeks flush. "I just wanted to talk for a minute."

"Sure. Come with me." He led her through the boxcar, past wooden crates stacked against the walls and secured with heavy rope. The air was humid and smelled of sawdust. Whatever the cargo was, it filled the entire car from floor to ceiling, with only a narrow space to walk in between. "It's usually not this packed in here," Gee said as if he'd read her thoughts. "This cargo's been with us since Tevshal. Even I don't know everything that's in it."

"Don't you have to know?" Piper asked. "I mean,

isn't whoever's shipping the goods supposed to let you look at it in case it's dangerous?"

"Not if the price is right," Gee said. "Aron will ship anything, no questions asked." His scowl told Piper what he thought of that policy. "We get a manifest, but it's never complete. The Merrow Kingdom doesn't tell us any more than necessary."

"I'm surprised Merrow and Dragonfly are still willing to deal with each other at all," Piper said. There hadn't yet been open conflict, but relations between the two places had been strained to near breaking point ever since the king stopped trading them iron.

"You were right—neither of them cares enough about what's happening to their own people these days," Gee said, shaking his head in disgust. "All Merrow wants is weapons, and the Dragonfly's too busy with his factories. Do you know he wants to have a fleet of steamships ready to set sail for the uncharted lands by next summer? The summer after that, he wants five skyships to cross the Hiterian Mountains."

"He's crazy," Piper said. "No one's ever crossed the mountains, and all the exploration ships that have gone beyond the coastlands never came back."

"That just makes the Dragonfly more determined," Gee said. "It won't be him going on any of these expeditions, so what does he care if they fail? It's not his neck that's at risk."

They passed through another cargo area and into

the mail car. Piper recognized this area from her first night on the train. It was where they'd snuck on board. "Where are we going?" she asked.

"Oh, sorry," Gee answered. "I should have said before. I want you to show me how you and Anna got on the train. As far as I can tell, all our defenses were working that night, but obviously something went wrong."

Piper felt a rush of fear, remembering that night. "Good thing it did." She shivered. "I almost got burned to a crisp."

Gee glanced at her, but Piper couldn't read his expression. "The vestibules are our weakest points," he explained. "The fire vents keep raiders from boarding the train and attacking the guards and passengers."

It was still a terrible system, Piper thought, when innocent people had as much chance of being burned as the raiders did. "But there has to be a better way to protect the train," she said, "one that isn't dangerous for your people too."

For a minute, Gee said nothing, and Piper thought he might be angry. But then he nodded. "You're right," he said sadly. "It *is* dangerous, but it's all we have."

Piper had no answer for that. They stood in awkward silence, Piper staring at the floor, at a loss for what to do next. Gee coughed, and when she glanced up at him, she noticed he was sweating; trickles of moisture were running down his forehead.

"Are you all right?" The train jolted, and Gee staggered in place. Piper grabbed his shoulder to steady him and felt a tremor go through his body. "You look awful. Maybe you should sit down."

"I'm fine," he said, but Piper didn't believe it. He was visibly shaking now. He coughed again, and the sound that came from his chest was a loud, harsh wheeze.

"It's the dust, isn't it?" Piper said. "You've still got it swimming in your lungs." Holding him by the shoulder, Piper guided him to a seat on one of the mail crates. Gee coughed again, only it was a longer fit that had him bent over, his head between his knees. Piper held on to him so he didn't fall off the crate; otherwise she could do nothing but watch helplessly.

Gee finally caught his breath. "I thought it would be better by now, but . . ."

"I'm no healer, but it sounds like it's getting worse," Piper said. She felt the flush of guilt again and couldn't meet his eyes. "I'm sorry. It's my fault. If we'd stayed on the train when you told us to, you wouldn't have been smacked with the dust."

Gee laughed weakly. "I knew you were going to be trouble the instant I saw you. Stubborn, hard-headed—"

"Well, you weren't exactly a charmer yourself," Piper interrupted. "Remember the part where you were going to throw us off the train?"

"I remember." His humor faded. "I'm sorry about

that. If I hadn't been so harsh, maybe you would have told me the truth right then about why you were running."

Maybe it had worked out for the best, Piper thought. If Gee had found out it was the Dragonfly's head machinist chasing them that first night, he would have had no choice but to turn them over. "Doloman's never going to stop looking for Anna," she said. The truth made her sick to her stomach. "I don't know what's going to happen once we get to Noveen."

Gee studied her face. "You care about her, don't you?"

Piper nodded. "Is that surprising?" she asked.

"No, it's not that. It's just . . . the two of you are so different."

Piper gave a rueful laugh. "That's the truth—a scrapper from the north and one of Dragonfly's own from the south. We couldn't be any more apart in the world." Her expression turned serious. "I think she's been through some terrible things. Maybe it's a blessing that she doesn't remember most of it. I want her to be safe, to find a home. Everyone should have that, especially at her age."

"She's not much younger than you," Gee pointed out. "What will you do after she's back with her family?"

"Well, I don't think I'm ever going back to the scrap town." As much as Piper longed to see Micah again, she didn't have the money to get there, and she knew she had to move forward with her life, no matter how hard it was to let go of the past. "I'll stay in the capital, maybe, or move on to somewhere along the coast. I've never seen the ocean before." Piper tried to summon the excitement she used to feel when she'd dreamt about these plans back in Scrap Town Sixteen, but she couldn't banish the empty feeling that came when she imagined leaving Anna behind. "What about you?" she said, needing to change the subject. "Do you have family in the south?"

Gee shook his head. "My parents sold me when I was seven."

"What?" Piper thought she must have heard him wrong.

Gee ran a finger over the twin scars that slashed his neck. "These marks are how the slavers value their purchases. Slaves as young as I was don't usually get more than one slash, but since I'm a chamelin, I was considered a novelty."

Piper stared at the scars, her own problems forgotten. "You didn't tell me that part."

"About the scars?"

"That you were a slave! I mean, you warned me about the slavers, but I didn't know . . . your parents . . . they *sold* you?" The idea was incomprehensible to Piper. Her own father had loved her more than anything in the world. "What happened? How did you end up on the 401?"

"Luck, mostly. Turned out, the slavers who bought

me weren't equipped to handle a chamelin, even a young one," Gee said. A shutter had closed over his expression and his body had gone tense, but he kept scratching absently at the scars, as if a part of him still hoped to obliterate the marks. "I escaped six times. They always caught me, though. The last time I got away, I was sure they were going to kill me. Jeyne found me first."

"She helped you escape?"

"No, she couldn't. The slavers were right on top of me. I flew into a rail yard where the 401 was being repaired." With his other hand, Gee made a little soaring motion in the air. "Jeyne pulled me out of the corner of a boxcar. I was still in my other form, scratching, biting—I'm sure I gave her a couple scars of her own in that fight, but I was desperate. Instead of handing me over to the slavers, she negotiated a price." Gee's mouth twisted in a mixture of humor and pain. "I never asked, but I'm sure she got me cheap. The slavers were tired of dealing with me."

"Then she set you free?" The thought of Gee as a slave, of someone tying down his wings and using the dust on him, made Piper feel queasy.

The slavers could have taken him again that night in the field, she realized. He must have known it was possible, but he followed them anyway. He came for both of them.

"She tried to," Gee said, interrupting Piper's thoughts. "When I changed back to my human form, she said she'd take me home. I was so angry—at my parents, the slavers, the world—I just screamed at her, told her I didn't have parents or a home. When I couldn't scream anymore, she said she'd give me a place on the 401. I've been here ever since."

"I'm sorry," Piper said again. "I misjudged you."

"No, you got me right," Gee said. He stopped rubbing the scars and wiped the sweat from his forehead, smearing the soot mark into a long dark streak. "I've been afraid for a while that Aron is going to shut down the 401. The train's powerful but old. Aron's factories have already churned out faster trains with deadlier defenses that run some of the major routes around the capital. Now he's strictly working on steamships and airships. In a few years, he'll probably abandon the railroads. We've avoided being shut down so far because we haven't given them a reason. We deliver our cargo on time and we make sure our passengers are safe. Everything was going well. When you and Anna snuck on the train that night, I saw you as a threat to that."

"We are a threat." Piper's heart thumped painfully. "If Doloman finds out that you're protecting us, he'll do a lot more than shut you down. You could all be thrown in prison."

"He won't find out," Gee said. "We'll get you to the capital and make sure you're safe."

"How can you be sure?" Piper said, trying to quell the fear that rose inside her. "Anything could happen."

She ticked the possibilities off on her fingers. "Doloman could change his mind, decide to come after us here, maybe bring an army with him this time."

"He won't risk it."

Piper couldn't stop—her mind spun with all the possible disasters. "You just said the 401 is old. Well, what if we break down, or the train derails, or we get attacked by vicious raccoons—"

Lips twitching, he cocked an eyebrow at her. "We don't see too many of those along the coast."

Piper crossed her arms. "Well, I wasn't expecting to see a chamelin on this trip either. And the train actually *could* break down."

"Yeah, about that." Gee gave her a searching look, and just as she had last night, Piper squirmed, as if Gee were staring right down inside of her. Something fluttered through her stomach. "The 401's been running smoother on this trip than it ever has before," Gee said. "I'm not worried about us breaking down." He stood and headed for the door at the back of the car. "I've rested enough. We should get going."

"Are you sure—" Piper started, but Gee was already out in the vestibule, and Piper scrambled to follow. She wanted to say something, to ask him why in the world he was risking his home and his freedom for her and Anna when he barely knew them, but the words caught in her throat.

Gee had his back to her, and he was inspecting

the canvas bellows connecting the cars. Light filtered through a hastily mended tear in the canvas. Piper recognized her knife slash. This was the spot where she and Anna had boarded the train.

"I'll mend it better when we get to Noveen," Gee said. "I'm more concerned about the pressure plates."

"Pressure plates?" Piper stood at Gee's shoulder and looked down at the metal platform where the canvas ended. By the dim light coming from outside, she saw a thin seam in the metal. "Is that what triggers the alarm?"

"Among other things," Gee said. "The plate runs all the way underneath the canvas to the outside. If someone wants to get onto the train through the vestibule, they have to step on it, and when they do, it triggers the alarm and the flame vents."

"That's what happened to me," Piper said. "I triggered the alarm, but I didn't realize I'd done it by stepping on the pressure plate."

"You did. I saw your boot prints on the pressure plate when I checked the vestibule over afterward." Gee looked at the tear in consternation. "But how did you disable the vents and stop the alarm?"

"I didn't," Piper said. "They must have malfunctioned or something."

Gee shook his head. "I checked the connections a dozen times. The vents to the fuel pipes were closed, but the igniter was still warm, as if it started to fire and then just shut down, which triggered the alarm to shut off too.

But there's nothing wrong with the system. It should have worked." He looked at her askance. "I thought maybe you'd done something to it, used a trick that you'd learned in the scrap towns, something we hadn't thought of, to get past the system."

"I *couldn't* do anything," Piper said, exasperated. "My coat sleeve caught on a bolt, and I wasn't able to get it untangled in time. The last thing I remember is . . ." She hesitated, embarrassed to admit how stupid she'd been.

"What?" Gee said. "What is it?"

Piper felt her cheeks get hot. "I put my hand over the vent. I knew it wouldn't stop me getting a stream of fire in the face, but I was scared out of my mind, so I just closed my eyes and hoped the thing wouldn't go off." She shot Gee a sideways glance, expecting him to be looking at her as if she were the queen of the idiots. Instead, she saw his pupils dilate and turn that same yellow color at the edges she'd seen before. Had she made him angry?

"Will you wait here a minute?" Gee asked her, and there was a note of excitement in his voice. "I'll be right back." He stepped around her and opened the door to the adjacent car.

"Wait, what's going on?" Piper demanded, starting to follow him out of the vestibule.

"Just stay here," Gee said, holding up a hand to stop her. "I'll tell you when I get back, I promise."

Reluctantly, Piper nodded and stepped back into the vestibule as Gee took off back toward the cargo areas.

What could he possibly be up to? she wondered. His moods changed so quickly Piper had a hard time keeping up. Maybe it was a chamelin trait.

She didn't have long to wait. A few minutes later, Piper heard footsteps coming from the mail car, and Gee poked his head into the vestibule. His eyes were still alight with that strange excitement, and Trimble was with him.

"Piper, tell the fireman what you just told me," Gee said.

A dozen questions filled Piper's head, but she managed to hold her tongue. She showed Trimble how she'd cut through the canvas and told him what had happened with the vent. The fireman wore a thoughtful expression as he listened to Piper's explanation. He and Gee exchanged several glances while she talked, and Piper found herself fidgeting, talking fast to get to the end of her story. Finally, after the fourth or fifth time they looked at each other, she couldn't stand it any longer. "What?" she demanded. "Look, I'm sorry if I messed up your fire trap, or whatever it is, but we were running for our lives that night. We were desperate."

"That's usually how it happens," Trimble remarked.

"What is he talking about?" Piper said, looking at Gee.

Instead of answering, Gee turned and checked the doors on either side of him to make sure they were closed securely. The air stank of burning coal, and there was hardly enough room for the three of them in the vestibule. Sweat ran down Piper's back in itchy little rivers. She couldn't shake feeling like a trapped animal in the small space.

Trimble took a vial of black liquid off his belt and shook it. "Sarnuns made this chemical—intended to put it in their tobacco," he said, "but it hardens too much under heat." He popped the stopper and reached in his pocket with his free hand. He pulled out a match and struck it against the metal car. "Little help, Green-Eye?"

Gee nodded, but he coughed a couple of times, shoulders shaking, before he took the vial and poured the liquid into Trimble's palm. The black substance was thick like molasses, allowing Trimble to hold a bit in one hand. He dropped the match into the middle of the black puddle.

Flames engulfed the liquid, burning brightly in the center of the fireman's palm. Piper's hands flew to her mouth. She stifled a cry at the fire licking along Trimble's skin, but the man didn't even flinch. Orange flames reflected in his blue eyes. Trimble made a fist, then opened it, revealing that the puddle of liquid had solidified into a ball. He rolled the fiery marble from hand to hand while Piper stared, transfixed. After a moment, he cupped his hands over the flaming ball and the fire went out in a soft huff of smoke.

The spell broken, Piper blinked and took a step forward. She uncupped Trimble's hands and turned his palms up. She already knew what she would see—a charred black ball—but the unmarked skin around it, not even hot, made her breath catch in her chest.

"How did you do that?" she said. "No, wait, don't tell me. It has to be a trick, right? Something in the chemical that takes away the heat. Anna would know. She reads those science books." She brushed the black ball with her finger, and jumped at the spike of pain. "Ouch! How did that not burn you?"

Trimble grinned lopsidedly. "Makes minding the firebox a lot easier, I can tell you that."

A wave of dizziness passed over Piper and she had to lean back against the wall of the train car. She tried to think. There had to be an explanation, some deception behind what Trimble had shown her. But the longer she stood there staring at him and Gee—their calm expressions and that charred black ball—the more Piper had the creeping feeling it wasn't a trick. But if that was so, then . . . "What are you?" she blurted.

"A fireman," Trimble said helpfully. He still wore that lopsided grin.

"He's just like you and me," Gee said. His voice was hoarse from coughing. "But he has a special talent."

"Not everyone thinks so," Trimble said. "I don't just go around showing everybody what I can do. The few that I have shown usually end up doing all this yelling and carrying on, and then I have to worry that they think I'm some kind of monster."

"Are you?" Piper couldn't help asking.

"Hey, I'm— No!" Trimble put on a hurt expression. "I just have magic inside me that the fire responds to. It makes me immune to it, and I can manipulate it like a baker molds his dough." His blue eyes pierced her. "I have a connection to it, the same way you do with machines."

Piper shook her head. "Uh-uh. What I do is *fix* machines—with tools, with my hands. There's nothing magic about it."

"You closed the vents," Gee said, "just by touching them and asking it to happen. The best machinists in Solace couldn't have done that. And you made that slaver's gun explode when he pointed it at you."

"I didn't have anything to do with the gun," Piper insisted. "It was probably just poorly made. I got lucky, that's all."

"I don't think so," Gee said. "I think you were scared, and you protected yourself on instinct. The gun reacted to your will, to what's inside you, the same way the fire responds to Trimble."

"It's a kind of synergy," Trimble explained. "Your will speaks to machines in ways that normal people's can't. You're a synergist—that's what we're called."

Piper had never heard the word before or heard of

anyone in the world having magic powers. She would have scoffed at the idea if she hadn't just seen Trimble calmly juggle a ball of fire. "You're saying there are more people like you?" she asked.

"Like *us*," Trimble said, "and yes, I think so, though I've never met any until now. But I've heard stories and rumors—it's hard to separate truth from wild tales when you're dealing with magic."

"This is crazy," Piper said. She heard her voice rising, the fear in it. "If I had magic powers, you think I'd waste them on machines? I'd use them for something important, like conjuring food whenever I wanted it—steak dinners, caramel apples, mushroom soup."

"Caramel and mushroom?" Gee raised an eyebrow.

"Not all at once, but yeah, something like that." Piper thumped her fist against the metal wall in frustration. She had to make them understand they had it wrong. Her, have magic powers? It was impossible. "You're just making excuses because the 401's traps didn't work for once, and a couple of girls outsmarted you."

"Things like this have happened to you before, haven't they?" Gee's voice was surprisingly gentle considering she'd just insulted him again. "Machines reacting in just the way you want them to?"

Piper thought of the music box she'd fixed for Micah, how he'd said she was weird with machines. *"You're like a healer with them."* Her hand went instinctively to the watch around her neck. The second hand ticked away steadily, the mechanism that ever since she'd fixed it had kept perfect time.

Only for her.

"A power like this is a good thing," Gee pressed. "It's helped you survive. It's nothing to be afraid of."

"Is that so?" Piper nodded at the black ball in Trimble's hand. "What about the people who call him a monster for what he can do? That's all it takes, you know. They find something about you that they don't like, something different, or some weakness—maybe you're poor, you're a scrapper, you'll work any job at a factory even if it kills you because you're desperate, desperate like a girl who's alone and running from someone with enough money to buy her like so many pounds of meat— and they take advantage. *They take everything from you!*"

Chest heaving, Piper forced her fists to unclench. She'd tried to hold it back, but the storm inside her was too strong. Didn't she have enough to be afraid of without adding some freakish magical talent? She looked at the fireman and the chamelin. Why were they saying this?

The tiny space went silent, and Gee looked down. Trimble bit his lip, but then he said, "I'm sorry. It's just that, when I finally accepted that I had this talent, even though it made me different, I was happier. We thought you might feel the same way. If you change your mind and want to know for sure, we can test you." Trimble tapped his foot lightly on the pressure plate but didn't put his weight on it. "We'll be stopping for a supply drop in Phirimor," he offered. "All we have to do is re-create the conditions of that night, see if you can do the same trick twice."

Piper couldn't believe what she was hearing. "Did you listen to anything I just said? You think I'm going to stand in front of the fire vent again, maybe whistle a pretty tune while I wait for it to turn me crispy? No, thank you." She pushed past Trimble to get to the door. "You two are crazy."

"We'd shut it down before it actually fired," Trimble said. "You wouldn't be—"

Gee put a hand on his shoulder. "No, she's right," he said. "This wasn't a good idea. We're sorry—" He stopped, pressed his hands to his chest, and coughed hard enough to shake his entire body. Pain twisted his face.

Piper took a step toward him and froze. Blood coated Gee's lower lip. Before she could speak, the chamelin drew a wheezing breath, and his eyes rolled back in his head.

He collapsed in the middle of the vestibule.

≥ THIRTEEN ≥

Trimble shouted for the guards. Two of them came to help carry Gee to his room. Heart pounding, Piper followed close behind.

They took him to the last car on the train. Maps of Solace covered the walls of Gee's room, the various train routes marked off in red ink. The rest of the room consisted of a berth, a washstand, and a small table, where the remnants of Gee's breakfast sat cooling on a plate. The smell of fried eggs lingered in the air.

Piper moved to a corner to stay out of the way while Trimble and the guards got Gee into bed just as another fit of coughing overtook him. They had to hold on to his shoulders to keep him from falling out of the bed until it passed, and when they stepped away, Piper saw that blood flecked the white sheets tucked under Gee's chin.

"He needs a healer," Piper said tightly. "The slavers' dust is tearing up his lungs."

"I'm the train's healer," Trimble said, "but there's not much I can do for this." He took a vial of yellow liquid from his belt and pulled out the stopper. The smell of burnt peanuts mingled with the fried egg. "Chamelins may look like humans on the outside, but inside they're a whole lot different. If we had a chamelin healer, that'd be a good start, but we don't." He held the vial to Gee's lips and forced the rim into his mouth. "Drink," he said, leaning close to Gee's ear. "Drink. I know you can hear me. Don't be stubborn."

He lifted the vial, and Gee swallowed the thick yellow liquid. Halfway through, he coughed again, spraying yellow liquid down his chin. Trimble cursed and wiped Gee's mouth with his sleeve.

"Will that cure him?" Piper asked anxiously.

"It'll ease the cough, but the damage is already done," Trimble said. Piper noted the tension in the fireman's body, his lips pressed into a hard line. "You can go," he told the guards. "Give us some space."

The guards filed out of the room, and Trimble took the single chair from the table and put it next to Gee's bed, indicating that Piper should sit. Piper came forward and perched on the edge of the chair. Gee's face was pale, and though he wasn't coughing now, every breath he took was a heavy, wheezing labor.

"Is he going to die?" Piper didn't want to ask it, was terrified of the answer, but she had to know.

"He isn't breathing well at all," Trimble said. His blue eyes were huge. "I can't . . . I didn't realize he was this bad off. He never said . . ." In a sudden, violent motion, he turned and kicked the table leg. Gee's plate and silverware rattled; his glass overturned and shattered on the floor. Piper stared at the broken pieces, the little drops of juice still clinging to them. "Can you stay with him for a few minutes?" Trimble said, his voice unsteady. "I need to get Jeyne."

"I'll stay," Piper said.

"Thank you." Trimble swept out of the room without another word.

Alone, Piper bent, picked up the broken pieces of Gee's glass, and placed them on the table. The juice drops made her fingers sticky. When she turned back to the bed, she noticed Gee's hand lay open near the edge of the blanket. Tentatively, Piper reached out and laid her palm across his. Gee's hand was warm, rough with callouses and stained by coal dust, but it fit comfortably into hers. Blood rushed into Piper's cheeks. Would Gee wake up when he felt the touch? But his fingers stayed slack, and he gave no sign that he was even aware she was there. Piper sat, holding his hand, listening to the sound of his breathing, as if she could keep his chest rising and falling by sheer force of will.

The silence became unbearable. Piper cleared her

throat. "You called me stubborn," she said to Gee, "but you know, you're just as bad as I am. Why didn't you tell anyone how sick you are? You could have at least told Trimble, even if you didn't want to say it to me." She swallowed. "I mean, of course you wouldn't confide in me; you barely know me. We're not friends or anything. Not that I wouldn't *want* to be . . ." She was babbling. "Look, I know I'm a nuisance, that it's my fault you're sick, but we're going to fix it. Somehow, we'll make you better."

Piper's mind was spinning. Just how was she going to do that? She was the girl who worked miracles with machines. She'd never met one she couldn't fix. What had Trimble called her? A synergist. But people— like Micah—she couldn't do anything for people. Piper clenched her other fist in frustration. Healing machines—what was that kind of magic worth? Gee needed someone who knew about chamelin anatomy, someone who could tell what the dust was doing to him inside.

The hairs on the back of Piper's neck stood up. Anatomy, science, nature—a walking encyclopedia, that was what she needed.

Quivering with excitement and the beginnings of hope, Piper gently let go of Gee's hand and jumped out of her chair. "I'm going to leave you for a minute," she told him, "but I'll be back as fast as I can, I promise. I'm bringing reinforcements."

*   *   *

When Piper returned to Gee's room with Anna in tow, Trimble and Jeyne were already there. The engineer shot Piper a severe glance. "Why did you leave him? Trimble told you to stay here."

"I went to get Anna," Piper said, trying not to flinch under the older woman's glare. "I think she can help."

Jeyne and Trimble exchanged disbelieving glances. "More likely you'll both be in the way," Jeyne said. She looked down at Gee, and the lines in her face deepened. "But since it looks like it's time for miracles, what did you have in mind?"

"A small miracle, that's all." Piper turned to Anna. The girl clutched a stack of books against her chest, but her gaze was fixed on Gee and the blood speckling his blanket. "Anna, look at me," Piper said. "I need you to tap that limitless brain of yours and find some way to cure Gee."

Anna shook her head helplessly. "I don't know anything about chamelin anatomy. Human anatomy, yes, as well as small mammals like squirrels, raccoons, pitikas, voles, moskweps—and also reptiles, amphibians, several insects and arachnids—"

"Good," Piper interrupted. "That's good. You know a lot about a lot of critters. Maybe one of them is similar to a chamelin, close enough that what clears one set of lungs will clear the other. There, that's my theory, now what can you do with it?"

"That's . . . possible," Anna conceded, "even logical, but it's not tested. I'd have to extrapolate, make a guess based on a set of conditions not fully known."

"*Try*, Anna—that's all I'm asking," Piper said.

"All right." Anna sat on the floor and spread the books out in front of her. She selected one volume, *A Catalog of Mountainous Regions and Native Inhabitants*, and opened it. "Chamelins are mountain dwellers, so the environment's right. It's a start." She bent her head to read.

"What can we do?" Trimble asked Piper.

Piper thought for a minute. "That medicine you gave Gee—where did it come from? And do you have anything else like it?"

"I made it," Trimble said. "I can mix medicines and make poultices, stitch wounds, whatever you need."

"If Anna comes up with a treatment, can you make it?"

Trimble nodded. "Shouldn't be a problem, unless she comes up with some rare ingredient I've never heard of."

"Mmmm," Anna said, her nose buried in the book. "Not likely. None of these entries is very detailed. That could be a problem—understanding simple physiology might not be enough to treat a chamelin."

"Do the best you can," Jeyne said. She glanced at

Trimble. "I'll be up front. Let me know if his condition changes, better or worse, you understand?"

The fireman nodded. Jeyne touched Gee's shoulder briefly, but he didn't move. His eyes were closed, and all his strength seemed focused on breathing. Jeyne leaned over and whispered something to Gee that Piper didn't hear. Then she turned and left the car.

When she was gone, Piper and Trimble sat cross-legged on the floor next to Anna. They watched her read for several minutes in silence. Impatience welled in Piper. She tapped her fingers absently against the floor.

Anna glanced up from her book, shooting Piper a distressed look. "Piper, the noise. I can't concentrate."

"Sorry." Piper buried her hands in her lap. "Have you found anything?"

Anna looked up again. "I've been searching for approximately three and a half minutes," she said, flustered. "That's hardly enough time to consult the table of contents, let alone cross-reference what little I know of Gee's physiology with that of potential mammal counterparts and factor in his symptoms with—"

"Fine, fine, I just thought if you had a lead, you could tell us—"

"I'm trying, but—"

"Make this excruciating waiting a little easier—"

"Piper, some theories take *years* to formulate and properly test!"

"Obviously, we don't have years!"

"Hey!" Trimble leaned in between the two of them, a hand on each of their shoulders. "Both of you calm down. Take your time," he told Anna, "just, like she said, not years. Anna, we'll leave you alone so you can concentrate." He shot Piper a will-you-please-shut-up-and-keep-quiet look. Piper threw up her hands and lapsed into sullen silence.

After a whole five minutes of sitting still, Piper checked her watch, slipped it back under her shirt, then dug it out and checked it again. Her heart beat so loudly in her ears she was surprised Anna didn't complain about that noise too.

Another minute and Piper realized that if she didn't do something, she was definitely going to go insane and would most likely take Anna and Trimble over the edge with her. "Tell us what you're looking for," she said to Anna. "We'll start on the other books." She might not have been a great reader, but Piper knew any help was better than none.

Anna looked up from the page she was reading and shoved a couple of books in Piper and Trimble's direction. "Bats," she said distractedly.

"Bats?" Trimble looked doubtful. "I don't think Gee's—"

"Not a bat, *I know*, but he's a flying mammal!" Anna said impatiently. It was the first time Piper had ever heard her express irritation at anything. "That's the closest equivalent, so look for bats. And please be quiet!"

Piper opened the book and began to read.

For the next several hours, Piper tried to concentrate on what she was reading, but most of it was beyond her understanding. It didn't help that the room was completely silent except for the sound of Gee's breathing, which became increasingly labored and intermittent as the hours passed.

When Piper got to the end of her book, she'd found nothing of substance on bats or any other mammals remotely similar to Gee. She tossed the book aside in disgust and stood to check on him. Lifting the blanket, she found his hand again and clutched it tightly.

Another stupid idea, Piper thought. Why had she even dared to hope she could change anything? Gee wasn't a machine. She couldn't fix this, no matter how much she wanted to.

"I'm sorry," she whispered to Gee. "I'm sorry I can't save you." Piper wondered if Jeyne had said something similar to him. Or had she said she was sorry she'd ever brought the two troublemakers on board, that if not for them everything would have been all right? Would she change her mind now and order them off the train, give them over to Doloman and King Aron?

Maybe I can convince her to spare Anna, Piper thought.

It's not her fault that she's with a stubborn, hardheaded, idiot scrapper who never should have left Scrap Town Sixteen in the first place.

"Aha!" Anna's chirruping cry broke through Piper's misery. "The simplest, simplest explanation—Braetoc's Theory all over again. I should have known!"

Trimble looked up, bleary-eyed, from his book on nocturnal species. "What is she talking about?" he asked.

"Did you find something?" Piper tamped down the hope that clawed at her insides. "Come on, tell us!" The one time Piper wanted the girl to spill her guts, and all Anna could do was wave her book around like a banner.

"I was studying the animal," Anna said, calming a bit. "I should have been looking at the dust."

"The slavers' dust?" Trimble suddenly looked much more alert. "What did you find?"

"An essay detailing the history of the dust's use and how the slavers came to make it," Anna said. "According to this, they tested it on a variety of small animals."

"Darn gruesome stuff," Trimble muttered. "Darn all goddess-cursed slavers too."

"Look," Anna said, holding out the opened book and pointing to a page. "There's a detailed breakdown of the chemicals used to make the dust. Apparently," she went on, "the slavers use a small amount of tiferi in their recipe, which caused their animal subjects to develop an infection in the lungs when they breathed in the dust, but for some reason it had no effect on humans."

"Because humans have the strongest immune systems," Trimble said. He seized the book from Anna and turned it so he could read. "It says that sarnuns were susceptible too because their immune systems are so weak. One dose kills them almost instantly."

"So you think the slavers used tiferi in the dust that Gee breathed?" Piper said. "You think he's susceptible to it too?"

"It makes sense," Trimble said grimly.

"This is fantastic," Piper said, squeezing Anna's shoulder excitedly, "but now we need to find a way to get rid of the infection. Can you do that?"

Lost in thought, Anna didn't reply. She tugged at one of her braids as she read back over the essay. "The problem is the bacteria in the tiferi," she said at last. "Gee's body can't get rid of it. If we could somehow help him fight it off, I think the infection would clear up, and he'll be able to breathe again."

"I think I can take care of that," Trimble said thoughtfully. "Now that I know tiferi is the problem, I think I can make a treatment to get rid of the bacteria."

"How long will it take to make?" Piper asked, worried they might not have enough time. Gee was looking worse than he had before.

"Not long," Trimble said. "I just need to get some ingredients." He jumped to his feet and ran out of the car.

When he was gone, Anna stood up and made her

way over to stand next to Piper. "I think this will work," she said reassuringly.

Piper nodded. She stared down at Gee, willing him to keep breathing. "Just a little longer," she said, speaking to herself as much to him. The waiting and worrying were driving her crazy. "Goddess, please. Just a little longer."

The next thirty minutes were the longest of Piper's life. Every few seconds, she checked her watch. More than once, she thought the stupid machine must be broken again. There was no way time could move so slowly.

Anna sat quietly on the floor next to her, her hand resting on Piper's boot. Piper almost wished the girl would talk—chatter on about nothing, just to fill the silence.

Finally, Piper couldn't take it anymore. "I'm going to see what's keeping him," she said. She stood and headed for the door. She was just reaching for the handle when Trimble slid the door open from the other side.

"I've got it!" the fireman said excitedly, holding up a vial of milky liquid and a syringe.

Piper was so relieved she could have kissed him. Trimble crossed the room and knelt down at Gee's side. Carefully, he filled the syringe, then lifted Gee's arm. He inserted the needle and pressed the plunger. Gee's faced creased briefly in pain, but otherwise he didn't stir.

"When will he wake up?" Piper asked. She wanted the medicine to work instantly.

"I don't know," Trimble said, looking at her, "but when you stop hearing the wheezing sound in his breathing, you'll know the treatment's doing some good." He glanced out the window, and Piper followed his gaze. Darkness had fallen while they'd worked to find a cure. When Piper looked down at her watch, she saw that it was well past dinnertime.

Anna's stomach growled. "You should go to the dining car and get something to eat," Piper told her. "I'll stay here and keep an eye on him."

"I can stay with him," Trimble offered, but Piper didn't move.

Anna gathered up her books to leave, and paused beside Piper's chair. "I'll bring you something to eat," she said.

"That'd be great," Piper said, though eating was the furthest thing from her mind at that moment. She laid a hand on Anna's arm, stopping the girl before she walked away. Anna turned and Piper wrapped her other arm around Anna's waist, hugging her tightly. "Thanks," she whispered.

"Oh, well, I just read the books," Anna said, sounding embarrassed. "I'm starting to think I may have read a lot of books. When I read them now, it's as if I'm getting reacquainted with old friends. Does that sound strange?"

For the first time in what felt like days, a smile spread across Piper's face. "Not for you. Not at all."

"We're lucky to have you," Trimble murmured.

"Thank you—I mean, you're welcome." Anna blushed, looking at her feet. "I should go now." Juggling her books, she hurried from the car before anyone could say anything else.

"Are you sure you don't want to go with her?" Trimble asked Piper. "You need to rest. We can take shifts watching him."

"It's all right," Piper said. She didn't want to be anywhere else. "I'm not tired. You go."

But Trimble stayed, and an hour later, Anna returned with plates of chicken and boiled potatoes and carrots. Piper's stomach growled when she smelled the pungent rosemary speckling the chicken. The three of them crowded around Gee's small table to eat.

The night wore on, and Piper and Anna took turns reading aloud to each other from the books Anna had brought back with her from the library. At least they intended to take turns, until it became clear that Anna was a far better reader than Piper was, so she had the book most of the time.

Piper passed the hours pacing the room and watching Gee. Once, she caught Trimble smiling at her from his seat next to Gee's bed.

"What?" she asked. "What's the grin for?" And how could he be grinning at a time like this? she thought with a flash of irritation.

"Nothing," Trimble said. "I can see why he likes you, though."

Piper stopped pacing. "What are you talking about?"

"I'm talking about Gee. He likes you."

Piper blinked in surprise. Trimble must be sleep deprived, she thought, to come up with that one. She shook her head. "I don't think so."

"I'm telling you—"

"And I'm saying you've been breathing too much coal dust," Piper interrupted. Her irritation increased. "Gee and I don't exactly get along. Every time we're in a room together, there's shouting. Lots of shouting."

"Uh-huh, I noticed." Trimble's grin made Piper want to set his hair on fire—not that it would do any good. "But you two are a lot alike," he said. "You're protective of the people you care about."

"He's right," Anna said, looking up from her book.

"You stay out of this," Piper said. She turned her back on the fireman so he wouldn't see the color rising in her cheeks. No way did Gee think of her like that. True, there had been a moment after he'd told her about being a slave . . . All right, Piper realized, maybe they did have some things in common, but that didn't mean there was anything more to it than that.

"Should I start another book?" Anna asked, interrupting Piper's thoughts.

"If you're not too tired," Piper said, grateful for the change of subject. Reflexively, she went to the bed and listened to Gee's breathing. Was she imagining it, or did his breathing sound wispy and deep, rather than harsh and shallow as it had only an hour ago? She leaned in close, stopping short of resting her head against Gee's chest. His heartbeat was strong—that was a good sign. Maybe the treatment was working.

"Don't you two have your own room?"

Piper jumped at the voice. Gee was smiling at her, his eyes half-open.

Relief, sudden and overwhelming, washed over Piper. He was all right. All she could do was stare into those bright green eyes while she fought to hold back tears.

"You're awake!" Anna slammed her book shut and scrambled to the bed. "How do you feel?"

"Like I've been run over by a train," Gee said. He rubbed his chest. "At least somebody put out the fire here."

"Anna and Trimble did it," Piper said, finding her voice. "They found a cure for the dust."

"All I really did was mix up some chemicals," Trimble offered. "Anna did the hard work. She saved your life, Green-Eye."

Gee tried to sit up, but he was still weak. Piper supported him and propped up his pillows so he could sit up in bed. "I owe you one," he said to Anna. He held out his hand.

Anna turned scarlet. She wouldn't meet his eyes, but she took his hand. "You don't owe me—not really. It was the least I could do after you saved me from the slavers, and you took me flying at the same time. And studying all that science, discovering that they used tiferi and it's what made you so sick—it was fascinating." She looked up and her eyes were sparkling. "I'd love to try it again sometime."

Gee smiled faintly. "Next time I'm dying, we'll work something out."

Trimble was on the other side of the room, holding open the door. "Okay, now that Gee's awake, it's time you girls got some rest. And you too," he ordered Gee. The chamelin saluted him weakly and lay back on the bed. Almost as soon as he did, his eyes drifted closed.

Reluctantly, Piper stood, taking one last look at Gee to assure herself he was really going to be all right. The chamelin was already asleep again, his breathing deep and steady now. It was a relief to hear. Piper turned to go and a wall of exhaustion hit her. She moved stiffly, her muscles sore from the tension.

Trimble closed the door behind them, but instead of crossing the vestibule to the opposite door, he turned to face Piper and Anna. He wore a serious expression, and Piper was suddenly uneasy.

"I talked to Jeyne earlier," Trimble said, "while I was mixing the treatment. I'll tell her that Gee's going to be all right, thank the goddess. But she wanted me to tell both of you that if Doloman wants you, he'll have to come through her, me, and our whole crew first."

Saying nothing more, the fireman turned and entered the other door, leaving Piper and Anna alone between the cars. Piper swallowed a lump that had risen in her throat. She was overwhelmed by Jeyne and Trimble's support, and for once, she had no idea what to say. She looked at Anna. "What do you think?"

Anna looked as if she might cry. "I wish we could stay here forever," she said.

"I know," Piper agreed. Her voice was husky with emotion. "Trimble's right, that was a miracle—what you did for Gee. I wish I had half your brains."

Anna shook her head. "It wasn't me; it was the books. They're a part of me. When I read them, I feel like I'm remembering a little of who I am. Having those memories makes me not so scared of the ones I'm still missing."

"That's good," Piper said. "You shouldn't be scared of who you are."

They lapsed into silence as they made their way through the passenger cars. All the worrying and exhaustion was catching up to Piper—and she hadn't fully recovered from their ordeal with the slavers. Her tiredness made the walk back to their suite seem to stretch on for miles.

When they finally reached their room, Anna collapsed in bed still holding her precious books and immediately fell asleep curled up around them. Piper climbed into bed as well, but tired as she was, she couldn't sleep. She lay awake, thinking about what she'd said to Anna, and what Gee and Trimble had told her earlier about her power with machines. During all the upheaval and worry surrounding Gee's sickness, Piper had been able to forget temporarily what had happened in the mail car's vestibule. But now, in the quiet darkness, she could no longer hide from her thoughts.

Were Trimble and Gee right? Was it more than just a talent that made machines work for her? And if it was magic—Piper's heartbeat sped up with fear and bewilderment at the thought—then what did that make her? What was she? She tossed and turned in her bed, the questions haunting her until she finally fell into an uneasy sleep, unable to escape her thoughts even in her dreams.

Sometime before dawn, the 401 pulled into Phirimor for supplies. Piper woke up when the train stopped. She got out of bed and dressed quietly, careful not to wake Anna, then slipped out of the room. A few minutes later, she stepped off the train into the predawn darkness. The air was dry and thick with dust clouds.

Trimble had said they could test her to find out if she really was a synergist. At first Piper had been terrified at the prospect. Suspecting she had magic was one thing; having the possibility confirmed was something else entirely. But she'd gone over it in her head for most of the night, and she'd realized she wanted to know one way or another—she *had* to know. She'd been the one to tell

Anna not to be scared of who she was, after all. It was time to follow her own advice.

Piper walked along the line of cars until she reached the mail car. She realized she should wait for the fireman's help—goddess knew it would be safer that way—but she didn't want to wake him, and besides, this was something she needed to do on her own.

She found the slit in the canvas between cars and—now that she knew what to look for—the pressure plate that would trigger the fire defenses.

She'd dealt with the alarm before getting off the train. The warning bell was fastened above the vestibule door. Piper didn't want to damage the mechanism permanently, so she had decided to keep things simple and removed the clapper from inside the bell. Without that crucial piece, the alarm wouldn't sound when she triggered it. She'd reattach the clapper later, after her experiment.

Carefully, Piper climbed the ladder and braced herself with a hand on one rung; then, trying to ignore the scorch marks on the train's exterior, she stretched out her other hand to the fire vent. Piper took two deep breaths, counted to three, then brought her foot down firmly on the pressure plate.

The vents made a shrill squeaking as they opened, and a rush of heat blasted Piper in the face as the igniter fired. In a few seconds, the pipes would spray the flammable liquid across the igniter, sending a sheet of flame straight at her.

Piper kept her hand over the vent, though everything in her was telling her to yank it away. "You're not going to fire," she said, her voice trembling with fear. "You're going to close." The heat intensified, beading sweat on Piper's forehead. Her heart beat furiously. And nothing happened. She slammed her open palm against the vent. "I said you're going to close, do you hear me?" Still nothing. A liquid rushing sound filled Piper's ears. Every muscle in her body tensed to jump, to throw herself to safety on the ground.

"*Close!*" she commanded with all her will.

The shriek of grinding metal shattered the air like a banshee's wail. The vents slammed shut, and the igniter sputtered and died.

Piper's face was slick with sweat, her palms slippery. Dimly, she became aware that her hand had slipped from its grip on the ladder. Then she was falling, her body weightless in midair. Angling her head, she saw the bare ground rush up to meet her. She landed on her back, knocking the wind out of her lungs.

For what seemed like an eternity, Piper lay on the ground, trying to breathe, staring blankly up at the stars. Nausea and weakness fluttered through her. It was as if an invisible hand had reached inside her and yanked out her energy, leaving a hollow sensation behind. She thought back to the times she'd worked on other machines and tried to remember if she'd ever felt such a weakness. Often she'd work late into the night fixing a machine, so of course she was tired afterward, but could it be possible that the toll working late into the night had taken on her was greater than it should have been? Could it depend on the machine? A big effect cost a lot of energy, but keeping the antique watch running cost only a little? No matter what, one thing was certain: she definitely had magic inside her.

A thousand questions swirled in Piper's mind at this revelation. She'd never known that magic existed in the world. Had she been born with it, or did it come from somewhere else? And how many others might there be in the world with similar gifts? Were they keeping them a secret, like Trimble, or were they ignorant—as Piper had been until now—that they even possessed anything special? If Gee hadn't told her, Piper might have lived the rest of her life without discovering it. And now that she knew the truth, Piper knew she would never look at herself or the world in quite the same way again.

With an effort, Piper brought her thoughts back to the present. She had to get up. She'd disabled the alarm, but the guards might have heard the grinding of the vents opening and closing. If they came to investigate, Piper didn't want them to find her here. How could she explain to them what had happened, what she'd done— twice?

Piper rolled onto her side and pushed herself up from

the ground. A thread of fiery pain went up her leg. She'd landed on it harder than she thought. Limping along the line of cars, Piper worked her way back to the station entrance where she'd gotten off. She held on to the handrails as she climbed the steps onto the 401. The guard at the door recognized her and nodded.

Piper moved slowly through the passenger cars, keeping as quiet as she could so as not to disturb the other passengers. She hoped she wouldn't run into Gee or Jeyne or Trimble. She wasn't ready to tell them what she'd discovered about herself, but she knew she wouldn't be able to hide it if they stopped her. Piper opened the door to the suite and was relieved to see that Anna was still asleep. She undressed and climbed back into the upper berth, careful not to jostle her aching leg.

Serves you right, Piper chided herself. *You wanted to know the truth, and now you do.* She opened the small cabinet behind her pillow, where she'd stored her satchel. As quietly as she could, she lifted the flap and drew out her tool belt. Wrenches, a pair of small hammers, screwdrivers, glue, and a pocket of nails and screws—they'd all come from Arno Weir's general store. Her father used to buy her a new tool anytime he could afford it, even if it meant he had less food for a few days. He never complained.

"I'll bring you the broken things, and you fix them up," he'd told her. *"We'll be a great team."*

Piper had happily done her part, and together they

had salvaged the broken things that came from other worlds, making them into machines that worked, that people valued. Her father had been proud of her talent.

Now all of that felt like a lie.

Piper bit her lip, folded up the tool belt, and put it away. All those years she'd spent working with machines, learning their insides and seeing how their parts worked together, making Micah's music box sing, even that stupid watch that wouldn't keep time when it wasn't with her—had she fixed any of those things with her own talent? Or had it always been the strange magic inside her that the machines had responded to? What was she? Where had this power come from?

Piper pressed her forehead against the window and stared out. Moonlight spilled onto rocky, barren ground. The area they were in now was remote, cleared of trees and plant life, choked with dust. She'd expected scenic coastlines and fragrant orange trees once they got to the southern territories. None of it had turned out the way she figured.

The train blew its whistle, and soon after, the big steam engine started moving again, pulling away from the station and continuing its stubborn push southward. Piper lay down on her side and listened to the rattle of the wheels on the tracks. The sound lulled her, but before she drifted off to sleep, she rolled over to look down at Anna, asleep in the lower berth. The girl slept deeply, and if she dreamed, it must have been a good dream, for she looked at peace—so different from the night they'd first met.

Gee was right about one thing: her power had helped her and Anna survive. Without it, she would have been burned to a crisp or swallowed a bullet. She couldn't argue its usefulness, but what would happen if people found out what she could do? Would they call her a monster, as they'd done to Trimble? Was it too much to hope that she could start a new life somewhere, one where she wasn't a poor, starving scrapper or a freak with strange powers? Where she wasn't alone?

Piper fell asleep with that thought in her head, and she dreamed. In the dream, she was flying, or it felt like flying. She stood on the roof of a train car and glimpsed the black mass of the 401's engine reaching out into the distance, blasting clouds of steam into the air that drifted back to curl around her, so thick she could almost cup it in her hands.

Above her flew a dark shadow with leathery wings and glowing green eyes, and all around them spread a vast field. Hot dust tickled her nose, and her eyes burned in the dry air. Despite that, Piper's heart pounded with excitement. Her father's coat snapped in the wind behind her. She was afraid and exhilarated and at peace, all at the same time.

Lifting her arms in the air, Piper jumped. The wind caught her up and bore her alongside the winged shadow.

The land below raced by at dizzying speeds, a whole world spread out before her.

This is where I belong, where I've always belonged, she realized.

She felt certain of it in her heart.

⇒ FOURTEEN ⇐

The next day, Piper's thoughts were still a confused jumble, but she tried not to let it show in front of Anna. Breakfast helped distract her and revive her at the same time. The girls sat at the table eating oatmeal sprinkled with brown sugar and sliced strawberries. Piper had never thought a fruit could be so juicy, sticky, and sweet.

They'd been eating so well on the train that Piper noticed Anna had started to gain weight around her face; she no longer had that gaunt look. And when Piper examined herself in the washroom mirror, she noticed a similar transformation. Her cheeks were more rounded, and her hair seemed thicker, shinier. She'd started tending her hair every morning, so her spirals were actually spiral and not tangles. Seeing her new image reminded Piper again what it meant to have food and security, a place where she could thrive. Living in the scrap town, especially after her father had died, she'd never cared about her appearance. What was the point of arranging your hair every day if there was no one to see? And dark circles under the eyes were just a fact of life when you were hungry, and thus tired all the time.

Piper again wished that the train could just keep traveling on and on forever, that it would never reach the coast or the capital. This time between destinations had been some of the best of her life.

It was going on midday before Piper worked up the courage to find Gee to tell him what had happened with the fire vent. She left Anna in the library again, surrounded by her books. Piper had never seen the girl so happy as when she was there, which was just as well. Piper didn't think she could talk to Gee with Anna listening. She wasn't ready for anyone else to know about her power.

When she knocked on Gee's door, she had to wait a moment before she heard his muffled voice say, "Come in."

Piper slid the door open, then shut it behind her. The door at the other end of the car was ajar, and Gee stood out in the open air on a short observation platform at the end of the last car. A hot wind blew from the doorway. Tentatively, Piper crossed the car and stepped outside. An iron railing enclosed the platform, with metal gates to her right and left, but she still felt odd, weightless standing at the end of the train while the barren land flew out from under her feet.

Gee wore his usual rumpled shirt and overalls. He had one bare foot propped against the railing, and he leaned out so far that Piper felt dizzy watching him. A healthy flush had returned to his olive skin, and his eyes were bright and alert when he turned to look at Piper.

"You're better," Piper said by way of greeting. The relief she felt at seeing him well again distracted her from her own worries.

"Looks that way," Gee said. "I think in the future I'll try to stay away from slavers, though. Trimble told me I was pretty far gone."

"You were." Piper didn't like to think how close they'd come to losing him. She stood next to him and leaned against the railing, letting the wind tease her hair. Glancing at Gee out of the corner of her eye, Piper noticed the familiar soot mark smudged across his jaw near his right earlobe. She couldn't help smiling.

"What is it?" Gee said.

"Nothing." Quickly, Piper turned away and the wind blew her hair across her face.

I can see why he likes you. Trimble's words rang inside her head, followed by a warm sensation spreading through her chest.

Oh, no. No no no no and no. Piper bit her lip. It was nothing. So what if she liked looking for a soot smudge on his face every time she saw him? And just because she'd been driven half out of her mind worrying when he was sick, it didn't mean she had a crush on Gee. Her life was too complicated already.

"Are you all right?" Gee asked. She felt his gaze on her, though her hair obscured him from view. A tingling sensation worked its way along Piper's scalp.

Who was she kidding? Piper thought. She couldn't even look Gee in the eye without blushing. Of course she had a crush, she just hadn't been able to admit it.

Oh, this is going to be all kinds of trouble.

"I'm fine," she said. Piper cleared her throat. She forced herself to peel her hair back from her face and look at him. "I'm glad you're better—I mean we all are. Jeyne is, and Trimble too, and Anna . . . everyone . . ." *Stop talking*, she willed herself. *Please, just stop.*

Gee nodded. "Yeah, Jeyne already put me back to work. We hit Cutting Gap tomorrow."

Piper jumped on the change of topic. "What does that mean?"

Gee swept a hand to encompass the barren landscape, the rock hills, and patches of scrub grass. "We're traveling through mining country. Nothing grows out here. People used to farm this land, or hunt on it, until the king's people found rich iron deposits here. Strip mining sucked every bit of life out of this place just a few years ago."

"Why am I not surprised?" Piper muttered. The

landscape was yet another casualty of the factories. "What happened to the farmers and the hunters?"

"They became sky raiders," Gee said. "Cutting Gap is a narrow pass through a canyon dotted with caves. The raiders attack on gliders that they hide in the caves. They always hit us on this route, especially when we're loaded down with cargo, like we are now."

Piper's stomach did a little flip. "Wait a minute— you're saying we're going to be attacked? By sky raiders?" She couldn't believe it. First Doloman, then the slavers, and now raiders? No wonder the passengers had been tense yesterday. They knew the train was coming up on dangerous territory.

"But with all the guards you've got, you'll be able to fight them off—won't you?" Piper said anxiously.

"We always have before," Gee said. "I'm still a little weak, but Trimble says the train's defenses are working perfectly—well, all except for the alarm by the mail car." Gee shot her a look. "He told me someone disabled it. You wouldn't know anything about that, would you?"

Piper blushed. "Actually, yeah." She reached in her pocket and pulled out the clapper from the alarm bell. "I decided to test myself like Trimble said, but I didn't want anyone to hear." She handed the clapper to Gee and caught him fighting a smile. "You're laughing at me!" she accused him, though she wasn't really angry.

"Sorry." Gee smothered a chuckle by pretending to

clear his throat. "It's just you look so miserable about it, but I think it's incredible."

"You do?" Piper said. She'd never expected that reaction. "Why?"

Gee shrugged. "Why not? You have a power that no one else has—at least, I've never heard of anyone who could do what you do with machines. Ever since you and Anna came onboard, the 401 has never run smoother or faster. You've been like a lucky charm for us."

"You can't be serious," Piper said in disbelief. "We've been nothing but trouble for you. And now that you're protecting us, the train could get shut down. Where exactly is the luck in that?"

Gee tilted his head in consideration. "I'm not denying you're a lot of work, but Anna saved my neck, and she's under King Aron's protection, so we owe her as much as we owe Doloman—more, actually, because Doloman betrayed his duty when he hired the slavers."

Piper could see where it did make sense. In many ways, Anna belonged on the train. She was from the capital, marked by the Dragonfly. But Piper was still the odd girl, the scrapper who didn't belong. She remembered her dream from the night before, when she'd stood atop the train while Gee's dark shadow flew over her. She had felt like the 401 was where she was meant to be, but it was, after all, just a dream.

No, that wasn't all, Piper thought stubbornly. She

had something to contribute—her magic. She didn't know how her power worked, but she made machines run better, and when she needed to, she could make them stop running. That was worth something, even if it set her apart or made her strange.

Piper gripped the iron railing tighter. She was tired of feeling sorry for herself. If having this magical talent meant she could help the 401's crew, well, that was worth exploring.

Gee nudged her. "What are you thinking about?" Piper blinked, coming out of her thoughts. "You look . . . determined."

"You're right," Piper said. "If machines react to me, if I'm a synergist or whatever, then it's a gift I should be able to use." And use it she would. "Tell me what I can do to help you fight off the raiders."

Gee stepped back. "Who said anything about fighting? The train's already running great because of you. Let me handle the rest."

Piper shook her head impatiently. "There must be something else I can do."

"You're too young. Jeyne would kill me if I let a kid like you get hurt fighting raiders."

Piper snorted. "A kid? How old are you, security man?"

Gee turned away, and Piper heard him sigh. "I'm thirteen," Gee admitted, "but it's different for a chamelin. We may look like humans, but we're physically much stronger."

"Fine, you won't let me fight, but what about the defenses?" she said. "If I help operate them, maybe they'll work better."

Gee looked at her thoughtfully. "There might be something in that," he conceded. "Trimble and Jeyne control most things from up front, but there's a security station back here in the last cargo area. If the raiders get past the first- and second-tier defenses, Trimble has to haul his butt back here to activate the backup systems. He's had to do it a few times, and it's dangerous for him to make the run while the train's under attack."

"So I'll stay back here and be the third tier," Piper said simply. "Trimble won't have to make the run."

"It's not quite as easy as that," Gee said. "I'd need to teach you what the defenses do and how they're activated. Also there are certain signals we use so you'll know when to set them off."

"Well, you said we have a day, so let's use it."

Gee pushed off the rail and looked her in the eyes. "Why are you so eager to do this?"

The answer was easy for Piper. She wanted to prove that she belonged there. That it wasn't a mistake leaving the scrap town. "I owe you," she said simply. "You and Anna are square, but you saved my neck too."

Gee frowned. "So you're just paying a debt?"

"It's not just that," Piper sputtered. "It's everything. Everything about this train has been good for us, for me." And it had. She'd had food, protection—in the last few weeks, she'd seen more of the world than she'd ever dreamed. Piper was horrified to feel tears pricking her eyes. She would *not* let Gee see her cry. "It sounds crazy, but this train feels like home sometimes."

Gee kept his gaze locked on hers, but Piper had to look away. "It's not crazy," he said after a moment. "Maybe you could stay here." He added quickly, "I mean, I know you said you might settle in Noveen, but your gift with machines is worth a lot. I'm sure Jeyne would hire you on if that was what you wanted."

"I don't know," Piper said, feeling suddenly breathless at the possibility. "I have to make sure Anna's safe first, but that sounds . . ." *Amazing*, she thought. The idea of staying on the train, of seeing the world, a new place every day, and doing it alongside people who helped each other and treated each other decently— Piper's heart lurched hopefully at the thought. She was almost afraid to want it, afraid to think about how happy it would make her.

She realized that she hadn't felt this alive—as if she were truly living and breathing—since her father left for the factory. Two years of letting the loneliness of the scrap town eat away at her—now there were so many possibilities, yet the future was still so uncertain.

Piper pushed those thoughts away. They hadn't

reached the capital yet. Sky raiders stood between the 401 and Noveen. They had to take things one step at a time.

Gee put a hand on her shoulder, shaking her out of her thoughts. "Come on, I'll show you the defense station, and we'll get started."

Piper nodded. He was right. For the time being, all she needed to do was focus on helping defend the train.

Gee led her back into the train and to the next car, into a small room cordoned off by a heavy black curtain. Piper gasped at the mess around her. Levers, valves, and pipes covered the walls and floor, labeled with hastily scrawled pencil marks—arrows pointing up, down, left, and right as if they were clues in a vague sort of scavenger hunt.

Piper squinted at the markings. "Are these meant for someone to actually read?" she asked.

Gee laughed. "Only Trimble. He's the one who made them, though he doesn't need them anymore." He leaned over Piper's shoulder and pointed to a red valve with a smudged mark beside it. "Flame turrets," he said. "Look, you can see where Trimble drew a fire."

Piper took a step back to see the marking from his angle, and she bumped against Gee's chest in the process. "Sorry," she mumbled, her face reddening.

"It's all right," he said quickly, putting a hand on her

back to steady her. He laughed nervously. "There's not much room in here."

Was it Piper's imagination, or did Gee's face look as red as hers felt? She tried to ignore it—it was slightly harder to ignore the warmth where his hand had been—and focus on the levers and valves. "What does this one do?" she asked, pointing to a copper lever with a worn leather grip in the center of the floor.

"That controls the spikes. Sets of them jut from the ceiling and sides of the cars," Gee said. He pointed to the set of pipes and valves just above the lever. "Those are the—"

"Smoke screens," Piper said, starting to get excited. She could see it now. "It's to throw the gliders off, right? Everything is designed to keep raiders from latching on to the train." She followed the path of the pipes and valves with her eyes, imagining where they would come out on top of the cars. Instinctively, she could see how the system worked. "You tied some of these defenses in with the heating and cooling systems, didn't you? They use the same ducts?"

"Very good," Gee said. "We close off the bonnet and ducts and stop the water jets that wash the air. Means it can get pretty hot in here for a while, though."

"I'll bet." But anyone who tried to land on top of the cars with a glider would be in for a nasty surprise when the train's ventilation system turned against them. "Do they always attack with gliders?"

"Not always. Sometimes they use horses, but Cutting Gap is narrow—lots of curves. Once we make it through the canyon, we can get out of range of their gliders quick. Their engines are small, mostly used for support and meant for short range only. The challenge is getting through without too many of the raiders boarding us."

"What about stopping the train? Have they ever tried that?" Piper asked. As she spoke, her attention was drawn to a square crack in the ceiling through which pale sunlight filtered.

"In the past, they have," Gee admitted. "They've torn up sections of track, but that tactic actually worked against them in the long run, so they stopped doing it."

"How could it work against them?" As interested as she was in the story, Piper found she couldn't focus. The crack in the ceiling was calling to her. It looked like a trapdoor.

"We're not the only train that makes Cutting Gap part of its route," Gee explained. "Tearing up the track or trying to derail the train slows everything down, delays the other trains coming through. It's more efficient for the raiders to hit multiple trains while they're on the move. They board them at strategic points, grab what cargo they can, and get out. In the end, they get more out of those kinds of attacks, and the 401 always has valuable cargo, so they make sure to hit us whenever they can."

"But the 401 has an advantage the other trains don't," Piper said, glancing at Gee as an image of him in his chamelin form went through her mind. "You can protect the train from the air and attack the gliders."

"That's my job."

Piper pointed to the ceiling. "What's that for? Is it part of the defenses?"

Gee frowned and shook his head. "You don't need to worry about the hatch. You won't be using it."

Now Piper was really interested. "Oh no?" She raised an eyebrow. "It's for going topside, isn't it?"

"Only in emergencies." Gee pointed to a corner where three crossbows hung on a rack against the wall. The weapons were as long as Piper's arm and obviously expensive. Bolts covered in wicked silver barbs hung beside them. "If too many of the raiders get on the train, somebody has to go up top with a crossbow," Gee said.

"Can I try?" Piper said, shooting him a hopeful look. She thought of her dream—how exciting it had been to stand on top of a train car with the wind in her face.

"No," Gee said firmly, squashing her hope.

"I don't mean fire a crossbow," Piper said, exasperated. She put her hands on her hips. "I just want to go up top."

"Well . . ." Gee glanced uncertainly at the trapdoor. "As long as you let me make sure you're strapped to a safety harness—"

Piper was already moving across the train car to grab

a safety harness from behind the weapon rack. She fastened it to her belt as Gee reluctantly pulled a short stool from the corner of the room and stood on it to open the trapdoor.

"I'll give you a boost, but stay on your knees when you get up there," Gee instructed.

Piper stood in the square of sunlight coming through the open hatch and waited while Gee checked the harness on her belt. He nodded, satisfied, and reached up to attach the other end to a metal loop on the trapdoor. "You sure you want to do this?" he asked. "You're not afraid of heights?"

"Nope," Piper said, unable to conceal her excitement. "Hoist me up."

"Watch yourself." Gee bent and cupped his hands for Piper to step into them. Without effort, he boosted her up through the trapdoor and out into the open.

Piper lifted her face to the blue sky as she emerged from the top of the car, and a gust of wind hit her, stealing her breath. The sun shone bright and hot on the metal roof; the whole train stretched out in front of her. Exhilarated, Piper brushed her hair back from her face. She felt like she was riding on the back of a huge metal dragon. The land sped past on either side at breathtaking speed, and the roar of the wind drowned out all sound.

Just like my dream, she repeated to herself. Filled with a daring she never knew she had, Piper put both hands on the hot metal roof and slowly, carefully pulled herself out. Then, bracing one foot slightly in front of the other and holding her breath, she pushed herself up and stood on the roof of the car. The safety harness pulled at her waist and helped to steady her, but she still felt as if she were one step from falling off the edge of the world.

Yet it was worth it. She lifted her arms and leaned into the wind, letting it push against her body. She was flying.

Piper caught movement out of the corner of her eye; then she saw the flash of leathery green wings glowing against the sun. Gee swooped down and landed on the car in front of her, his thick claws digging small gouges into the metal roof. He nodded to her as if to make sure she was all right, and Piper grinned back.

Gee launched himself back into the sky, wings effortlessly beating the air. Piper watched him go, her heart thumping in her chest. *This is where you belong*, an inner voice whispered to her. *Where you've always belonged.*

FIFTEEN

Gee stood in the engine cab with Trimble and Jeyne. He had transformed, so he couldn't speak to the engineer or the fireman, but it hardly mattered. Trimble watched the temperature gauges, and Jeyne had her head out the open window, watching the track before them with the intensity of a hawk. Ahead of them, less than ten miles away, loomed Cutting Gap.

"You put the girls in place in the back?" Jeyne asked without turning her attention from the track.

Gee grunted an affirmative. Trimble checked the firebox and nodded to Gee. "Be careful out there, Green-Eye. They'll be aiming a lot of their firepower at you. Keep your eyes open."

Lifting a clawed hand in acknowledgment, Gee went to the window and climbed out onto the ledge. He'd had to keep his wings tucked close to his body in the small cab, but now he could spread them wide. He let the wind pluck him away and flew upward, circling back to get a good view of the 401. With his keen vision, he could see the individual cars clearly, but he intended to be high and out of sight of the raider gliders before the attack. Surprise was the main advantage in making it through the Gap. Gee would strike as soon as the raiders made their move, hopefully scattering them and ruining their plan.

Gee slowed, coasting on the wind and letting the train get ahead of him, until he was hovering over the two back cars. Piper and Anna would be at the defense station by now. They were as ready as they were ever going to be.

In that moment, Gee felt a surge of foreboding. Maybe he shouldn't have let Piper help with the defenses. Goddess knew those girls were always getting themselves into some kind of trouble. If anything happened to them . . .

Don't get distracted, Gee chided himself. If he didn't concentrate, he'd end up dead, or worse, he might get someone else killed.

On a burst of wing beats, Gee flew away from the cars and took up his position high above the cliffs. He just had to do what he'd always done: protect the train, its passengers, and its crew.

Protect his family.

* * *

"Let's go over it one more time—tell me what this lever does," Piper said. Nerves clawed at her stomach as she squinted at the pencil drawings. It was almost time. They were approaching the Gap, and she wanted to make sure they were ready.

Anna looked up from where she sat in front of the crossbow rack. "Mmm . . . pressurized darts," she said. "I wonder if Trimble tipped them with any sort of sedative. He's been telling me about some of his experiments. He's quite good with alchemy, hardly ever makes anything explode unless he means to."

"We can stagger the darts' release," Piper said excitedly. "Three, no, four sets. This . . . this is an incredible set of systems." Despite her nervousness, Piper was thrilled at the idea of figuring out a plan for the defenses. She could be good at this. She knew it. "I mean, I could take these things apart and be a week sorting out what each individual mechanism does—maybe I could find a way to make some improvements here and there—but it would be the best sort of scavenger hunt, I can tell you that."

"But we won't need the defenses once we get through Cutting Gap, will we?" Anna asked.

"No, but I mean for the future," Piper said distractedly. She ran her hands over a set of pipes, mentally removing the walls of the car so she could picture where they went. "There aren't enough windows in here either," she added with a scowl. "We don't have a clear view of where the raiders will attack. Maybe Gee would consider putting in some more glass. It would make me feel a lot better."

"Are you—" Anna hesitated.

"Mmm?" Piper turned to look at her. "What's wrong?"

"Nothing, it's just . . . you sound like you're staying— on the train, I mean." Anna looked away, running her hands over the crossbow bolts.

Piper saw the girl's expression and felt a pang of remorse. In all her excitement over the possibility of taking a job on the 401, she hadn't thought about how Anna might react to the news. Piper left the defense station and sat down next to Anna. "Gee said that Jeyne might hire me on once we get you settled in Noveen. I haven't decided yet, but I'm thinking about it."

"I see." Anna nodded her head, but she still wouldn't look at Piper.

"Don't worry," Piper said, "I'm going to make sure you're safe first. That's the most important thing."

"I thought you were going to stay in Noveen," Anna said, clenching her hands in her lap. "If you go with the train, who knows when I'll see you again?"

Piper's chest got tight. "Hey, look at me." Piper laid her hand on Anna's shoulder. "Believe me, I'm not wild about the idea of leaving you either, but you've got a family in Noveen—"

"We don't know that."

"*I* know that," Piper said firmly. "I'm going to get you back to them. Point is, you've got a home waiting for you, and I've got to find one of my own." Piper cleared her throat, not trusting her voice. "Do you understand? I have to earn my own money and build a life somewhere, and I think I can do that here. I'd like to try, anyway."

The thought of that opportunity filled Piper with such excitement that she thought she would burst. She hadn't felt so much hope about the future since she'd first made her plans to leave the scrap town. But mixed with that hope was sorrow too. It would be hard leaving Anna.

Anna sat silently, staring at her hands. Piper bit her lip as she felt tears coming on. She couldn't cry now. She had to be strong. Gently, she nudged her friend with her elbow. "Listen," she said. Her voice wavered. "No matter what I decide, I promise we'll see each other again. I'll come back to Noveen and visit as often as I can." She tried to smile. "You can't get rid of me that easy."

"You promise?" Anna looked up. Her pleading expression almost undid Piper.

"Absolutely. Now, what are you doing over here?" Piper nodded to the weapons rack. She desperately needed a distraction.

Anna reached over and lifted a crossbow off the rack. "I remembered something," she said. "I think I've used one of these before."

"Really?" That was definitely a surprise. Piper tried

to picture Anna wielding a crossbow, but she just couldn't conjure the image. Anna was so small and fragile. "Do you remember why you used it—or who taught you how?" she asked.

"I don't know, but the parts feel familiar. Look— they fit in my hands, and my hands know what to do." Anna traced the trigger and the groove where the bolt was supposed to go.

It did look like Anna knew what she was doing, Piper thought. "Have you remembered anything else?" she asked.

"Sometimes I see things in my dreams," Anna said. "I don't always tell you, because I'm not sure what parts of them are memories and what aren't. But sometimes they're about Doloman and the scar, and other times I see myself doing things, like talking to the man whose voice I told you about—the one I remember reading to me before I went to sleep at night. I can't see his face—he feels very far away—but I think he might be a scientist."

"That fits," Piper said, nodding, excited that her friend was getting more of her memories back. "You have a scientific mind. He could be your father."

"I'd like that," Anna said wistfully. "Another time, I saw myself holding a crossbow—I thought that had to be a dream, but when I touched the crossbow just now, I knew I'd held one before." She closed her eyes. "In my dream, I see myself standing in the snow and firing it at a round target off in the distance. There are pine trees all around me, cones crunching under my feet. I can see my breath it's so cold."

Those were the most vivid memories Anna had recalled so far, Piper thought. It was a promising sign. "That sounds like the far north," Piper said. "That's good. You're remembering the details. About the crossbow— you think you would be able to fire it?"

"Yes, I think so," Anna said. "I thought the skill might come in handy, but then Gee said he didn't want us touching the weapons—"

"Never mind that." Piper stopped Anna before she could put the crossbow back. She hoped they wouldn't have to use the weapons, but she didn't want to rule out any possible defense. "Keep that close," Piper said. She glanced out the small windows to see that rock walls had replaced the open plains. They'd passed into Cutting Gap. "We're here," she said nervously. "I'm going to check the view from outside."

Quickly, Piper crossed the vestibule into Gee's car and out onto the observation deck. Sheer canyon walls reached up into the sky on either side of the train, casting shadows down on the valley floor. A tremor of fear went through Piper as the caves Gee mentioned came into view.

The caves were wide and deep, like enormous dark mouths gaping open. Wide enough to accommodate glider wings, Piper realized. All the raiders had to do was slide the gliders out of the cave mouths and let them fall to catch the wind.

Anna stepped out onto the platform and looked over Piper's shoulder. "I see five caves—no wait, seven . . . now nine," she said. "They go all the way up to the top."

"A lot more than I thought there'd be." Piper's initial excitement at the prospect of manning the defenses was quickly turning to anxiety. The Gap was also narrower than she'd expected. She glanced up at a cloudless strip of blue sky. There was no sign of Gee, but she knew he was up there somewhere. The sounds of the train were amplified by the narrow canyon, making it impossible to hear anything coming. They'd be relying on him to signal Trimble and Jeyne in the engine cab, and they in turn would signal the guards in the cargo areas and trigger the defenses in those sections. Piper and Anna's section at the rear was the least likely to be attacked first—there was very little of value to the raiders back there. They would focus their attacks on the cargo areas.

Her eyes on the sky, Piper caught a flash of light from one of the cave mouths. The sunlight reflected off something metallic that slid out into the sun as Piper watched. A long, sleek metal body and cloth wings. She squinted and could see that two men piloted the craft, one at the front and one facing the rear.

This isn't right, Piper thought, the beginnings of real panic stirring in her chest. They'd expected the raiders to focus their attack near the front and middle of the train, not the rear.

But here they were. The glider emerged from the cave and dropped toward them.

"Get back inside!" Piper yelled. She pushed Anna into Gee's car. "Signal Jeyne that they're attacking back here!"

"They must be attacking the front too!" Anna cried as she ran back up the car. "Look—Trimble set off the smoke screens up there." She pointed to the windows. The view out was obscured by plumes of thick white smoke that drifted from the front of the train.

"Let's add more smoke, then," Piper said. They needed to make it as hard as possible for the raiders to see the train and latch on to it with grappling hooks. She ran through Gee's car and back to the defense room. She grabbed a red valve and twisted it left to release the smoke screen at the rear; then she pointed to the fire valve. "We have to keep them off the back car. They'll try to board us on the observation platform. I'm going to lock the door back there. Can you start the fire?"

Wide-eyed, Anna nodded. Piper sprinted back to the observation deck and saw a glider approaching, its nose pointed directly at the space between the metal railing and the covered deck. One of the raiders leaned over the side of his craft and aimed a crossbow at Piper.

"Fire!" Piper yelled back at Anna.

At that moment, vents on either side of the door slid

open, and Piper heard the rush of the igniter. Flames burst from the vents, shooting out streams of fire. The raider swerved, but not far enough. The glider's left wing caught fire. The man with the crossbow dropped his weapon and dove forward to try to put the flames out with his hands, but the fire had already consumed most of the silk covering the wings, leaving behind a blackened metal skeleton. The pilot dropped the controls and crash-landed the glider into the dirt.

"Great shot, Anna!" Piper charged back inside the car, locked the door, and ran to close off the fire vents.

Anna's eyes were huge, her cheeks flushed. "How many of them do you think there are?" she asked.

"I don't know." Piper hated not being able to see what was going on. The smoke helped obscure the train from the gliders, but it also made it impossible to see what was coming out the windows. "I'm going to take a look topside." Maybe she could get above the smoke.

She dragged the stool over beneath the trapdoor. Anna grabbed her arm as she jumped up on it. "Piper, don't. If you can see them, they can see you, and they've got crossbows."

"You're right," Piper said. Anna looked relieved until Piper added, "Hand me one of the crossbows."

"You don't know how to fire it!" Anna wailed. Piper pulled open the trapdoor and thick threads of smoke leaked in from outside. "What if another glider comes back here?"

"All the more reason to have a weapon. And I've fired one before—Dad showed me once—it's just been a few years." Piper attached the safety harness to her belt. Climbing onto the top of a moving train while raiders were attacking it might be the single craziest thing she'd ever done—and that was saying something, considering what she'd done so far on this trip—yet her hands trembled with as much excitement as fear. "You think you can load one of those bolts and get it ready for me?"

"Theoretically," Anna said. "But, Piper—"

"You can do it." Piper smiled. "Just don't shoot yourself in the foot."

"I'm more scared of what'll happen to you!"

It was a fair point, Piper thought, but she had to take the risk. "Anna," she said seriously, "it's all right to be afraid, but you can't let that stop you from doing what you have to do. I've seen you put that incredible brain to work under pressure, and I have faith in you. We can do this."

Anna picked up the crossbow. She looked at the weapon and then back up at Piper. Finally, she nodded. "All right. I'll get it ready."

"Fantastic," Piper said. "Well, here goes." She hoisted her body through the opening in the ceiling. At first, all she could see was smoke. She coughed on the thick clouds, but then a gust of wind blew the white curtain back, and she gasped.

The sky was full of gliders.

Piper counted a dozen before the smoke obscured her view again. Just like the first glider she'd seen, each craft held at least two men, and the one in the rear was armed with a crossbow. Piper sat up on her knees, poking her head above the thick layer of smoke to get another look. Just as she peeked out of the cloud, a glider dove down, flying alongside the train two cars ahead of her. The man in the rear heaved something big and heavy over its side at the car nearest him, and Piper squinted to make it out as it bounced and clung to the roof of the train. A grappling hook!

Oh no you don't, Piper thought, her heart pounding. "Anna," she called down, "give me darts!"

Almost as soon as she'd given the order, dozens of tiny vents slid back along the roof of the car, exposing sharpened metal tips, poised to fire. From his position hovering beside the train, the pilot swerved, almost dislodging the rear man as he was getting out of the craft to climb down the rope attached to the hook. The darts fired, slicing holes in the glider's silk wings and sending the craft spinning away into the dirt.

Piper didn't have time to celebrate the victory. Ahead of her, two gliders flew side by side, a large net dangling between them, headed toward the front of the train.

The net's for Gee, Piper realized. It had to be. Two more gliders fell in behind the first for what looked like a coordinated attack. Piper crawled forward to the limit of her harness, trying to see if she could find Gee, but all the smoke made it impossible.

She knew she should get back inside the car. Every minute she spent exposed, she risked becoming a pincushion. Still, she lingered, crawling on her knees as close to either side of the car as she dared, looking for the chamelin.

As far as she could tell, he wasn't flying next to the cars either. Anxiety flooded Piper as the minutes passed. Where was he? Gee had a world of trouble coming his way, and she couldn't even warn him.

Finally, giving up the idea of finding him, Piper turned and crawled carefully back to the trapdoor. The canyon walls raced by in a blur of rock. She dropped into the car, balancing on the stool. "Anna, how are you doing loading that crossbow?" she asked.

"I've got it!" Anna ran over to her and held up the weapon, loaded and ready with a bolt fitted to the groove on the stock.

"Perfect." Piper stood, cradling the crossbow in her hands. "I'm going up again."

Anna bit her lip, but she didn't argue. "Be careful."

"I promise." Piper smiled at Anna reassuringly. She checked the roof, but she couldn't see anything from where she stood. She handed the crossbow back to Anna to hold while she hoisted herself up and out into the wind and the smoke and chaos.

This time, she caught a glimpse of Gee almost immediately. He was in the distance, perched on a rocky outcropping halfway up the canyon wall, his feet clutching the stone as he swiped at a glider passing by. She watched as his claws caught a wing and tore it to shreds, sending the craft spiraling away. The pilots abandoned the glider at the last minute and rolled onto the rocky ground.

Piper hadn't realized she was holding her breath until she exhaled, relief flooding her. She smiled down at Anna and looked back up. Gee had pushed off the wall into empty air and was beating his wings hard to lift his body high above the train. And then Piper saw the gliders with the net. They'd circled and were headed right at him. Two other gliders approached from the opposite direction.

Quickly, Piper reached down and took the crossbow from Anna. Bracing herself, she hefted the crossbow and, squinting through its sight, aimed for the raiders with the net. Her arms shook under the weight of the bulky weapon, and the sighting tilted crazily. Piper strained to hold the crossbow steady against the wind. Maybe this wasn't going to be as simple as she'd thought.

All you have to do is hit the glider, Piper told herself. *Just hold it steady long enough . . .*

Suddenly, one of the gliders dipped, putting its right wing directly in Piper's sights. The pilot's attention was focused on Gee. He didn't see her through the thinning smoke. Piper didn't hesitate. She fired.

The bolt flew with a loud twang. The recoil was sharper than she expected. Piper almost dropped the weapon. She rocked back against the safety harness and ended up flat on her back beside the trapdoor. The sky tilted, and her stomach lurched. She grabbed the safety harness to reassure herself that she wasn't going to fall off the side of the car. Carefully, she sat up, trying to see if her shot had hit anything, but the glider she'd been aiming at was gone. Piper had no idea if she'd hit its wing or not.

She was about to call down to Anna for another bolt when an engine growled directly behind her. Piper recognized that sound. A compact engine, modified with sarnun stretch coils to give it an extra power boost. She'd been working on one that sounded just like it for Arno Weir before she left Scrap Town Sixteen. Gee had said the raiders used the engines for supplementary power to the gliders.

Instinctively, Piper dropped flat on her stomach. She looked up to see the glider pass right over her. The pilot shouted to his partner, pointing at where she lay, and the glider turned in a wide arc and flew straight at her.

"Anna!" Piper screamed. "I need more darts!"

To her left was another set of vents, open, with the dart tips visible. Either Anna couldn't hear Piper's shout above the roar of the train or the mechanism was jammed. Piper reached out and touched one of the dart tips gently, mindful of the wickedly sharp point.

Fire, she told it silently. The glider's shadow fell over her. *Fire!* she commanded, and jerked her hand back.

The darts exploded from the vents. Piper rolled away hastily. The glider bearing down on her swerved, managing to dodge all but a few of the darts. It was still airborne, but at least it was no longer aimed right at her. She was safe. Or so she thought, until the glider swerved and the man in the rear of it leaned out and reached for her.

Piper tried to roll away, but her harness tangled around her. She ripped the hook off her belt and scrambled for the safety of the trapdoor, but the man grabbed her arm and hauled her off her feet.

A second of terrifying weightlessness followed. Piper couldn't move, couldn't breathe, until she felt her feet come down on the glider's metal surface. She saw the train pass beneath her, and then a pair of hands pushed her roughly forward toward the pilot.

"Sit down!" a voice yelled in her ear, and sour breath hit her in the face.

Piper was pressed between the front and rear seats, her legs dangling free just behind the wings. The craft pulled sharply to the left, forcing her to fall forward and hug the glider's body. The pilot cursed as he tried to steady the craft. The left wingtip skin had been shredded by the darts. He could no longer control it properly, and the engine couldn't compensate for Piper's added weight.

Before she had time to think too much about the utter stupidity of what she was about to do, Piper leaned far to the left, letting her leg dangle off the side of the glider. She grabbed the left wing and leaned on it as hard as she could.

"Are you crazy?" the man behind her shrieked as he grabbed Piper by the shoulder and wrenched her back, but the damage was done. Both men screamed as the glider flipped in the air, launching the rear man out of his seat and toward the earth. Piper felt the weight of her body pulling her down as the pilot righted the glider. She held on to the wing, but her feet dangled in empty air.

They were flying toward the train again. Piper didn't think the pilot intended to attack. The way he jerked the craft, he barely had control of the glider at all. The engine stalled, and Piper saw the train below her, tantalizingly close.

You really are crazy, scrapper, she thought, *but if you're going to do this, it's now or never.*

Piper let go.

⇒ SIXTEEN ⇐

The train rushed up to meet her. Her feet hit the roof of the car, and Piper was immediately skittering backward, unable to find her balance on the moving surface. She threw her arms behind her, fingers searching for something to hold on to. When she felt a piece of smooth metal under her left hand, she grabbed it without thinking. The handgrip stopped her from toppling off the side of the train.

Piper turned to look at what had saved her and saw the blood. Then the pain hit her in a wave of agony.

She'd grabbed hold of one of the blades protruding from the train's metal skin, barbs that protected it from raiders dropping onto the cars exactly as she'd just done. Looking around, Piper cringed. She sat in a nest of the blades—luck alone had saved her from impaling herself when she fell.

It felt like her hand was on fire. Warm blood filled her palm and spilled over. Gingerly, Piper let go of the blade and clutched her sleeve to try to staunch some of the bleeding. With her other hand, she braced herself against the roof of the car, acutely aware that there was no safety harness to keep her from falling.

Piper struggled to get her bearings. She was near the front of the train. The smoke had cleared somewhat, and she saw there were fewer gliders, but Gee had disappeared too. Behind her, toward the middle of the train, two gliders had managed to latch on to the cars with grappling hooks, and the raiders were swinging down the ropes.

As Piper watched, trapdoors popped open up and down the cars, and guards stuck their heads out with crossbows. Bolts filled the air. The raiders saw them and ran, charging recklessly along the roofs and jumping from car to car. Piper thought they were trying to dodge the crossbow shots, but then she realized they were trying to get *to* the trapdoors. They were running *toward* the crossbow bolts.

A shadow fell over Piper's shoulder. Instinctively she ducked, but then she saw the outline of wings against the sun right before Gee landed in front of her. He turned, and his green eyes burned with a fierceness she hadn't seen before. Piper assumed he was angry with her for being on top of the train—and rightfully so, she conceded. This was another of her not-so-smart plans. Then he reached for her bloodied hand with his clawed one. A red stain had soaked the hem of Piper's shirt, making it look like the wound was much worse.

"I'm all right," she said, waving him off, but Gee took her hand and put it across his shoulder. He slid his claws gently under her knees and lifted her. Piper felt that weightless, giddy sensation pull at her stomach again as Gee jumped off the roof and propelled them into the air. Holding on tight, she tucked her head against his shoulder, which in this form was hard as granite, and closed her eyes against the dizzying view of the canyon.

"The raiders are on the train," Piper said. She had to yell into his ear to make herself heard above the roar of the engine. She didn't know if the rear defenses would be enough to keep the raiders away if they decided to attack there again.

Suddenly, something slammed into them from behind, sending Piper lurching forward. She bit her tongue, tasting blood, and tightened her grip on Gee, but it didn't matter. They were falling out of the sky. Piper looked up as a glider soared over their heads—it must have struck them from behind.

Gee grunted in pain and beat his wings desperately, but his left wing was crooked. Piper choked back a sob at the sight. The pain must have been excruciating, yet Gee tried to use his wings to slow their descent.

But they were still going to hit the ground hard, Piper

realized, her heart in her throat—very hard. She braced herself as the ground surged up to meet them. The last thing she saw before sand and dirt sprayed her in the eyes was the glider that had hit them landing a few feet away.

Piper rolled on the ground, tucking into a ball, trying to protect her injured hand. Breathless, terrified, her body roaring in pain as she tumbled over rocks and scraped her skin raw, she finally came to a stop. Gee fetched up next to her, his wings caught beneath him in a twisted mess. For a few seconds, Piper could do nothing but lie there, panting. Her whole body felt like it was on fire, but at least she was alive. Wiping the grit from her eyes, Piper sat up and bent over Gee to see how badly he was hurt. His wing had to be broken, she thought, tears stinging her eyes.

A sudden noise made Piper look up. Several yards away, the raiders jumped off their glider with crossbows pointed at her and Gee.

To Piper's shock, despite his injuries, Gee sat up, crawling forward to put his body in front of hers. He got halfway to his feet and straightened his wings before Piper noticed two other gliders coming up behind them.

"No!" she cried, but it was too late. The raiders dropped their thick net over Gee. The added weight, combined with the wounds to his wing, was too much. Gee collapsed in the dirt, panting.

Fury exploded in Piper. She crawled to her feet and ran to Gee, clawing at the net. *How dare they*, she thought as her tears blinded her. *How dare they hurt him!*

"Stand up!" one of the raiders shouted at Piper in the Trader's Speech. "Step away from the chamelin!"

Piper knew that stepping away from Gee was a bad idea. Even trapped in the net, he towered over the raiders and their gliders, and none of the raiders seemed too eager to venture any closer to him. She glanced over her shoulder and saw the other pilots jump from their craft, clutching their crossbows. In the sky, there was one glider left—which made four gliders, not counting the ones that might still be attached to the train or that had crashed.

In the distance, Piper heard the 401 blow its whistle, but the sound was faint, not echoing off the canyon walls anymore. The train was out of Cutting Gap and getting farther and farther away from them. She and Gee were in a world of trouble.

"Are you deaf?" a raider yelled. "I said step away!"

Piper tamped down the panic inside her and put her hand on Gee's shoulder. His body was rigid with tension. "Not a chance," she said.

As if to drive the point home, the man walked forward until he stood directly in front of them. He laid the tip of his crossbow against the hollow of Piper's throat. Beside her, Gee growled, a rumble like a small earthquake, but the raider shot him a quieting look. He wore a tattered shirt and trousers that molded perfectly to his body, as if he hadn't taken them off in years. Sunlight reflected off his bald head, and he had a flat, smashed-in look to his face, as if he'd come out on the wrong end of more than a few fights. Still, his heavily muscled arms and the comfortable way he held his crossbow told Piper he'd collected enough victories to earn the respect of the others.

"I hope your pet understands that if he makes a move on me or any of mine, he'll be digging this bolt out of your neck," the man said.

Piper swallowed hard and the bolt's sharp tip scraped along her throat. Clenching her jaw, she concentrated on keeping her face expressionless. "I think my pet's trying to tell you the same thing about his claws," she said calmly.

Muffled titters of laughter came from the gathered raiders. Even the man with the crossbow seemed to regard her with grudging approval. Then he glanced at Gee, and his expression hardened. "We'll let you go," he told him. "You fly on back to the train and tell them to stop. Tell them to give up the cargo without a fight, or I'll kill this girl."

"No." The word came out before Piper had time to think. The raider glanced at her and nudged the bolt. The barbed tip scratched her throat again and she felt a small dot of blood run down her chest. Piper forced aside the panic rising inside her. "What I mean is, you don't actually think they'll stop the train, give up all that cargo, just for one scrapper?" Piper forced a laugh. "I might be the only thing on the 401 worth less than you are."

Some of the raiders exchanged glances, but the man with the crossbow didn't waver. "I think he'll make them stop," he said, nodding at Gee. "Won't you, chamelin?"

Gee was utterly still inside the net. Piper didn't look at him. She knew he would never give up the train or its cargo, not for her, not for anything. Protecting the train was his duty.

"You're wasting your time," Piper said.

The raider's eyes narrowed. He curled his finger around the crossbow's trigger, and suddenly, Gee stirred. To Piper's horror, he bent and put his claws down on the ground and bowed his head in acquiescence.

"That's what I thought." The raider lowered his weapon.

"No, you can't!" Piper shrieked as two of the other men came forward and lifted the net off Gee. The chamelin ignored her and spread his wings, stretching them out and testing them gingerly, checking to see if they were too badly damaged to carry him. His left wing still didn't seem as strong as the other, but it didn't look like that was going to hold Gee back. He was going to fly to the train so he could deliver it into the hands of the raiders.

Piper's heart sank at the realization of what was happening.

"Hurry up," the raider said, turning from Piper to Gee and nudging him with the butt of his crossbow. "Don't keep your friend waiting."

Furious, Piper grabbed Gee's arm before he could take off. "Don't do this," she begged.

Gee growled at her, but his eyes weren't angry. If anything, he looked resigned and scared. He stepped away from her and, in a powerful flash of wings, soared away.

"No," Piper called weakly. She watched Gee's shrinking form disappear behind the ring of men surrounding her, their weapons gleaming in the hot sun. She thought of Doloman hunting them, and the slavers, always someone, threatening with their crossbows and their guns and their dust. Anger took hold in Piper's gut and began to seep into her veins. It poured out of her in waves that she could almost see like a heat mirage in the air. She felt dizzy and strange—and then she heard a sharp cry.

"Goddess!" The bald raider dropped his crossbow. The trigger mechanism had exploded, showering parts across the dusty ground.

But it wasn't just his. All around Piper, raiders dropped their ruined crossbows. It looked like they'd been hit by one of Anna's whirlwind dismantling sessions. The bald man stepped back and surveyed the scattered pieces, cursing violently—some of the words he used Piper had never even heard of.

Then he turned his fury on her. *"What are you?"* he screamed.

At that moment, Piper swayed on her feet. She'd never used her power on such an enormous scale before, and her body was letting her know it. Her knees wobbled, threatening to give out. Darkness danced at the edges of her vision. *Please don't let me pass out,* she begged the universe. And from the edge of her consciousness, she could hear all the raiders yelling now.

Piper fell, gravel and dirt digging through her trousers into the skin of her knees, her shoulder, and her cheek. The sun beat down on her neck. She smelled raider sweat and her own blood from her injured hand. The pain was a distant throbbing, and the raiders' voices narrowed to a hollow echo.

She was going to pass out. She couldn't help it. Maybe it was even for the best.

Then, in the distance, she saw a large shadow, like another mirage, descending into the canyon. A dark shape with leathery wings. And the men were too preoccupied shouting to see it.

Gee came at two of the raiders from behind, knocking them flat with his outstretched wings. He kept flying, aiming straight at Piper. Never slowing, he reached out for her, and Piper raised shaking arms to meet him. He lifted her off her knees, and Piper was flying again, the raiders and their weapons receding to small dots on the ground.

Weakness finally overcame Piper while they were in the air. She had no strength left in her body. She closed her eyes and gave in to it, hanging limp in her friend's grasp. The world spun into blackness, and when she came to, she was lying on granite boulders again, cradled in Gee's arms, her head supported against his shoulder. Distantly, she heard the 401's whistle, the most welcoming sound in the world. It had to have been what woke her.

She looked down and saw the train appear on the horizon, a dot that steadily grew larger, though from this height it still looked like a toy. Piper searched for the raiders that had latched on to the train earlier, but there was nothing. Everything looked normal. Even the spikes that had been jutting from the roofs of the cars had been retracted.

As they approached the 401, Gee dipped low and Piper realized he intended to land on the observation deck at the rear of the train. It was actually where he always landed when he finished his scouting forays, she decided.

As they neared the deck, Gee growled with the effort of keeping them steady. His injured wing trembled. "Almost there," Piper encouraged, squeezing his shoulder. "Look, there's Anna."

Her friend stood in the doorway waiting for them, waving her arms frantically. Piper waved back to let

Anna know they were fine, but the girl didn't stop, and then she was pointing too, at something in the sky. Piper turned to look over Gee's shoulder and saw it: a lone glider that had followed them from the canyon.

"Behind us!" Piper yelled.

Gee was too close to the train to pull up—suddenly Piper was flying through the air as Gee tossed her straight toward Anna and the observation deck. A scream welled up inside Piper. If she landed wrong, this could be very bad. Anna reached out her arms as if to catch Piper, but the girl was too small to do anything but slow her momentum. Piper slammed into her, and both girls went down in a heap on the platform. Piper closed her eyes and breathed a quick sigh of relief. She was bruised and dizzy, but the landing could have been much worse. She pushed herself up to her knees and looked back for Gee and the glider. Her breath caught in her chest when she saw the pilot—it was the bald raider who'd threatened her with the crossbow.

One raider against the whole train seemed like suicide. Unless he wasn't planning on attacking the train. Then Piper realized, *What if he just wants to kill Gee?*

Piper stood up, blood pounding in her ears as she fought back her terror. They'd been so close to escaping.

In the distance, Gee made a tight circle and flew back toward the train, soaring over the glider. He came in fast and landed hard on the observation deck a few feet in front of Piper and Anna. Turning, he leaped up to perch on the railing while the girls huddled behind him on the platform. Gee let out a roar and swiped out at the approaching glider with his claws. The craft swerved at the last moment, pulling beside the train, and the raider leaned out the side of the glider, slashing at Gee with a long-bladed dagger. Gee jerked back, but not in time. The blade left a thin cut across his chest. Gee snarled and lashed out, digging his claws into the glider's wing. He yanked upward and tore the wing off the craft.

The tension in Piper's body receded; there was no coming back from damage that bad. Then, to her shock, the raider stood up and jumped, grabbing the iron railing of the observation deck as his craft hit the dirt and broke apart. Using his momentum, he swung into Gee's body with a loud thud. The impact pushed Gee off balance and allowed the raider to swing his dagger at the chamelin's throat. Gee managed to dodge, but the raider pulled back for another strike.

"No!" Piper screamed. She ran to the end of the platform and grabbed the raider's arm, wrenching backward, anything to keep the dagger from slicing into Gee. Anna ran up and attached herself to his other arm, yanking as hard as she could.

The raider threw Piper off, sending her flying across the platform so that she struck her head on the iron railing. For a moment, her vision darkened, stars blinking in her sight line, and when they cleared, she saw that Gee had regained his balance. He reached for the raider, who was trying to retreat, but Anna still clung to his other arm.

Piper saw what was going to happen next. She tried to get up, but her head swam. She couldn't seem to move fast enough and her tongue lay thick and heavy in her mouth. Helpless, Piper watched as the raider turned and slashed at Anna with his dagger. By some miracle, the girl saw the strike coming and leaped backward, half falling through the doorway behind her to avoid the blade.

As she fell, Piper saw that her friend hadn't been fast enough. The dagger had sliced open her left arm; there was a long gash from shoulder to elbow. Piper found her voice then, and screamed. She jumped up, head pounding, throat raw, and tried to reach for Anna. A wave of nausea and dizziness washed over her, and this time Piper couldn't shake it off. Her body had had enough. She slipped into darkness, her screams turning to whimpers in her ears. The last thing she heard was Gee's bestial roar.

≈ SEVENTEEN ≈

W hen she awoke, for a minute Piper thought she was flying again, carried in Gee's strong arms. No, that wasn't right. The surface she lay upon was softer. Puzzled, she opened her eyes.

Slowly, Piper recognized her surroundings. She was back on the 401. She was in Gee's room, lying on his bed, and her arm was stiff and sore. When she looked down at it, she saw there were white bandages wrapped around her hand. And someone had removed her blood-soaked shirt and replaced it with one of her clean ones. She tried to sit up, but her head felt as if it weighed a ton, and she was dizzy and a little queasy.

How had she gotten here? Piper tried to remember the last thing that happened before she'd lost consciousness. She remembered the canyon, Gee coming back to rescue her from the raiders, and then . . . something felt wrong. A spasm of fear went through Piper's body. Something bad had happened. Why didn't she remember? She tried to sit up again, slower this time.

"Don't try to move," said a voice.

Startled, Piper rolled onto her side and saw Gee sitting in the chair at his little table. He was back in his human form, and he looked terrible. His left arm was tied close to his body in a sling, and his shirt collar was pulled back, revealing bandages wrapped around his shoulder.

"What happened?" Piper croaked. Her throat burned for a drink of water, but she needed to know that everything was all right first. "How bad are you hurt?"

Gee smiled wanly. "It's not as bad as it looks. Nothing's broken, but it made Trimble feel better to truss me up with bandages. I'll have them off by tomorrow."

Piper breathed a sigh of relief. Gee would be fine. If he'd been hurt badly, she'd never have forgiven herself. She opened her mouth to ask why he'd risked his neck for her like that, when her memory flooded back in a horrible rush, and she blurted out, "Anna!"

Gee's face clouded. "She's up front in Jeyne's room. Trimble looked after her too. She'll be fine."

"Then why do you look like that?" Piper heard her voice, high and frightened like a child's. "I want to see her!"

"You should rest for a while longer," Gee said. He stood up and came to sit on the edge of the bed. "Trimble thinks you might have a concussion. You hit your head pretty hard on the railing."

"You saw that?"

"I saw everything," he said with a sad smile.

The memories were still fragmented, but Piper vaguely recalled the raider throwing her off, and then hitting her head, then Anna, falling through the doorway as the dagger cut into her arm. . . .

"I want to see Anna," Piper repeated. "I have to know she's all right." Gee ducked his head and muttered something. Piper raised an eyebrow. "What was that?"

"Nothing, it's just—I thought hitting your head might have knocked the stubbornness out of you, but I guess it was too much to hope for," he said. "I'll get you some water, and then, if you can prove to me you can get up without fainting, I'll take you to Jeyne. She'll explain about Anna."

"Explain what?" Now Piper was really scared. "You said she was all right!"

"She *is*," Gee said sharply. "It's complicated. Just be patient, and I'll take you to her."

"I— Sorry," Piper said, ashamed that she'd snapped at him. Gee was hurt too, and he'd obviously been sitting up with her. The last thing he needed was for her to badger him. She tried to be patient while Gee filled a glass of water from his washstand and brought it to her. He waited while she drank it.

"Do you feel like eating?" Gee asked. "I brought

some fruit from the kitchen." He held out a small plate of sliced apples. Piper took one and bit into it. The fruit was crisp and juicy and tasted delicious. "That's good," he said. "Food will help you get your strength back. After what you did to those crossbows, you must be starving."

Piper stopped chewing as she remembered. "I was angry and so scared," she said, "and the next thing I knew, everything was in pieces."

Gee nodded. "Once there was a fire in the engine cab, and Trimble brought it under control all by himself. He said he didn't plan it—he just reacted, like you did, and it was over just like that. It took a lot of energy, though. Afterward, I watched him wolf down a whole chicken and three baked potatoes, skins and all." Gee whistled in admiration. "I've never seen anyone eat so much."

Piper wrinkled her nose. "I'm fine with the apples, thanks."

"It was a good thing, what you did," Gee said. "When I heard all those men screaming, I circled back and saw I had a clear path to you."

Piper clutched an apple slice in her hand, her fingernail piercing the peel. "Would you really have gone back to stop the train?" she asked nervously. When Gee didn't respond, Piper realized he would have. She couldn't believe it. "But you would have given up all that cargo, put everyone on the train in danger, just for me? What were you thinking?"

Gee's jaw tightened. "I wasn't thinking," he said,

shaking his head, clearly frustrated at himself. "I didn't know what I was going to do. All I could think was . . . was . . ."

"What?" Piper demanded.

Gee stood up suddenly, pacing the car like a caged animal. "I didn't want you to get hurt," he snapped. "Seeing you out there with that crossbow bolt at your throat—it twisted my insides, and I couldn't think straight. You just . . . you can't imagine how scared I was."

A fire spread across Piper's cheeks. "Yes, I can." She stared at the blanket, unable to meet Gee's eyes. "I felt the same way when they dropped the net on you," she said in a small voice.

Gee said nothing, but he'd stopped pacing and stood in front of her. Piper still couldn't look up at him. She was afraid if she did, she would see him laughing at her. Why should she worry for his safety—a chamelin with twice her strength? He didn't need her help. All she'd done was get herself caught again and make him come rescue her.

She heard Gee utter a quiet sigh, and before Piper knew what was happening, he was kneeling in front of her. Gently, he untangled her hands from the blanket and held them in his own, being especially careful with the bandaged one. Piper's heartbeat sped up. The fire in her cheeks raced down her neck.

Slowly, he leaned toward her, releasing one of her hands so he could wrap his uninjured arm around her and pull her into a hug. Piper let out a breath she hadn't realized she'd been holding, closed her eyes, and rested her chin on Gee's shoulder. She could feel his heart beating fast as he turned his head and pressed a kiss against her cheek.

Safe, Piper realized. *I feel safe.* She wanted to stay like that, listening to Gee's fluttering heartbeat. But she couldn't because . . .

Anna.

Gently, Piper pulled away. Gee leaned back, and this time Piper was able to meet his eyes. Now that she'd found the courage, she couldn't stop staring into that vivid green field, ringed with yellow at the pupils. The more emotion he felt, the more the yellow came through, Piper realized. Then there was that soot smudge. She reached up and touched it gently before she noticed what she was doing. Suddenly shy, she buried her hands in her lap.

"I'm sorry, but please take me to Anna," Piper said. "I need to see her."

Gee nodded solemnly. He stepped back and, without a word, stood next to the bed while Piper got up. She moved slowly—it felt like every muscle in her body had been bruised—but gradually she got to her feet. She wavered a bit, but Gee put an arm around her waist, pulling her toward him. Leaning on him gratefully, Piper limped to the door.

They made slow progress up the train. In the cargo areas, guards were stacking and resealing crates that had been torn open. It looked like some of the raiders had managed to get inside the train during the attack.

"They almost got the cargo," Piper said, surprised. "How did they get inside the train?"

"They attacked at three different points, took us all by surprise," Gee said. "We spread ourselves too thin in the defense."

"But they weren't just after the cargo. They came after you too," Piper said, remembering the last raider's desperate flight on the glider and his attack on Gee. She didn't ask what had become of the man. She didn't want to know.

"Yeah, and if I'd figured that out a little sooner, I could have led that last raider away from the train. Then you and Anna wouldn't have gotten hurt," Gee said, scowling.

Piper opened her mouth to argue, but they had reached the front of the train, and her attention was taken by fear of what she would soon discover. Standing at the door to Jeyne and Trimble's car, Piper suddenly couldn't bring herself to go in. Something was terribly wrong; she could feel it in her bones. And she knew Gee wouldn't have been acting so strangely otherwise.

Gee knocked on the door.

"Come in," Jeyne's voice called from inside.

Gee opened the door and helped Piper inside. Jeyne was sitting at Trimble's bedside, where Anna lay under a pile of blankets. The girl's eyes were closed, her face deathly pale. Her left arm, the injured one, was uncovered and had been laid across a small table next to the bed. Trimble bent over the table, partially obscuring Piper's view. Piper's heart sped up. Anna was hurt badly and Piper wanted to cross the room, take her hand, but she couldn't make her feet move.

"How is she?" Piper asked, unable to keep the fear out of her voice.

Jeyne looked up. The older woman had dark circles under her eyes. "She doesn't have much more color than you do. Goddess, we're all pretty beat up, but we're still here." Piper heard the determination in her voice and knew where her nickname had come from. "How are you feeling?"

"Better," Piper said.

"Well then, come over here." Jeyne pulled up a chair for her.

Gee helped her to the engineer's side and steadied her as she sat down, then retreated to a corner. Without him standing there, supporting her, Piper felt even shakier. She also noticed Trimble hadn't spoken since she'd come into the room. He remained bent over Anna's arm, intent on something Piper couldn't see.

"Will she be all right?" Piper asked. She directed the question at Trimble, but the fireman didn't reply. "How's her arm?" she tried again, but he still didn't answer. Panic gripped Piper. "She's not going to lose her arm, is she?"

"Calm down, honey." Jeyne put her hand on Piper's shoulder. Piper had never heard the stern engineer's voice sound so gentle. It terrified her. Jeyne had lost part of her own arm—was she preparing to tell Piper that the same thing was about to happen to Anna?

"Tell me what's going on!" Piper's voice was louder than she'd meant, but she could barely hold herself together.

"Let her look," Trimble said. He straightened and turned to Piper. "We might need you. Goddess knows I can't figure out what to do here. This is way beyond me."

Jeyne nodded. "At first we thought Anna's cut wasn't that deep," she explained. "There wasn't hardly any blood, so we brought her back here to patch her up. When she wouldn't wake up, we realized that the cut was worse than we thought. We took a closer look and . . . well . . ." Jeyne paused while Trimble stepped out of the way, making room for Piper to lean in.

The room went dead quiet. Piper's vision darkened at the corners, leaving only the small gaslight glow shining on Anna's arm. The knife slash was an angry, jagged line from her shoulder to the curve of her elbow. Jeyne was right, Piper thought faintly, there was very little blood, and as she looked closer, she could see why.

Beneath the surface wound, where deeper layers of skin and tissue should have been, was instead a mass of metal—machine parts, interwoven gears and wires that were more complex than anything she'd ever seen before. Piper sucked in a breath, shocked by what she saw.

Tentatively, Piper reached out and touched Anna's arm. Her skin was warm and soft, like that of any normal human, and covered in small hairs like anyone else's. Piper traced her hand upward and stopped shy of the wound revealing the metal parts. The silence in the room, combined with what she was seeing, strained every nerve in Piper's body.

She hesitated, then gently touched the machine parts before her with her fingertip. Again, the warmth, but with an unyielding rigidity that made Piper recoil. She stepped back quickly and bumped into Jeyne's chest. The engineer steadied her, holding her in place by her shoulders so she couldn't run.

"You have to help her, honey," Jeyne said. "That knife cut into her pretty deep, and something's not right with her. You're the only one who can do anything for her."

"But what do you want me to do?" Piper could barely recognize her own voice. She was trembling so badly, she thought she might have fallen over if Jeyne hadn't been holding her upright. One human hand and one made of metal kept her in place. "I'm only a machinist," Piper murmured.

"Yes, you are," Trimble said, "and Anna's at least part machine herself. And just looking at this small slice of her inner workings, I can tell you she's far more complicated than any machine we've ever encountered before."

Sudden anger burned in Piper's chest. "Would you stop talking about her as if she's some kind of mechanical toy!" she snapped.

"What I'm trying to say is that I believe that what you can do is the best chance Anna's got for healing," Trimble said.

Piper thought back to that night in her house when Micah said she was a healer with machines. It seemed so long ago now, back when she was just a local scrapper with a big mouth, proud of her work tinkering with machines. She hadn't known anything back then.

She hadn't known they walked around in human skin.

"I have to . . . have to get out of here," Piper stammered. How could she possibly help her friend? "I can't do this. I'm not a healer—"

"For her, you are." Jeyne gripped Piper's shoulders harder and turned her, forcing her to look at Anna's arm again. "Trimble's right. You're the only one who can fix her."

"Fix her?" Piper exploded. "I told you she's not a steam engine or a . . . or a pocket watch or a music box! She's a human being—or at least, I thought she was until about thirty seconds ago! I can't just grab a wrench and go to work on her. What if something goes wrong and I"— her voice trailed off to a whisper—"kill her?"

"You won't," Trimble said. "I think she's been reacting to you since you first met. You said when you found her she was unconscious and then you brought her home and she got better. Your magic probably revived her without you even being aware of it. The longer you were around her, the stronger she became. I bet she would have died if you hadn't been the one to pull her out of that caravan wreck."

The caravan. Slowly, Trimble's words penetrated the panicked haze blanketing Piper's mind. Anna had been in a deep sleep that day in her house, and Doloman had said she was half-dead, broken, when she came to him. When he'd seen her awake and alive, he'd acted as if it was some sort of miracle. Except it wasn't—it had been Piper's magic all along. Somehow, she'd fixed Anna the same way she'd fixed all the other machines.

"Goddess," Piper murmured. Was this real? She looked at Anna's wound again, trying to reconcile that the girl lying motionless in the bed and the arm with the machine parts buried in the skin really belonged to each other. Anna's arm seemed disconnected from the rest of her, lying on the table under the light. Piper looked from one to the other, and suddenly she saw Anna's eyelids flicker. The smallest movement, but it drew Piper. She knelt between the bed and the table, not able to look at the arm, just staring at her friend's face.

Slowly, Anna's eyes fluttered open and focused on her. "Piper," she said. "There you are."

"That's right," Piper answered, her voice catching in her throat. "Here I am." She reached up and brushed a strand of hair off Anna's forehead. "How are you feeling?"

"Tired," Anna said. She blinked several times. "I've never been this tired—wait, maybe once. It feels like a long time ago."

"You go ahead and sleep as long as you need to," Piper said. "We beat those raiders up one side of the canyon and down the other, so you don't have anything more to worry about."

A little smile crossed the girl's face. "The crossbow worked . . . fascinating weapon . . . strength of the bow . . . but . . . you don't have to be so strong to use it . . . machinery helps it work. Needs more study . . . could improve it further . . ."

"That's my girl," Piper whispered. "Always thinking, always working that mouth."

"My arm hurts," Anna said, making Piper's insides go cold. "And—I can't move it."

"Then don't try," Piper said, fighting to keep her voice steady. "Lie still, and Trimble and I . . ." She cleared her throat. "We're going to take care of you. You just go back to sleep, and you won't feel a thing."

"All right." Anna's eyes slid shut as if they were weighted. "You'll stay, though, won't you, Piper?" she mumbled.

"I'll be right here," Piper answered. When she was

certain that Anna had fallen asleep again, Piper turned to look at Anna's arm closer. "Trimble," she said, and then, louder, "Trimble, will you help me? I'm going to need . . . aw, I don't know what I'll need yet, just stay close." She glanced up at Jeyne and Gee. "I'll do whatever I can to save her, but I don't know if it'll be enough."

"We're all out of our depth here," Jeyne said. "I know you'll do the best you can."

"I have some tools," Trimble said. He laid a tray of metal instruments on the table at Piper's elbow. Glancing at them, Piper thought they looked like a cross between machinist's tools and healer's instruments. She supposed that was appropriate. She would have rather had her own tools, but she could tell Trimble's were clean, and she didn't want to risk the wound becoming infected—if that was possible.

"We'll let you two get to work," Jeyne said. "Come on, Green-Eye, let's give them some space."

Piper was so absorbed in sorting through the tools, she didn't realize at first that Gee hadn't answered Jeyne. Piper glanced up and saw the chamelin still in the far corner, watching them silently. Jeyne walked over to him and said something too low for Piper to hear, and Gee narrowed his eyes at Jeyne.

"I'm not leaving," he said.

"It's all right." Piper gave him a look, trying to put everything she felt into it—hope, fear, gratitude . . . and more. Something must have gotten through, because

Gee nodded and left the room with Jeyne. The engineer touched Piper's shoulder as she passed her, and Piper looked up at the older woman. "Thank you," she said.

Jeyne nodded, and then they were both gone, and she and Trimble were alone with Anna's wounded arm between them on the table.

⋙ EIGHTEEN ⋘

"How do you want to do this?" Trimble asked in a low voice.

Piper let out a big breath. "To be honest, fireman, I don't have the faintest idea," she said.

When she'd looked at just the small bit of machinery visible beneath Anna's skin, Piper had felt lost. Attempting to fix this would be like Micah trying to fix Piper's broken watch or Arno Weir's engine. To someone who wasn't a machinist, all the gears and springs inside ordinary objects like those would seem like an impossible puzzle. That was what the machine parts inside Anna looked like to Piper. They were so complex—so far outside her experience—she didn't know where to begin. All she knew was that she had to try, so she might as well get on with it.

"I'll get some more light over here." Trimble lit another lantern and pointed to the washstand in the corner. "Wash your hands," he said. "You're a healer now, and healers have to have clean hands."

Piper went to the basin and ran some water. She took the soap and scrubbed, digging her fingernails into the bar to wash away all the dirt that had collected there. She washed her arms to the elbows, grateful that whoever had tended to her injuries earlier had also cleaned her up some from the fight with the raiders. When she finished, her hands were bright red and probably cleaner than they had ever been in her life. She wiped her hands on a towel lying beside the basin and went back to stand on the opposite side of the table from Trimble.

Trimble handed her a scalpel. "Hold this in your hand. Get the feel of it before we start," he instructed.

"Won't she wake up?" Piper asked, casting an uneasy glance at Anna. "If we start messing with . . . I mean a human would . . . won't it hurt her?"

"I'll give her something that should keep her out for several hours," Trimble said. "Go ahead and get used to the scalpel. I'll take care of it."

Piper held the scalpel and leaned in to take a closer look at the wound as Trimble administered the sedative. That was when she saw it—movement among the metal plates and gears, the flowing wires and bolts. Like a thread of liquid gold, it wove among the machine parts, passing in and out of view.

319

"Look at that," she breathed.

Trimble leaned in close. "What do you think it is?" Trimble asked. "Something like blood, maybe?"

Piper shook her head. Instinct sparked in her—it hummed in her veins and raised gooseflesh on her arms. "We've already seen that she has blood, just not as much as a human does. Maybe this other stuff is a supplement to her blood, something that performs a similar function, only for a machine—like an energy source."

"You mean, the way our hearts pump blood in arteries and veins—"

Piper nodded. "Since she has some blood, it means she has a heart, but maybe she also has something else that pumps the gold fluid. Whatever it is, maybe it's also a power source, her fuel." After all, a machine needed a power source to function, Piper thought, and a human being needed a heart. She laid her ear against Anna's chest, hearing the familiar thumping of a human heart. "It doesn't sound any different from one of our hearts," she said.

"Here, listen with this." Trimble handed her an amplifying scope. Piper put the hooked ends into her ears while Trimble laid the rounded knob against Anna's chest. "Now see if it sounds the same as a human heart."

Piper listened. The beating got louder, but it still sounded the same as any other human heartbeat. Maybe her theory was wrong and Anna had no supplementary power source. She was about to say so—then she had an idea. Gently, she moved aside Anna's pillow and positioned the scope at the back of Anna's neck, over her scar. And there it was. Faintly, Piper heard a low, almost inaudible humming sound. She handed the scope to Trimble to make sure she wasn't imagining something. The fireman listened, and his eyes widened.

"So we think that in addition to a human heart and blood, she's got something extra giving her energy," Piper said. Her hands were shaking a little as she picked up the scalpel again. "Hold the light close."

Trimble brought the lantern to the table. "Just relax and go slowly."

Sweat beaded Piper's forehead as she bent over Anna's arm and touched the blade to the wires, moving them gently aside, probing the metal plates beneath. A tingling sensation traveled through the scalpel up to her fingertips. Just below Anna's shoulder, she found a gouge in the metalwork. The raider's dagger cut had severed one bundle of the wires, the torn ends sticking out in all directions.

"I'll need to weave those back together," Piper said. "They might be . . . tendons, or something. Maybe that's why she can't move her arm. I can't be sure."

"It's a place to start," Trimble said. "Concentrate, and let your magic do the rest."

Piper nodded, and they went to work.

* * *

"Wearing yourself out isn't going to do anyone any good," Jeyne said as Gee passed her for the third time on his journey around the small engine room. The fire burned hot in the firebox, but a cool night breeze from the open window lifted Jeyne's gray hair and blew the strands around her face. The coolness helped keep her awake. She hadn't slept since the raider attack. Thank the goddess they were only a few days out from Noveen. Jeyne had had enough excitement on this run to last her until retirement.

Be careful what you wish for, Jeyne told herself. Retirement might come sooner than any of them expected with Doloman waiting for them in Noveen. And now they had another crisis to deal with.

Before the revelations about Anna's identity, Jeyne had been sure Doloman wouldn't risk coming for the girls himself, not after the disaster in Tevshal. She'd thought they would have time to hide them somewhere in Noveen and plead ignorance later when questioned by the authorities. It had been a fool's hope. Doloman obviously knew what Anna was, and Piper was sure he would risk anything to get her back. He'd probably be waiting for them at the train station in the capital with a full contingent of guards.

It was time for a new plan, Jeyne decided. They'd have

to get the girls off the train and far away as soon as possible. Derghesh was a small farming village that supplied food to the capital. Jeyne had some friends there, folks she knew she could trust. It was far from their route, but not so far that Gee couldn't fly them. The girls would be safe there until they could find a more permanent place for them to hide.

What a pair of strays they'd picked up. Jeyne couldn't help smiling to herself at the thought. Hadn't she told Gee at the beginning of this mess that if all she had to worry about on this trip was a couple of little girls, she'd thank the goddess?

"What can you possibly be happy about?" Gee stopped his prowling and was staring at Jeyne.

"I was just thinking that in all my years on the railroad, I've never encountered anything quite like those girls," Jeyne said, then added, "Well, maybe one other time." She shot Gee a significant glance.

"They're in a world of trouble," Gee murmured. A look of misery creased his face. "Why can't we just keep them on the 401? They could earn their keep as well as anyone else."

"You know I can't do that, Gee," Jeyne said gently.

"Why not?" Gee burst out. He kicked a trash bin in frustration. The metal basket clattered across the floor. "You did the same for me once. You know I would have died if you hadn't taken me in."

"Never regretted it a day since," Jeyne said, "but this is different. Doloman knows they're here. There's no hiding them. We have to offload them outside the capital."

"Just like a pallet of cargo," Gee muttered.

"Stop it," Jeyne snapped. "We're all tired, Green-Eye, and you're not the only one who cares about what happens to those girls."

"I should be able to protect them," Gee said. "It's what I'm supposed to do."

"You have protected them," Jeyne said. "And you'll get your chance again when it really counts."

"What do you mean?"

Jeyne looked solemn. "King Aron says the future of Solace is in machines, that we need to expand and explore our world. That little girl in there is something we've never seen before, something new. She may just be that future. Doloman must know it too, how valuable she is. He won't quit until he gets her. Somehow, we've got to stop that from happening."

Piper and Trimble worked long into the night. Piper glanced up once when the sun went down, and when she looked up again, gray dawn light was visible through the window. Her shoulders were stiff from hunching over the table, her injured hand ached, and her eyeballs felt like they'd been rolled in sand.

"I don't think we can do much more," Piper said at

last. Her throat was so dry. She desperately needed a glass of water.

"Let me stitch up the knife cut," Trimble said. "You've done more than enough. You need to rest."

He was right. Piper had been working for hours, her magic subtly taking hold and slowly helping her mend broken coils and wiring. Healing wasn't nearly as fast and dramatic as the destruction Piper had caused when she blew up the raiders' crossbows. She still didn't fully understand how her magic worked, but in a way, it made sense. Destroying a machine, whether smashing it with a hammer or sending a burst of magic at it, was relatively easy. But fixing a machine was harder, requiring subtlety and her own skills as a machinist. In fact, Piper might not have noticed the healing magic at work at all had they not been working so long on so many minute details.

The inner workings of Anna's arm were composed of a system of parts so finely integrated and in tune with each other that as soon as Piper fixed one part, another had to be seen to immediately or the whole system threatened to break down. She had worked with a few complex machines like that in the past, but nothing close to this scale before. At first, the task had seemed impossible, but gradually, as the night wore on, the work got easier. Piper's magic combined with her own skills as a machinist created the healing process. The longer she and Trimble worked, the easier the repairs became, until Piper felt as if the machine parts responded to her thoughts rather than her touch. She'd never experienced anything like it before. If she hadn't been terrified of hurting Anna, Piper would have been thrilled at the challenge before her and at what she'd accomplished.

She'd helped heal Anna, and Piper knew in her heart that her magic, on its own, wouldn't have been able to do that. She'd needed all the skill and experience with machines that she'd gained during her years in the scrap town. The magic was a part of her, but it wasn't everything—her own talents were just as important.

The light outside had turned pink by the time Trimble finished putting the last stitch in Anna's arm. He cleaned the area around the wound, bandaged it, and arranged Anna's arm against her side on top of the blanket.

"Good work," Piper said, rubbing her bleary eyes.

"Thanks, but she's going to have a bit of a nasty scar there," Trimble said.

"It won't be the first," Piper said, thinking of the scar at the back of Anna's neck. "It doesn't matter anyway, as long as she's fixed."

She was so tired. Her head throbbed, and the room looked blurry around the edges. Piper wanted to sleep, but she had to go see Jeyne and Gee first, let them know that she thought Anna was going to be all right.

Trimble put a hand on her arm as she moved unsteadily to the door. "I mean it—you need to rest. You used up a lot of energy, and it's not something you have an infinite supply of—magic takes its toll on us. Remember that."

Piper nodded. Casting one more glance at Anna's sleeping form, she left the car. As she expected, Jeyne and Gee were waiting for her in the next car, a place used as dry food storage. It was strange to see them sitting there side by side on sacks of rice, not speaking. They looked up when Piper walked through the door, worry creasing their faces.

"She's going to be all right," Piper said. It felt strange echoing the same statement Gee had made earlier. Of course, he must have known that Piper would be able to help Anna. He'd believed in her. "She's asleep, but when she wakes up, her arm should be fine."

Gee's solemn face split into a grin, and Jeyne's expression softened. "Good work," she said. "Well done, both of you."

Trimble came up behind Piper. "This one needs food and sleep," he said firmly. "I'll take her back to her room."

"Wait," Piper said. Though she wanted nothing more than to collapse in her bed and sleep for a week, she knew she couldn't. Finding out that Anna was part machine had changed everything. "We have to talk about Anna."

"Agreed," Jeyne said. She and Piper ignored Trimble's scowl. "Now we know why she's so important to Doloman. And that gives us an advantage."

"We can't stay on the train or go to the capital,"

Piper said. She'd had all night to think, and the realization that both the 401 and Noveen were lost to them hurt her more than all her other injuries. "Where can we go that Doloman won't find us?"

"Gee and I have been talking about that," Jeyne said. "Tomorrow night, Gee's going to fly you off the train and take you to some friends of mine. They used to be farmers before Aron strip-mined their land. They don't have any love for the Dragonfly. You can stay with them until we figure out where to move you for good."

Despite her worry and fear, Piper warmed when she thought about what Jeyne was willing to do for them. She'd probably been planning their escape all night. "You've risked so much for us already," Piper said. "Wherever we go, we'll have to earn our keep." She looked at Jeyne, and her face burned with shame. She needed to tell her the truth. "I came on the 401 with Anna because I thought I could get something out of it. I thought that if I took Anna back to her family, they'd give me some kind of reward, something that would buy me a new life. I thought everything was going to be so simple. Then Anna—well, she messed it all up. The girl talks more than anyone I've ever met. I don't understand her half the time, and the other half she drives me crazy. She's so smart and determined, yet she's fragile too." Piper needed them to understand. "I never wanted to be a burden on you or anyone else. I was just so tired of being poor, of being nothing but a scrapper in a tiny little town in one corner of the world. But it's different now. I always wanted to earn my place. Now I know there's more to it than that. I need to look out for more than just myself. I want to help you all however I can, and to help Anna. She's like a sister to me, no matter what she's made of."

Jeyne nodded approvingly. "You've defended this train and looked out for its people more than once," she said. "If I could give you a place here, I would, and give you both the chance to earn your keep. As it is, the least we can do is make sure you're safe. Will you let us do that?"

Piper nodded, tears burning in her eyes. "Thank you."

"You need to rest now." Gee came forward and supported her as she crossed the room. Piper hadn't realized how much strength it was taking to stay on her feet until Gee put his arm around her. *Careful*, Piper warned herself. *You might come to rely on that too much. Then when it's gone . . .*

She refused to consider being separated from Gee right then. It was just too painful. Maybe when she'd rested, when she could think clearly. For now, she leaned on Gee and let him lead her back to her room. She was too tired even to climb into the upper berth, so she stretched out on Anna's bed. The last thing she remembered was Gee helping her draw up the covers, and then she was asleep.

* * *

Piper woke late in the day just long enough to fumble her way to the washroom, catch a frightening glimpse of herself in the mirror, and then stumble back to bed. She was still sore all over, but at least her head no longer ached.

When she woke again, it was dark. She'd slept the whole day away. Piper pushed her tangled hair back from her face and stared bleary-eyed at the moonlight coming in through the window. Why had no one come to wake her? Piper supposed Gee and the others were either still making repairs to the 401 after the raider attack or they were busy planning Piper and Anna's secret escape. Probably both.

As Piper gazed out the window, she drifted between sleep and wakefulness. Worry and fear gnawed at her, fighting with the exhaustion. Would they really be able to hide from Doloman? She thought of everything they'd seen on their journey to the capital. The land around King Aron's iron mines, stripped bare of trees and grass, and she already knew what the factory in Noveen was like. The Dragonfly was obsessed with building the best machines in all of Solace—tools that would help him explore beyond the known world. All those grand plans and accomplishments, yet Aron's chief machinist had done him one better. In Anna, Doloman had discovered the most incredible machine of all.

But *machine* wasn't the right word for Anna. She might have machine parts running the show under her skin, but her mind and her heart were just like any other human's—and better than most.

Piper wouldn't let Doloman hurt any of them. He hadn't counted on Piper being a synergist. She would use all the magic she had in her to protect Anna, Gee, and the rest of her friends.

But she had to get her strength back first. Right now, she was too weak to protect anyone. Piper dozed and suddenly she was dreaming again, flying low over a vast blue-green ocean and then rising at dizzying speed toward a cliff. It was just like Raenoll's vision. When she crested the top, the city of Noveen spread out before her. A layer of thick gray fog clung to the stone buildings, shredding in the ocean wind and then re-forming like angry ghosts. The source of the fog was the factory, a sprawling mass of buildings and smoke stacks that filled an entire neighborhood. From her vantage, she saw people scurrying between the buildings like insects.

Piper descended toward the factory. She didn't want to, but a weight pulled her down, shaking her, tearing her out of the dream. The factory and the city dissolved into the anxious face of Jeyne. At first Piper didn't recognize the woman. Her clothes were all askew, and her hair hung in tangles around her head as if someone had yanked her out of bed as roughly as she was now trying to yank Piper.

"Get up, girl! Come on, we've lost too much time already," Jeyne said.

"What is it?" Piper sat up, groggy and still half held by the dream.

"It's Anna," Jeyne said. "She's gone."

NINETEEN

"What?" Piper's mind snapped into focus as dread washed over her. She sat up and grabbed Jeyne's arms, fingers closing tightly around the metal one. "What do you mean 'gone'? Where did she go?"

"She's not on the train. Get up; we've got to hurry."

Doloman—oh goddess, no! Piper sprang from the bed, yanked on her clothes, and grabbed her boots. Sore muscles screaming in protest, she half ran, half limped after Jeyne out of the car and up to the engine cab. Trimble and Gee were already there. They still looked tired, but Piper noticed Gee had removed his bandages just as he'd promised. He stood by the window, a bundle of barely contained energy. His expression was furious.

"I put a guard at her door," Gee said to Jeyne when she and Piper walked in. "He says he didn't see or hear anything. I'll have him packed up and off the train before we get to the capital."

"You don't get a say in that, Green-Eye," Jeyne said firmly. She laid a hand on his arm. "He was doing his job, trying to protect her. How was he supposed to know she'd try to slip away?"

"Wait—you mean she ran off?" Piper was stunned. "I thought . . . But surely Doloman took her. It had to be him!"

"It wasn't," Trimble said. "She must have gotten off the train at our last stop." He handed Piper a folded piece of paper. Piper took it, unfolded it, and stared at the page blankly for a moment. It looked like Anna had torn the paper from one of her encyclopedias. She'd scrawled a note in the margin. She must have been in an awful hurry. Piper could barely read the handwriting, but she recognized that it was addressed to her.

> *Piper,*
> *Don't be angry. You will be anyway, I know, but try not to throw things. By the time you read this, I will have caught an express train to Noveen to find Doloman. I'm pretty sure he lives in the big house on the hill, the one in Raenoll's vision. I know you say that's where my family is, but I don't think so.*
> *I remembered some more things while I was asleep this time. Not everything, but I know what I am. I'm sure Doloman won't hurt me, but I can't be sure he*

won't hurt you, Gee, or the others. That's why I have to do this alone. Maybe the way to get Doloman to stop chasing us is to stop running. Until we do, we won't ever be free. And maybe if I find out what he wants, I can give it to him and somehow make him leave us alone.

I hope this will make things better, but if I'm wrong, I hope you won't be angry with me. I don't have that many memories, but the ones I have of you are the most important. I'll come back as soon as I can.

Anna

For a long time, Piper didn't say anything. She was aware of Gee and the others watching her, but she didn't pay them any attention, she just clutched the paper and read it over again, hoping that if she read it enough times, the words might start to make sense. Outwardly, she was calm, but inside her head, she was screaming. Fear and panic clawed at her like a wild animal.

Why did they all leave? The thought drifted up out of the storm raging inside her. Her father had gone off to the factory, Micah had run off into the scrap fields, and now Anna had abandoned her too. Why did they all leave to do monumentally stupid things? Didn't they know that they weren't helping her by leaving her behind?

"Piper." Gee's voice broke through her thoughts.

"We'll get to the capital as soon as we can. With luck we'll catch her in the city before Doloman finds her."

Gee's voice was flat. Piper knew he was just trying to make her feel better—Anna had been gone too long. An express train would have her in Noveen and at Doloman's doorstep long before the 401 got near the city.

Burying her face in her hands, Piper took a shuddering breath. No, she couldn't lose control now. She needed to think. If she was going to rescue Anna, she would have to be ready to face Doloman.

Piper looked up and met Gee's tense expression. Her gaze swept his overalls, bare feet, and tangled hair. Looking at him now, at the soot smudge on his face, no one would ever guess what he was. A chamelin, so powerful, fierce, and beautiful. No one would ever guess he had wings under his skin.

Just like no one would ever guess that Anna had machine parts under hers, or that Piper had magic in her hands that only machines could feel. It made Piper realize how little she really knew about her world and the people who inhabited it.

But maybe Doloman was just as ignorant about certain things. An idea started to take shape in Piper's mind, a vague notion that became clearer minute by minute. "I have to go to the house," she said, "the one on top of the hill. That's where Raenoll's vision ended. That's where Anna said she's going."

"Doloman will never let you get close," Jeyne said. "Once he's got Anna, he won't risk letting her go again."

"I have to try," Piper said. "If I go alone, maybe he'll let me in." She saw Gee stiffen. He opened his mouth to speak, but Piper headed him off. "Don't you see? He has to be curious, wondering how a scrapper managed to revive Anna when everything he tried failed. He doesn't know what I can do. If I offer to show him my magic, it would at least keep me alive long enough to get to her."

"That's crazy." Jeyne shook her head. "The last thing you want to do is tell the king's chief machinist what kind of power you have. Bad enough he knows what Anna is. Goddess knows what he would try to do with the two of you together."

"I'm not going to give Doloman anything," Piper said. "I'm going to rescue Anna. Like I said"—she glanced at Gee as she spoke—"he doesn't know what I can do. The raiders didn't either. That's our advantage."

Gee met Piper's gaze. The two of them stared at each other for a long time as a quiet understanding flickered in Gee's eyes and his expression softened. Slowly, he nodded. "The key will be to take him by surprise," he said. "We'll only get one chance."

"Then we're going to have to make sure we come up with an amazing plan," Piper said.

•

TWENTY

Just as Piper had imagined a hundred different ways in which she might burn down King Aron's factory, she had, since she started the journey with Anna, imagined at least a hundred different ways she might arrive in the capital. The 401 steaming into town, its shrill whistle a herald of Piper's presence—*Look here*, the whistle proclaimed, *here's someone new in town, and are you ready for her?*

Those times when she'd really let her imagination run wild, she'd pictured herself striding into Anna's house, pushing her way past guards and servants to announce to the grieving parents within that she'd brought their lost daughter home to them. Then the grateful parents would fall all over themselves to hug Piper and shake her hand, offering her anything and everything they owned as a reward for returning their precious daughter.

At more subdued moments, she'd just hoped the guards and servants wouldn't throw her out on her backside before she could explain herself.

Recently, she'd been hoping and hoping that inside the house on the hill they'd find someone who cared about Anna and would have the power to keep her safe.

None of those daydreams was going to come true.

When Piper arrived in Noveen, she wasn't even on the 401. Gee flew her away before the train reached the city outskirts in case Doloman had assigned guards to stop the train. Her first glimpse of the capital was from the edge of the ocean, looking up at the city that perched on a cliff.

In the distance, she heard the 401's whistle as it pulled into the city. The sound had a mournful note to it, as if the big old engine were wishing them to be safe, or maybe that was just Piper's imagination acting up because she was scared.

The city view distracted her. Noveen was bigger than Piper had ever dreamed. Redbrick and cream-colored stone houses covered the base of the cliff. Situated next to them were the factories. They grew out of the lower part of the city like a black, oozing sore, and the smoke spread even farther, carried on the wind to twine around the houses and cast a pall over dozens of neighborhoods. Gradually, as the land sloped upward, the smoke thinned and disappeared altogether. The royal palace with its fortified stone walls occupied the city center, and everything else had grown up around it, the buildings and streets taking root on the cliff like a thick blanket of multicolored moss. The houses, Piper noticed, also got bigger and newer farther up the cliff. It wasn't hard to guess where the house she'd seen in Rae-noll's vision would be—right at the peak, with the best view of the ocean.

The cliff itself fascinated Piper almost as much as the factories repelled her. Some industrious souls had tunneled passages up and down the rock face, and Piper could see lights and movement coming from within.

Gee saw where she was looking and pointed. "Those tunnels come out at different points in the city," he explained. "They're all sarnun homes."

Of course, Piper thought. Underground homes just like in Tevshal, but here the view was so much better. The sarnuns could step to the mouths of the caves and smell the salt water, just soak it up with their feelers. The briny scent tickled Piper's nose. She'd never smelled anything quite like the ocean. The movement of the water and her boots sinking in the sand combined to put her off balance, but she didn't mind the sensation. Under different circumstances, she thought she could sit for hours staring at the blue expanse that stretched to the horizon. She felt peaceful listening to the waves crashing against the shore.

"We should go," Piper said, turning away from the view. "Anna's waiting for us."

"You'll know the house when you see it?" Gee asked.

"I'll know," Piper said.

Gee stepped away until he was standing up to his ankles in the water. Piper watched his shadow lengthen and widen, the wings unfold from his back. She turned and looked up at him as the tips of his wings temporarily blocked the sun. He leaned toward her and stretched out his clawed hands to lift her into his arms. Not long ago, Piper had been frightened at the thought of what those claws could do, but now she felt comforted by Gee's arms around her.

They took off. The ocean swirled away beneath Piper's feet. The colors of the distant city got brighter, the buildings taller. Gee beat his wings, and Piper clutched his granite shoulders as the cliff face rushed past. They cleared it and soared high above the city. The houses slipped by beneath them so fast, Piper had trouble making out many details, but she knew what she was looking for: columns around the entrance, fountain, opulent gardens. And she hoped they would find it fast. Every minute they were in the air was a chance Gee would be seen by someone on the ground.

"There!" she cried excitedly after Gee had circled the city once. "The gardens—see them? That's the house. Try to land in those trees over there."

Gee inclined his head and dove until they were gliding between trees in what appeared to be a small park nestled amid the houses in a private neighborhood.

They touched down near a small pond hidden from the main street. Gee set Piper down and crouched beside the drooping pika branches.

Piper lifted her silver watch and checked the time. "I think an hour ought to do it," she said. "Don't try to come onto the grounds until you see my signal. Stay near the cliffs." Gee inclined his head again and reached out to touch her shoulder. Piper laid her hand over his claw, squeezed, and smiled. "Let's see how much trouble I can get into."

The mansion was some distance away from where they'd landed. Piper set out along the wide cobblestone avenue, forcing herself to walk at a leisurely pace, when all she really wanted to do was run full out up to the mansion's front gate.

Doloman's house was bigger than Raenoll's vision had suggested. The manicured lawns and carefully sculpted gardens enclosed the lower stories, and the upper windows facing the ocean ran from floor to ceiling. As Piper neared, she saw that an imposing wrought-iron fence enclosed the whole property, complete with a guarded gate. Only one man on watch, Piper noticed. That was unexpected—and suspicious.

She walked up to the gate, where the guard stood, and she noticed that he carried a revolver at his belt. "Can I help you, miss?" he asked.

Piper was careful to keep her expression serious. "Yes. I have an appointment to see Master Doloman," she announced irritably—as if it was ridiculous that she'd already been kept waiting half a minute.

"I'm sorry, miss, but if you did, that appointment's been canceled," the guard said. "Master Doloman left strict orders that he wasn't to be disturbed today."

"Oh, really?" Piper had to struggle to stay calm—this *was* Doloman's house. She put her hands on her hips and prayed the guard couldn't see how she trembled. "I guess it's pretty important if he thinks he can ignore an appointment with someone who has the mark of the Dragonfly." She pulled up her sleeve to give the guard a brief glimpse of the dragonfly tattoo on her left arm before quickly covering it. She had to admit, Trimble had done a fantastic job on the fake, but it was still a fake— one the guard would be able to spot if he demanded a closer look. Piper hoped he wouldn't.

"Look, I'm sorry, but I have my orders. Master Doloman is entertaining a very important guest today."

"An important guest?" Piper's heart sped up. The guard had to be talking about Anna—she was *here*. She pressed her lips together and nodded solemnly. "Well, then I suppose you're going to have to give Master Doloman my message," she said. Piper reached into her pocket and pulled out a tightly rolled piece of paper tied with a ribbon. "I'll need you to read it back to me so that I can be sure you understand the message correctly."

Obediently, the guard removed the ribbon and unrolled the piece of paper. It was blank and covered with a fine film of green dust. Before the guard could react, Piper took a step back, drew a deep breath, and blew out as hard as she could.

The dust hit the guard in the face. He sneezed wildly, waving his hands in front of his nose, but it was too late. His eyes glazed over, and his arms dropped to his sides. The paper drifted to the ground.

Piper felt sick to her stomach at what she'd just done. "I'm really sorry about this," she said. She reached through the wrought-iron bars and unlatched the gate. The guard watched her pass with a blank expression. "All right, now you and I are going to walk up to the house."

Piper put her hand through the guard's arm and towed him across the lawn. She kept a smile plastered on her face and pretended to chat with him. She felt silly as she told him how lovely the gardens were with the flowers blooming.

Trimble had told her the slaver's dust would be strong, but even having seen its effects on Doloman, Piper was shocked at how completely helpless it made the guard. She hoped it would wear off soon. "I'm sorry," she whispered again, knowing the man wouldn't remember her words later but needing to say it just the same. "But I have to get inside. It's a matter of life and death."

As they made their way slowly across the lawn, Piper noticed a small door on the side of the house, half hidden behind a trellis of climbing roses. It might be a servants' entrance, she thought. If so, that was probably her best way in, or the way that was least likely to get her noticed.

Piper slipped the guard's revolver off his belt and held it awkwardly at her side. She knew how to shoot a gun—she'd practiced a little with her dad's old rifle—but maybe just pointing it would be enough to get her past any more obstacles that presented themselves.

When they reached the door, she positioned the guard on the opposite side of it, facing the lawn. With any luck, she'd have a few minutes' head start before someone noticed he wasn't where he was supposed to be.

Gently, she tried the door and found it unlocked. Again, a tremor of suspicion gripped Piper. This was too easy. Doloman should have had everyone on alert for a break-in. And why weren't there more guards?

It doesn't matter, Piper told herself. *Even if it's a trap. As long as it gets me to Anna.*

She slipped inside and found herself in the middle of a narrow hallway running the length of the rear of the house. Now all she had to do was find her friend. She stood quietly, listening for signs of other people in the house. A house this size probably had several servants. She turned left and moved slowly along the hall.

A few feet ahead of her was an open doorway, and she heard faint voices and the clank of pots and pans echoing from within.

Piper froze, and her heartbeat picked up. She took a deep breath to calm herself. Probably the kitchen, she thought. Since she wasn't eager to try to cross in front of the open doorway unseen, she decided to turn back and go right. Keeping close to the wall, she crept along the length of the hall in the opposite direction, hoping as she went that a servant didn't decide to pop his head out of the kitchen and see her.

Thankfully, she made it to the end of the hall without encountering anyone. There, Piper found another door that was also unlocked. She eased it open and found herself in a larger hallway adjacent to the main foyer. There was no one in sight.

Quickly, Piper crossed the foyer, passing beneath a huge crystal chandelier, to the base of a grand winding staircase. Sunlight streamed in through the upper windows, pooling on the white marble floor. She started up the stairs, past three portraits of aging men, some of them with black beards similar to the machinist's.

At the top of the stairs, a hallway curved off to either side. Before she could decide which direction to take, movement from the far end of the left hall caught Piper's attention. She crouched down by the stair rail as a woman came out of one of the rooms, followed closely by a man. They were dressed in identical gray slacks and white shirts with work aprons tied around their waists. The woman was agitated, gesturing sharply with her hands. Piper shrank lower as they came near.

"If he doesn't want to come out, that's his business, but the least he could do is offer his guest some refreshment. It's just good manners is all I'm saying." The man replied in a low voice Piper couldn't hear, and the woman sniffed. "Yes, I left the tray outside the door for him, but if he comes for it in an hour, the tea will be cold and the biscuits hard. What good is it then?"

The woman kept talking as the pair passed Piper's hiding place, oblivious to her crouched against the rail, and continued down the opposite hall. Piper waited until they were far enough away, then darted down the left hall and slipped through the door they'd come through.

To her surprise, she found herself in another passage—very small, almost a closet, with two doors situated adjacent to the hall door. A silver tray rested in front of the door on the right.

Piper stepped over the tray of goodies. The revolver held carefully in one hand, she laid her other hand on the doorknob. For a moment, Piper felt a surge of fear at what she might find behind the door. But before she had time to let any doubts creep in, she gripped the knob and turned it.

The room beyond was lit by sunlight streaming in through the ocean-view windows. A crimson and mahogany rug covered the floor, and between the broad windows was a white marble fireplace. A bronze statue—an elephant fighting a dravisht raptor—stood at one end of the mantel, a clock at the other. In the center of the timepiece was a painting of a mechanical dragonfly.

Piper had expected some kind of lab—a metal room with examining tables, vials of chemicals, vats of strange mixtures bubbling over a fire—but not this . . . sitting room? Her gaze took in a large desk against the right-hand wall. A sofa covered in gold and crimson brocade stood opposite it near the fireplace.

Lying on the sofa, covered to her chin by a red wool blanket, was Anna. And she appeared to be asleep. Time seemed to stop, and for a second Piper couldn't move; she just stood frozen in the doorway. Then a door behind the desk opened with a soft creaking sound. Piper hadn't noticed the door on her first sweeping glance of the room. She tensed, clutching the revolver, as Doloman stepped through.

He carried a stack of papers, which he laid on the desk. He stopped in the middle of arranging them and slowly raised his head to look at Piper.

"Well, hello, little scrapper," Doloman said.

⇒ TWENTY-ONE ⇐

J eyne stood in the engine room of the 401, letting her
metal fingers trace the words written on the piece of
paper the guard had given her. The king's guards had
boarded the train almost as soon as they'd pulled into
the station—not that Jeyne was surprised. She said as
much to the man in charge.

"What does surprise me," she went on as she scanned
the paper, "is that I'm not seeing King Aron's signature
on this request."

The guard's face reddened. "With respect, ma'am,
this isn't a request. The chief machinist orders you to
turn over the girl who accompanied Miss Anna on her
journey to the capital."

"Well, that's where we disagree, sir," Jeyne said. "My
'orders' as regards this train come from King Aron.
Notes from his chief lackey are 'requests' as far as I'm

concerned. I'm not obliged to hand over anything to you."

Jeyne knew she should just tell the guard that Piper wasn't on the 401, but she didn't like the way he and the others had stormed onto the train as if they owned it, bossing her and everyone else around. She was still in charge here, until the king himself told her differently.

"You're defying the Dragonfly's own advisor," the guard sputtered. "I could haul your entire crew off this train and—"

"Yes, that would be a brilliant plan." Trimble spoke up, arms crossed, near the engine. "Leave the train and its cargo unattended and put our whole operation off schedule for who knows how long. I'm sure you'll have a lovely time explaining to King Aron how the huge loss of revenue and time was worth it just to catch one little girl."

"Where is your security chief?" the guard said. "I want him with me personally while we search every inch of this train."

"Oh, he's under the weather at the moment," Jeyne said, assuming a fake tone of regret. "But I'll open up the train to you and the rest of your guards. Search for the girl all you want, but she's not here. I won't have you disturbing the cargo or the other passengers, and you'd better be finished by the time we're ready to pull out."

She handed the man back the message signed by Doloman, but the guard ignored it. He spun on his heel and stormed out, pausing at the door to sneer at Jeyne. "King Aron will hear about this, and then we'll see what happens to this run-down metal shrieker."

With great effort, Jeyne tamped down her anger and kept her face expressionless as she nodded. "Give my regards to the king, then."

When the guard had gone, Trimble took a vial of black powder off his belt and held it in his hands. "Call the 401 a shrieker? You know, I could rig up a couple of my experiments, show him a few surprises from the old girl. How about it, Jeyne?"

Jeyne sighed. "I appreciate the sentiment, but we've got to lie low for now," she said. "The more time we can give Piper and Gee, the better."

"It's no fun sitting around here waiting for something to happen," Trimble muttered. He turned to check the pressure gauges. "I wish I could be there when Piper tries out my mixture. It's going to be fantastic."

"And probably land us all in prison," Jeyne reminded him. She glanced out the window of the engine cab to make sure the guards weren't harassing any of the passengers disembarking from the train.

"True, but if you're going to lose your job and your freedom all at once, you might as well do it with some style," Trimble said. "Besides, maybe old Aron will take pity on us poor railroad folk."

"That's an interesting thought, fireman," Jeyne said thoughtfully, turning to look at him. "I've wondered for a long time now what the king would think of all this business. We've heard a lot of noise from Doloman over Anna. Why haven't we heard anything from the boss yet?"

Trimble's eyes went wide. "You think Doloman's kept Anna a secret from him?" he asked. "Why would he do that?"

Jeyne shrugged. "All I know for sure is she's better off away from both of them."

"Then let's hope Piper and Gee make it to her in time," Trimble said.

Piper raised the revolver. Doloman stood behind his desk as Piper pointed the gun at him with shaking hands. "What did you do to her?" Piper demanded. Anna was so still it was hard to tell if she was even breathing. "Tell me what you did!"

"I believe you'll find that Anna's condition is *your* doing," Doloman said calmly, "not mine."

Piper's face went hot with rage. "You're a liar, and you're even crazier than I thought. How could I have ever thought this place was Anna's home?"

"But it is her home." Doloman came around to the front of the desk. Piper hurried to the sofa, still pointing the gun at Doloman, putting her body between him and Anna. The machinist scowled at her. "I'm not going to hurt her, ignorant child," he snapped.

"Why won't she wake up?" The sound of their raised voices should have woken Anna by now, Piper thought. Doloman must have given her something, some kind of sedative.

"Because you were not here." Doloman clenched his fists, as if the words were difficult for him to say. He moved to the fireplace, leaning his good arm on the mantel. The other was no longer in a sling, but he obviously favored it, keeping it close against his side. "You see, I know what you are—synergist."

Piper fought to keep her expression neutral. Inwardly, she was starting to panic. *How can he know that?* she screamed to herself. To her knowledge, Doloman had never seen her use her powers.

"I've suspected for some time." He nodded to the papers on his desk. "The research I accumulated on Anna—and you, once I returned to the city—confirms these suspicions. I've encountered a handful of individuals who had magic in various forms, but your gift is exceptionally rare. Machines feed off the energy inside you and grow stronger. Your magic emanates like a beacon— even the most hopelessly broken machine will return to life at your touch." He stared at her, and Piper realized with a jolt that there was admiration in his gaze. "Your power has been a great gift to me."

Hopelessly broken machines . . . But her magic had *healed* Anna; she . . . she should be better. Piper looked down at her friend, and suddenly a horrible understanding filled her, so quickly and completely that she was dizzy with it. She clutched the revolver tighter, sweat slicking her palms. No, it couldn't be like that. It couldn't. "Anna, please wake up," she whispered.

"She can't," Doloman said. The gentleness in his voice sickened Piper. "A trader from a scrap town to the east of yours—Scrap Town Eighteen, I believe it was—brought Anna to me a little over a year ago. She was unconscious and appeared near death. At first, I thought the trader was just a common slaver when he tried to sell me the girl. I was prepared to have him arrested, but then he told me of the girl's true nature and showed me—"

"Her insides," Piper finished, realizing at that moment what had probably happened. "He cut her on the back of her neck and gave her that scar." She sank down on the edge of the sofa next to Anna. She thought if she didn't, her legs might give out. She kept the revolver close in her right hand. With her other hand, she touched Anna's shoulder, adjusting the blanket. At least Doloman had made her comfortable. "Anna said you used to hurt her because of her scar. You were trying to get at her power source, weren't you?"

"That and more," Doloman said. "She is the most advanced machine I have ever seen, with an energy source that mimics and works alongside a human heart. The technological improvements that might come from studying her—more powerful engines, new medical treatments, advanced defense systems—they're too great to count. But I encountered a problem. Essentially, her heart had been broken. It sounds morbidly poetic, I realize, but it's true. Something, some trauma, had injured her so grievously that she no longer functioned. I dared not operate on her power source directly until I understood more about her and the extent of the damage."

"So for a year, you poked and prodded at her, sticking her with needles, experimenting on her, and all the while she felt everything!" Piper said.

"I didn't know that." Doloman spun from the mantel to glare at Piper. "How could I know she was aware of what was happening to her? I was trying to save her life!"

"And study her—but you couldn't figure out how to revive her, could you?" Piper said, not bothering to hide the scorn in her voice. "That's why you brought her back to the scrap towns, isn't it? You were looking for the trader who sold her to you. You wanted to find out what he knew about Anna—where she came from."

"Very good," Doloman said. "The trader was cagey when I first asked him where he had acquired Anna. I suspect he pulled her from the scrap fields with the other bits of broken machines."

"Wait a minute. You think she came in a meteor shower?" Piper scoffed. "I've seen those meteors hit. She would have been torn to pieces."

"You don't know everything about the meteor storms," Doloman said, waving an impatient hand. "Based on my research into the phenomenon, when objects come through to our world, they are initially protected by a dense shielding substance, which starts to dissolve as the object enters our atmosphere, forming—"

"The dust," Piper said, making the connection. "The shielding is poisonous, and it changes into the dust as it dissolves."

"Yes, but occasionally, the shielding remains intact until impact, protecting the object and bringing it into our world safe and whole," Doloman said. "I believe this is what happened to Anna, how the trader found her. But I needed to know for certain, to make sure the trader didn't know any more than he claimed, so I bought passage for us on the caravan, pushed the drivers through the days and nights and countless scrap towns. I had to find that trader. I was so close." He looked at Anna with a wistful expression. Then his features hardened. "He was always one step ahead of us, leaving the scrap towns before we arrived, almost as if he knew I was coming. I thought I could head him off by cutting through the scrap fields, but the storm came up too quickly, too violently." He glanced up at Piper, a speculative light in his eyes. "Perhaps it was the goddess's will. She led Anna to you, and you revived her with your powers. But in the end, she is too broken. She can't live unless she has you near her." Doloman paused to look at Piper closely. "You understand. I can see it in your eyes."

Piper's hand involuntarily went to the watch around her neck, clutching it protectively. The watch refused to work for anyone else because it was too broken. It functioned only when it was near Piper, exposed to her magic. Anna was the same. Piper thought she'd healed her, but it was only temporary. Hadn't Raenoll told her that Anna was too fragile, that she would die if Piper abandoned her?

It owes you its existence. The seer's words echoed in her head. But she'd been talking about the pocket watch—an object! Not a person. Goddess, how could this be?

"So, if you knew all that . . . you wanted me here," Piper said. She'd been right, she realized. She hadn't tricked anyone to get inside that house. Doloman had let her walk right in.

"Don't you see what an opportunity lies in front of you?" Doloman asked. He took a step toward the sofa. Piper raised the revolver automatically, but Doloman acted as if it weren't there. "The two of you will become my adopted daughters. And in exchange for your coop- eration with my research, I can reward you beyond your wildest dreams."

"My cooperation?" Piper echoed. She couldn't be- lieve what she was hearing. "You mean you want me to be some kind of power source you keep around for Anna."

"You're just a child," Doloman said. "You couldn't possibly understand what's at stake, what a discovery like Anna means for the Dragonfly territories."

"But she's a person, not a steamboat or an

airship," Piper said. "I thought that's what the king's interested in."

"True enough," Doloman said grimly. "Aron would depart for the uncharted lands in his machines, leaving his people to wallow in the factory smoke. However, there are other leaders, stronger men and women, who could unite Dragonfly with the Merrow Kingdom. All they need is an army and sufficient resources."

Piper stared at Doloman, stunned, as his words sank in. "An army? You mean . . ." Of course. She was stupid not to have realized it sooner. "You don't work for Aron, you're working for the Merrow Kingdom." Piper looked from Anna's face to the revolver, the length of its iron barrel. "You want to build your own set of weapons and war machines with what you learn by studying Anna and her power source, an arsenal for Merrow to use to take over. You just need to get hold of the iron trade down here to help you do it."

"That plan is already in motion," Doloman said, "but only for our short-term goals. If I can discover the secret of *organic* machines, there'll no longer be a need to strip-mine vast quantities of iron for weapons or ship hulls. You must see how many lives this will save. Solace will be united under one power instead of two squabbling nations trying to hoard resources from each other. Scrappers like you, starving in the wilderness, will have a place again, and not just in Aron's factories. We'll reseed the land and abandon these fruitless plans for exploration. All balances will be restored." Doloman spoke almost to himself now, but he continued to stare at Anna in a kind of dazed rapture. "Anna is the key to everything."

Of course she is, Piper thought. It was clear now. Raenoll's prediction, the reward Piper hoped she would get for returning Anna to Noveen. Doloman would take Piper and Anna into his care, make them the richest two girls in Solace, and provide for their every need while he studied Anna. On top of everything, he'd have a synergist around to make sure his war machines were in the best shape possible for Merrow to take over the world.

Piper stood speechless as Doloman regarded her expectantly. *He thinks I'm going to take his offer,* Piper realized. And why wouldn't he? Doloman had just offered her everything she'd ever wanted and more. She would never be poor again, never have to worry about where her next meal was coming from or how hard the winter was going to be. And he planned to unite the two kingdoms, meaning the Dragonfly territories and the Merrow Kingdom would never again be in conflict over land or resources. If that happened, maybe they would start to look after the people again and save them from starving in the scrap towns.

Maybe no more fathers would have to die in factories breathing deadly smoke.

Piper's chest tightened as she thought of her dad. What would he say to Doloman's plan? She wished more than anything that he were with her right now. That he could tell her the right thing to do. But he was gone, and Piper had to decide not just for herself but for Anna and everyone else too.

Piper looked down at her friend, Doloman's promises echoing in her head. Would Anna truly be safe and happy in the new life he was offering them? She'd never go hungry, Piper told herself, and she'd have a home, just as Piper had wanted for her. They'd also never be separated. But was that enough? What would happen after the Merrow Kingdom finally took over? Would they be as kind and generous to the people of the Dragonfly territories as Doloman claimed, reseeding the land and dividing resources fairly? Or would they take the iron and use it to make more guns and war machines, ignoring the people starving in the scrap towns, as they had been doing already?

Neither one of them deserves to have all the power, Piper realized. Both Aron and the Merrow Kingdom had wronged their people, and no matter how rosy a picture Doloman painted of Merrow's intention, Piper didn't trust them. And she knew beyond anything that she could never trust Doloman—not after everything he'd done.

Piper looked at Doloman and slowly shook her head. "No," she said.

A muscle in Doloman's jaw tightened. "Excuse me?"

"It's a good offer for a scrapper, but the thing

is—I don't believe the world will be like you say it will. Besides that, I don't like your price." Doloman opened his mouth to speak, but Piper rushed on before he could interrupt her. "You didn't mention that part—this new world you want to create costs us our freedom. You'd put us in a cage. It'll be a soft, pretty cage, I'm sure, but there'll still be needles for Anna, and pain." Anger burned in her chest, and she tightened her grip on the revolver. "Won't there?"

Doloman raised his hands in an appeasing gesture. "Only until I learn more. The experiments, the pain, are temporary."

Piper ignored him. "And what if in the end you find out that the only way to do the research you need is to take her apart piece by piece? Would you sacrifice Anna for your new world?" She stared him down, waiting while he opened his mouth and closed it again. For a long time, he didn't answer.

Finally, his expression hardened. "If it became necessary, yes," he said.

"That's what I thought," Piper said. She leaned down and touched Anna's cheek. The girl sighed in her sleep. Her eyelids fluttered, and suddenly she was staring up at Piper dazedly. In the silence, Piper heard Doloman's excited gasp.

"Oh," Anna said, rubbing her eyes. "Hello, Piper. I heard your voice, but I thought I must have been dreaming this time. You got here so fast."

"As fast as I could," Piper said, smiling at her. "You know you're in trouble, don't you? So much trouble, I can't even begin to describe the tonnage of it."

Anna smiled back. "I'm happy to see you."

"If you're up to it, you'd better try to stand," Piper said, looking up at Doloman. "We're leaving soon."

"You fool!" Doloman roared. "Why make this harder on yourselves? Any life you want, I can give it to you. You'll be safe, secure, fed, and happy. What more could someone like you ask for?"

"Someone like me," Piper echoed, fury making her tremble. "My father wanted to give me all those things you named. That's why he went to work in the factory and let the black smoke eat away at his lungs. You say your world would be better than Aron's, but I don't think either the Merrow Kingdom or the Dragonfly territories care enough about their people to rule the world, and the price for what you're offering us is too high. In the end, it'll kill us."

"What about you, Anna?" Doloman asked. He watched as Piper helped Anna to sit up on the sofa. Every movement she made, his eyes tracked her with the same wonder and intensity Piper had seen that first night in her house. "I took care of you when you were hurt. I put the mark of the Dragonfly on you for your protection. I only wanted the best for you. You are like a daughter to me."

Anna flinched at the word "daughter" and leaned

in closer to Piper. "I know what you were trying to do, and I guess I should thank you for protecting me," Anna said. "But you've never felt like my family. Piper feels like home to me. I want to go where she goes."

Anna had no idea how important that was, Piper thought. If being away from Piper for the two days it had taken the 401 to reach the capital had caused her to fall unconscious, they really did have to stick together from here on out.

Piper helped Anna stand. She was unsteady on her feet, which would slow them down, but they were running out of time. Piper knew Doloman's patience was almost gone. She nudged Anna behind her, and as she did so, she slipped a small tubular object into Anna's trouser pocket. Anna squeezed her arm to let Piper know she felt it.

Piper faced Doloman. "Let us go," she said. "If you try to keep us here, eventually Aron's going to find out what you're up to." Her eyes narrowed. "One of us will make sure of that."

Doloman laughed, a sharp, ugly bark that echoed in the quiet room. "You think you can threaten me? You're not leaving this room."

Behind her, Anna trembled. "Piper," she pleaded.

"It's all right," Piper said. "He's just trying to scare us. Anyway, don't you have something you want to give your 'father'?"

"Enough," Doloman growled. "Guard!"

"Anna, get back!" Piper raised the revolver, but Doloman slapped it out of her hand and sent it skittering across the floor under the desk. She tried to dodge as he lunged at her, but he was too fast. He backhanded her across the face. Pain exploded in her cheek and jaw, and she staggered and fell, tasting blood in her mouth as she hit the floor.

"Don't hurt her!" Anna shouted. She reached into her pocket and pulled out the slender glass vial Piper had slipped there. Before Doloman could react, she smashed it on the floor at his feet.

Piper dove aside as tongues of blue flame leaped from the shattered vial, burning through Doloman's trousers and suit coat. The machinist shrieked, slapping at his clothing to try to put the fire out. Sparks flew to the desk, catching the papers stacked there and setting them ablaze.

Piper ran to the mantel and grabbed the bronze statue of the elephant and raptor. The metal was slick in her sweaty palms. She reared back and hurled the statue at one of the enormous windows. With a crash, the bronze block tore through the glass, and a shower of glittering shards rained down on the floor and the balcony beyond the window.

"Come on!" Piper yelled at Anna.

Anna ran to Piper and grabbed her hand. "Where are we going?" she asked as Piper pulled her through the broken window and out to the narrow balcony. "The prey should never back itself into a corner. Logically, we should have run for the door to the hall."

"We haven't done anything logical on this trip. Why start now?" Piper squinted at the horizon, the dazzling sunlight glinting off the ocean. She waved her arms frantically. For a heart-stopping moment, she saw nothing. Then a speck of movement caught her eye—a figure gliding over the water toward them. "When I tell you to, jump!"

"What?" Anna clutched Piper's arm, digging her fingernails into Piper's skin. "That's . . . that's . . ."

"Trust me." Piper glanced back inside the house. Doloman had put the flames out and was scrambling up from the floor. Trimble's chemical cocktail hadn't been as potent as she'd hoped. It was now or never. "Jump!" she screamed.

Piper didn't really expect Anna to jump. She had her hand at Anna's back, prepared to give her a shove, so she was surprised when Anna launched herself off the balcony.

Piper watched as Anna fell toward the gliding figure. Gee soared up and snatched Anna out of the air, holding her tightly against his chest. Then he flew away toward the gardens and the stone fountain on the lawn. Piper counted the seconds in her head. Gee had warned her to give him at least a twenty count before she jumped.

At thirteen, Piper felt a hand close on her upper arm. She screamed as Doloman yanked her back into the room and threw her to the floor. She caught herself on her hands and rolled, ending up on her back, sprawled in front of the machinist.

Doloman had retrieved the revolver from beneath the desk, and he crouched over her, pointing it at her. A crazed light shone in his eyes. "The worst part is that I can't kill you," he said. "Not if it will endanger her. But I can hurt you. And I assure you, I will do that happily."

At that moment, the hall door burst open, and a pair of guards came rushing into the room. "Sir, King Aron's guards are at the gates. They're demanding you come to the palace at once—"

"Don't let them up here!" Doloman screamed. His face drained of color but for twin splotches of red on his cheeks. He swung the revolver around and pointed it at the closest guard. "Get out! Get out!"

The guards backed out of the room, their hands in the air, shocked expressions on their faces. Piper heard raised voices coming from somewhere downstairs. "You're the one who's backed into a corner now," she said. "How are you going to explain all this to the king?"

Before Doloman could reply, movement flashed across the shattered window. Hope surged within Piper as Gee landed on the edge of the balcony. As she watched, he ripped away what was left of the window frame with his clawed hands. He tried to force his way in through the opening, but his body was still too big to fit through it in his beast form. He snarled at Doloman, but the voices coming from downstairs had distracted the machinist. He stood frozen, unsure.

Piper seized the moment. She scrambled to her feet and took off running toward the window. Out of the corner of her eye, she saw Doloman spin and raise the revolver. Panic clawed at her insides. Piper stopped and turned, trying to focus her power on the gun, willing it to explode just as the slaver's gun had, but Doloman was too fast.

"Gee, watch out!"

The crack of the gunshot drowned out Piper's scream. Terror overcame her as she braced for the pain, but none came. The bullet struck the far wall just above her head, raising a puff of plaster dust. Doloman fired again, but this time Piper heard only a click. No more bullets.

Piper didn't waste a second. She scrambled to the window, but just as she threw one leg out, Doloman slammed into her back, knocking her off balance. Piper yelped as the breath whooshed out of her body, and Doloman drove them both through the broken window onto the balcony.

Piper had a brief, dizzying view of the sky and the gardens below, and for a terrifying second she thought she was going to fall. Then it seemed as if a wall rose up in front of her, and Gee was there, catching her against his chest. Piper's knees went weak with relief as she wrapped her arms around his shoulders.

Gee's weight steadied her and kept them all from

plunging off the balcony, but they were nowhere near safe yet. Piper stood in a pile of broken glass, Doloman so close she could feel his breath on her neck. Gee pulled her securely against him, and Piper felt him trying to push off the ledge with his feet. All they had to do was get airborne and they'd be free, Piper thought as she struggled to hold on to Gee.

Suddenly, Piper's head wrenched back, a fire spreading across her scalp as Doloman grabbed her by the hair. She screamed as he pulled her back inside through the window. Panic swept through her. She was slipping from Gee's grasp.

A loud crash sounded from the far end of the room, as if the door had been ripped off its hinges. Footsteps pounded across the floor, and Piper felt Doloman's grip on her hair loosen. She turned to see what the commotion was.

Her mouth fell open. Armed guards filled the room—there had to be at least a dozen of them—and they weren't dressed like Doloman's guards. These men and women wore green and gold livery, just like the colors of Anna's tattoo.

One of the guards stepped forward. "Master Doloman," he said, "I am here to place you and your household under arrest on suspicion of treason. You will surrender yourselves and accompany us to the palace for questioning."

Treason, Piper echoed silently, her thoughts whirling.

Did that mean the king had somehow discovered Doloman's plan to conspire with the Merrow Kingdom?

Doloman let go of Piper and turned to face the guards. Outwardly, he appeared unafraid, but Piper saw that his hands, held slackly at his sides, trembled ever so slightly. "What is this nonsense?" he shouted. "As the king's advisor, I demand you leave my property at once! I bear the mark of the Dragonfly—I am beyond your authority!"

"It was the king himself who commanded that we take you," said the guard. "If you surrender yourself without violence, we will not put you in chains."

Doloman was visibly trembling now. "How dare you!" he cried.

Piper felt Gee tugging at her arm insistently, and her heart pounded as she surveyed the room. Most of the guards had fixed their eyes on Doloman, but several were watching her.

She wouldn't get out the window. Gee was a different story. The guards' view of him was blocked, but as soon as either of them moved, the guards would see him and he'd be caught. Piper couldn't let that happen. She cared about her friend too much to let him be arrested.

"Go," she whispered to Gee, keeping her eyes on the guards, "before they see you." Piper wasn't surprised to hear Gee's soft growl of protest. He wouldn't leave her. Tears pricked her eyes as she reached behind her out the window and gently pushed his chest. "Please, Gee. I'll be all right. Get back to the 401 and come up with a new plan."

The guards started to surround Doloman. Piper felt a surge of panic and pushed harder against Gee's chest. "Go," she hissed quietly.

Gee growled again, and Piper thought he wasn't going to listen to her. Her heart sank, but then suddenly, she felt a rush of wind at the back of her neck as Gee spread his wings and jumped off the balcony into the air. She closed her eyes as a mixture of relief and fear washed over her. Gee was safe, but she wasn't. In only a moment, the guards were pulling her away from the window. They didn't put chains on her, but their grip on her arms was rough and unbreakable. Piper stared at the floor as they led her and Doloman out of the room. It was going to take the best plan in the world to get her out of this mess.

≈ TWENTY-TWO ≈

Things were worse than Piper had thought.

The guards marched her back through the house, down the stairs, and out the front door to where several carriages waited. Standing there on the drive was another guard, holding Anna by the arm.

Piper felt as if someone had knocked the wind out of her. She'd hoped that Anna had gotten away, but the king's guards must have found her in the gardens. The plan had been for Gee to leave Anna hiding near the fountain while he came back for Piper, and then they would all escape together.

But nothing had happened like she'd planned, Piper thought sadly. And now they were going to the palace—the last place in the world she'd ever expected or wanted to be.

The guards put the girls in one of the carriages, and

Anna sat down next to Piper, immediately taking her hand. "Are you all right?" she asked.

Piper tried to come up with something reassuring to say, but she was all out of ideas, so she just squeezed Anna's hand and smiled weakly. "I'm fine," she said.

As the carriage pulled away from the house, Piper glanced out the window and saw Doloman being herded into another carriage by a pair of guards. There were iron manacles on his wrists. He must have put up a fight in the end. Seeing the wolf finally in chains made her feel a little bit safer, though not much.

She had heard the guards talking about Doloman as they led her through the house. The king's spies had intercepted messages sent by him to the royal palace in Ardra. The messages revealed that he'd been conspiring with the Merrow Kingdom for months, feeding them detailed information about the Dragonfly territories' military strength and the layout of the palace, and letting them know when iron shipments were scheduled to come from the mines so that the Merrow Kingdom could hire raiders to try to steal them.

Piper had listened closely for any mention of Anna in Doloman's list of crimes, but so far she'd heard nothing from the guards. As far as she could tell, they were confused about who the girls were, and Doloman had refused to answer when the guards questioned him about their identities. Piper wondered if that meant that even the Merrow Kingdom didn't know about Anna. If so, that was no small thing to be grateful for. It meant Doloman had been very careful about keeping her a secret.

But what would Doloman tell the king? And what would Aron do with Anna once he learned what she was? Would he be like Doloman and try to reap as much technology from her as he could? Piper shuddered at the thought. There was no use speculating right now. All Piper could do was keep quiet herself while she tried to come up with a plan.

The journey to the palace seemed to take forever as their carriage wound through the city streets. When they finally arrived, Piper expected the guards to throw them directly into a cell and lock them up, so she was surprised when they led her and Anna through the front entrance and to a small gallery off the main receiving hall. There they were told to wait for King Aron himself.

Piper tried to distract herself from her fear by examining the portraits that lined the gallery walls, pictures of past monarchs of the Dragonfly territories. A pair of glass display cases stood in the center of the room. Inside were two models. One was of a huge steamship, a steel-hulled behemoth that in real life would be bigger than any man-made craft Piper had ever seen. The other model was a sky ship. Its hull was similar in size and design to the ocean vessel, but it had huge wings that sprouted from its sides, making it look a bit like a dragonfly. These wings were bigger than the mountain ice dragon's, though, and made of silk and veined with metal like the mechanical dragonfly from Anna's tattoo. Piper had to admit they were impressive, but she still preferred the 401.

"Beautiful, aren't they?" said a voice from the doorway. "You're looking at the future of Solace right there."

A prickling sensation touched the back of Piper's neck. She and Anna turned. A man stood in the gallery doorway, tall and slender, dressed in a tailored gray suit with a gold watch fob.

King Aron was younger than Piper had expected. His hair and mustache were honey-colored, with light streaks of gray running through them. He wore spectacles, and his boots clicked on the marble floor as he approached. A sparkle at his chest caught Piper's eye. Attached to the lapel of the king's jacket was a gold dragonfly broach.

There he is, Piper thought, with an oddly detached calm. *The man who killed my father.* She clenched her jaw and forced aside the burning anger before it rose within her. She needed a clear head if she was going to get them out of this.

Anna curtseyed to the king, and Piper tried to imitate her as best she could. Nervousness made her stumble, but the king didn't seem to notice.

"I've spoken to Master Doloman," Aron said, "and he has confessed to conspiring with the Merrow Kingdom to overthrow me." The king spoke matter-of-factly, but there was an icy glint of anger in his eyes. "In exchange for his confession, I have decided to show mercy and not sentence him to death. He will, however, be imprisoned for the rest of his life. You will not see him again." The king watched them as he spoke, and now there was a hint of confusion in his blue eyes. "He was less forthcoming about who the two of you are," he said, "and what you were doing at his house."

Surprised, Piper fought to keep her expression neutral, but she felt a flutter of hope for the first time since she'd entered the palace. Doloman hadn't revealed Anna's secret. For whatever reason, he'd chosen to protect her.

Pinned by the king's icy gaze, Piper swallowed and scrambled to decide what she should say. She decided to keep things simple. "Anna and I are part of the 401's crew," she said, glancing quickly at her friend to make sure her sleeve was covering the dragonfly tattoo. Thankfully, it was. "We work for Jeyne Steel."

"I see," the king said. Piper couldn't guess what he might be thinking. "And how did you come to be in Master Doloman's home? My guards told me you and he were fighting like savage animals when they found you."

"That's . . . true," Piper said, trying to stall. "I was—"

"It was my fault," Anna interrupted, taking a step forward. "She was protecting me." Piper turned to look at her, trying to keep the surprise off her face. What was her friend up to? Piper begged Anna with her eyes not to tell the king the truth.

"Oh?" The king looked at Anna expectantly. "Explain, please."

"W-well," Anna stammered, "Master Doloman was traveling to Noveen on the 401, staying in the private suite. And I was in charge of cleaning it and the other passenger areas." Anna glanced at Piper as she spoke, and Piper saw in her wide eyes the fear she was trying to hide. She nodded at her friend, silently encouraging her.

"Go on," the king said, sounding impatient. He seemed to believe the story—so far.

Anna took a breath and continued. "One day while I was cleaning, I found one of Master Doloman's letters on the floor under the table. I read the letter—I know I shouldn't have. It said that he was working with the Merrow Kingdom. I was scared, and I didn't know what to do, so I showed the letter to Piper. But before we could tell anyone, Master Doloman found out. He kidnapped us and took us back to his house."

"We were trying to escape when your guards broke into the house," Piper said, finishing the story. Her heart pounded as she waited for the king's reaction. Would he believe them?

The king stroked the edges of his mustache as he gazed at the two of them in silence.

Finally, the king nodded. "It sounds like it was very

lucky for you that my guards arrived when they did," he said.

"Yes, sir, it was," Anna said, and beside her, Piper breathed a quiet sigh of relief. Unbelievably, it looked like Anna's secret was safe.

We might actually escape this mess, Piper thought.

"Sir," she said, addressing the king, "if that's all you need from us, we really should get back to the 401. They'll be missing us." Actually, Gee was probably going out of his mind right about now. Piper hoped they could escape before the chamelin mounted an assault on the palace.

"I'll need to send word to the 401, confirm your identities, but after that, yes, I believe it's fine for you to go," Aron said. "Now that that's settled, I have matters I must attend to."

With a nod, he headed for the door to the gallery. *Matters to attend to*, Piper echoed silently. *Like the Merrow Kingdom.* What would happen now that Doloman's plan had failed? Before she'd fully considered what she was doing, Piper turned and spoke to the king's retreating back. "Will there be a war?" she asked, her voice echoing through the quiet gallery. "With the Merrow Kingdom?"

The king paused and glanced back at her. "You shouldn't worry about that right now," he said. "All you need to know is that I will do whatever is necessary to protect the Dragonfly territories." He turned and walked out of the gallery without another word.

Piper watched him go, a jumble of conflicting

emotions swirling inside her. Though she believed in her heart that she had made the right decision rejecting Doloman's plan, she wondered now what the future held. Would Dragonfly and the Merrow Kingdom someday realize how much their people were suffering because of their power struggle? Would this obsession with weapons and factories and machines never end, except in war?

And how ironic, Piper couldn't help but think, that the most valuable machine in all of Solace was about to walk out King Aron's front door.

It wasn't until they were safely outside and far away from the palace that Piper finally started to relax. She was bumped and bruised, but the knots of tension that had sprung up all over her body began to loosen. As they followed the signs back to the train station, Piper turned to ask Anna if she was feeling all right now too, and caught her friend watching her surreptitiously out of the corner of her eye.

"What is it?" Piper asked, suddenly worried. "Is something wrong?"

"No," Anna said quickly. "It's just . . ." She trailed off, looking at Piper uncertainly.

"It's all right," Piper said. "Tell me."

"Well, I thought you'd be angry at me—for running off."

"Oh, that," Piper said. A wry smile tugged at her lips.

Anna nodded. "I thought there would be yelling—lots of yelling."

"I do yell sometimes," Piper agreed. Her smile broadened. "Listen, I'm just glad you're all right. I'll let you off easy this time, if you'll answer a question for me."

Now that she knew she wasn't in trouble, Anna's expression brightened. "Anything," she said.

"Why didn't you let me come with you to confront Doloman?" Piper asked, her humor fading. "If you'd told me, I would have."

"I know. I'm sorry," Anna said, ducking her head. "But once I realized that I had to face him, I thought it would be better if I went alone, because I knew he didn't want to hurt me. But you, Piper . . . I couldn't risk him hurting you. I thought if I went to him, he would help me remember the rest of my past. In exchange for whatever it was he wanted with me, I thought I could get you your reward."

"My—" Piper opened her mouth, but she couldn't find any words. Anna had gone to confront Doloman for *her* sake? It was the last thing in the world Piper had wanted. She put a hand on Anna's shoulder. "How do you even know about that?" she asked.

"I heard you talking to Gee and the others," Anna explained. "I wasn't asleep. I don't think I ever really do sleep, at least not like you do. I sort of drift in a fog, a place where there's no light and sometimes I can hear sounds but not always." She added, "I can feel pain too.

When I was with Doloman, I was in that place, that sort-of-sleeping place, but I couldn't wake up. It was so long, that time I spent in the dark. I thought I wouldn't ever wake up, not until I heard your voice, Piper."

Piper's chest ached. "You must have heard me say that I didn't care about a reward anymore."

"Yes, but you were right," Anna said. "Your plan was logical, even—I was shocked you'd come up with it."

"Thanks," Piper said dryly.

"I mean, if we're going to live on our own, we'll have to have money," Anna said. "If I couldn't get a reward, I knew we'd have to be able to earn our keep, and we couldn't do that with Doloman chasing us. You said you didn't want to be a scrapper anymore. I wanted to give you your wish. I wanted us to be together on the 401. You've done so much for me, it was the least I could do for you."

"I've got everything I need," Piper said, her heart full. "Don't worry about me." She wrapped her arms around Anna and hugged her. She didn't know what the future held, but no matter what happened, she knew she wasn't alone anymore. She'd protected her friends and found a new life for herself. Right now, that was all she needed.

"We should go," Anna said when Piper pulled away. "They'll be waiting for us on the train."

"In a minute," Piper said. "There's one more thing we need to talk about." But that "one more thing" was big, Piper thought as a knot of worry formed in her stomach. She hadn't yet told Anna what Doloman had said, about Anna being too broken to live without Piper. How would her friend react? Did she want to be so tied to Piper that she couldn't leave her for more than a day or go farther than a city away? She hoped Anna could live with that—Anna had to know the truth.

"What's wrong, Piper?" Anna asked. "You look sad all of a sudden."

"I'm fine," Piper said. Her throat tightened. "It's just there's something you have to know, about what happened when you went to see Doloman."

Anna's forehead wrinkled. "What do you mean? I remember. Guards took me to the house. The servants gave me a room and told me to wait for Doloman. Then I was back in that gray nothing-place again, the place I was in when you first found me. I still don't remember where I came from, but after I got hurt by the raider, I remembered what I am—part machine, part human." Anna held up her hands and looked at the backs, as if she saw through to the machine beneath.

"There's a reason you go to that place," Piper said, feeling tears well up in her eyes. "You were . . . hurt . . . when Doloman found you. Sometimes when people get hurt, even the best healer can't fix them." Her voice shook as she said the last part.

"Piper, don't cry," Anna pleaded, but there were tears in her eyes too. "We don't have to talk about this. Let's just go back to the train."

"Not yet," Piper insisted. "I have to tell you what Do-loman said."

"You mean that I can't live without you—that I'll stop working?" Anna sniffed and wiped her eyes. "I didn't need Doloman to tell me that. You're my sister. I don't want to leave you, Piper, not ever."

Her voice broke, and then they were hugging again, standing on the street corner, sobbing and hugging. People walking by were probably staring, but Piper didn't care.

Through her tears, Piper glanced up at the sky and saw a dark shape briefly dip out of the clouds. Gee flew high above their heads. He circled, and when he saw Piper looking, he dipped his wing. Piper nodded back, letting him know they were all right.

TWENTY-THREE

Trimble was there to meet them when they arrived at the train station.

"Thank the goddess you're both safe," he said, and grinned. "I mean, I'm glad to see you and all, but Gee was climbing the walls—literally—until he saw you coming."

Jeyne was in the engine room. Trimble brought the girls to her as soon as he'd had a chance to look at Piper's head and bandage a few cuts she'd gotten in the fight with Doloman. The engineer confirmed that one of Aron's guards had been to the train asking about the girls, and Jeyne listened as Piper related what had happened at Aron's palace. When she finished, Jeyne shook her head and grinned. Piper didn't think she'd ever seen the woman smile like that.

"Welcome to the 401," Jeyne said, touching Piper and Anna on the shoulder. The girls beamed at each other.

After they'd told their story, Jeyne sent them to eat and rest and gave them an extra day to recover before they started their new duties as members of the train's crew. Piper slept more soundly that night than she ever remembered sleeping in her life. When she woke the next morning, the train had left Noveen behind and was headed north again.

Anna was already up and wanted Piper to come to the library. "Jeyne says we're going to be paid a weekly wage since we're members of the crew," she said excitedly. "I want to buy some new books for the library."

Piper laughed. "At the rate you're reading them, that's probably a good idea. I'll meet you there. I have something I want to do first."

She left Anna happily ensconced with her books and headed back to the observation platform. She wasn't surprised to see Gee standing outside, leaning against the rail.

"It'll probably still be cold up north," Gee said when she came to stand next to him. "You'll need this."

He held her dad's coat in his hands. She'd known all along that he had it, but for some reason, she'd never asked for it back. He held it out to her, and she took the worn garment, rubbing the soft fabric against her cheek.

"We'll be making a stop at Scrap Town Sixteen again," Gee said. "It'll be a chance for you to pick up anything you left behind when you ran that night."

Piper thought about her father's drawings and letters, her tool belt, and the other supplies she'd grabbed before leaving her house. In some ways, it seemed like a long time ago. She'd taken all the things that were important to her—except one.

"There's someone I'd like to visit," Piper said. "His name is Micah. He got hurt right before I left. I have to see if he's all right."

"Micah," Gee said. "He's your friend?"

"Yes." Her heart warmed at the thought of seeing Micah again.

"I see."

Piper heard the uncertain note in Gee's voice. She turned to look at him, but he was staring off into the distance. The train was running parallel to the coast, and the sun on the crystal blue water dazzled Piper's eyes, but Gee didn't seem bothered by the intensity of the glare. She looked at Gee's hands resting on the rail. Hesitantly, she reached out and laid her hand over his.

"You know, you're stuck with me now," she said, trying to keep her voice from quavering. "You had your chance to throw me off the train."

Gee went very still. Then he stood straight and leaned toward Piper, putting his arm around her. Piper slipped her hand around his waist and laid her head against his shoulder.

They stood like that for a long time while the wind and the salt air rushed over them, blocking out all sound.

After a while Piper felt the train jostle them, and she shifted her feet, holding on tighter to Gee. She heard footsteps behind them and turned to see Anna run out onto the platform, her face flushed with excitement.

"Piper, Gee, come quick!" she said. "Trimble's going to show me an experiment he's been working on, something about mixing black powder with a sarnun perfume recipe. He says it makes this amazing explosion, and the smoke smells like lilies."

"Sounds great," Piper said, grinning. "Just try not to blow up the train—or each other."

Hand in hand, she and Gee walked back inside. The big black engine blew its whistle and continued its journey north. Piper thought of her father. After he died, she'd dreamed about escaping aboard the 401, but she never thought she'd be calling it her home. Yet here she was—a scrapper, a machinist, a synergist. A chamelin walked next to her, holding her hand. Her sister was half human, half machine.

Miles and miles of track, and the whole world spread out before them, waiting.

⫸ ACKNOWLEDGMENTS ⫷

A lot of people had a hand in making this book possible, going all the way back to when it was just a vague notion of a dragonfly, a train, and a girl with a stubborn streak who lived in a world of forgotten things. I don't even know all their names—the people who helped me—but I can start with the names I do know.

Elizabeth, Gary, and Kelly, my critique partners and friends, helped guide this book from the beginning. They made sure my world, characters, plot, and all the other details were just right. And I like to think they screamed the loudest when I told them the book was going to be published. Thank you for that and so much more.

My parents and my brother, Jeff, have seen every high and low of my writing adventures. They put up with all of it and never complained, and they claimed they weren't at all surprised when I told them the book was going to be published. Thank you for everything.

My incredible agent, Sara Megibow, gave me the best Christmas present ever, and the best New Year's present too. She calls me a rock star, but she's the real star.

My editor, Krista Marino, and her team at Delacorte Press understood exactly what I wanted this book to be and helped make it even better. All of you rock.

Two women I respect a great deal, Susan Morris and Erin Evans, helped bring me to this point in my writing career. I thought of you both while writing this book, hoping you would like it.

And now some of those whose names I don't know: thank you to the crew at the Monticello Railway Museum who spent fifteen years bringing an old steam engine back to life, at the same time sparking an idea in my head about a very different train in a very different world.

Last, thank you to the group of Girl Scouts who heard me speak on a panel about women in gaming at the Gen Con games convention in 2011. You won't remember me, but you listened to me talk about some of those vague notions about dragonflies and lost things and other worlds, and your eyes lit up. That was the moment I first thought there might be something to this story. Thank you for listening.

Read a sneak peek of Jaleigh Johnson's new book,

THE SECRETS OF SOLACE

On Sale Spring 2016

———

"Apprentices, quiet!" The excited chatter in the classroom almost drowned out Tolwin's exasperated shout. "You'd think none of you had ever seen a simple box before."

From her seat near the back of the classroom, Lina Winterbock snorted in amusement. An archivist, even a junior apprentice like her, knew there was no such thing as a "simple box." Not when that box had been shipped from the meteor fields up north.

The classroom for Archival Studies was an amphitheater, the desks arranged in a semicircle on stone tiers carved out of the cavern's natural rock formations. At the bottom, in the teaching pit, there was a scarred oak table and a podium beside it for the teacher. The box that had caused the pandemonium sat in the middle of the table. Lina's teacher, the archivist Tolwin, stood behind the podium, his apprentice-assistant, Simon, beside him, scowling at all the noise. Though to be fair, the sour expression could just be Simon's version of a smile. With him, it was hard to tell.

Tolwin swept his gaze over the fifty-odd students assembled in the classroom. Lina turned her attention away from the box and sank as low in her seat as she could manage without actually falling to the floor. It didn't matter. The teacher's sharp eyes found her anyway, and narrowed, his lips pressing into a thin line of displeasure. Lina forced herself to stare back at him without flinching, but it wasn't easy. Tolwin's glare felt like a spider skittering down her spine. A large, hairy spider with fangs.

Given the *incident* last year, Tolwin's reaction wasn't surprising, but Lina kept hoping that maybe he would fall and hit his head and somehow forget the whole unpleasant business. Normally, she wouldn't wish a head injury on anyone, but it might make her days in Archival Studies a bit easier.

Lina released a tense breath as Tolwin finally looked away from her and she eagerly refocused her attention on the mysterious box. What *was* he hiding in there? Some new bit of technology, or maybe a painting or even a manuscript? Mystery poured from the depths of the box, filling Lina's mind and quickening her heart.

Where do you come from? How far have you traveled? What secrets do you hold?

Lina had never been to the meteor fields or the scrap towns where all these strange objects were gathered. They were located far to the north of the archivists' strongholds, in the Merrow Kingdom. But she'd heard plenty of stories about the violent meteor storms that ravaged the land up there. For reasons that even the wisest archivists hadn't been able to discover, the boundary between their world—Solace—and other lands was thin in the meteor fields, and on the night of each full moon, it dissolved completely. With no barrier, objects from these other worlds tumbled from the sky in clouds of poisonous green dust. It was the poorest people in the north, the scrappers, who bravely took on the task of harvesting these meteorites. They cleaned up whatever objects were still intact and sold them at local trade markets to make money to live on.

The archivists were the scrappers' best customers. They bought up as many otherworldly artifacts as they could and paid special attention to any object that might reveal hints of what life was like in those unknown worlds. It was their mission to preserve the artifacts and record whatever knowledge they gleaned from them, not only for its own sake but also because they believed that the more people learned about these other worlds, the more they'd come to understand their own. It was a unique calling, one that made Lina's life, even as an apprentice, very different from the lives of people in other lands.

"I said *quiet!*" Tolwin barked, shaking Lina from her thoughts. Anger deepened the crisscrossing lines on the instructor's face. Even his bushy brown-gray hair seemed unhappy. As he glared at the students, the noise level in the room gradually dropped to a quiet murmur.

"Today I'm going to conduct a hands-on experiment, the purpose of which is to test your understanding of the archivist principles you've been taught so far." Tolwin gestured to the box on the table. "You're all wondering what I've got in here, yes? I hear you whispering about it, trying to guess which division it came from."

Naturally, Lina thought. It was the first thing any archivist would wonder. The six general divisions—Flora, Fauna, Technology, Language/Literature, Cultural Artifacts, and Medicine—formed the basis for all the archivists' work. At the end of their long years of study and apprenticeship, each student in this room would end up working in one of those divisions.

Tolwin rubbed his hands together as if to build suspense. "All I will tell you to start is that there is an object inside the box that was discovered in the meteor fields only two weeks ago."

An astonished hush fell over the classroom, and Lina sat up straighter in her seat. Apprentices rarely got the opportunity to *see*, let alone *study*, an object newly recovered from the meteor fields. That privilege was usually reserved for the senior archivists.

"Well, now that we've finally achieved silence," Tolwin said dryly, "we can begin the lesson. First, I will require a volunteer. Simon, would you care to select someone?"

Hands shot up all over the room, the students squirming in their seats and casting pleading looks at Tolwin's apprentice. They all wanted to be the first to examine the object inside the box.

Only Lina sat with her hands folded on top of her desk. Her heart banged against her ribs, begging her with each unsteady beat to raise her hand and volunteer. But as curious as she was about the secrets and wonders contained within the box, she didn't trust Tolwin. She didn't trust anyone who made her feel spider legs on her spine.

Then Simon said something that made Lina's heart stand still. "I think . . . I think Lina Winterbock looks eager to volunteer."

Lina's stomach dropped, and she caught the malicious glint in Simon's eyes as he motioned for her to come down and join them in the teaching pit.

"Ah, yes, I believe you're right," Tolwin said, glancing up at her. A slight smile curved his thin lips. "Come down and stand in front of the table here, Miss Winterbock."

Lina's mind raced even as she slid her chair away from her desk with a quiet scraping sound. All eyes in the classroom fixed on her, bringing a deep flush of embarrassment to her cheeks.

At times like this, Lina wished more than anything that she could look across the room and meet the eyes of a best friend, someone who would giggle and stick her tongue out at Tolwin when his back was turned, and who would mouth a few encouraging words to her while she faced down the teacher. She'd even settle for a temporary friend, one who appeared only under the most dire of circumstances. She wasn't picky.

Focus, Lina.

Whatever game Tolwin and Simon were playing by choosing her for the experiment, the way Lina saw it, she had three possible counter moves. She could refuse to volunteer, which would thwart Tolwin but also probably get her kicked out of class. Lina considered feigning sickness as she stood up and made her way down the stairs. All she had to do was clutch her stomach and run out of the room as if she were about to vomit. If she played it up enough, Tolwin might even believe her.

But that would give Tolwin the satisfaction of knowing he'd scared her off.

Which left option three. Lina squared her shoulders and approached the box on the table, prepared to play along with whatever Tolwin had in store. Maybe, if she was good enough, she'd find a way to outsmart him and avoid the trap he and Simon had set.

Excerpt copyright © 2015 by Jaleigh Johnson. Published by Delacorte Press, an imprint of Random House Children's Books, a division of Penguin Random House LLC, New York.